Mystery at the Thirteen Sycamores

Frank R. Faunce

Frank R. Faunce

Joe C. Rudé

For more information about *Mystery at the Thirteen Sycamores*, its characters, the book's authors, and sequels in the works, visit the author website at **www.frankfaunce.com**.

Cover design by Mike McDowell

Interior design by Kerry Faunce

ISBN-13: 978-1537740614
ISBN-10: 153774061X

FOREWORD

Thirteen Sycamores is a book about little known modern chivalric organizations who have unbroken traditions and history that reach all the way back to the First Crusade and the fall of Jerusalem in 1099 A.D. It is also a modern adventure wrapped in a mystery laced with threads of counterterrorism interwoven with the remarkably rich history of the chivalric organizations that was discovered, painstakingly researched, and assembled over the past two decades. Finally, and surprisingly, *Thirteen Sycamores* is a book that provides a thorough, descriptive, and accurate travelogue of many beautiful locations around the world that you may want to visit as well as providing the reader with a non-stop culinary adventure and description of fine gourmet menu combinations will make you hungry just to read them.

By now you may be thinking, Chivalry! Isn't it dead? That is a question that was debated for much of the 20th century and is still being debated today in the 21st century as cultures, manners, and acceptable behaviors between genders evolve. However, a simple query on the internet or a book website will reveal many offerings outlining proposed chivalric behaviors or rules for true chivalric gentlemen in the 21st century. There are no fewer than several dozen books in print offering well-reasoned and modern codes of chivalry—making an appeal to men to adopt such behavior in a 21st century context. So, chivalry is still alive and the concept of chivalry in the popular mind is far from dead with many advocates actively engaged.

Meanwhile, there are individuals who are actual knights and dames and who daily practice and live by the traditional code of chivalry—doing good deeds on behalf of the Christian faith and for the benefit of mankind. These individuals are associated with modern orders of chivalry that are continuations of the original military Crusading Orders or belong to orders created by a monarch in the past that continue into the present. *Thirteen Sycamores* will acquaint the reader with a tiny bit of the new and remarkable history associated with two of the modern continuations from the original Order of Saint John of Jerusalem that survived after the Order was expelled from Malta by Napoleon in 1798. These modern continuations have a better unbroken lineage than some of the fragments of the Order of Saint John that landed in England, France, and elsewhere in Europe. For example, from 1826 to January 29, 1831, a French Knight of the French Capitular Commission helped revive the English langue of the Order of Saint John in England, but it was not until 1888 that Queen Victoria recognized the "Venerable Order of Saint John" and gave them a revival charter under the British crown—90 years after Malta. Ironically, the Venerable Order has individuals today who with extreme bias and selective scholarship aggressively pursue and presume to pass judgment on the validity of other Order of Saint John post-1798 fragments.

So what is *chivalry* and what is an *order of chivalry?* The definition of chivalry is complex. In fact, whole books have been spent describing its many facets and complexities from inception and across history, martial aspects, religious aspects, romantic ideal aspects, political aspects, and so forth. Such scholarly works are often offered as a whole as "the definition" of chivalry, but that does not satisfy readers who want something pithy. My favored definition comes from Kenelm Henry Digby, who in 1822 published a multi-volume comprehensive treatise on chivalry, *The Broadstone of Honour,* that some scholars credit with sparking a revival of chivalry in the 19th century.

His definition was:

"Chivalry is only a name for that general spirit or state of man which disposes men to heroic and generous actions and keeps them conversant with all that is beautiful and sublime in the intellectual and moral world."

An order of chivalry is much easier to define. It is simply a society of knights—individuals who have received the accolade of knighthood and embrace the ideals of "chivalry" and who are governed by a Charter or Rule.

Why should you read *Thirteen Sycamores?* Because you will be entertained and educated, especially if you like action and adventure, murder mysteries, travel to exotic locations, history, historic puzzles, historic fiction, culinary adventure, fine wine, and are a gourmet. Any one of these interest areas would be a good reason to read the book, but if you are blessed with more than one or all of these interests, you should devour the book and will find yourself wanting the next installment.

I have personally known and had the pleasure of working with the authors of *Thirteen Sycamores* for over 20 years in various chivalric endeavors. They are scholars who have searched for and dug up original documents in dusty archives in order to assemble the historic facts that provide structure to this novel—learning a bit of new history is another reason to read their book. They are also honorable knights who live their daily lives according to the code of chivalry. Therefore, and without reservation, I commend *Thirteen Sycamores* to you and hope you get as much pleasure as I did when you read it.

H.E. Bailiff David Hanson, KH Grand Prior USA Hospitaller
Order of Saint John of Jerusalem Knights Hospitaller

PREFACE

This book is based on carefully documented research. There really are Christian chivalric Orders of Saint John operating today that are the inheritors of the legacies of the original medieval crusading Knights Templars and the Hospital Order of Saint John of Jerusalem.

There really is a Muslim Brotherhood whose goal is to convert the world to their brand of Islam by the means of immigration, proliferation, and finally subjugation rather than an outright invasion by a Muslim army.

And there really was a member of that Brotherhood named Al-Haj Amin al Hussaini, the Grand Mufti of Jerusalem in Palestine who was a General in Hitler's murderous SS and commanded Muslim SS troops in the Balkans during World War II. It is thought that he recommended to Hitler prior to the infamous Wannsee Conference in 1941 that the Jews be "killed where they stand!" It may be the Genesis of the final solution that led to the Holocaust!

The Grand Mufti escaped from the French authorities after the war with the aid of the secret Nazi organization, ODESSA. He fled to Egypt to avoid the Nuremberg Trials and was given a warm reception and protection by the Egyptian President, Gamal Abdel Nasser Hussein. By the end of World War II, there were an estimated 2 million members of the Muslim Brotherhood. The Grand Mufti's family was part of the Black September terrorist group that committed the heinous killing of Jewish athletes during the Munich Olympics.

The Muslim Brotherhood and their affiliates have planned and executed numerous acts of terror with their underground cells in many areas around the world, and specifically the West, to bring about the destruction of those cultures using their own laws of tolerance and fair play in order to institute a new Islamic Caliphate. All of this funded by Middle East oil money. For obvious reasons, the names of some people and places have been changed.

Frank R. Faunce

ACKNOWLEDGMENTS

In writing any modern mystery novel, sharing history is sometimes more exciting than fiction. This novel is based on historical information that is relevant in today's world. For that reason we would like to acknowledge a few people who inspired us to write our story.

Col. Oscar Stroh was a retired professor at the United States Army War College on the Carlisle Barracks Campus at Carlisle, Pennsylvania, and the senior aerial intelligence officer for General of the Army Douglas MacArthur during the Korean War. Col. Stroh encouraged us to write a series of novels based on the history of the Hospitaller Order of Saint John and their colleagues, the Knights Templar.

As a close personal friend of King Peter II of Yugoslavia, Dr. Robert Formhals, heard the story of his escape from the Royal Palace in Belgrade, April 1941, and his harrowing journey into exile in London during World War II. Dr. Formhals relayed that story to us so we could share it with you.

We would like to acknowledge Dr. Fran S. Watkins who inspired us early on to write this book and to press on whenever we became discouraged. She also was an encouraging line editor throughout the writing process.

We would be remiss if we didn't include Ray Pelosi in our acknowledgements. He taught us what raconteur meant and throughout the writing served as our continuity editor. His intelligence and wit kept us on our toes! He was a gentle teacher of the craft of writing, and he was always most supportive during the hardest of times as our story unfolded.

Cledith Alsing was tireless getting copies of our book out to readers whose reviews helped us in the final revisions of our book and which you can read on our website.

We are grateful to Kerry Faunce, our senior editor, who put the final polish on the book to prepare it for publication. We are thankful for his wisdom and guidance to help us finish this book and provide many suggestions for the prequel and sequels on which we are currently working. We hope you will enjoy this opening book in our continuing story.

Respectfully, the authors
Frank R. Faunce
Joe C. Rudé

CONTENTS

Mystery at the
Thirteen Sycamores

1 SHADOWS AT DAWN

Awispy thin cloud slid across the face of the orange full moon in the western sky silhouetting the thirteen sycamores and ruins of the ancient Saint Mary Chapel that capped the crest of Mount Lothian, a hill in the middle of a vast meadow across the road from the Elliott family farmhouse. They bred and raised sheep and Scottish cattle. The sheep and cattle were lying peacefully in the meadow near the sycamores.

The eastern sky, still covered with stars, was beginning to lighten with the first rays of the sun that were creeping above the eastern horizon. It was 5:00 a.m. Wednesday, the sixth of June, 2012. The air was cool and crisp with a slight breeze that brushed the hair of the dark male figure struggling to push a pole topped with a round glass disc into the grassy soil. The young man, Maj. Dietrich von Schoenfeld of the German Luftwaffe, was working just outside the eastern foundation of the ancient Cistercian chapel of the long departed, twelfth century Abbey of Saint Mary of Magdalene. Nestled in a grove of thirteen sycamores, it was the very same chapel in which William Wallace was knighted in 1307!

Von Schoenfeld told the older man huddled next to him that he needed help to push the pole to a depth where the

1

glass disc could easily focus the sun's rays onto the chapel floor at precisely 5:39 a.m. The disc and pole had to be the same height and position as the chapel's original eastern round glass rose window had been. The two men were talking to each other in whispers so as not to disturb the cattle nestled around the ruins of the historic chapel.

Upon looking at his watch, Dietrich suddenly leaped up and shouted, "There it is!" ran to the far side of the western part of the chapel's foundation, and eagerly scraped away the dirt over the stone floor where the image of the sun was focused. The cattle moved slightly.

Just as he declared to the older man that he had found the stone, he turned just in time to see the glint of the curved dagger in the sun's early rays as it sliced through the air toward his neck. Blood spurted onto the chapel's stone floor.

He heard the older man mutter "Allah Akbar" as he tried to turn toward the now menacing figure.

The man pushed von Schoenfeld to the floor of the chapel and in an instant buried the dagger into his back. Dietrich felt a sharp pain in his ribs as a dark pool of unconsciousness opened up and swallowed him. He slumped to the floor gasping for air. The assailant tried to remove the dagger from the young man's back, but it was wedged between two of his ribs.

A cow began to move and moan her disapproval of her sleep being interrupted by the two men. A barking collie that had been approaching the two men, ran past the assailant and started sniffing around the body of the bleeding young man.

Limping, the older man shuffled down the hill toward a black Mercedes sedan that had just arrived at the gate to the meadow and jumped inside. The black and white Border Collie, sensing that something was terribly wrong, ran down the hill after the fleeing man and reached the black Mercedes just as the back door slammed shut. The cattle started to stir and make noise. Maj. Dietrich von Schoenfeld was left bleeding to death on the floor of Saint Mary Chapel with the ornate curved dagger protruding from his back.

The black Mercedes sedan sped off down the road with the collie barking and chasing after it. It raced over the bridge and past the Mercedes roadster in which the older man and von Schoenfeld had arrived an hour earlier. Sean, the Border Collie and family dog of the Elliotts, stopped chasing it after the car disappeared over the hill and ran back to the driveway of the farmhouse, barking to the family inside.

Mrs. Annie Elliott, a tanned trim blonde dressed in a pale blue dress that matched her eyes, had wavy blond hair which hung down over her right eye making it resemble the Veronica Lake peekaboo look in the 1940s. She had been in her kitchen starting to fix breakfast for her family when she heard Sean barking. She ran to the kitchen window just in time to see the dark figure of the older man jump into the back of the black Mercedes sedan as it sped away with Sean running after it. She couldn't make out the license number of the automobile because of the mud smudged on its surface. A thought that it was a rental car flashed into her mind. She didn't notice the roadster that was pulled off beside the road. She saw nothing else and dismissed the event from her mind and went back to fixing breakfast for her family.

Sean ran to the farmhouse kitchen door, still barking, and started to scratch at the kitchen door. Annie opened the door and instinctively knew that Sean wanted her to follow him. He tugged at her apron, pulling her down the driveway toward the hill. He then ran up the hill toward the chapel as the cattle and sheep moved away from the speeding dog with Mrs. Elliott in hot pursuit.

As they reached the top of the hill, Annie heard the unconscious figure on the chapel floor breathing heavily. She ran to him and saw the ugly scene with Dietrich bleeding profusely and the dagger protruding from his back. Realizing that the young man on the floor of the chapel was still alive, she ran quickly down the path from the chapel to the country road in front of her house—a distance of about a hundred yards. Sean was running ahead of her as if he realized that an emergency was in progress.

When she and Sean reached the front door to their house, Annie threw the door open and darted for the telephone. She grabbed the phone and hurriedly called the emergency number.

"A man has been stabbed and needs an ambulance immediately!" she gasped into the phone at the operator.

"Where are you and what has happened?"

After giving her the address, Annie blurted, "I think he's bleeding to death and that someone has tried to murder him. Please call the police in Temple; it's the nearest town."

The operator sensing the immediacy of the situation said that she would do so.

At this time, her husband Sam, rubbing his blue eyes in bewilderment at the commotion, was standing in the door of their hallway and kitchen.

"What's going on?" he asked.

Sam and their kids, Brian and Susan, who had heard the noise, burst into the kitchen and saw the worried look on their mother's face.

She gasped and said, "Sam, there's a man up at the chapel with a dagger in his back bleeding to death and I've just called for an ambulance and the police in Temple. Please, don't let the children see it!"

Sam immediately looked at the children and pointed to the chairs around the kitchen table and told them to stay put while he went to see what was going on. Brian, who at ten years resembled a smaller version of his father, and Susan, who was two years younger and the spitting image of her mother, silently obeyed their father and sat down at the kitchen table. Sam put on a coat and went out the kitchen door with Sean close behind. Annie told her children she would finish fixing their breakfast before the ambulance and police got there.

Meanwhile, the operator who had received the emergency call realized that the situation was critical and called the Royal Infirmary of Edinburgh, which serves the mid Lothian area of Scotland for accidents and severe injuries. She knew that time was of the essence and informed the emergency operator at the infirmary that a man was severely wounded, but was still alive and needed immediate attention. She gave them the location of the emergency and they told her a life flight helicopter and an emergency doctor with help had been dispatched and was on the way. It would arrive there within thirty minutes or less. The operator then called the police at Temple and told them what had happened.

The Royal Infirmary is the oldest voluntary hospital in Scotland and is associated with the University of Edinburgh Medical School.

Sam followed Sean up the hill as the collie headed for the ruins of Saint Mary Chapel. The sheep and the cattle sensed that something was amiss and scattered safely away from the chapel. Sam reached the slumped over figure of von Schoenfeld, who was breathing laboriously. He tugged at his coat trying to arouse the unconscious man. Seeing the elaborate and obviously decorated curved dagger sticking from his back, Sam decided that he should only try to stop any more bleeding from the gash on the side of Dietrich's neck next to his ear. He took a handkerchief that he pulled from his pocket and pressed it against the wound on the man's neck. He was relieved that the unconscious man was still breathing. He decided to stay there until help arrived to make sure that there wasn't any more bleeding from the neck wound.

About fifteen minutes later, a helicopter approached the meadow and the cattle and sheep again moved away from the grove of sycamores to a safer distance down the hill. The helicopter quickly found some flat ground just to the north of the grove of trees and settled down onto the grass of the meadow.

Just as the helicopter landed and a doctor jumped onto the ground with two medical assistants, a police car arrived at the gate to the meadow and a tall man in a tan trench coat got out of the car with a smaller man in a police uniform with sergeant's stripes following him.

The two men ran up the path toward the grove and again the sheep moved out of the way not quite figuring out what all of the excitement was about. The cattle had already moved some distance from the grove so that they would not be disturbed any more. The two men were yelling something that Sam could not quite understand and they were waving their arms anxiously in the air. The police car was parked near the gate to the meadow and another man exited the back seat of the car running behind the other two men. He had a camera slung over his shoulder and a leather bag in his hand.

Inspector Ed MacGregor, a tall man in his early thirties with sandy hair and blue eyes to go along with a face full of freckles, and Sgt. Roland Young, who was younger and shorter, but looked older with his dark hair, pale face and intense grey eyes, reached the grove just as Dr. Jamie Macadam and his assistants were beginning to assess the medical condition of the injured man on the chapel floor.

"Please, this is a crime scene," barked MacGregor, who anxiously pleaded to everyone there, "We need some photographs, so don't destroy any possible evidence."

"Look," said the doctor who resembled a taller James Dean, "We are trying to save this man's life. He has a thoracic wound with tension pneumothorax and needs immediate care."

"Alright," conceded MacGregor, "but let us get a photograph of the victim with the knife in place before it's removed and record the position of the injured man before you move him."

While the inspector was pleading his case, the police photographer, John Smedley, a young man in his twenties, moved rapidly to the scene and started expertly taking photographs before being told otherwise. After taking about a dozen or more photos, he muttered, "All done sir, the doc can finish what he was doing."

Dr. Macadam, who was busy treating his patient, bristled, "Thanks for letting me go about saving this man's life."

Dr. Macadam, who knew Ed MacGregor, was obviously

used to working with the police and a smile crept begrudgingly over his face as he saluted the inspector and his men with his gloved right hand and then immediately tore open Dietrich's shirt, pulled two eighteen-gauge needles from his doctor's bag, and plunged them expertly into the injured man's chest to the horrified expression on Sam's face.

Built up air rushed out of the pleural cavity with a terrific whoosh and Dietrich's labored breathing began to ease. Dr. Macadam noticed Sam's concern and with a patient smile explained that it was necessary to let air out of the pleural cavity surrounding the lung to eliminate the tension pneumothorax in Dietrich's left lung and stabilize the pressure that was building up in his chest. He further explained as he cut off the left sleeves of the man's coat and shirt and put an IV into the man's arm that if he had not relieved the built-up pressure that Dietrich's heart would have stopped beating.

Sam breathed a sigh of relief at this news that apparently had not phased the policemen. Dr. Macadam then expertly pulled the dagger from between the ribs of the man's back and handed it to Sgt. Smedley who already had rubber gloves on his hands. He then calmly removed the rest of Dietrich's coat and shirt, cleaned the wounds, inserted a tube with a one way valve into the wound in his back, and bandaged his neck and back. He and his assistants had quickly placed an oxygen mask over the patient's mouth and nose, placed him on a gurney, silently covered him with blankets, and moved him into the helicopter.

Jamie Macadam then leaned out of the open door of the helicopter and waved at Sam and the policemen and yelled, "Thanks!"

Just as swiftly as they had arrived, the helicopter lifted into the air and sped northeast towards Edinburgh and the Royal Infirmary at Little France. The three policemen, Sam, and Sean looked up and followed the mercy flight as it disappeared toward Edinburgh about fifty miles distant.

Inspector MacGregor turned toward Sam and introduced

Sgt. Young and the young police photographer who was still busy at the crime scene collecting evidence and placing it into plastic bags with his gloved hands.

The young man waved a gloved hand at Sam and smiled, "Don't mind me, I just need to get a few more photos and items and then I'll be through. I wonder what this pole is all about," he said as he photographed the scene, carefully wrapped the pole with the lens and the dagger, and carefully placed the items into plastic bags so as not to damage them or any fingerprints or DNA.

Inspector MacGregor smiled and shook Sam's hand as he explained, "I've worked with Dr. Macadam on several cases and have never worked with anyone as conscientious or more compassionate in his work. You know, he is a veteran of the Afghanistan War where he was stationed, doing "dust-off" operations as he called these emergency flight evacuations."

Sgt. Young interrupted the conversation as he had just noticed that Sean was digging at the ground and had uncovered a strange metal object with a piece of black cloth clinging to it.

"Hello, what is this?" he asked as he pointed it out to Smedley who was gathering evidence.

"It looks like a Maltese cross."

"Yes, there is also a small flashlight and measuring tape close by where the dirt had been cleared off of a portion of a stone tile in the floor," said Smedley.

"Get a photo of that cleared area!" Ed MacGregor yelled. He then muttered to them, "Something very mysterious has happened here."

Inspector MacGregor then pointed out the Mercedes convertible parked off the road just past the small bridge over the tiny creek that meandered through the meadow. They all looked in the direction of the Mercedes roadster that he had just pointed out.

Then it dawned on Sam, "I think that's the same car your victim and his bride were in when they stopped yesterday afternoon and asked my wife Annie about Mount Lothian and the Chapel of Saint Mary. It must be the same guy!"

The others looked at Sam, who continued, "I didn't think anything about it because we sometimes get strangers stopping wanting to visit the chapel. Annie told me they seemed so much in love and that he had said it would mean a lot to them since it is an ancient historic holy place."

Inspector MacGregor looked at Sgt. Young and then at Sam. "Do you think that Annie might be able to answer a few questions at this time?"

"Yes, I believe so," said Sam.

"We're going down to the farmhouse," MacGregor said to Smedley. "You go ahead and finish up here—we'll meet you at the car when we're done."

"Okay!" said Smedley as he scarcely looked up from his work collecting the items they had just seen.

The four of them, MacGregor, Sgt. Young, Sam, and Sean all went to the farmhouse.

"Darling, could you fix some tea for the inspector and sergeant?" Sam shouted as they entered the kitchen.

"Of course dear, straight away."

2 EXPLANATIONS AT THE FARMHOUSE

The two policemen seated themselves comfortably on the sofa in the living room as Sam settled himself into his favorite overstuffed chair. He glanced around the room to make sure that everything was in place and he had not left any old shoes or other embarrassing items around.

"Nice place you have here," MacGregor said as he looked around the room.

It was a large room with walnut paneled walls and a large painting of the old Saint Mary Chapel on Mount Lothian with its sycamore trees hanging above the flagstone fireplace. There was a scarlet throw rug in front of the fireplace where the children had apparently been putting a jig saw puzzle together. The floor was made of well waxed oak, slightly scuffed by the children's play.

As MacGregor returned his gaze to Sam, Annie entered the room with a tray filled with a tea pitcher, some cups, a pitcher of milk, and some scones. The children were by her side as she laid the tray down on a coffee table in front of the couch.

The children started to lie down on the rug to work the puzzle when Annie spoke to them, "I want you to go outside with Sean and play, but don't go up toward the hill, just play around the house."

The children nodded their approval and said simultaneously, "Yes ma'am," and obediently left the room.

Ed MacGregor picked up one of the scones and bit off a corner. He smiled and said, "Home cooked? It's delicious."

The sergeant immediately picked up a scone and stuffed it into his mouth and nodded his approval.

Annie grinned as Sam said, "Best cook hereabouts."

She knew Ed MacGregor from when they all were friends in school. She took the pitcher and poured two cups of tea for the men, saying that Sam liked his tea without milk, but if the policemen wanted milk they were welcome to add it. She took a cup of tea for herself, poured some milk into it, poured a cup for Sam, and then sat down on the rug in front of the fireplace.

"What do you think is going on?" she said, looking at Ed.

The inspector looked at her and said, "Have you seen that man before?"

"Yes," she replied. "I think he is the same nice young man who showed up with his wife yesterday afternoon and that is their car parked next to the bridge. They knocked on my door while I was cleaning the kitchen and doing a laundry. They were very polite and asked if the ruins of the old Saint Mary Chapel were on the top of the hill across the road. I told them yes, but there wasn't much there to see now. They didn't seem to mind.

"I think the man was from Germany by his slight accent, but the woman spoke perfect English with no accent. They were surprised when I asked them if they wanted tea. They said no at first, then changed their minds. When we sat down at the kitchen table, they thanked me for the tea and crumpets. I asked them if they were strangers to Scotland, and they replied they were.

"The man was about six feet tall with wavy blond hair and blue eyes. He was tanned, very good looking, dressed well, and had a military bearing. She was tall—about five feet eight—and seemed to have a calm look in her hazel eyes. She had long black hair and a milky complexion. She spoke softly with a slight lilt in her speech. She seemed so much in love when she looked at her husband.

"We talked for about a half hour about the history and legends of the old chapel where William Wallace had been knighted and of the mysterious thirteen sycamore trees that surrounded the old ruins and harkened back to the times of the Knights Templar and Robert the Bruce. They asked if they could go up the hill and take photos of the ruins and trees and I gave them my permission.

"I watched as they went up the hill holding hands, and then they started taking pictures. I saw them drive away after they had finished and that's the last I saw of them or the car until this awful morning."

By this time, Annie's eyes had started to cloud and she covered them with her handkerchief. She sobbed quietly and said softly, "Ed, what do you make of all of this?"

"Well, it's certainly puzzling," Ed replied. "But one thing is for sure. The knife in his back was an elaborate ceremonial Hanjar dagger!"

"A what dagger?" Sam blurted out.

"A Hanjar dagger that was used by jihadist assassins during the Crusades to kill specific enemies when they wanted to make a political statement," Ed explained. "It meant that whoever it was that wanted to kill that young man had a deliberate agenda that he was proclaiming to the world and specifically to the Arab world. That young man was singled out for a purpose."

"I don't understand," said Annie. "Why would anyone want to do such a thing?" She looked at her husband in disbelief at the statement the inspector had made.

Sam shrugged his shoulders and nodded his head in agreement.

MacGregor continued, "This has all the earmarks of a jihadist branch of the Muslim Brotherhood that was founded in 1928 to resist British colonialism and spread the doctrine of socialist jihad. One of its founders was Haj Amin al-Hussaini, the Grand Mufti of Jerusalem. He had fled to Germany from Palestine after his attempt to overthrow British influence in Iraq in 1939. He was introduced by Adolph Eichmann to Heinrich Himmler and Adolph Hitler. Hitler made him a general in the SS and assigned him to command several regiments of Muslim SS that were recruited in Bosnia, Yugoslavia. Those regiments were called the Hanjar regiments after the symbolic dagger that they wore in their uniform belts. The dagger we found in that young man's back looks like one of those daggers.

"Those regiments ran the concentration camps in Hungary and Yugoslavia. It was Haj Amin who recommended in a letter to Hitler that he should not export the Jews to Palestine to be executed after the war, but rather to execute them in Europe as they conquered territory. This was in 1941 while Haj Amin was living in Berlin. Because of his activities, he was indicted at Nuremberg after the war, but was secreted out of Europe to Egypt by the ODESSA—the SS secret organization that arranged for Adolph Eichmann and others to flee to Argentina and other safe countries.

"Haj Amin died on July 4, 1974, at the age of 80 of a heart attack in Al Mansuriyah, Beirut, Lebanon. He was buried in the cemetery of The Fallen of the Palestinian Revolution on July 7. He was eulogized by the Palestine Liberation Organization and the Muslim Brotherhood. The funeral procession numbered in the hundreds and the funeral celebrations were attended by many prominent Arab leaders saddened by his loss.

"You know, many Muslims still consider westerners as Crusaders, and the jihadist organizations relate to the ancient cult of the assassins who were mortal enemies of the Crusading Orders."

"Whoa," sighed Sam. "I had no idea that this was going on today! What should we do or say to anyone?"

Ed put his finger to his lips and said, "Nothing!" And he emphasized, "Not to anyone until we find out exactly what happened here. We don't want these criminals to think that they have not succeeded. When our victim regains consciousness, he might be able to shed some light on all of this. Did you notice the Maltese cross medal? It had the Prussian eagle between the arms of the cross and was attached to a black ribbon. That is the emblem of the Johanniter Ordenung—the German Order of Saint John, which is a Lutheran branch of the ancient Hospitaller Order of Saint John. It was one of the original Christian military orders during the Crusades, along with the Knights Templars and the Teutonic Knights! I think that this guy who was stabbed might possibly be a knight of that German order."

Sam again whistled and then said, "This is really getting strange. What does this have to do with the chapel?"

Ed said, "I don't know yet, but the chapel was a Knights Templar historic site and the Knights Templar were close to the Order of Saint John and the Cistercian Order that built many of the cathedrals, abbeys, and chapels in Europe after the Crusades. They are also linked to the Masons and the Freemasons of recent years. When the Knights Templar were suppressed on Friday, October 13, 1307, their properties were given to the Hospitaller Order of Saint John.

"In Scotland, the headquarters of the Knights of Saint John was at Torphican, not too far from the headquarters of the Knights Templar at Temple! It is said that the knights of the Temple joined with the Saint John knights in a secret alliance that later led to the Masonic movements of the 1600s and the 1700s."

Annie said that she understood there are modern versions of these Orders around, but didn't know anyone in them.

The inspector blushed, then explained, "I must confess. I'm a member of one of the early offshoots of the Temple-Malta alliance, the Black Knights of Malta in Scotland, which is now headquartered in Edinburgh. There also the Venerable Order of Saint John headquartered at Saint John's Gate in London. Queen Elizabeth II is the head of that Order and is the patron of our Scottish branch of the

Fraternal Order of the Black Knights of Malta. That's how I recognized the medal from the German Order."

Annie's eyes grew large and she covered her mouth with her hand.

He continued, "We'll have to keep this under wraps so the assailants believe they have killed this man, since we don't want them trying this again. An inspector of Scotland's security forces I know in Edinburgh, Steve Grant, is a close friend of mine in the Order. I'll call him and explain what has happened and to keep this under wraps for the time being until we can get everything under control. He'll call the hospital and our friend, Dr. Macadam. We don't want them to try again, do we? I can depend on your silence on this whole affair, can't I?"

Annie and Sam nodded their heads.

As MacGregor and Sgt. Young rose from their seats and thanked the Elliotts for the tea and scones and for their cooperation in the affair, MacGregor said, "For good measure, I'll call the Scottish Historical Society and explain to them that there has been some amateur archeology at the chapel site and ask them to watch over the area."

MacGregor gave Sam his card and asked them to let him know if anyone else showed up to look at the chapel or if they remembered anything more to please let him know.

As they all exited through the kitchen door, MacGregor turned to his old schoolmates and friends, Annie and Sam, and said, "Both of you don't mind if they help you watchdog the area, do you?"

They both nodded their approval and they watched MacGregor and Sgt. Young disappear down the driveway toward the police car and Sgt. Smedley, who was already sitting in the back seat of the vehicle.

Upon reaching the car and entering it, Inspector MacGregor reached for his cell phone and paused, saying to the other two policemen, "Boys, we're going to keep this case quiet and downplay it as an ordinary death in the country until we can get more facts. I don't want the criminals behind this to get a second chance at this lucky young man, so I'm going to call Dr. Macadam at the hospital and Inspector Grant in Edinburgh and get them to go along with it without any publicity or newspaper coverage other than a small notice in the local Temple newspaper of the death of a stranger and that his body is being returned to his native country."

"I've gone over the Mercedes roadster with a fine tooth comb and gathered more evidence," said Smedley. "I found out where the man and his wife were staying in Edinburgh. The registration of the car and the rental agreement in the car along with the information in his wallet indicated that it had been rented to a Maj. Dietrich von Schoenfeld of the German Luftwaffe. Also, a hotel key that I had found with the personal effects that I removed from the man's pockets indicated that he was staying in Balmoral Suite 420 at the Balmoral Hotel in Edinburgh. The police lab is on their way to collect the roadster and haul it back to the police garage for a more thorough inspection."

Without saying a word, Inspector MacGregor turned to his cell phone and dialed Dr. Macadam at the hospital in Edinburgh.

3 SETTING THE BAIT

Ed MacGregor smiled when Dr. Macadam answered the phone and explained to him that they had just arrived at the hospital and that the patient was stable and they were on their way to the operating room for surgery.

"Jamie, we're going to put a lid on this case—it may be terrorism—we need to have the hospital admit your patient anonymously and we need police security for this patient," MacGregor said. "I'll call our friend, Inspector Steve Grant, and get the okay. I know that your hospital has its problems with this current Legionnaires Disease outbreak, but I would certainly appreciate your and the hospital's cooperation."

"You got it!"

Jamie was not known for his verbosity. He just simply did his job without questions. They said their goodbyes and hung up.

Now that he knew that the emergency flight would be hushed up, he turned to the job of getting the Edinburgh police on board. His friend Steve Grant was an old friend from college and he could rely on his discretion and help.

MacGregor dialed Steve Grant's personal cell phone number and got an immediate answer.

"Hello, Steve, this is Ed MacGregor."

"Yeah, I recognized your voice. What's up?" Steve asked, pleased to hear from his friend.

"I'm not sure," replied Ed, "But I think we might have a case of terrorism and attempted murder—a Hanjar dagger is involved and I think it also involves the Order of Saint John! Could you put a security guard on Jamie Macadam's patient at the Royal Infirmary at Little France? I've already tipped off Jamie and he said he and the hospital would cooperate and keep a lid on this affair. We're keeping this patient anonymous, but he is a major in the German Luftwaffe by the name of Dietrich von Schoenfeld. And get this, he's a member—I'm pretty sure—a knight of the Johanniter Ordnung!"

Steve was part of the Scottish branch of police for homeland security that handled terrorism in Scotland.

"Whew!" was Inspector Grant's immediate response. "Are you sure? Did he contact our Order's office here in Edinburgh when he arrived?"

"I don't think so and I don't think he's contacted the Venerable Order in London either, but I'll check," was Ed's reply. "Something's up."

"This may have international consequences," Steve pointedly said.

Jamie, Ed and Steve were all members of the Order of Black Knights of Malta—the descendant of the ancient Templar-Saint John alliance in Scotland. Grant also was a Knight of the Venerable Order of Saint John.

"I'll send what we've got up to Edinburgh today and all of the evidence that we have, including a strange pole with a glass lens, a medal, and the dagger that was used," said MacGregor. "We'll send the rest as we get it. We'll need to run them through DNA and fingerprint analysis."

"You're right, we can run the analysis faster here in Edinburgh." Steve added, "Do you know where the major was staying?"

"Yes, he and his bride are staying at the Balmoral Hotel in Edinburgh, Balmoral Suite 420," Ed answered. "We haven't called her yet. I hope she's still there with all this breakout of Legionnaire's Disease."

Steve replied, "I'll call the hotel immediately to see if she is still there, and if so, I'll personally go over and talk to her. Jamie did say that he thought her husband would pull through, didn't he?" He added, with a slight quiver to his voice, "I don't want to go over to the hotel with encouragement if she's going to be a widow!"

"Well, you know Jamie, he wouldn't be so positive that Maj. von Schoenfeld would pull through if he thought he wouldn't. He's the best they have at the Royal Infirmary!" Ed exclaimed.

Steve sighed in relief with Ed's assurances and told his friend he would call him later after talking with Maj. von Schoenfeld's wife. They then hung up and Inspector Grant looked over his appointment calendar and called his secretary.

His secretary, Katharine Sue Winslow, a beautiful slender woman with blonde hair, blue eyes, and a winsome smile, came through his door. She was a charmer who knew Grant's mind almost before he did.

"I know, an emergency has come up and you need to cancel your appointments for the day!" she exclaimed. "I've already cleared your calendar and called for your car. Is there anything else I can do?"

Grant winced in amusement at her perceptiveness and leaned back in his chair with his usual surprised look on his face when Ms. Winslow performed her mind reading feats.

"It must be ESP, you're a doll!"

"I know," she replied and proceeded to his closet to get his hat and coat.

"Do call and let me know what she has to say!" she ended, gently teasing him.

Steve Grant was a bachelor and he noted a slight bit of sarcasm in Ms. Kate Winslow's voice. "No, this really is serious business that I can't talk to you about now, but it may involve national security—I'll tell you later!"

Kate rolled her eyes at him as he headed for the door. As

he passed by her, she patted him on the shoulder and sighed, "Later!"

She followed behind him toward the door and casually asked him, "Shall I call her now and arrange your meeting with..." and she paused as Steve filled in the blanks, "Mrs. Natalie von Schoenfeld at the Balmoral Hotel, Balmoral Suite 420. Her husband is a member of the Order of Saint John and has been injured, but don't tell her that he's been injured!"

He paused at the door while Kate called the Balmoral Hotel.

The Balmoral Hotel is located at the corner of Princes and North Bridge Roads at 1 Princes Street overlooking Edinburgh Castle and close by the National Gallery and Library of Scotland. It opened its doors in 1902 as the North British Hotel, a traditional railway hotel adjacent to Waverly Station in Edinburgh. It has a majestic clock tower which can be seen all around. Its clock is always set two minutes fast to ensure that people don't miss their trains!

Grant had always wanted to stay at the Balmoral, but he thought the five-star hotel that had been a favorite of the Queen Mother and many film stars and celebrities was a bit above his salary. He welcomed the opportunity to see the hotel and meet Mrs. von Schoenfeld.

Kate had called the hotel before he left his office and confirmed that Natalie von Schoenfeld was indeed still in her room at the hotel and would speak with him.

"What is this all about?" she had asked Kate.

"Oh everything is okay," Kate said. "Inspector Grant just wanted to bring you a message from your husband. As a Knight of the Order of the Black Knights of Malta, he wanted to welcome you to Edinburgh."

Steve marveled at the way Katie, his pet name for her, had managed to smoothly arrange the meeting with Natalie von Schoenfeld and he pondered at the thought of asking Katie for a drink and possibly dinner at the hotel at a later time.

Inspector Grant had driven his personal car—a silver

Jaguar XF, 240 hp, 2.0 liter, i4 turbocharged four-door sedan—that he had received from a rich aunt who thought the car might prove to be a way to attract a wife to her favorite nephew who was apparently content to remain a bachelor.

As he drove up to the main entrance of the hotel on Princes Street, a young valet popped out of nowhere to park his car. Grant flipped open his wallet revealing that he was an inspector of the Scottish Security Force as he stepped out of the car. The valet's eyes opened wide as he looked at it. Then Grant put it back into his pocket and pulled his blue Harris Tweed sports coat close about him. He held on to his dark blue fedora hat as a brisk cold wind swept around him.

The weather had been cool and sunny that day, but still the wind was brisk at times and penetrated through any light clothing. Steve remembered that he had debated wearing his tweed coat this morning, but now he was glad that he had.

He handed the key of his car to the eager boy and cautioned him about being careful when he parked the car.

The boy nodded and grinned a smart, "Yes sir!" and drove the car away.

Steve Grant hurried up the walk to the front door and entered the spacious lobby and walked over to the concierge and asked, "Which elevator goes to Balmoral Suite 420?"

The elderly man behind the desk pointed to an elevator directly opposite and down a small hallway. "That one right there, just push the fourth floor button that lists Balmoral Suite 420," he said as he nodded his greying head toward the elevator.

Steve walked over to the elevators and entered an empty one and punched the number four button that listed the Balmoral Suite 420 among its other listings. He had not noticed an older man in a dark blue suit with greying hair and a swarthy complexion watching him from behind a pillar in the lobby while he asked the concierge about Balmoral Suite 420. The man watched as Steve went to the elevator and entered it. He saw the elevator rise to the fourth floor and stop. An angry scowl crept across his face and he clenched his fists.

The elevator immediately rose to the fourth floor and opened its door and Inspector Grant stepped out. He was about six feet two inches tall with black hair that he parted on the right side, blue eyes that twinkled when he smiled, a perpetual tan, and a dimple in his chin. He was athletic and quite a good swimmer when he was in college. He never thought of himself as handsome and was rather shy around women, even though they seemed to find him attractive.

As he disembarked on the fourth floor and gazed down the hall, he saw a sign that pointed him to the right, down to the Balmoral Suite. He walked the short distance to the door and knocked on it. He could hear some scuffling of shoes and then the door opened to reveal a startlingly beautiful young lady with pale hazel eyes that had blue speckles around the edges and a dreamy look. She resembled the American movie actress, Ali Cobrin.

She was tall, about five feet eight, Steve guessed, wearing Jimmy Choo dark blue high heel shoes that made her look even taller. She was slender and athletic with a milky complexion and smooth skin. Her long, dark brown hair fell around her face and shoulders like a halo. She was wearing a grey skirt and ivory white silk blouse with no bra and a navy blue silk scarf that wrapped around her shoulders in a large bow slightly off center. She had a quizzical smile that revealed perfect teeth that sparkled when she spoke.

"Hello, are you Inspector Grant?" she purred in perfect English with no accent that revealed her origin. "I'm Natalie Novak." Then she tossed her head and laughed, "No, von Schoenfeld, I mean. You see, we were just married this last week and I haven't gotten used to my new name. Please forgive me," she said as she extended her hand to shake Steve's hand.

They shook hands and Steve was impressed by the firmness of her handshake.

"Are you an athlete?" he said.

"No, I used to be a gymnast and studied ballet when I was younger, but I grew too tall. Now, I just ski." She laughed again and said, "Shall we sit down? Can I get you anything to drink?"

Steve replied, "Just Scotch."

They walked into the spacious suite of rooms and he sat down in one of the two convenient large chairs next to a table as Natalie walked over to the bar and picked up a bottle of 12-year-old Glenlivet Scotch.

"No ice, neat, and with water on the side," she said as she turned her head around to speak to him.

"That's correct—how did you know?" he said.

Natalie smiled again, "Dietrich said that was the way whiskey was drunk in Scotland."

She poured the Scotch, one for Steve and one for her, placed them on a tray with the water and brought them to the small walnut table between the two stuffed blue leather chairs.

As she sat down and took a small sip of her drink, she asked, "Well, what is this about? What is the message from Dietrich, and how did you know that he was a Knight of the Order of Saint John, and what are the Black Knights of Malta?"

"Whoa, slow down," Steve said. "Dietrich has had an accident, but he is okay and he is in the best hospital in Scotland, here in Edinburgh. His doctor is Dr. Jamie Macadam, the best doctor in Scotland and he assures me that Dietrich is recovering and that we can visit him later tonight."

Natalie started to swoon as her eyes clouded over with tears and her lips began to tremble. She laid the glass down on the table and Steve quickly got up and held her shoulders and tried to reassure her that her husband was just fine.

She looked up at him with tears running down her face and her body trembling. "Are you sure that he's going to be all right," she sobbed.

Steve put an arm around her shoulders and comforted her with a pat of his hand on her arm. "He'll be just fine, I'm waiting for his doctor to call me soon."

Steve's reassurances seemed to work.

Natalie took a few deep breaths and sighed, "I didn't want him to go alone last night to meet Mr. Smythe from the Venerable Order of Saint John in London. He was supposed to meet him last night in Roslyn and then they were going to Saint Mary Chapel for the sunrise this morning. I wanted to be there for the eclipse of Venus, but he didn't want me to have to stay awake all night and insisted that he bring me back to the hotel. He said that he would be back in time for a late lunch. Was there an automobile accident—how badly was he hurt?"

Her words tumbled over each other and she was desperate for some answers. She seemed to be recovering from the initial shock and her tears were beginning to dry. She dabbed a small handkerchief at her eyes and looked longingly for some answers in the inspector's eyes.

Steve sensed her bewilderment and anguish and sought how to phrase what he had to tell her and how to reassure her and yet not frighten her with the events of last night. He decided to let her talk about what her husband and Mr. Smythe were doing at Mount Lothian and the chapel last night.

"Dr. Macadam has not told me what Dietrich and Mr. Smythe were doing at the Chapel of Saint Mary last night," he said. "Could you tell me?"

Steve was not ready for the answer to that question when it came.

"You are familiar with the Order of Saint John and the Knights Templar, aren't you?" she asked. "I understand from your secretary and your lapel pin that you are a member of the Venerable Order of Saint John. You must understand the significance of the transit of Venus and the Chapel?" she said inquiringly.

"No," Steve answered.

She looked at him intensely and slightly bewildered and said, "The Holy Grail!"

Steve repeated what she said without realizing that he had said it in almost a whisper. "You don't mean the actual Holy Grail, do you?" he asked in a slow clipped voice.

"Yes, of course, I do. I thought that all of you in the Order knew of its existence," she said. "Dietrich had been contacted by one of the members of the Venerable Order of Saint John at Saint John's Gate in London and he seemed to know all about it and the Chapel of Saint Mary of Magdalene and its relationship to the rose line and with Rosslyn Chapel. Dietrich told me that with the exact time of the midpoint in the eclipse of Venus at this morning's sunrise that the location of the hiding place of the Holy Grail would be seen in the chapel. He said that such an eclipse would not be seen for another two hundred years."

"So that was what this is all about," Steve said to himself. "Another one of those legends that have inspired so many books and that movie about the DaVinci Code."

"You don't really believe all of that, do you?" murmured Steve to Natalie, not wanting to upset her.

Natalie looked startled with Steve's remark. "You are a Knight of Saint John, aren't you?" she said with a questioning look.

"Well, sort of. I'm a Knight of the Venerable Order of Saint John which is the reconstituted English Langue of the Order."

"Reconstituted. What does that mean?"

"It was reorganized by the Capitular Commission of the former Langues of the original Saint John Order after Napoleon forced them from Malta in 1798," Steve explained. "As you now know, I also belong to the fraternal Order of the Black Knights of Malta which is descended from the ancient Order of Saint John in Scotland and Ireland that protected and assimilated the Order of the Knights Templar in Scotland and Ireland when they were outlawed in 1312."

He continued, "We were also outlawed in 1560 by the Knox Parliament and converted to the Protestant cause and the Church of Scotland and England, and then later we affiliated with the Orange Movement and became a fraternal Order with a branch in Canada and the United States. So I guess we are part of the Saint John and the Knights Templar tradition."

Natalie could not quite understand what Steve had just said, but nodded nevertheless that she understood. He looked at her and decided that he could now tell her that this Mr. Smythe, whoever he actually was, had tried to murder her husband, but had luckily failed.

"Natalie, I don't want shock you, but I think you can take what I am going to tell you now. Your husband quite likely saved your life last night. We think that this Smythe fellow wanted to kill you and your husband because he is a Christian Knight and you are his wife. Mr. Smythe is probably a Muslim jihadist assassin. He failed and we are trying to keep it quiet from the press so he will not make a second attempt."

Natalie looked at him with big incredulous eyes and simply said, "I understand!"

It took a minute for both of them to digest the conversation that had just occurred.

Finally, Steve drank the rest of his Scotch without a water chaser and said, "We are going to pretend that this Smythe fellow has succeeded in killing your husband, so we are going to make it appear that you are claiming Dietrich's body in Temple in a routine fashion and have it flown back to his home in Germany. Where is he from anyway?"

"His family is from Marburg an der Lahn. Do you want me to call them?"

"No, not just yet," Steve replied. "We need to have check out of this hotel after you claim the 'body' of your husband in Temple and make the necessary arrangements for you and 'the body' to be flown quietly to Germany.

"We'll have the Temple newspaper print a small back page story of a German national accidentally dying and his body being flown back to Germany. We'll create false funeral and burial arrangements in Marburg and afterwards arrange for you secretly to return to Edinburg to be with your husband as he recovers at the hospital and we unravel this puzzle. We'll create a cover story that you are in private mourning so no one will know where you are.

"Whoever these people are and why they wanted to kill your husband is a total mystery now and we need time for your husband to recover, and then, with his help and yours, figure out what this is all about. It may have international implications. We are going to touch base with Scotland Yard in London and Interpol to find out what connections, if any, this Smythe may have with Saint John's Gate or the Venerable Order or any jihadist groups. We won't bring the German police or anyone else into this until we have more information. So, will you please help us?"

"Of course I will," she said with a glimmer of a smile.

Steve's cell phone rang and he pulled the phone from his shirt pocket. His iPhone was in a leather cover that looked like a leather covered small appointment book. He looked at the phone's screen that told him who it was.

"Hello, Jamie, how's our patient?"

He smiled and winked at Natalie when Dr. Macadam replied that Dietrich was awake, his lung reinflated by a small tube with a one-way valve and that he was weakly asking about Natalie.

"That's great," replied Steve. "Can he talk on the telephone and reassure his wife not to worry?"

"Yep," was the singular reply from Dr. Macadam and Steve could hear him talking in the background, when suddenly the weak voice of Dietrich asked from Steve's phone, "Natalie?"

"Wait a second," replied Steve as he turned to Natalie who was anxiously listening to the conversation. He put the phone on speaker and handed his phone to Natalie.

"Dietrich, darling," she whispered quietly into the phone. "Are you okay?"

He replied firmly, "Yes, the doctor and nurses have got me patched up like a mummy, but I'm still breathing—a little weak, but wanting to see you!"

She could hear Dr. Macadam in the background telling Dietrich, "Later tonight when you're stronger. We'll have Inspector Grant bring her to you. Let me talk to your wife."

"Bye darling, got to go," rasped Dietrich. "Here's Dr. Macadam."

"Mrs. von Schoenfeld?"

"Yes."

"Would you like to see your husband later tonight?"

"Oh, yes. When?"

"Tell Steve to bring you here around four o'clock tonight to the emergency room entrance."

She turned to Grant and said, "Dr. Macadam wants you to take me to Dietrich's room about four o'clock—is that all right?"

"Right-O," Steve replied loud enough for Jamie to hear him.

"Okay, I'll see you both later at four," said Macadam.

As she hung up, Natalie turned to Steve with a sigh of relief as the color came back into her face, and said "Well, I guess that we'd better go downstairs to Hadrian's for that late lunch Dietrich had promised me we were going to have when he returned." She went to the closet and put on a navy blue half jacket, and smiled, "Let's go!"

Steve straightened up and smiled, realizing that he was going to sample some Balmoral cuisine sooner than he had thought. He knew that Balmoral's chic and stylish Brasserie was famous for delicious cuisine in an informal ambience. The luncheon menu offered a mix of Scottish dishes and international dishes. He was ready for some Haggis and Scotch!

4 THE GATHERING

When Steve and Natalie entered Hadrian's Brasserie, Steve noticed that it had a distinct 1930s Art Deco influence. This was the first time that he had actually been here for lunch even though he had lived in Edinburgh for ten years while going to law school and the police academy. Natalie had obviously been there before with Dietrich.

The waiter smiled at her and asked, "Hello, Mrs. von Schoenfeld, so nice to see you again. Will your husband be joining you?"

"Later, I hope, he's been delayed." She smiled as they were seated at a table for three by the waiter.

"Very smart," Steve thought. "She's three steps ahead!"

Always observant, as Steve seated her he had noticed an older man with greying hair and dark complexion in a blue suit, staring at them or perhaps it was Natalie. She looked stunning in her grey skirt and ivory silk blouse and blue jacket with the navy blue silk scarf that was wrapped around her shoulders. He seated Natalie with her back to the man at the walnut bar as the waiter handed them the menu. He seated himself opposite from her with his back to the wall since he wanted to casually observe everyone in the room. His police training had kicked in without a conscious thought.

The waiter returned and Natalie ordered the French onion soup with Gruyere cheese to start and the Isle of Gigha Halibut with Crab Brandade and dill sauce, topped off with a glass of Piesporter Goldtropfchen Riesling, Spatlese wine. Steve decided on the Traditional Haggis, Neeps, and Tatties with Braised Shallots and Whiskey Cream with Lismore single malt Scotch to wash it down.

Steve confided to Natalie that they must be discreet when they leave to go to the Royal Infirmary. He didn't know if she was being watched, but the older man at the bar that he had first noticed when they sat down had been looking over at them quite often. He didn't like the look of it.

As they made small talk, Steve took his cell phone in its notebook disguise and pulled a pen from his pocket as if to write a note in the book. He quietly murmured to Natalie that he was going to videotape the man at the bar as he pretended to look at something in the book and then write in it. He wanted her not to turn or appear to notice anything askew as they continued their conversation. As he went through the charade and he got his pictures, the old man appeared not to notice that his picture was being taken. Natalie calmly performed her role very well.

She asked Steve, "Did I do okay?"

He smiled back at her and quipped, "You'd make a great detective!"

They finished their delicious meals and Steve paid the bill. He thought, "This would be a perfect setting for a date with Katie!"

As they left the restaurant, Steve said he would have his car brought around to the front of the hotel and then he would drive to the corner of Market Street and North Bridge and pick her up there in fifteen minutes and for her to bring her cell phone. He asked her if she knew where the hotel exit to that corner was located and she nodded her head and said that she did. He then entered her cell phone number into his phone directory and asked her to go to her room and get a hat and coat.

"You do have a suitable hat and coat for our weather, don't you?" he chided.

"Of course!" she answered.

They took the elevator to the fourth floor and he walked her to her room.

While they were walking, he pulled out his cell phone and played the video that he had taken of the older man in the bar and showed it to her. She replied that she didn't recognize him and that she had never met Mr. Smythe.

He said, "No matter, we'll run his picture through identification to find out who he is."

As they reached her door, she took her electronic key out of her bag and handed it to him so he could unlock her door. He was slightly startled at this gesture that he thought had disappeared so long ago in the morass of political correctness.

He took the key, and as he unlocked the door and handed her key back to her, he smiled and gave her a wink of appreciation for her good manners, "I'll see you in fifteen minutes at the corner of Market and North Bridge Road, is that sufficient time?"

She nodded in the affirmative and said simply, "Yes, I'll be wearing my dark brown leather coat with a mauve fedora," as she waved her hand and disappeared into her rooms. The door clicked as it closed.

Steve turned and walked the short distance to the elevator and pushed the down button. When the elevator arrived and opened, he appreciated the fact that it was empty. He entered it and rode down to the lobby in silence with the thought of Natalie and how charming she is! As he exited the elevator, he turned and sauntered toward the lobby and the valet service to retrieve his Jaguar. He did not notice that the man from the Brasserie was standing behind one of the pillars in the lobby watching his every move.

It took about fifteen minutes for the car to arrive. The man behind the pillar moved toward the elevator and as he walked he pulled a piece of paper from his pocket and glanced at it. The number on the paper read Suite 420. He smiled, pressed the up button and waited for the elevator to arrive. When the elevator door opened, he entered and punched the button for the fourth floor. As the door for his elevator was closing, the door to an adjacent elevator opened and Natalie stepped out in her hat and coat. She turned toward the hotel exit to North Bridge Road and swiftly walked toward it.

Meanwhile the man from the Brasserie had exited his elevator cab on the fourth floor and walked to Suite 420. He knocked on the door and waited two minutes and then knocked again. When there was no answer, he took a small electronic device from his pocket and passed it over the door's electronic lock. There was a clicking noise and he turned the handle. The door opened, revealing the darkened rooms. He pulled a small flashlight from his pocket along with a bottle of chloroform and a handkerchief which he then soaked with the chloroform. He turned on the flashlight and silently moved toward the bedroom where he expected Natalie to be asleep. He turned off the flashlight and waited briefly for his eyes to become accustomed to the darkness and to make sure she was asleep, then entered the bedroom. To his surprise the room was empty and the bed unoccupied.

He cursed, then put the bottle of chloroform and handkerchief back in his pocket and ran to the front door of the suite and to the elevator and repeatedly pushed the down button. When it arrived, he pressed the button for the lobby and waited impatiently for it to descend.

Meanwhile, the valet had already handed Steve the key to his Jaguar and tipped his cap.

Steve handed the young man a sizable tip with a smile and said, "I sincerely appreciate your efficiency!" and slid into the right side driver's seat as the valet closed the door smoothly after him.

Steve started the car. The Jaguar growled, and then he slipped the transmission into drive and the car purred and moved forward onto Princes Street. Steve drove the short distance to the corner of Princes Street and North Bridge Street. He turned right onto North Bridge, and looked down the block toward Market Street.

There she was. Natalie was waiting patiently on the corner dressed in a dark brown leather coat and a broad brimmed Hildegarde Neff mauve felt fedora hat pulled down and slightly tilted toward the right side of her brow. As he pulled up to her and stopped, she opened the passenger door and quipped, "What kept you?"

He chuckled at her remark as she settled into the leather seat next to him. "Oh, you know we Scots, we take the time to do it right and on time!"

The door to the elevator opened and the man from the Brasserie ran limping to the valet service desk. He asked the valet if a man and a woman had just left and the young man answered, "No, just Inspector Grant in his Jaguar who gave me a large tip."

The swarthy man in the blue suit clenched his fists and swore under his breath, "Damn!"

The sedan, a few minutes before, had slid into traffic and purred southeast toward the new Royal Infirmary at Little France. As they pulled into the drive leading to the emergency room, Natalie leaned forward hoping to see the emergency room entrance faster.

She exclaimed, "Is that Dr. Macadam standing there?"

Steve looked and could just see Jamie waving at him. He thought to himself that Natalie certainly has good eyesight, he could just barely make out Jamie's figure.

"I believe it is," he said. "We are here and it is just now precisely four o'clock!"

They pulled up to Dr. Macadam and Steve lowered the window on Natalie's side of the car. Dr. Macadam peered into the car and extended his hand to Natalie as the passenger window slid down. He nodded a "hello" to Steve and he returned the nod.

"A pleasure to meet you Mrs. von Schoenfeld," Jamie said. "You have no idea how desperate that husband of yours is to see you and ease any concerns you might have about him."

"That sounds just like my Dietrich, always concerned about my feelings!" she exclaimed as she thankfully shook Jamie's hand with both of her hands.

"Steve, park your car over there," Jamie said as he opened the left side door to let Natalie out.

As she exited the car, Jamie helped her. She extended her hand and grasped his hand. It was a firm grasp, like a skier grasping a ski pole. He looked into her hazel eyes glimmering with hope.

"Is he really okay?" she asked hesitantly.

"Yes, he is a very strong young man." He brushed his long, blond hair from his eyes as a strong wind was freshening from the west and he muttered, "It might rain tonight."

Inspector Grant had finished parking his car and was walking toward them. He looked at the clouds gathering in the west. "Yes," he breathed quietly to himself, "It sure feels like rain."

The three of them walked through the electric doors that had swung open as if by magic. They entered a large hallway leading toward the emergency rooms, and twenty paces down they turned into another hallway that led to a group of private suites. As they started to enter one of the suites, Dr. Macadam prepared Natalie for what she'd see.

"Don't be alarmed, Dietrich is firmly bandaged to keep the chest tube and stabilizing valve in place during the healing process. Try not to excite him, he's a very determined young man who is most anxious to see his wife." He turned to Natalie and with a wink of his twinkling blue eyes, he softly told her, "Try not to embrace him too tightly!"

"I understand, I'm a nurse," she said.

They entered the apartment, crossed the living room and entered the bedroom. Dietrich was lying up in his bed and could hardly constrain himself when he saw Natalie.

"Liebchen, bitte, kommst du hier!"

He held his arms up weakly as she ran across the room

and kissed him. He moaned slightly, trying not to alarm her as she embraced him.

"Oh, I'm so sorry, schatzy, I'm so happy to see you. I've been worried all afternoon."

"Es ist nichts!" he declared unconvincingly.

Jamie took control of the events, saying, "I'm the doctor now and we will have plenty of time to talk tomorrow. I must insist that we not excite the patient too much tonight; he needs some rest. Dietrich has told me that he wants to call his cousin, Dr. Christopher Rood in Austin, Texas, and tell him what happened last night, but I told him that Inspector Grant and I will call Dr. Rood. Tonight, Natalie, you'll be the best medicine and nurse for Dietrich."

Grant voiced his approval, "That's good. We'll arrange to have your clothes and other effects brought here to the hospital from the hotel and make it look like you have checked out of your suite."

"Okay," agreed Natalie. "I'll give the security guards a list of our belongings and where they are located in our hotel suite."

Jamie continued, "Steve, you and I have another private apartment that we'll use as a command post and also accommodations for Dr. Rood and his wife if they can come immediately to Edinburgh!"

With that, Jamie motioned for Steve to follow him and leave Natalie and Dietrich alone for the night. As he and Steve started for the door, the normally taciturn doctor turned and told them both, "We will get whatever you both need while you are here. Then he smiled, "And remember— no excitement!"

With that, Steve and Jamie left the room and walked down the hall to another private apartment and entered. Jamie had gathered a few essentials such as a desk with telephone and computer and an apartment refrigerator and microwave. He had done the same for Dietrich's rooms. Both apartments had a private bath and a small kitchenette with a dining room, living room and bedroom.

They sat down in two leather stuffed chairs on either side of a small table with a lamp and telephone on it. Macadam then shared what he'd been told by his patient.

"Dietrich told me he had been working on a thesis that the Holy Grail had been recovered from the Jesus family tomb south of Jerusalem by the Templars 1,000 years ago after the conquest of Jerusalem by the first crusaders in 1099 AD. He explained that the tomb had been rediscovered on Friday, March 28, 1980, by a construction company that was building modern apartments on old sites. If it had not been for Rivka Maoz and a couple of engineers who recognized the importance of the discovery, everything could have been lost.

"Dietrich and his cousin, Dr. Rood, evidently, had both read the book, *The Jesus Family Tomb*, about that discovery and read that one of the things noted from the research by James D. Tabor and other archeologists was that the tomb had been entered around the time of the first crusade and that there was evidence that the Templars had been the intruders. Some of the things missing from the tomb were eating utensils and plates, but more importantly a stone cup—the Holy Grail!

"Legend has it that evidence recently found in the Vatican archives document that the Templars actually had such a cup and artifacts from the tomb of Jesus and his family, which they hid possibly in Scotland from the time of their Inquisition on Friday, October 13, 1307!

"It seems that a Templar fleet had been anchored at La Rochell on the west coast of France and the Templar treasure that had been seen by the king of France two weeks earlier in the Temple in Paris had mysteriously disappeared. It was not found by the king's soldiers on that same morning of Friday 13, 1307. Some of the Knights Templar escaped arrest and joined up with the Knights of Saint John, including Dietrich's ancestor, a knight by the name of Schoenfeld. He, too had survived an assassination attempt!

"Many historians, Dietrich continued, have written that the only safe haven for the fleet was Scotland since Robert the Bruce and his entire kingdom had been excommunicated by the Pope! For that reason, treasures and documents from the Templars may have been hidden in Scotland. He said that his ancestor had hidden a secret lead box beneath the floor of Saint Mary Chapel at the time of a Venus eclipse of the sun. Even Mary, Queen of Scots' mother, Mary of Guise, wrote in a letter about a secret of the Templars that she would never divulge! Anyway, one thing for sure, Dietrich and his cousin Dr. Rood may be able to shed some light on what is going on and why Dietrich was attacked at Saint Mary Chapel."

"Whew!" exclaimed Steve. "This is getting more and more interesting. Let's call Dr. Rood and tell him what has happened and see if he can come to Edinburgh as soon as possible. Do you have Dr. Rood's number?" he asked Jamie.

"Yes," Jamie replied. "After I told Dietrich about our scheme and he readily approved it, he gave me Dr. Rood's home number in Austin, Texas. He will call his family tomorrow and advise them what we have planned and the utmost need for secrecy."

After Jamie handed Steve the number in Austin for Dr. Rood, Steve punched the number into the phone and he could hear the phone on the opposite end ringing. It was seven hours earlier in Texas—1:30 in the afternoon. After what seemed an extremely long period of time, a female voice answered the phone.

"Hello, who is it?"

"Sorry to disturb you, this is Inspector Steven Grant in Edinburgh, Scotland. Is Dr. Rood there by any chance?"

"Yes, speaking!"

"No, I mean your husband."

"Yes, he's here too," came the reply, then he heard feminine laughter. "Yes, we are both doctors, that mistake is made all of the time. Wait a minute, I'll get him."

Steve could hear her footsteps and then garbled conversation and then a man's voice answered, "Hello, Christopher Rood here, what can I do for you?"

"I'm sorry sir, I didn't know that there were two of you who are doctors."

"Yes, I feel that way sometimes, too," chuckled Dr. Rood. "What's happened?"

"I'm sorry sir, I have some good news and some bad news for you. The bad news is that your cousin Dietrich von Schoenfeld has been attacked and stabbed. The good news is that the attack failed and Dietrich is in stable condition and is now with his wife in a private apartment in a hospital here in Edinburgh. He'll recover, but it will take some time. His left lung was collapsed but we have reinflated the lung and he is breathing normally. We need you and your wife here to help us unravel this mystery and we also need the utmost secrecy. Can you come immediately?"

The instant answer was, "Yes!"

Steve heard some muffled conversation on the other end of the phone as the two Drs. Rood conversed.

"I'll call you right back and let you know the name, number and time of our flight. We'll probably fly to Atlanta and then take a Delta flight directly to Edinburgh. What is your number?"

Steve gave him Jamie's cell phone number and the number of the telephone on the table and they both said their goodbyes and hung up.

"Well, that's that!" sighed Steve. "I need to get home and get some sleep and sort this all out." He looked at Jamie and asked, "You'll take the call from Dr. Rood, won't you?"

Jamie nodded that he would.

"Good, call me and let me know when to pick them up at the airport and I'll rearrange my schedule. Katie's pretty good at that, you know. She'll ask some questions so you'll have to cover for me so we can hush this thing up. You know of course, that we'll have to let her in on all of this sooner or later, don't you?"

"Later," replied Jamie.

Steve ambled toward the door, dreading his drive back to his townhouse. It's at times like this when he'd wished that he were married and could get some solace.

Maybe he should call Kate, but he knew that she could

weasel the information out of him. "Oh, what the hell," he convinced himself and called Kate's number.

"Well, it's about time you called!" she purred. "Jamie just called. I've got coffee, brandy and a soft shoulder waiting for you. I've been on pins and needles all day."

"What's it all about?" Steve sighed and gave in. He simply could not resist her logic and besides that soft shoulder sounded pretty good!

"Okay. But all of this has to be hush-hush. Jamie's going to call me later and give me some information that I need for tomorrow. I'll be there in thirty minutes!"

5 THE PLOT THICKENS

Col. Rood was an athletic man now in his 40s who had been a young flight surgeon serving voluntarily in "Desert Storm" as a backseat weapons systems officer in the Phantom II RF-4C "Wild Weasel" tactical reconnaissance aircraft. It was the last manned aircraft of its kind in the US Air Force inventory. The Phantom had served well in Vietnam and had still served ably in Desert Shield and Desert Storm. It was capable of mach two flight.

Dr. Christopher Rood was deployed late in theater with the 12th TRS from Bergstrom Air Force Base in Texas. The RFC's began flying combat missions on the first night of Operation Desert Storm, January 17, 1991. They began with a limited daylight mission, but increasingly were repeatedly diverted from their photographic missions to go and look for Scud missile launchers hiding in western Iraq. They had great success just as they had in Viet Nam. The versatility of the aircraft and crew made them formidable fighters. No Iraqi MIG, missile or gun ever touched an RFC-4C throughout the war!

Col. Rood later said after Desert Storm that he was well suited for the Phantom jet tactical reconnaissance missions since he was a photographer, a radiologist, pathology expert, and most of all a fighter. He wasn't exaggerating since he had been Texas state champion in martial arts and judo!

As Dr. Rood hung up the telephone, he turned to his wife. Carolyn and murmured, "Babe, I hope I haven't been wrong in this theory that Dietrich and I have about the Holy Grail and gotten Dietrich in real bad trouble."

Carolyn, a diminutive but resourceful and doggedly determined Scot, moved to his side and put her arms around him soothingly.

"It will be all right. Tell me about it. Is Dietrich okay?"

He put his arms around her waist and held her. Christopher was almost six feet tall and she was only five feet three inches, but what she lacked in height was more than made up by her dogged Scottish determination—her maiden name was MacIntosh! She carried herself proudly with a stubborn lilt to her chin when a problem presented itself—an affectionate friend, but a formidable foe!

Christopher said, "You remember when the three of us, Randall, you and I were at Roslyn Chapel and I said to the two of you that the carvings at the top of the master's column resembled the notes of a song, and I had the sudden epiphany about the Song of Solomon, Saint Bernard, and his sponsorship of the Knights Templar. Saint Bernard's favorite part of the Bible was the Song of Solomon. And remember when the next morning at breakfast, Randall casually informed us that the number of verses in the Song of Solomon were the same as the number of notes at the master's column?"

Puzzled, Carolyn looked at him and said, "What's that got to do with Dietrich?"

"Well, I told Dietrich about our theories about Roslyn Chapel being on the Rose line and that Saint Mary Chapel was also on the Rose line, twelve miles due south of Roslyn Chapel's South Door—the Woman's Door. Remember that Roslyn Chapel was originally known as Saint Matthew's, and the Gospel of Saint Matthew mentions Mary Magdalene and the Song of Solomon are supposed to carry a code about hidden treasures of the Knights Templar. Dietrich had convinced Natalie that it would be fun if they planned their honeymoon in Edinburgh, Scotland, a city just a few miles northeast of Roslyn and Saint Mary Chapel. He told me that he was going to test out a theory of his own and then talk to us. He mentioned that our friend Randall Fox, a PhD in history and anthropology, was on an archeological investigation of his own at Fountains Abbey in England and that he was going to talk to him after his visit to Saint Mary if his quest was successful."

"So what happened to Dietrich?"

"Someone stabbed him while he was checking out Saint Mary Chapel. Fortunately, Natalie was not with him."

Carolyn signed and held her hand over her mouth as she looked anxiously at Christopher.

"The police are investigating the crime. Dietrich will survive, and they are keeping everything silent since there appears to be some foreign intrigue. They don't want the assailants to know that Dietrich is alive and is recovering. The police and Dietrich want us to come over to Edinburgh and give them a hand in this case."

"So, what are we waiting for? Let's get a move on. You call the airlines and I'll get us packed. I just have a few calls to make and I'll be ready in an hour; besides, you know that I always love going to my Scotland!"

With that, she grabbed Christopher around his neck and pulled all five feet three inches of herself up on her toes and kissed him squarely on his lips. She abruptly turned and with a smile and a wink, she hurried off to their bedroom to prepare for their trip.

Dr. Rood collected himself, called Delta airlines and got the reservations for the flight. Then he called Dr. Macadam's cell phone and got a prompt answer.

"Is that you, Dr. Rood?"

"Yes," answered Christopher. "We are packing right now and we'll be arriving on Delta's connecting KLM flight DL9633 out of Amsterdam at 5:30 p.m., your time, tomorrow. Will someone be meeting us?"

Jamie thanked him for the information and told him that Inspector Grant had said that he would personally pick them up at the airport and drive them to their apartment in the hospital. He mentioned that Dietrich was doing well and looked considerably better now that Natalie has joined him in their apartment. He also mentioned that Inspector Grant had already assigned inconspicuous Scottish homeland security agents to that area of the hospital and quietly checked Natalie out of the Balmoral Hotel and brought their belongings to the hospital.

"I am looking forward to meeting you and your wife, particularly since you belong to the older American offshoot of our Scottish Branch of the Order of Saint John."

Dr. Rood thanked him for calling them about Dietrich. They both said their goodbyes and Jamie retired to his emergency room quarters in the hospital.

Meanwhile, Carolyn had finished the packing and was waiting on her husband to finish getting ready for their departure. She had just finished pouring a Scotch for both of them when Christopher appeared in the living room. He was just finishing tying a full Windsor knot to his tie and straightening the Harris Tweed jacket that Carolyn had laid out for him.

She instinctively knew the weather would be stiffening in Scotland and would be considerably cooler than the warmer spring weather in Austin. Christopher complained that it was too warm for the coat, but she assured him that he would appreciate the extra warmth the Scottish coat would give him when he arrived in Europe! With that he picked up his Scotch and drank it down. The bracing effect of the Scotch was immediate.

About that time, their taxi had arrived and they picked up their luggage and opened the front door just as the driver approached them to help with the baggage. Christopher put his bag down and locked the front door after setting the alarm system as the driver picked up Carolyn's bags and reached for Dr. Rood's bag. He thanked the driver, but said that he would carry his own bag since he had noticed that the driver was already struggling with Carolyn's three bags!

The flight to Atlanta and connection with their flight to Amsterdam proved to be uneventful. Christopher had taken a sedative so that he could peacefully sleep as they crossed the Atlantic Ocean. Carolyn passed her time reading and napping in between the dinner and snacks that were served.

When they arrived at Schiphol airport, they found that their flight would not be leaving for an hour and a half, so they decided to find a restaurant and have a good meal before they got to Edinburgh.

They were just finishing the meal, when their flight to Edinburgh was announced. Christopher paid the bill and they hurried to the gate and got there just as they started to board the flight. Their seats were announced and they boarded the aircraft without incident and settled comfortably down for the short trip to Edinburgh.

The announcement of their arrival at Edinburgh woke Christopher from a light nap and caught Carolyn on the final page of the book that she had been reading. She was happy to hear that they had arrived in her beloved Scotland!

"Well, we're finally here," she said. "I can hardly wait to meet Inspector Grant. He sounded very charming on the phone."

She smiled as she looked at Christopher and winked! He laughed. He knew her appealing and coquettish mannerisms completely dumbfounded many people that didn't know her. She mesmerized everyone she met!

Carolyn stood up after they landed and taxied to the gate and the "all clear" sign was illuminated. After gathering their bags and swiftly clearing customs, to their delight they saw Steve Grant standing directly in front of them at the exit gate waving a sign with their names emblazoned upon it.

Steve smiled as he waved the placard. He was pleased that there had been no delays or waits. He motioned to a porter who was ready with a baggage cart to take their bags. He then exchanged handshakes with both of his charges. As he shook Carolyn's hand, he looked into her blue-green eyes.

"Inspector Grant, I presume?" and then she smiled in a demure fashion.

Steve was completely captivated.

Steve had been impressed with the firmness of Christopher' handshake and intrigued by the assured grasp of Carolyn.

"This way, I have my car outside."

And as they entered the back seat of Steve's Jaguar sedan, Steve brightly announced, "Natalie and Dietrich are so happy that you have come. They can't wait to see you again. Your coming has really lifted Dietrich's spirit and he has shown definite improvement with seeing Natalie and hearing of your arrival. They just knew that you would be starved after that long flight, so they persuaded Jamie to pick up a complete dinner from their favorite restaurant in Edinburgh—'Number One' at the Balmoral Hotel where they had been staying. Jamie has pulled out all of the stops and picked up a full course dinner for you. You'll find the hospital also has a fine menu for honored guests such as yourselves. You know that the Queen has been our guest in the past."

With this, Carolyn and Christopher, remembering the meal at Schiphol, looked at each other and simultaneously puffed out their cheeks and sighed, "How nice!"

The Jaguar pulled up to the curb next to the hospital with a quiet purr and stopped. Dr. Macadam was waiting patiently for them and when Steve exited the automobile and opened the back door on Carolyn's side of the car, Dr. Macadam had already seized the handle of Christopher's door and opened it.

Christopher stepped into the brisk wind that was picking up and swirling around him and the car. He thought to himself, "How right, she was. Carolyn knew her Scotland!"

"Dietrich has told me that you both had flown similar types of missions— you, when you were in 'Desert Storm' and him, when he was in Afghanistan," Macadam said as he shook Christopher's hand.

"Yes, I guess that's right, only I wasn't the pilot like Dietrich was."

Jamie grinned, "Yeah, I know Afghanistan, I was in quite a few 'dust-off' missions in Kandahar."

They looked at each other as comrades in arms and smiled knowingly.

The 'boot' of the Jaguar flipped open as if by magic, revealing its contents.

Steve, Jamie and Christopher removed the luggage, closed and locked the doors. They carried the luggage through the hospital doors where some security men, wearing white orderly uniforms, promptly secured it and swiftly carried it toward the apartment that had been selected for Carolyn and Christopher.

Once inside their apartment with their clothes neatly hung in the bedroom closet by the security men, Carolyn looked at her husband and voiced her admiration of their treatment.

"This is really okay. I wish we had something like this when we were on call as residents, don't you? Christus Spohn Memorial Hospital in Corpus Christi was never like this! I remember that we were lucky to even find an empty bed to snatch a few Zs."

Carolyn and Christopher had gone to undergraduate school at the University of Texas in Austin where he had been a member of the "Silver Spurs," but they had not met each other until they were residents at Spohn Hospital and Driscoll Children's Hospital, respectively in Corpus Christi on the eve of Desert Storm.

In the late 80s, they were all working frantically, going some weeks with little or no sleep. She was in Pediatrics and he was in Radiology. They had met at a fluid rounds party given for the new residents at the hospital. Also at that party was an archeologist that was studying some old Spanish ships that had sunk in a hurricane in 1561 just off the coast of Padre Island. Dr. Randall Fox, who was a friend of the hospital's chief of staff, was working on his PhD and was using the shipwreck of the galleons for his thesis.

They had met each other while they were standing at a makeshift bar in a lecture room at the hospital. Alcoholic beverages were not allowed in the hospital, but nobody had said anything about the 99 percent ethyl alcohol that was in use in the research laboratories! Their discussion about the wreckage of the ancient ships had begun a friendship that had lasted over the years since that meeting in Corpus Christi.

Carolyn and Christopher had married as had Randall, but his marriage had not lasted, partly because he was a PhD that was oblivious to everything but his real loves—history and archeology—and partly because of his long absences at various archeological digs around the world. He was an expert on the Crusades and the Middle Ages as well as the Middle East, but not marriage.

Christopher put his arm around Carolyn as Jamie proudly escorted them and Steve to the dining room where the meal from the Number One Restaurant had been delivered and laid out.

Jamie and Steve had planned to just drink some wine as Carolyn and Christopher ate their meals—to get better acquainted before they went down to Natalie and Dietrich's apartment. But Carolyn said that they couldn't possibly eat all of it and insisted that the two of them share the meal. Jamie and Steve looked at each other as Christopher piped in and echoed his wife's pleas.

"Okay!" muttered Steve. He had not eaten any lunch and couldn't resist the temptation to try some food from another top rated restaurant—especially this one that had an outstanding reputation!

"Me too," chimed in Jamie, who was known more for action than words.

Carolyn and Christopher both sighed in relief, and Jamie and Steve laid out two more plates and silverware from the pantry for themselves.

During the course of the meal, Steve and Jamie filled their guests in on all of the facts that they had in the case and they were anxious to learn what it was that he and Dietrich had going on with the chapel on Mount Lothian. Christopher's answers to their questions all pretty much matched what they had been told by Natalie and Dietrich. Steve said that he had just a few more questions for Dietrich and Natalie when they would all meet later for just a short time that evening. Dietrich was still quite weak and they didn't want to wear him out.

Steve suggested that they discuss some things with Dietrich and Natalie over brandy. They all agreed and left the "headquarters" apartment after locking the door. Jamie then handed Carolyn and Christopher the electronic keys to their apartment.

Steve knocked on the door to Dietrich and Natalie's apartment and there was a shuffling of footsteps just before the door opened and Natalie appeared with the same calm look in her eyes and sparkling smile that had captivated him so when he first met her.

"Inspector Grant, it's so pleasant to see you again," and then she noticed Carolyn, Christopher and Jamie standing behind Steve.

"Oh!" she burst out and rushed to Carolyn and Christopher and threw her arms around them both. "I am so glad to see you. We haven't seen you since our wedding in Germany! Dietrich and I both need you to help us in this affair. I'm so frightened—they nearly killed Dietrich!"

By this time big tears were rolling down her face as she embraced Carolyn and looked desperately into Carolyn's eyes. She broke down in her arms and started to collapse. Carolyn and Christopher together put their arms around her and helped her to the sofa in the living room. Jamie by this time had entered the room and was kneeling by her side and holding her hand. Carolyn got a moistened towel from the kitchen and laid it across her forehead. Dr. Macadam looked at Carolyn and Christopher.

"I guess she's been building up to this and was so relieved at seeing the two of you. I've seen this type of delayed hysteria on the battlefield when a soldier finally knows that he's been rescued!"

After a few minutes of consoling her, Carolyn patted her shoulder and said, "Everything is going to be okay. The cavalry has arrived!" With that she left the living room and walked into the bedroom where Dietrich was anxiously waiting.

When he saw Carolyn, a great rush of relief passed across his face and he asked, "Is Natalie okay?"

Carolyn answered him in a soothing manner, "Yes, she's just a little tired, worrying about you and everything that has happened over the last two days. It was just a little too much and when she saw us, it was just a rush of relief over all of the building up of fear and anxiety that she was holding inside of her."

Carolyn said softly, "Now, we can rally all of the forces and solve this problem. But this has been a little too much today and I think a little sedative given to Natalie by Dr. Macadam will help both of you relax, and we can begin to tackle this situation tomorrow when everyone feels better." And with that, Carolyn went to the bedroom door and asked Christopher to come into the bedroom and talk with Dietrich for a little while.

He walked over to his wife and put his arm around her waist as he looked in at Dietrich and said, "Alles ist gut. Natalie ist sehr mude and musten zum bett gehen, nicht war?"

All Dietrich could do was smile at his favorite cousin and say, "Ja, Ich verstehe."

And with this, they went back into the living room and Christopher said to everyone, "You know, I think that we are all tired and Carolyn and I are going to our rooms and get a good night's sleep. Jamie, would you mind staying with Natalie for a few more minutes while she gains her composure? What do you think, would a little sedative help her tonight?"

Jamie nodded in the affirmative.

Natalie said, "I feel better now and would welcome a little quiet and sleep. I think a good night's rest would be just the ticket for everyone. Dietrich and I would love to have breakfast with our favorite cousins tomorrow morning. Maybe all of us could get together for lunch and an afternoon discussion of what's going on."

"Do you mind if I walk you to your door?" Steve said to Carolyn and Christopher. I think I'll go home to bed now, myself. And with that, the three of them left the room waving goodbyes until tomorrow.

As soon as the door closed and they walked down the corridor towards the Drs. Rood's apartment, Steve stopped, shook both Carolyn's and Christopher's hands and said, "You know, I'm pretty tired myself. I'll say goodnight now and go home and try to get some sleep."

He turned and walked a few steps down the corridor and then stopped, and turned toward Carolyn and Christopher who were still watching him. And he said thoughtfully, "You know, I think that I may have some pictures of Dietrich's assailant." He then turned, walked down the corridor and went out the door to his waiting Jaguar.

6 A LITTLE UNDERSTANDING

The sun crept above the horizon and revealed a clear crisp Scottish morning. There was a hint of the rain that had fallen a few hours before still on the streets and the birds were already flitting about in their morning duties.

Christopher was up and busy in the kitchen making their morning coffee when Carolyn poked her head from beneath the covers and exclaimed, "You certainly are a morning glory. I thought you might still be tired from yesterday's trip and all of the excitement from last night."

Christopher grinned and replied, "Yeah, I thought that I would be too, but I've been thinking about what Inspector Grant had said last night when he was leaving. Do you think that he might actually have a picture of Dietrich's assailant?"

He had hardly gotten the words from his mouth when there was a knock at the door. Christopher walked over to the door with a hot cup of coffee in his hand.

When he opened it, he was surprised to see Dietrich standing there!

"Good morning, sleepy heads," Dietrich said. "Natalie has just about finished making breakfast and wanted me to invite you over to our apartment for a little morning repast. She is feeling much better since she has gotten a good night's sleep. I think the sedative that Dr. Macadam gave her last night was just what she needed."

Christopher looked at Dietrich and said that he was surprised about how chipper he looked and remarked, "Apparently Natalie was just what you needed and I'm happy to see you up and about."

"I'm tired of being in bed and I'm ready to get on with trying to find out why I was attacked."

With that being said, Dietrich entered the apartment and Christopher walked over to the kitchenette and poured Dietrich a cup of coffee. "You like it black, don't you?"

"Jawohl," Dietrich replied as he took the cup. "You remembered."

"Aber naturlich!" Christopher smiled.

Carolyn appeared in the doorway to the bedroom dressed in a pale blue nightgown with a dark blue robe wrapped around her. She waved at Dietrich and said, "We were just getting up, would it be okay if we came to your apartment in our robes?"

Dietrich smiled and said, "But of course, we don't want the food to get cold, do we? And besides, the two of you look so ravishing in your night clothes!" He laughed and then said, "Seriously, Natalie is anxious to see you both!"

Carolyn walked over to Christopher and took the cup of coffee that Christopher was holding out to her. Christopher kissed her as she took the cup and said, "Let's go."

The three of them then walked out of the door and into the hallway with Christopher locking the door behind him and stuffing the key that he had taken from the kitchen table into the pocket of his robe. They walked the short distance to the other apartment and Christopher noticed the security agent in an orderly uniform out of the corner of his eye who was leaning against the wall a few meters down the hall. Dr. Rood nodded in his direction and the agent nodded back.

Dietrich opened the door to his apartment and entered with a strong voice proclaiming to Natalie, "Liebchen, wir sind hier!"

As they entered the apartment, they could see that Natalie had breakfast fully prepared. It was a breakfast of orange juice, scrambled eggs with toast and butter with orange marmalade and bacon on the side. There was a bouquet of roses in a vase in the middle of the table.

"Did I do okay?" Natalie said, "I was trying to make breakfast as American as I could!"

"What no grape jam!" Christopher laughed. "Just kidding," he added quickly as he noticed a slight frown cover Carolyn's face and then quickly disappear.

Natalie observed the nonverbal communication and she understood. She smiled at Dietrich, knowingly, and as they all sat down at the table she poured her cup of coffee with cream and sugar and smiled at them, "Bon appetit!"

Christopher expressed their pleasure at seeing the two of them again since their wedding two weeks ago and quickly followed up with the question that he had asked Carolyn earlier that morning. He related what Inspector Grant had said the night before as he was leaving the hospital.

"He thinks that he may have a picture of the guy that stabbed Dietrich."

Natalie immediately remarked as she looked at Dietrich, "He must be talking about the photographs that he took of an older man in the restaurant where we had gone to have a late lunch after he told me about the attack by that awful man you were with."

"You mean, Mr. Smythe?" Dietrich replied.

"Yes!" she gasped. "He had noticed this man looking repeatedly at us and said that he wanted to get some pictures of him. Then he drew a cell phone with a camera that was disguised as a notebook and took some video."

Dietrich rubbed his chin and said, "Could be, yes, it could be! What did he look like, Natalie?"

"Well", she said, "he was sitting at the bar in the Brasserie and I couldn't tell how tall he was, but I don't think that he was very tall—certainly not as tall as you are—he was dark complected. You know, like someone from the Middle East and he had greying hair around the temples, deep set dark eyes that were shifty. When Inspector Grant showed me the video, it appeared that he was nervous. He was dressed in a dark blue business suit that did not fit him very well and with an absolutely hideous patterned tie that didn't match!"

"Darling you could have been a detective!" pronounced Dietrich. "That exactly matches Smythe's description. I'll be able to confirm it if I see Inspector Grant's video. But the question is, why? I've never met this fellow before. All I know is that he called me in Marburg and wanted to know if he could meet me in Scotland. He said that he knew something about Templar treasure. I told him that I was interested in the possible location of historical objects from the Templars and asked if we could meet at the Chapel in Roslyn sometime during our honeymoon. He said that could be arranged and I told him the best time would be on the evening of June fifth since I needed to be at the Chapel of St. Mary at dawn on the sixth of June. He said that would be perfect and that we could meet in the bookstore at the chapel at five o'clock. He said he was of medium height and that he had greying hair and would be wearing a blue suit and green patterned tie."

Natalie remarked, "That's exactly what the man in the video looked like!" "But why would he want to kill you?"

"I don't know, I never met him before and all we discussed that night in Roslyn was the Knights Templar and the treasure that he said the Knights Templar took from Jerusalem and their digging under the Holy Temple there. He didn't seem to know anything about the possibility of the Holy Grail being buried at Saint Mary Chapel and I did not want to say anything more about it. He didn't really seem to be all that interested in anything except the Knights Cross I had from the Johanniter Order that I was wearing.

"He continually talked about the Crusaders in the Holy Land looting and pillaging everywhere they went. When I asked about the Venerable Order, he said that he was actually only a member of the Ambulance Corps at St. John's Gate in London and had gotten my name from one of the members there. I thought at the time that it was peculiar since I had only been at Saint John's Gate one time before, you know," nodding his head towards Christopher. "That was when I went there with you several years before, and we were doing some of our early research on the relationship between the Hospitallers and the Templars after their inquisition from 1307 to 1312.

"He really was mostly silent with chit chat until we left for the Saint Mary Chapel. I remember, before we left for the chapel, that he excused himself for a few minutes and went to call a friend that he would not be back in Glasgow until the next day. He seemed to be genuinely interested in going with me to the chapel that morning. The last thing I remember as the early morning sun's rays caught the steel of the blade of a knife as it slashed across my neck and then plunged into my ribs was him muttering Allah Akbar! I felt just like a lamb that had been led to the slaughter. Just before I blacked out, I thought to myself, 'Dumkopf!' The next thing I remembered was when I became aware of my being in a helicopter and Dr. Macadam leaning over me and reassuring me that I was okay and on my way to the hospital."

Christopher leaned forward just after he took a deep drink of coffee and said, "This is not about our search for the Holy Grail; this is a deep personal vendetta that somehow is mixed up with you being a Knight of Saint John, the Crusades and the current deadly Jihadist movement worldwide. Did Mr. Smythe, or whatever his real name is, seem interested in Natalie or her absence when he met you at the bookshop at Roslyn Chapel?"

"Well, I don't know," replied Dietrich. "He did seem a little disappointed that she wasn't with me when we met at the bookshop. But I just thought it was a matter of courtesy rather than real disappointment. You don't think that he had designs on Natalie?"

"Yes I do!" said Christopher. "There must have been a

reason for his being at the Brasserie instead of leaving the country. I believe that Inspector Grant's hunch about possible danger to Natalie is well founded and I believe that it was on his mind when he made that statement last night that he just may have taken a picture of the assailant."

For the first time, a shiver ran down Natalie's spine as she took in the full meaning of what was going on. She had just finished taking a bite of toast and marmalade and had picked up her coffee cup when Christopher had spoken about the possible dangers. Her cup shook and a little coffee spilled onto the table. She quickly took her napkin, dabbed at the spilled coffee and choked an apology, "I'm sorry," and looked down at her plate. "I'm suddenly not hungry."

Dietrich reached over and patted her shoulder at the same time that Carolyn held her hand.

"It's okay," Carolyn assured her. "Remember, I told you that the cavalry is here. Don't worry, we're ahead of the game. Inspector Grant is on top of this and we'll have plenty more to talk about when he gets here at noon. Meanwhile, let's finish breakfast."

She had no sooner spoken, than there was a knock at the door and Dr. Macadam announced his presence.

"Is breakfast ready?"

Natalie could not hide her joy at his voice as she answered, laughing, "Come in, you're not too late—yet." Then she whispered to Carolyn, "I think he's just a little boy who thinks he's grown up, but he is nice."

Jamie opened the door and peered around it just as if he were the mischievous boy that Natalie had alluded to.

"I brought some fresh fruit in case anyone had forgotten."

With that he entered through the door with a basket of mixed fruit that he had pilfered from the hospital's kitchen. Someone had tied a bow around the handle, but Jamie would not admit to doing that. Instead, he said that he had found the basket lying on top of a cabinet and felt that it needed a more worthy home.

Everyone laughed. It had been just the right thing at the

right time to counter the seriousness of the situation. He placed the fruit on the table, grabbed an extra chair and sat down between Carolyn and Natalie, who poured him a cup of coffee and declared that she felt like one of the six musketeers. With that observation, everyone laughed again, but didn't correct her numbers and welcomed Jamie into the group discussion of events and bid that he help them eat breakfast.

Jamie gave an instant apology to Dietrich, "I'm sorry, I didn't mean to cause so much humor."

He turned to Natalie, "I hope that I didn't cause our patient too much pain."

He looked back at Dietrich and said, "How are your ribs this morning? It looks like you're strong enough to walk, but take it easy!"

Dietrich smiled and faked a false wincing, "They were okay just a minute ago!"

Jamie laughed out loud and exclaimed, "You are an amazing young man—just two days ago you were in Death's grips and now you are raring to go! I'm glad you're feeling better. Please let me know if you're feeling tired." Then Jamie put on his best serious doctor face and quietly whispered to Dietrich, "You're not out of the woods yet and you are very important to all of us."

Dietrich thanked him and said, "I believe that Inspector Grant may have a handle on all of this. Perhaps he'll know who's responsible for the attack when he meets us at noon."

7 EUREKA!

The sun had scarcely reached its zenith when Inspector Grant's Jaguar purred into its comfortable berth in the hospital parking lot. Just then his cell phone rang and he answered it with an easy, "Hello Katie! What have you got for me?"

Kate's soft, but self-assured voice answered, "I had the pictures you sent me run through face identity at Interpol, the security cameras at Glasgow and Edinburgh airports, Scotland Yard, and the FBI and we've got ourselves a real live fish! This bad guy has a record a mile long and he is no less than an operative for—get this—the Muslim Brotherhood."

At that, Grant gave a start. He knew that the Muslim Brotherhood preaches Wahhabi Islam, an extreme strain of the faith that justifies violent means to rid the world of nonbelievers and establish a world where strict Sharia law rules.

"And not only that, he is the grandson of one of its original supporters, the Grand Mufti of Jerusalem, Haj Amin al-Hussaini," she continued. "His name is Mohammad al Hussaini and he has been working in Afghanistan for the Muslim Brotherhood and al-Qaeda teaching the Taliban how to make improvised explosive devices! He currently lives in

Saudi Arabia under assumed names, but frequently uses the name John Smythe when traveling in Europe on a Swiss passport. He was educated in England and attended The London School of Economics. He left Edinburgh yesterday for Prague, Czech Republic. Interpol lost him there and assumed that he is headed for Saudi Arabia through Turkey.

"He also has a son and a daughter. The son's name is Ahmed ali al Hussaini and the daughter's name is Rania al Hussaini. We don't have anything on them yet, but her father Mohammad is a leader in the Muslim Brotherhood that his grandfather had supported since its founding in 1928. His grandfather, Amin al Hussaini was an admirer of Hitler and the Nazis and was the Grand Mufti of Jerusalem since 1921. His grandfather, the Grand Mufti was a co-founder and president of the Arab League. He was the uncle of Yasser Arafat, who was the leader of the PLO. And he was also an SS general in charge of Muslim Waffen SS troops recruited from Bosnia that persecuted Jews and Serbian Christians. They ran the concentration camps in Yugoslavia and Hungary during World War II. They were the Hanzar Divisions.

"On March 1, 1944, Amin al Hussaini made a speech from Berlin addressing his Muslim SS troops to 'Kill the Jews where you find them.' Apparently he expanded this to all Christians as well. Orthodox Christian Serbs were forced to wear blue armbands and Jewish Serbs were forced to wear yellow armbands."

The history lesson was dizzying and depressing, but Katie pressed on. "While in Bosnia, Amin al Hussaini was given the title 'Protector of Islam' and thousands of Muslims joined the Nazi cause. It is estimated that 200,000 Serbian Christians were killed, 22,000 Jewish Bosnians were killed and over 40,000 gypsies were killed. This set the stage for the reprisals later in the Balkans during the Serbian-Bosnia-Herzegovinian Croatian Wars between 1992 and 1995.

"He was also on the Nuremberg criminals list after World War II! Heinrich Himmler, the head of the SS, financed and established the Islamic Institute in Dresden for al Hussaini with the purpose of creating Islamic leaders who would use Islam as a means to spread the Nazi ideology into the Islamic world. After World War II, he fled to Egypt from Paris with the help of the ODESSA and Francois Genoud, Hitler's Swiss banker. Hussaini was under the protection of the French in Paris and escaped to Egypt. In Egypt, he was given a hero's welcome by the Egyptian government and Gamal Abdul Nasser, the leader of the Arab Nazi Party known as 'Young Egypt.' Nasser later overthrew the Egyptian government in a coup in 1952 and made Egypt a safe haven for Nazi war criminals.

"In 1946, Yugoslavia had requested Egypt to extradite him for war crimes and crimes against humanity, but Egypt refused. There is also some evidence that Amin al Hussaini earlier had an active part in the Armenian genocide when he was a young officer in the Turkish army stationed in Smyrna. One and a half million Armenian Christians were slaughtered under the sword of Islamic jihad by the Ottoman army. His granddaughter married Ali Hassan Salameh, the founder of PLO's Black September, who was later killed by the Mossad for his involvement in the Munich Olympic Massacre!"

There was a long silence on the telephone and Kate responded with an anxious voice, "Steve, are you still there?"

She was always cautious and called him usually with the salutation, Inspector Grant. But the silence had been unusually long and she thought she had heard a gasp on the other end of the line.

A weakened voice answered, "Sorry Katie, but this information caught me off guard. Are you sure? Is it really the grandson of that Nazi war criminal?"

She assured him that the information checked out.

"When was he in Afghanistan?"

"Just a minute", she replied. "I've got it right here." There was a sound of rustling paper and soon Kate's voice came back on the line and said, "It appears that he was there in 2007 and was injured in an air raid by the Germans while he was working with a group of Taliban in the southern province of Kandahar. It seems that he was one of only two 'freedom fighters'"—she spat the words out with disdain and disgust—"to survive that attack."

When she said "freedom fighters" she mouthed the words in a fashion that she used when speaking of persons she considered to be criminal cowards.

After another long pause, Steve said in a soft voice that he usually reserved when they were alone, "This is really dangerous—does he have any confederates here in Scotland that we know about?"

Katie's voice came back on the phone sensing his anxiety for her safety and she replied, "We don't know, but he apparently had someone pick him up at Saint Mary Chapel. Mrs. Elliott said that she saw him picked up by a black Mercedes sedan and we've checked all of the rental agencies and hotels concerning his stay in Scotland and they can find no trace of him staying at any hotels or bed and breakfasts or renting any automobile. He was probably aided by one of the mosques in Glasgow. I promise you that we all are taking precautions for any possible reprisals." Then she said very softly, "Please be careful! These are really bad people!"

She emphasized the word bad!

"Okay," Steve replied and added, "You too, keep me informed on anything else that comes in."

"Will do," Kate murmured and then she hung up.

Steve sat in the automobile for what seemed a long time mulling over what he had just heard. He remembered that Dietrich was a pilot in the German Luftwaffe and wondered if he could make any sense of what Katie had told him. After all, Natalie was from Prague. What was Dietrich's connection with Prague and why did Mohammad fly to Prague? Why not directly to Istanbul, he mused. "This Mohammad is a chameleon," he said to himself. He knew that the face identification devices today could recognize people even with disguises. What did this Mohammad really look like? Were there any accurate photographs of him without disguise? He probably had multiple passports.

He shrugged his shoulders and decided that it was time for lunch and he sure didn't want to be late for lunch with the Roods, the von Schoenfelds and Jamie. He felt that perhaps they could now pull the loose ends together and solve the puzzle.

Grant retrieved his umbrella from the car's door as a hedge against the usual fickle Scottish weather. He exited his car and pulled his collar up on his coat as a stiff wind and some clouds were beginning to gather on what had appeared to be a perfectly beautiful spring day this morning. He turned on his heel and moved across the parking lot with long deliberate strides. He jumped across the curb and sidewalk and entered the hospital. He nodded to the security men and flashed his badge and then turned left from the entrance down the hall to the von Schoenfelds' apartment and knocked firmly on the door. He heard a woman's voice and the click of high heels as Natalie opened the door with a softly brisk voice.

"Good afternoon, inspector. So nice to see you again. Carolyn and I have just about finished preparing lunch. Jamie was kind enough to supply some fruit for a fruit salad appetizer! He and my husband are just starting on the Scotch. May I take your coat and umbrella? It looks like a rainstorm may be brewing."

He handed her his coat and umbrella and waved at Jamie, Christopher, and Dietrich. They were already pouring their Scotch neat into glasses with the seltzer bottle standing nearby ready for duty if need be.

They were trading stories about the research that the University of Edinburgh was doing in the treatment of burns. Dr. Rood recounted the work he was familiar with at the Burn Center in San Antonio, Texas and with the University of Texas Medical Center there. He was professor and chair of the Radiology Department at the University of Texas Medical School in San Antonio. Dr. Rood declared that the research methodology used in medicine, criminology, anthropology, and history were all similar and all relied on the null hypothesis.

Dietrich added that electronic surveillance and interdiction techniques were all about detection and were also similar to the logic they were talking about. He followed up that comment by saying that his squadron in Afghanistan had the best record among all of the NATO air squadrons in interdiction of Taliban terrorist activities, especially finding and destroying roadside bombs and improvised explosive devices that were being used to kill civilians and soldiers alike, particularly in the southern Kandahar Province. Dietrich was a squadron commander in the Aufklarungs Geschwader 51 Immelmann that did reconnaissance and attack sorties in the south of Afghanistan where the Taliban had their stronghold. They had been deployed by the German Luftwaffe in 2007 to Mazar-i-Sharif in Northern Afghanistan.

They had performed recon and combat missions similar to the missions that the 13th Tactical Fighter Squadron and 432nd Tactical Reconnaissance Wing of the United States Air Force had flown when they were stationed at the Udorn Royal Thai Air base in Thailand during the Vietnamese War.

Dr. Rood had gone into the US Air Force in 1986 just after his residency at Spohn Hospital in Corpus Christi and his marriage to Carolyn. Captain Christopher Rood had been assigned as flight surgeon to that squadron in 1987 and had later flown close to fifty combat missions as a weapons systems control officer in a RF-4C Phantom fighter during Desert Storm. He later received the Air Medal for his heroism in Desert Storm and was promoted to major after his stint in Iraq. He had remained in the Air Force Reserves, eventually obtaining the rank of colonel. His unit at Bergstrom Air Force Base in Austin, Texas, was the 12th Tactical Reconnaissance Squadron of the 67th Tactical Reconnaissance Wing, and they had been assigned to the Middle East during Desert Storm in 1990 and had returned to Bergstrom Air Base after Desert Storm highly decorated for their outstanding services.

It was this commonality of service to their countries that

had welded a firm warrior bond between Christopher and Dietrich. They were both members of the Order of Saint John, descended from that ancient Order that had defended Christianity during the Crusades and later. They also belonged to their country's air forces and had flown similar missions in different wars. Christopher had frequently talked to Dietrich about learning air tactics, such as the "Immelmann Maneuver" that had been developed by the outstanding German fighter ace of World War I. Dietrich's squadron was even named after that ace. And even best of all, they were both descendants of an historical warrior family from Germany!

Jamie had been listening to all of this and couldn't help but toss in the observation that Christopher's last name was Rood and that his wife's maiden name had been MacIntosh, which he opined that both were Scottish!

Christopher raised his eyebrow and laughed in the affirmative and said, "Well, you know we Americans are a mixed lot of all of the best elements of the human race!"

They all laughed and Carolyn chimed in, "Let's have lunch now."

Steve had taken in all of this information and said, "That's a good idea, I've been listening to all of this and I am just starting to sort this out."

Natalie asserted, "Let's talk about it after lunch. It would be better for our appetites!"

With that, they all sat down at the table and quietly began to eat lunch.

Jamie proposed a toast to all and they raised their wine glasses to each other. "May we all profit from this friendship that is beginning and that we solve the mystery at the thirteen sycamores soon."

With that they tipped their glasses to one another and smiled. However, Steve raised an eyebrow with the sudden realization that pieces of the puzzle were starting to fall into place and that he would have to save his revelations until after they had consumed their repast.

8 MORTAL DANGER

Natalie had just served coffee to everyone when she turned to Steve and queried, "What have you found out? Who do you think has done this terrible thing?"

Steve looked at Natalie and then at Dietrich and calmly said, "Do either of you know a Mohammad al Hussaini, Ahmed ali al Hussaini, Rania al Hussaini or know anything about the Muslim Brotherhood and their activities in Afghanistan in 2007?"

While he was speaking, Natalie sat up straight with the mention of Rania al Hussaini and Ahmed ali al Hussaini and looked desperately into Dietrich's eyes as he flinched with the mention of the Muslim Brotherhood and Afghanistan.

He too stiffened and gasped and then in a barely audible voice said, "We know Rania, she was at our wedding and I believe that Natalie has met her brother, but I don't believe that either of us have met Mohammad al Hussaini until I met Mr. Smythe in Roslyn."

Steve looked him squarely in his eyes and said, "Bingo! I believe you might also have met him on the battlefield in Kandahar Province in 2007! Look at this video," he said as he reached into his pocket, pulled his cell phone out and started the video that he had taken in the Brasserie.

By this time Carolyn, Jamie and Christopher had gathered around the screen of the iPhone and stared at the pictures.

Dietrich was the first to speak, "That's Smythe—he's still in the clothes that he wore the morning of the sixth!"

"That," Steve said slowly, "is Mohammad al Hussaini, the father of Rania and Ahmed ali. The face recognition capability of Scotland Yard, the FBI, Interpol, the Bundes Nachtrichten Dienst, the Mossad, and airport security all say the same thing. He is definitely Mohammad al Hussaini and I believe that he survived a raid that you and your comrades made in Kandahar on a group of Taliban that he had been training to plant roadside bombs to blow up NATO troops sweeping through that Taliban stronghold. Was there any distinguishing nose art or markings on your Tornado aircraft?"

Dietrich stammered, "I was the squadron commander, and the leader always marked their aircraft in some unique manner—just like General Adolph Galant, commander of a squadron of ME 262 jet fighters had done in the last months of World War II. He had a picture of Mickey Mouse on the nose of his fighter to show his contempt of Hitler. I painted the nose and wing tips of my Tornado red to honor the memory of Baron von Richthoven who had painted his fighter red in World War I, and in order for my comrades to be able to spot me in combat."

Steve looked at Dietrich. "I believe that Mohammad had also noticed those markings when you and your comrades wiped out the Taliban group that he was training," he said. "I don't know how he found out who you were or where you were. I haven't gotten enough information yet to figure that one out."

Natalie gasped and put her hand over her mouth as she took a breath and said, "I think I know. I believe it was when Rania and her brother visited my apartment in Prague while she and I were students at Karlova University Nursing School at the Karlova Medical Center. We were both graduating and I had been interviewing before graduation for a job at the

Phillips University, Gniessen/Marburg Hospital."

"I had met Dietrich when I was having lunch at an outside restaurant in the pedestrian center in Marburg," she continued. "He had strolled by my table and then returned with a bouquet of spring flowers in a crystal vase that he said perfectly set off my hazel eyes as if they were the setting for a diamond. He placed the bouquet in the middle of the table as he asked my permission to sit down and join me for lunch. He swept me off my feet and I've been in love with him ever since. He showed me around Marburg the next two days and when I was ready to return to Prague, he gave me a picture of himself in his uniform standing in front of his airplane with the crimson markings in Afghanistan. I put it into a gold frame and have kept it on my bedroom dresser ever since. Ahmed and Rania must have seen it when they visited my apartment in Prague after our graduation ceremonies before I moved to Marburg to be with Dietrich. I believe they are still in Prague, though. I know Rania said she was born and raised in Sarajevo in Bosnia."

"Aha!" exclaimed Steve. "That's why he booked a flight from Edinburg to Prague after we saw him at the Brasserie. There is no doubt in my mind that he has believed the story we put out that Dietrich is dead and that you are under the temporary protection of the Edinburgh police—me! We'll have to get you and Dietrich's 'body' back to Marburg for his funeral. They will probably be watching the whole thing. I think there may be a fatwa out for you," he said as he looked at Natalie. "I believe he intends to wipe out your family line by eliminating both you and Dietrich just in case you might be pregnant."

Natalie blushed and then, with a horrified look in her eyes, said, "That is positively revolting!"

"Nevertheless," said Steve, "we know that Dietrich is his family's only male child and that the al Hussaini family is from Bosnia where such a vengeful blood feud is commonplace. We believe that you, Natalie, are in mortal danger."

Natalie looked at Steve with fear now in her eyes. Dietrich, on the other hand, had set his jaw and there was anger burning in his blue eyes.

Christopher, by this time, had regained his composure and looked at Dietrich and Natalie with calm blue eyes and a quiet visage that portrayed careful thought and determined attitude. He composed his words carefully and then said, "I believe it might be time that we contacted our friend, the professor, who I believe is at Fountains Abbey in England on a 'dig.' He understands the Middle East and medieval history and will be able to tell us exactly what we are up against and how to defeat this evil. As you know, the Muslim Brotherhood is rooted in the past and is still fighting the Crusades. Their goal is to establish a worldwide Caliphate with everyone converted to the Muslim faith and with them at the head of this Nazi theocracy."

Christopher continued, "I know Randall Fox and once he gets on to something, he is like a badger. He never lets go until he has accomplished what he has set out to do."

Steve broke in and said as he looked at Jamie, "Do you think you might be able to persuade one of the pilots in your 'dust off' brigade to pop on down to the Fountains and pick up this chap, Fox."

"Yep," said Jamie. "But I think Christopher and I should make the trip together tomorrow."

He looked at Dr. Rood and asked him, "You don't mind doing a dust off do you? Do you have a telephone number for him?"

"Yes, I do," said Christopher, "We frequently converse about matters concerning the Order of Saint John. You know, he is also a member of the Order as well as all of us."

"Just a band of brothers," quipped Jamie with a broad smile on his face.

Immediately Carolyn admonished Jamie, "And sisters!"

She and Jamie looked at each other and Jamie dropped his head and admitted, "Touché!"

They then slapped their palms together and laughed.

Christopher flipped through the list of telephone numbers on his phone's directory and came up with Dr. Fox's cell phone number.

"Let's take a chance and call him now."

He tapped the number and it began ringing.

Presently, an inquiring voice answered, "Fox, here, is that you, Christopher? What's up? Must be something important to call me all the way over here."

"No, no. Randall, I'm over here. I'm in Edinburgh and I need you badly for a murderous mystery that I believe only you can solve!" Christopher knew that Randall would respond to the flattery.

"It must be something for you to flatter me so!"

They both laughed.

"You remember Dietrich, don't you?"

"Oh, yes. He and Natalie aren't mad at me for my forgetting the date of their wedding and showing up the day after it was all over, are they?"

"No, I believe they never were angry with you, even though you were a day late and a dollar short!"

They both laughed.

"Well, give them my blessing. I'm sorry I got there after they had already left for Scotland, I'm just an absent-minded professor. That's the story of my life."

"You're forgiven!" Natalie shouted at the phone that Christopher had put on speaker for all to hear.

"Please come help Dietrich and me. Someone is trying to kill us!"

There was silence for a moment on the other end of the phone and then the determined voice of Professor Fox said, "I'm on my way!"

"Not so quick," interjected Christopher. "Inspector Steve Grant with the Scottish Defense Force is sending Dr. Jamie Macadam, who saved Dietrich's life, and me to get you. We will be coming in a helicopter ambulance from the hospital here. What time and where should we pick you up?"

"What do you mean—saved his life?"

"I'll explain when we get there. Where will you be?"

"In the meadow beside the Abbey at noon. I'll have my trench coat, old fedora and an umbrella. I'll be easy to spot and there is plenty of room—about 800 acres! I'll be in my professor disguise."

"You know the old Irish saying: I realized fear one morning at the blare of the fox hunter's sound. When they're all chasing after the poor bloody fox, it's better to be dressed as a hound!"

With that, everyone in the room smiled. They knew that the crafty professor was relishing the thought of untangling the mystery and that they had a determined and resourceful friend coming to help them.

"See you then," Christopher replied. And then the old friends said their good-byes and hung up.

Steve turned toward Natalie. "Natalie, I need you to be strong and talk to your parents as well as Rania. We must make Rania believe that Dietrich is dead and that you are in deep mourning and seclusion. Tell your parents that they also must be strong and keep the secret about what is going on. Maybe it would be best to just let them believe that Dietrich is dead."

"No, no they can keep a secret and make the right impression of mourning and protect us," exclaimed Natalie.

Steve then turned toward Dietrich. "Do you think that you can persuade your parents the same and not inadvertently tip off our adversaries?"

"Yes, I know they can do this for Natalie and me."

Making his point adamantly, Steve poked his finger at both of them, "No one, and I mean no one, outside of this close circle can tip our hand. I believe Rania may be an unsuspecting pawn in this whole affair but we can't take any chances. We know that Ahmed ali and Mohammad are both on the terrorist lists worldwide. They will stop at nothing and will use all means at their disposal to kill Natalie and anyone else who gets in their way. They mean to kill all infidels and especially Christians and any person they consider crusaders!

Dietrich and Natalie fit the profile of those they are most anxious to annihilate!"

Christopher reminded everyone, "These fanatics believe they have killed Dietrich and they are in no hurry to accomplish the second half of their murderous plan. Right now, we have the advantage. We know that the assassins are Mohammad and his son Ahmed ali. We know that there are allied terrorist cells hiding out in many guises in most of the Christian countries and they are willing to help their fellow Muslims in jihad."

Speaking mainly to himself, "I'm wondering if we should have a public funeral in Marburg? They might try to plant explosives at the gravesite—Mohammad, after all, is an explosives expert and neither father nor son would be concerned if they killed a few innocent Christian bystanders!"

Then, remembering the others in the room, he turned to them. "Why don't we have Dietrich and Natalie go into deep cover? And we can plant a story in the Marburg newspaper and television about the tragedy, and that the ashes of the victim have been thrown into the sea as per the wishes of the widow and will of the victim. Natalie, Dietrich what do you think? Could you convince both of your parents to remain quiet and convince Rania of the burial at sea and the seclusion of a grieving widow?"

Christopher looked deep into their eyes and concluded that the nod they both gave him was an affirmative reply. He thought for a second and then said, "I'm not too sure, it sounds too contrived. Steve, what do you think? Do you think it could work?"

"Maybe, but it might be better to have the ashes consecrated at a small private family church memorial in Marburg. It might be safer than taking any chances with these madmen. It would probably be better to involve only the immediate family at a private chapel memorial service that can be closely contained and watched. Besides, if Rania tries to weasel any information out of Natalie as to where she might be during her mourning, then we could probably conclude that she would inform her brother. At any rate, we have to keep the number of people in the loop to a minimum if we're going to catch these two!"

"All right then, that's the plan," pronounced Christopher. "We'll have a small immediate family memorial service in Marburg to consecrate Dietrich's ashes. We'll get the stories planted right away. Natalie, you and Dietrich should call your parents this afternoon and tell them what's happened and what we're doing to catch these criminals. Also, tell them to inform us of anyone that might make any suspicious enquiries. Give them Natalie's cell phone number and please turn off the GPS on their phones. Everyone else, do the same with your phones so they can't be traced. Dietrich, don't use your cell phone at all—you're dead! We don't want anyone to know that we are at this hospital. I'll get everyone, including Dr. Fox, scrambled phones that can't be intercepted or tracked so we can all converse later safely from anywhere in the world."

"Okay, let's all get started with our plan," Steve concluded. "Jamie, you and Christopher need to get on down to Fountains tomorrow and get Dr. Fox. When you retrieve him, let's meet here. We can put him in one of the rooms here so that we can all be together at this command post in the hospital while Dietrich recovers from his wounds. Shall we say tomorrow, late afternoon when Dr. Fox gets here?"

9 DEN OF THIEVES

The KLM flight to Prague had just touched down in a morning drizzle of rain at the Vaclav Havel International Airport. Mohammad was weary and still wearing the disheveled blue suit from the morning of the sixth of June. He didn't have time to shave or relax since he had spotted Inspector Grant with Natalie at the Brasserie in the Balmoral Hotel in Edinburgh. He had surmised that he was a policeman and was telling her of the murder that morning at the Saint Mary Chapel.

He had been surprised how easy it was to dupe Maj. von Schoenfeld.

"These Westerners were so gullible! And that nonsense about the Holy Grail—the same quest of the medieval knights. What trash," he chuckled to himself. "How can these Christians believe such rubbish?"

He was glad that Dietrich believed in all that nonsense of the Order of Saint John. It was easy to make him believe that he was a member of the Ambulance Corps of the Venerable order of Saint John headquartered in London at Saint John's Gate. He gained Dietrich's trust by just mentioning that he knew something about the Holy Grail and Roslyn Chapel. He mused that he was glad that he had taken the time to read the book, *Holy Blood, Holy Grail.* These Christians are so naive!

Al Hussaini was happy in his heart that his adversary had been a knight of the Order of Saint John. It was a double satisfaction that he had eliminated a modern representative of that ancient order that his ancestors had struggled with a thousand years ago and the infidel that had commanded the squadron of fighter planes that had swooped down and wiped out his command in Afghanistan. He was happy that he was killed in the same mode as the assassins would have done. He was glad that his ancestors had kicked these infidel knights off of the island of Rhodes five hundred years ago and that Hitler's idol, Napoleon, had completed the task and scattered them to the four winds of their native countries when he conquered their home island of Malta in 1798. These infidels are too busy squabbling among themselves to realize that a great secret army of Holy jihad was rising under the ISIL black flag of Allah and his sacred sword! Secret cells of this army were scattered among the cities of the infidel worldwide under their very noses and they are sleeping so deep in their dream of material wealth and individualism that they can't comprehend their impending doom! They have lost their way in the faith of materialism!

He had just become aware of the signal to deplane when he remembered he needed to call his son Ahmed and let him know that he had just arrived. He had turned off the GPS system on his cell phone and decided that he would wait until he actually saw Ahmed to let him know of his partial success and that they should not mention any of this to Rania since she might tip off Natalie. He was suspicious that she had been swayed by the rights that the women of the Czech Republic have. He believed that she was becoming westernized since she had attended the Karlova School of Nursing and her best friend there was a Christian and had married his hated enemy! She was also seeing too much of a Christian boy and that angered him. He would have to watch her closely—she had a strong will that could inadvertently prove dangerous to his plans.

He had cleared customs and Ahmed was dutifully there to greet him and help carry his one checked bag.

Ahmed smiled expectantly and said, "Did everything go well—no one tailing you?"

"Everything was perfect, except Natalie was not with the major. I had to be satisfied with our primary target. When I went to her hotel, the police had already arrived and I was not able to reach her in time. A policeman got to her door before I could get to her. I saw them when they went to a restaurant and bar—the Brasserie. I watched her from the bar, but the policeman didn't leave her side. I followed them to her room and he left when she entered her room.

"I followed him down to the lobby and watched as the valet went to get his car and then I went back to her room and knocked on her door, but there was no answer. I didn't see any police guard, but guessed that there might be a policewoman with her, so I knocked again. When there was no answer, I used my electronic key decipherer to open the door. It was dark and I assumed that she had gone to bed, but when I went to the bedroom, she was gone. I left quickly before I could be identified by anyone.

"When I got to the lobby, I saw the policeman's car leave, and when I asked the valet if there was a woman with him, he said there was not. Somehow, she evaded me.

"I was extremely angry that I hadn't gotten to her before that damned policeman arrived. It would have been easy to kidnap her and hold her while we decided whether to kill her or sell her into the sex slave markets! We'll find her, and next time we'll succeed!"

Ahmed nodded his head in agreement with his father.

"There was no difficulty at the Edinburg International airport or here. It was a clean visit! Don't breathe a word of any of this to your sister," Mohammad warned. "I believe that she may have been westernized!"

They reached the parking lot where Ahmed had parked his black Toyota Camry automobile. They got into the automobile and Ahmed drove directly to his apartment which was not far from the airport.

"Did you get me a ticket to Jeddah, Saudi Arabia under my Swiss passport by way of Istanbul?" Mohammad asked. [He liked to take devious routes to where he really wanted to go.]

"I did. You leave early tomorrow morning."

"That," thought Mohammad, "will get me get back to friendly territory behind the Crescent Curtain as quickly as possible."

He had prepared his father's clothes together for the trip, so that he could pack quickly tomorrow morning.

"I haven't told Rania anything about your being here before you left for Scotland or that you are leaving here for Saudi Arabia," Ahmed said. "She thinks that you have been in Saudi Arabia all the time that you've been in Scotland. Using different names and passports was a good idea. With your disguise and new Swiss passport and leaving this early you should be able to get to Istanbul without anyone knowing where you have been. Rania knows nothing about what we are doing. I'll keep a close watch on her. We might get some information about Natalie from her, but I'll be careful not to arouse any suspicions."

Mohammad said with a wink to his son, "Good for you, my boy. Women must be seen and not heard as the English say about children! They're far too unreliable and emotional for our kind of work!"

Ahmed parked his car and dutifully took his father's luggage and they went inside his house. It was a small house in a quiet neighborhood where a small group of fellow Muslims also lived. He was a smaller and thinner version of his father with hard-set, dark, brown eyes, olive skin, and square jaw. He had kept a low profile and been neighborly enough while he attended a small college where he studied engineering on a part-time basis when it didn't interfere with his real work with the Muslim Brotherhood. He had a state scholarship that he managed to keep even though he was not a diligent student. Just enough to get by. The house was comfortably furnished and it had a small room for prayer that

Ahmed and Mohammad, when he was there, used regularly for the required prayers of the day.

Rania had her own apartment close to the Karlova Hospital where she now had a job in the pediatric wing. She was highly thought of by her superiors and she tried to fit in with her sister nurses and be a dutiful Czech citizen. She had embraced the culture in Prague which suited her independent nature. Her father was right, she was Muslim, but she was a Czech Muslim who followed the laws of that country and adopted its culture. She was small in stature with dark, waist-long hair that she kept up while she was on duty at the hospital, but that she let down while off duty and on the weekends. Her features were pleasant with large hazel eyes like her friend Natalie, but they made her look like a smaller version of Audrey Hepburn with her slender features, light olive skin and delicate face like her mother.

She had an infectious grin that made her eyes sparkle. She preferred European clothes, but covered her head with a scarf whenever she was around her father. However, she refused to take any special care around her brother. She kept reminding him that she intended to make her home in the Czech Republic and become a citizen of her new homeland. She also reminded her brother that their mother, who was Serbian, had been killed by stray bullets in the internecine conflicts that had consumed their native Bosnia and that she never intended to submit to the kind of life that had taken her! She would choose her own life and friends, and he could choose his!

The next morning found Ahmed ali driving his father to the airport and wishing him well on his trip to Saudi Arabia. His father embraced his son, and with a kiss on both cheeks and a wave of his hand, he disappeared into the airport.

"Just a reminder," Ahmed had told his father before he exited Ahmed's car, "I have to make a trip to the Muslim Brotherhood headquarters and affiliated groups in Romania soon and will keep in touch with you and let you know about the multiple agendas that are being followed in Europe."

As it happened, the various cells of the Brotherhood and their fellow jihadists in Europe were being run by the headquarters in Romania. On top of that, Ahmed also was a liaison agent for the Brotherhood in Saudi Arabia.

10 FOUNTAINS ABBEY

D r. Fox was true to his word, he was standing about a hundred yards from the Abbey when Jamie's dust off helicopter appeared overhead. He was dressed in a khaki trench coat wearing a well-used brown fedora and he was carrying a brief case and a black umbrella that resembled a cane. It was precisely noon and Dr. Fox was impressed with the promptness of its appearance. It reminded him of the Snell Zugs of Germany. But then, he remembered that he had been told Jamie was a doctor that had commanded military emergency rescue missions in Afghanistan and was highly successful and decorated because of his promptness in his missions of mercy. All of the members of the Order were known for their professionalism.

He could see his friend, Dr. Rood sitting beside Dr. Macadam as he stood in the open doorway of the helicopter. They waved at each other as the ambulance descended gracefully onto the meadow and waited for him to get in. Macadam motioned to him and Fox scrambled to the aircraft. Christopher and Jamie grabbed him by his arms as he stepped onto the steps and helped him inside.

"These things are noisy aren't they?" shouted Fox.

"I hadn't noticed!" quipped the taciturn emergency doctor.

They all grinned as they sat down on the seats and Jamie introduced himself.

"Dr. Fox, I presume."

Christopher shook his old friend's hand warmly and then Dr. Fox shook Jamie's hand.

"We are so glad that you are going to help us solve this mystery," said Christopher.

The helicopter began its ascent into the air and then leveled off at 2,000 feet to begin its flight to Edinburgh. Fox looked at his comrades and said, "I hope this flight has been registered as an emergency medical flight!"

"It certainly has, and I think you'll agree when you hear all the details of what is going on," shouted Dr. Rood over the roar of the helicopter's engines.

The conversation during the flight was minimal because of the noise, and they were all glad when the hospital came into view. The pilot, who had also been in Afghanistan with Jamie, waved his hand at the passengers that they were going to start the descent onto the hospital's landing pad.

As soon as they landed, the pilot cut his engines and the deafening roar subsided and all they could hear was the flapping of the rotor blades as they slowly began to stop turning. When the blades had stopped, they scrambled out of the door and thanked the pilot for a good flight and waved at him as they headed for the hospital. They all still had a ringing in their ears.

"Not to worry," assured Macadam, "That will subside shortly, particularly after we have a shot of Scotch!"

The trio entered the hospital emergency entrance just opposite the helicopter's landing pad that was marked by a huge white Maltese cross with a red outline designating it as a part of the Saint John's ambulance corps. As they entered the hospital, Jamie led them to a hall that led to the VIP apartments that the hospital had built for special patients such as celebrities and the royal family. They walked swiftly to the side corridor where Dr. Rood's apartment was located and entered. Their fellow sleuths were already there.

Grant had brought his secretary, Kate, with him and she had a briefcase filled with information that she had faithfully collected from her information sources. She was chatting with Carolyn, Natalie and Steve while Dietrich had opened the door and shook hands with his visitors.

Christopher introduced Dr. Fox to Kate and Steve as they all shook hands. Dr. Fox was impressed with the firmness of Dietrich's handshake and remarked that he had never met someone supposed to be dead who looked to be in such good health.

Dietrich blushed a little and said, "I owe it all to Dr. Macadam and his wonderful staff!"

Jamie looked embarrassed and replied, "It wasn't me—it was Annie Elliott and her collie Sean we all should thank."

Dietrich immediately seconded Jamie's remarks and thanked everyone gathered around who had come to his aid.

Natalie said that she, Carolyn and Kate had prepared a welcomed late lunch for everyone. Kate had brought some ham, liverwurst and all the trimmings for some sandwiches, salad and dessert. She had even brought some Mosel and Merlot wine. She laughed it off by saying that it was no problem since she had planned on a picnic anyway! Carolyn shook hands with Randall and gave him a hug. She relieved him of his satchel, trench coat and well-worn hat—his professorial disguise as he had described it.

Christopher then led his old friend and Jamie over to where Steve had already poured four glasses of welcomed single malt Lismore Scotch—neat of course!

Then Carolyn, Natalie and Kate raised their glasses to the five knights of Saint John and Carolyn toasted the gathered band and their resolve to bring Dietrich's assailant to justice!

They finished the strawberry and ice cream dessert that Kate had brought. Coffee had just been served, when Steve said that it was time to bring Dr. Fox up to speed. He turned to Kate and asked her, "Kate what is the latest information that you have for us?"

She got up from the table and walked over to her briefcase

that she had placed on the couch. She brought it back to the table and took a large file out of it. She opened the conversation by stating the assailant had been identified from the photos that Steve had gotten from the Brasserie in the Balmoral Hotel. "The good news is that they know he left Edinburgh Airport for Prague and had arrived before they could do anything. He had not been identified on any flights out of Prague this morning, but they will keep looking."

"At this point, Mohammad has completely disappeared," she continued. "They checked out Ahmed ali later this morning and he was at his college class, but they will keep a surveillance on his house and Rania's apartment. She was at work all night last night at her hospital and is at her apartment right now. There has been no suspicious movements by either of them as of eleven o'clock this morning when surveillance was begun. Mohammad apparently has disappeared into thin air. At last notice, he had been in Jeddah, Saudi Arabia, but we haven't been able to get any information on him this morning. He has simply vanished and may already be behind the Crescent Curtain!

"The dagger that was used in the attack on Dietrich has been identified as a 15th century ceremonial Assassin's dagger that had been owned by Mohammad's grandfather when he was an officer in the Turkish army during the First World War before he became the Grand Mufti of Jerusalem.

"We also have some leads that we are pursuing on a mosque outside of Glasgow. There is an Imam there that we have been watching that may have had a hand in this affair and he does own a black Mercedes sedan. We have planted a story about Dietrich's death in the local newspapers and have downplayed the incident as an accidental death and that the body is being returned to Germany where it will be cremated and buried with only the immediate family present. No word was printed as to where the burial will be. We will get a small obituary printed in the Marburg newspaper and the Kiel papers later in Germany two days from now. At the present we are keeping a lid on everything.

"Interpol is spreading a large net over Europe and the Middle East to see what they can get. Israel's Mossad is willing to help us find Mohammad so we have high hopes on that score. If we can find him, we'll get him arrested no matter where he is. We won't let him get away like his grandfather escaped the Nuremburg Commission with the help of the ODESSA after World War II. I know that Dr. Fox is an expert on medieval history, the Crusades and the Orders of Saint John and the Templars."

Kate turned toward Professor Fox and asked him, "Is there anything that you think we should know or do in addition to what we have done?"

Fox replied, "Well Christopher and Jamie pretty well told me the story of what happened during our flight from Fountains Abbey and what has occurred up until now, but I am still puzzled about this business at the Chapel."

He looked at Christopher and then Dietrich and asked, "What made you believe that the Holy Grail was at the Saint Mary Chapel?"

Dietrich and Christopher started to speak at the same time, but Christopher stopped and told Dietrich, "You go ahead, this was your theory that you had called me about and we discussed. You tell Randall."

"Okay," said Dietrich. "Christopher and I had read the book, *The Jesus Family Tomb*, and Dr. James D. Tabor's books, *The Jesus Discovery* and *The Jesus Dynasty*."

"Oh, I know about those books!" interjected Dr. Fox.

Dietrich continued, "And we know the legend of our ancestor, Schoenfeld, who was a Knight Templar who helped hide the Templar treasures. They used many codes and astronomical signs to point the way to the treasures. [He emphasized the word, treasures.]

"I had read about the eclipse of Venus at sunrise on June 6th, 2012, and when I calculated back to the time that the treasure must have been hidden, the time matched the cycle for that time! The Templars were noted for their puzzling secrets and mysterious codes and their devotion to the sacred

Feminine and that the reactivation of the Solar Feminine is a key marker for a new 2,600 year cycle of humanity. They would have developed some technique for illuminating the hiding place for the Holy Grail. I calculated from old manuscripts and drawings of the chapel the height of the round Venus window that was above the main chapel stained glass Rose window behind the Altar of the chapel. The morning sun would cast an image at the time of the midpoint of the Venus transit of the solar disc onto the correct stone of the floor of the chapel where the Holy Grail was hidden by my ancestor Schoenfeld.

"The legend that he had hidden some of the Templar treasure has been a part of our family history. This phenomenon would not be repeated for another 200 years! The Grail will be a rebirth of the consciousness of humankind. That was the purpose of the glass lens on the pole that I had at the chapel."

"You know, you may have something there!" exclaimed Fox, looking at Dietrich and Christopher. "I believe that if the Holy Grail is recovered as is postulated in the book, *The Jesus Family Tomb*, then there might be a new era of understanding between all of the branches of Judaism, Christianity and Islam. We first have to understand who our enemy is and understand how they think in order to defeat them. The enemy of all of the monotheistic religions is the radical fanatic Wahhabi Jihad and their ilk that has hijacked modern Islam and wants rigidly to recreate the authoritarian strictures of the Islamic Caliphate. They really are modern day Nazis. But they're not united yet.

"As Sun Tzu said in his treatise on the Art of War 800 years ago, in order to defeat your enemy, you must know who he is. The Wahhabi Sunni jihadists such as al Qaeda, PLO, ISIL, Hamas, al Shabab, Boca Haram, and the Muslim Brotherhood are in a struggle with the Shia Jihaddists such as Hezbollah. It's really a struggle for dominance between Saudi Arabia and their allies and Iran and their allies. But the Great Satan for both groups is the United States!"

Fox then turned the lesson to dogma. "To Muslims, God is one and incomparable and the purpose of existence is to love and serve the only God—Allah. They believe that Islam is the only true monotheistic religion and that Abraham, Moses and Jesus were merely early prophets of this primordial religion and the messages and revelations they had were flawed, misinterpreted or altered over time. They believe the last prophet of this religion and the only true messenger of God was Muhammad. Therefore, everyone should submit to the teachings of Muhammad and the word of God from the Qur'an or Koran. They believe it is the unaltered and final revelation of God.

"These concepts and practices of the Faith include the five pillars of Islam which are the basic obligatory acts of worship and the following of Islamic law or Sharia which dictates every aspect of life and society. This law is enforced by the rulings of learned clerics of the religion or Imams to ensure that it is the will of God that judges everyone as interpreted by these clerics! To the Sunni Wahhabi Muslims, Jihad is defined as the protection of the faith if not by peaceful teaching, then with force by holy war against the infidels who want to destroy the true faith!

"You know that Muhammad was raised in the Judeo-Christian tradition and had his visions of a new form of that tradition put into the Qur'an. Except that he felt that it was necessary to spell out every little detail of life and how it should be lived to glorify the God for which the Jews have no name and the Muslims use the name Allah. In that respect, Sharia Law uses the concepts of the Qur'an and the Sunnah and the Hadith that details the sayings and lifestyle of the Prophet Muhammad.

"The difference between the Sunni and the Shia is in the interpretation of these precepts. The Shiites went with the teachings of the clerics that Muhammad's favorite daughter, Fatima, and her husband Ali favored and the Sunnis went with the teachings of the clerics that Muhammad's paternal uncle and foster brother Hamza ibn Abdul-Muttalib, who was known as the 'Lion of God' favored. He is known as the Chief of Martyrs!"

Dr. Fox continued his lecture. "That reminds me Thomas Jefferson had studied Islam and recognized its faults, and was chiefly responsible for making sure that the United States was not a theocracy.

"Muslims believe that violations of Islamic Sharia law is a crime against God and nature, including a person's own human nature. They believe in predestination and the divine will of God, interpreted by the clerics, to govern through Sharia! Thus the elite few would dictate to the masses of humanity!"

Fox continued, "These Jihadists use the mosques as a place to teach hatred and death to nonbelievers. As a boy, I was taught in church the commandment of Jesus to do unto others as you would have them do unto you." He smiled and then added, "Oh, yes, I forgot—instead of how to build explosive devices, I was taught how to play basketball in the church gymnasium and sing in the choir. I was also a member of the church Christmas carolers that sang in front of neighborhood homes during the Christmas season praising God in the highest and extolling peace on Earth and goodwill toward man instead of building explosive devices!

"In the human experience, politics should never be hitched to religion, art or music! That's why, in the United States, we separate religion from politics and believe in the rights and freedom of the individual. We need to relight the flame of the Enlightenment that sparked the search for the freedom of mankind and led to the migration of downtrodden people to the United States in order to be free from tyranny."

Dietrich nodded his head in agreement and elaborated on the lesson, "Muhammed ibn Abd al-Wahhab was an Arabian Islamic Salafi scholar who was born in 1703 and died June 22, 1792. His pact with Muhamad bin Saud helped to establish the first Saudi state. It began a dynastic alliance and power sharing arrangement between their families that continues today. The descendants of Ibn Abd al Wahhab are called the Al ash-Sheikh and have led the ulama in Saudi Arabia and dominate the country's clerical institutions. They have established Wahhabi religious and Sharia schools all over the world. Within Saudi Arabia, the Wahhabi family is held in prestige similar to the Saudi Royal family, with whom they share power. The arrangement between the two families is based on the Al Saud maintaining the Al ash-Sheikh support of the Al Saud's political authority thus using its religious moral authority to legitimize the Royal Family's rule.

"Contemporary assessment of Ibn 'Abd al-Wahhab, as with the early Salafis, was criticized for disregarding Islamic history, monuments, traditions and the sanctity of Muslim life. His own brother, Sulayman, was particularly critical, claiming that he was ill-educated and intolerant, classing Ibn 'Abd al-Wahhab's views as fringe and fanatical."

At this point everyone's mouth was open and Natalie had her hand over her mouth in horror.

Fox picked up the narrative, "When you have these fanatics that are willing to lay down their lives and everybody else's in their way in order to obtain a first class ticket to a seventh heaven and bypass the hardships of a productive life simply by obtaining martyrdom with suicide and killing infidels in the process, you can understand why these individual cells of assassin lunatics are so dangerous!

"How much better it would be if they embraced peace and tolerance so that the world could learn the positive sides of their culture, history and religion. Even though they recognize Moses and Jesus as prophets, they laid aside the Ten Commandments of Moses and the Golden Rule of Jesus.

"The Muslim Brotherhood is a transitional, pan Islamic, religious, political and social movement founded by the Islamic scholar and teacher, Hassan al Bannah in Egypt in 1928. In 1935, Al-Haj Amin al Hussaini, the Grand Mufti of Jerusalem, and your man Smythe's grandfather, was the leader of the Brotherhood in Palestine. He later joined with the Nazis and lived in Berlin during World War II. He was an SS general and leader of Muslim Nazi SS troops in the Balkans. He was the voice of the Nazis in the Middle East and broadcasted Nazi propaganda to the Muslim world during the war. He was an Arab version of Lord Haw-Haw and Axis Sally. By the end of World War II, the Muslim Brotherhood had an estimated two million members.

"The Brotherhood's credo is, 'Allah is our objective, the Quran is our law, the Prophet is our leader, Jihad is our way, and dying in the way of Allah is the highest of our aspirations.' They believe in absolute obedience to the Brotherhood's leaders. They want to firstly infiltrate into all of the nations of the earth by immigration and multiplying and the introduction of the Islamic Sharia Law as the means of controlling the affairs of society and the state. They are influenced by both Sufism and Salafism. They have both Shia as well as Sunni members and seek unification of all elements of Islam to firstly reclaim Islam's manifest destiny, a Caliphate from Spain to Indonesia and the Philippines and then the entire world!

"The aim of the Brotherhood in America is 'The process of settlement in a Civilization-Jihadist Process' with all that it means. The Ikhwan must understand that their work in America is a kind of grand Jihad in eliminating and destroying western civilization from within and sabotaging its miserable house by their own hands and the hands of the believers so that it is eliminated and Allah's religion is made victorious over all other religions."

Christopher frowned and glanced at Randall with a swelling anger in his eyes, "In other words, they decided early on to defeat western civilization by using the west's own strengths as the means of conquest. They would be patient and like a cancer that would invade the west through their open borders and then metastasize throughout their society until it was changed into a Muslim neo-Nazi state with a supreme leader like an Ayatollah or a Fuhrer."

Dietrich turned his head toward his cousin Christopher and continued the thought, "Rather than invade a country with a recognizable army, they would use the open borders of America , the Great Satan, and their freedoms of religion, speech and sense of justice for all as a means of diversification through immigration and then proliferation to spread their doctrine. They would use local mosques to teach Sharia and local obedience and thus raise a home grown army of impressionable youths capable of spreading terror throughout the country as a means of Jihad, martyrdom and conquest. But first it would be an insidious and deceptive growth by different community organizing of the various races and ethnic groups using their own culture and the country's churches and free speech and freedom of religion to accept social justice and use racism as a means to welcome the new Muslim religion onto our shores.

"They would be secret about their real aims and deceptive in their methods to infiltrate all strata of society, education and politics. They would lull their enemy into submission by the reason of free speech and the common good for equality and justice. They would confuse and confound the population by exaggeration of racism and the perceived exploitation of minority groups by the white majority. In the confusion, perceived guilt and sense of justice by the white majority, it would go to extreme lengths to be politically correct and compensate any perceived wrongs. In this way, the majority would be marginalized and an activated and organized minority could win political power and America could be persuaded to change their social order to the new order of things and fundamentally change America, much the same way that Adolph Hitler gained control of Germany in the 1930's and changed it from a republic to a totalitarian state. The road to Hell is paved with the best of intentions."

After this exhaustive exposition of religious dogma and the political and cultural history and intentions of jihad, Grant brought the discussion back to the business at hand.

"We simply have to find this assassin that attempted to murder Dietrich and will also try to kill Natalie," he said.

"He wants to wipe out the future of your family," Dr. Fox

said as he looked at Natalie and Dietrich. Everyone in the room appeared to be visibly moved by these statements.

Steve was the first one to break the silence. "We have gotten a cover story out and for the time being, I think that Natalie and Dietrich are safe, but we can't sit on our laurels. We have to be proactive to flush this madman out of his hiding place. Any ideas how we can do this?"

Steve gazed around the table and Carolyn volunteered, "If we could entice Mohammad to the United States, we might be able to arrest him there."

She said that she had seen an article in the Chicago Tribune about the patron of the Hospitaller Order of Saint John in America, King Peter II of Yugoslavia. She went to her purse and pulled out the article that she was bringing to show to Natalie and Dietrich.

Addressing the group, she said, "His body is going to be flown to Belgrade in January 2013 and we thought that you might want to be our guests at a gathering of the Order in Libertyville to pay their last respects. I noticed in the news the other day that King Peter II's son, Crown Prince Alexander, and family were going to have his body disinterred from the Chapel of Saint Sava, that is in a Serbian Orthodox monastery in northern Libertyville, Illinois, and have it returned to Belgrade, Serbia, for temporary internment in St. Andrew Chapel near the Royal Palace until a formal state funeral on May 29, 2013. King Peter II had requested to be buried at St. Sava Chapel before he died from a failed liver transplant in a hospital in Denver, Colorado, in 1970 at the age of 47. The reburial will take place at the Royal Mausoleum of St. George in Oplenac together with the reburials of King Peter's mother Queen Marie, his wife Queen Alexandra, and his brother Prince Andrew."

She continued, "The article had mentioned that King Peter II had been a patron of the Hospitaller Order of Saint John in the Americas and its Grand Master for a while. He and his father Alexander I had been Knights and members of the Russian Grand Priory originating from the original Order of Saint John on Malta. King Peter, as a Knight of that Order, was a knight descendent of Tsar Paul I who was elected Grand Master of the Order of Saint John on October 27, 1798. Pope Pius VI bestowed his paternal and apostolic benediction upon Tsar Paul I shortly after he accepted the office of Grand Master.

"King Peter II had also been appointed an Honorary Associate Bailiff Grand Cross of the Venerable Order of Saint John by King George VI, his cousin and godfather, on June 21st, 1943, while in exile in England during World War II. It had been published in the London Gazette on Friday, June 25, 1943. While he was Grand Master of the Hospitaller Order in America, he had given the accolade of knighthood to over fifty Americans and Canadians in Chicago, the article continued.

"His sarcophagus can still be viewed there until he is removed in January. Thousands of visitors visit there every year and the site is on the Pilgrim Trail of the Hospitaller Order of Saint John. You know that he never abdicated his throne but remained a King in exile and is buried there with his entire cabinet of ministers in the churchyard! He had high hopes of returning to Yugoslavia as King and now he will."

Carolyn suggested, "If we could get the word out that Natalie will be in the United States visiting with Dr. Fox, Christopher, and me when we go to Libertyville with some members of our Order to give our last respects to King Peter, perhaps we can lure Mohammad and Ahmed into the United States. Col. William Harries who lives in Atlanta, Georgia, and is the Grand Commander of our Order called me to tell me that he was arranging a pilgrimage for Order members to King Peter's tomb in Libertyville sometime this fall before the disinterment. Since King Peter had been a Grand Master of our American Hospitaller Order of Saint John and the site is on our Pilgrimage Trail, we might be able to bait our trap and lure Mohammad and Ahmed to the United States where we can nab him."

Steve rubbed his chin and said, "It might work, but we

can't chance that he might injure bystanders in the process. How would we go about that? And besides, we wouldn't want to bring harm to the chapel or King Peter's tomb. Would it be possible for Natalie to visit with you and go to the chapel, but have it reported in the local Austin paper after the fact since you and Christopher are prominent citizens there! Maybe a photograph of the three of you could be published with the article. Natalie, you can't tell Rania until after the visit. Maybe you could call her from Texas."

Dietrich immediately exclaimed, "But I want to go there with Natalie so that we both can pay our respects to King Peter!"

Natalie interrupted and added, "We don't have to have you in the picture to be published and the story in the newspaper can describe me as your widow. I think that it would be good to set a trap for Mohammad in Texas after we go there from Libertyville. After all Texas is like a separate country that cherishes its history as a free and independent country before it joined the United States."

She then added, "Where is Libertyville?"

Everyone laughed and Christopher volunteered that it was thirty-five miles north of Chicago.

Natalie looked worried and with eyes wide she said, "We won't see any gangsters there will we?"

Carolyn and Christopher laughed together and Carolyn said, "No I don't think so—maybe just some politicians," and then she winked at Christopher who raised his eyebrows without saying a word.

Natalie immediately said, "Do you think that we might be able to meet some Texas Rangers while we're in Texas. I've heard so much about them."

Dietrich also seemed to be pleased with the possibility.

"Well, let's take care of the present situation," Steve proclaimed. "We need to have all of you, except Dietrich, go to Marburg for the church services with Dietrich's and Natalie's families. We don't want a fuss, and just a small affair for appearance sake, and then we'll get Natalie back here with

Dietrich right afterwards before word leaks out about her presence there. When you have left, you can call Rania and say that you have left Germany, but don't let her know where you are going and that you just want to be left alone for a while. Later, when Dietrich is well enough to travel, the two of you can go to the United States."

Kate added that she thought that it would be prudent for her to be with Steve more and assist him with all of the arrangements to get Natalie and Dietrich to the United States. She then held out her left hand so that everyone could see the diamond engagement ring that Steve had given her last night.

Steve blushed, looked at her, and said, "Are you sure?"

Her eyes twinkled as she put her arm around his waist and said firmly, "Yes, I'm sure!"

Jamie looked at his old friend and smiled, "I hope I can be your best man!"

Carolyn looked at Christopher and then said, "We all want to be at your wedding, especially since it will be in Scotland!"

11 MARBURG

The sun was just rising over the city of Marburg and the Landgrave's castle that overlooked the ancient city was beginning to glow with a bright grey from its walls. The castle predated the building of the Elizabeth Church which was begun in 1235 by the Order of the Teutonic Knights in honor of Saint Elizabeth. Her tomb made the church an important pilgrimage destination in the late Middle Ages. It was one of the earliest purely Gothic cathedrals in Germany. It was a model for the Cologne Cathedral and an inspiration for the Saint Paul's Cathedral in Strasbourg.

The Teutonic Knights were the third crusading order after the Order of Saint John and the Knights Templar. Many of the Knights Templar joined that order after they were suppressed in 1307. The ancient Phillips University was nestled below the castle on the small mountain that rose over the city. The Elizabeth Church was built next to the buildings of the Order of Knights Templar that are a part of the present Mineralogisches Museum. They were built on the banks of the Lahn River that runs through the city. It is the perfect picture of an old university town, like Heidleberg, that could have been the inspiration for Sigmund Romberg's 1924 operetta, *The Student Prince*.

Steve Grant had flown into Frankfurt, Germany earlier that morning and was going to check into the Europaischer Hof Marburg hotel that was located close to the Elizabeth Kirche at Elisabeth Strasse 12 in Marburg. He had rented a Mercedes C class automobile at the Frankfurt International airport and driven north to Marburg. It was not a terribly long drive and it was through incredibly beautiful country. He was anxious to get there so he could spend some time for lunch in the pedestrian market area that Natalie had described to him when she had told him about her first meeting there with Dietrich.

He entered the city and exited the autobahn onto the Friering Kurt Schumacher Bridge, crossed the Lahn River into the city and followed the signs to the Pilgrimstein Strasse that turned into the Elisabeth Strasse and passed the Cathedral on his right and drove directly to his hotel a few blocks past the church and on the left side of the street. He turned into the parking garage and parked the car conveniently in it.

After retrieving his bag and briefcase from the trunk, he walked to the lobby and checked into the hotel and went directly to his room and called long distance to his office in Edinburgh.

Kate answered the phone and he said, "Well, I've arrived and the city looks beautiful and the weather is perfect, I wish that you were here."

"Me too, darling!"

"Did anything else occur while I was gone?"

"No, everything is running smoothly."

"Okay, I'm going to lie down for a few minutes and then go to the old town center to have lunch. I have my new scrambled cell phone with me if anything comes up that I need to know about."

Steve was supposed to get a call from Dietrich's father later in the afternoon so that he could get the details of tomorrow's memorial services with Natalie and Dietrich's families. They were going to have the memorial in the morning at nine o'clock at the Saint John's altar in the Landgraves Choir which was the South Choir of the Cathedral.

"You know that the last President of the old German Reich before Hitler, Field Marshal Paul von Hindenburg and his wife are buried there in the corner of the South Aisle," he explained. "They were buried there after World War II after their remains were removed from the Tannenberg Memorial in former East Prussia."

I'm impressed," whispered Kate.

"I was reading about the Cathedral on my flight from Edinburgh."

"You have done your homework! Keep me posted, I'll have my new cell phone handy as well. I've been talking to your aunt, and she is thrilled that we are finally going to be married."

"Me too!"

"We are getting together later today with your mother to start making plans, I hope you are as anxious as we are!"

"That I am. It's a relief to finally make the decision."

He heard her laugh on the other end of the phone and she softly said, "Call me later tonight, please."

They said their goodbyes and he settled back onto the bed and thought to himself that he was pretty lucky!

It seemed that he had just rested his eyes for a few minutes when he woke up with a start and glanced at his watch. It was past noon and he had been asleep for almost two hours. He got up went to the bathroom and washed his face. He returned to the bedroom, unpacked his bag, placed his clothes into the dresser and kleiderschrank opposite his bed, put on his grey tweed coat and tightened his tie with the regimental alternating red and blue stripes. He looked into the mirror over the dresser and decided that his hair needed to be combed. After doing this, he picked up his keys and wallet, put his briefcase under the bed and placed the room's electronic key in his pocket and left the room closing the door quietly behind him.

He walked down the hall past a maid that looked up at him, smiled and said, "Guten Tag."

He thought for a second, then smiled back and replied as best he could, "Guten Tag." It had been a few years since he had studied German in school and he was pleased that his reply had come more easily than he had thought it would. Things were looking up! He walked briskly to the elevator and pushed the ground floor button. He was pleased with himself that he also remembered how the Germans counted their floors.

The elevator smoothly descended to the lobby of the hotel and he exited, and went to the concierge and got a map of the city. The man at the desk spoke perfect English and instructed him how to go to the pedestrian Markt Platz. Steve thanked him in German "Danke schoen," and the man replied, "Bitte schoen."

Steve left the hotel and turned right onto Elisabeth Strasse and walked south past the Elisabeth Gasthausbrauerei, the only brewery in Marburg. Most every town in Germany had a brewery and all of them were good! He continued on to the Steinweg Neustadt and then farther south to Wettergasse and then onto the Markt Platz where no automobiles were allowed.

The town center had many restaurants and shops that seemed to be filled with university students from Phillips University, tourists, and townspeople who reflected the kindness and courtesy that he had already encountered. He could understand why Natalie and Dietrich liked Marburg. He decided that he would have a light lunch and then walk up the hill toward the castle that covered the top of the hill like those in storybooks.

He saw a restaurant with an outside serving area that was covered with tables with their own colorful parasols for cover. Other restaurants had outside awnings, but he thought this one was the one that he and Kate would probably like if she were here. It was the Cafe Am Markt. He walked into the enclosure and took a table so that he could have a good view of the plaza and the castle.

A waitress who looked like she might be a student at the university, walked over to his table and smiled at him.

"Guten tag."

"Guten tag," he answered.

Then she said in perfect English, "Oh, you're English then?"

He felt a little embarrassed that she had spotted him so quickly and replied, "No, I'm actually from Edinburgh, Scotland."

She looked at him quizzically and then she said, "But you don't have a Scottish accent!"

He quickly answered, "Only when I want to!"

She put her hand to her mouth and said, "Now I know why I like the Scots!"

Both of them then laughed. She had completely won him over!

She handed him a menu and asked him what he would like to drink and if he wanted any appetizer? He replied that he thought he would like to have a Lauterbacher dunkel beer to start off. She replied that it was a good choice and that she would be right back with it while he looked over the menu. She turned and disappeared inside the restaurant. He quickly looked the menu over and decided that he would have some fried sausages with mustard and leek with a potato bake. He had heard about the German pastries and had already made up his mind to have an apple torte with coffee for dessert.

When she came back with the beer, she was impressed that he had been so decisive about his order. She said that she would remember and would tell the chef to be particularly diligent with his order to make sure that he was well pleased. She smiled again and disappeared again into the restaurant.

It wasn't long until she reappeared with his meal and after she laid it out on the table she smiled again, and with a quick curtsy she said, "Guten appetit!" She turned and then walked over to another table where an elderly couple had sat down. She looked back at him and then turned to her new customers.

Steve smiled to himself and murmured that maybe it was better if Kate weren't here right now. He took a bite of the sausages and they were delicious as were the leek and potato bake. He had just finished the last bite and the rest of his beer when his waitress reappeared with his coffee and dessert. He was impressed with her efficiency and politeness. He had noticed that she seemed to be equally diligent with her other customers. He finished his dessert and she appeared with the bill.

He smiled at her and after he looked at the bill, he said that the meal was wonderful and that she was too! And with that he gave her an extra-large tip and she gasped when she saw it and said, "That's too much!" He replied as he closed her hand around the money and told her that he had to work his way through college too and he appreciated the way that she had treated him.

"How did you know?"

He looked into her blue eyes and said, "Because I am a detective!" He rose and waved a kiss at her and left her standing there stunned and bewildered as he walked across the platz toward the path up to the castle. He mused to himself, "I guess she'll know that at least not all Scots are tight with money and do appreciate hard work."

He walked up the small road toward the castle and noted the Buchingsgarten beer garden that was located near the castle at the last steps of the most prominent path to hike up to it. The restaurant was a huge garden with tables of various dimensions with colorful large umbrellas scattered among the trees and lights. It was obviously a hangout for tourists and students alike. He noted it in his memory book for a return visit as he hiked up the path toward the castle. It was certainly impressive! He looked at his watch and discovered that he had spent nearly three hours with his walk. It was time to return to his hotel and check for any messages. He looked at his new iPhone and there were no messages.

He arrived at his hotel as the sun was just beginning to

duck behind the castle. He checked the desk for any messages and there were none. He took the elevator to his floor and walked down to his room and slid the electronic key into its slot and the door opened. He walked inside and his bed had already been turned down. The maid had been there and everything was still in its place. He sighed a welcome relief that he was back and even with the walk was still not hungry! The German food and drink had certainly hit the mark. He was just getting ready to put on his pajamas and robe when his cell phone rang. It was Natalie and she and her parents were staying with Dietrich's parents in their country house outside of town. She said that the Roods were there also and would be with them at the church tomorrow.

"Did you have any trouble with your new scrambled iPhone?" he asked.

"No, everything's working perfectly. I'm calling you instead of Dietrich's father. Everybody's been fully briefed on the charade memorial the next morning at nine o'clock at the Saint John's Altar. Have you been over to the cathedral yet?"

"No, but I walked past it this afternoon on my spatziergang."

She asked, "So you're getting into your German? Did anyone spot that you're not German?"

"Immediately!"

He could hear her laugh, then he continued, "I have a map of its interior and know where the Landgrave's Choir is located. I'll arrive a little early and you should be thinking about getting back to Edinburg and Dietrich as soon as you can and as discreetly as you can. Be doubly careful not to be spotted returning to Dietrich. Have you spoken to Kate and given her the airline flight number on which you will arrive?"

"I did, and Kate told me that she would go to the airport to personally pick me up and take me to Dietrich."

"Good girl!" Steve thought, "She thinks of everything!"

They both said their goodbyes and hung up. Steve felt greatly relieved. Everything was going well. He placed his cell phone on the dresser and started to turn on the television and see what was going on in the world, when his cell phone rang again. It was Kate checking to make sure that he was okay.

"Everything on my side's going along splendidly," she said enthusiastically. "Your aunt went with me, your mother and mine to help me pick out my wedding dress. You'll love it. We've also been over to the minister to make arrangements for the church and I've already cleared your schedule and made the necessary reassignments at the department as well as the arrangements for our honeymoon!"

"Is there anything she can't or won't do?" Steve wondered with admiration.

"I've contacted Col. Harries in Atlanta, Georgia, to find out when the pilgrimage to Libertyville will be. I thought you might want us to be there before visiting with the Roods in Texas."

Steve sighed in relief, He had thought that he would have to do some of the work, but as usual, Kate had come to his rescue.

She asked him to call and let her know if there were any changes in his schedule so that she might be able to help him if needed. Then she added, "Oh by the way, Natalie called and told me the flight number and airline for her return to Scotland."

"Good. Natalie called me at my hotel and said that she had called you."

"That was sweet of her," she answered.

Kate then whispered into the telephone, "I love you very much, please do be careful!"

"I love you, too, Can't wait to see you again. Goodnight, darling."

They hung up and Steve looked down at the bed and suddenly felt very tired. It had been a long day and he was ready to call it a day. He pulled his pajamas out of the drawer and slowly put them on, put on his slippers and then went to the bathroom to floss and brush his teeth. He hung his clothes up in the closet and then he sat down on the bed and stretched his tall frame out and pulled the covers over him.

He was asleep almost as soon as his head hit the pillow.

The morning sun had just started to peep through the half drawn drapes that covered his outside window. Steve crawled out of bed and slid into his slippers that he had left beside his bed and shuffled toward the window. He pulled the drapes open so that the daylight would pour into his room. He looked out and he could see the Elisabeth Kirche down the street. It was a beautiful day. He was glad that he did not have to drive that morning. The hotel was very convenient to the church. He quickly took a shower, shaved and dressed for breakfast. He had put on a black suit with his white Maltese cross in the lapel. He wore a white oxford cloth shirt with French cuffs with Maltese cross cufflinks and a plain black tie tied in a full Windsor knot.

He went to the restaurant downstairs in the hotel and had a light breakfast of fruit and a small biscuit with orange marmalade and coffee with cream and then went back to his room to wait for 9 a.m. to roll around.

There was a London newspaper shoved under his door when he got there and he wondered if all of the English speaking guests got the same service. The Germans were certainly efficient! He entered his room and his bed was already made up and the bedroom and bathroom cleaned! He shook his head in wonderment. He took off his coat and hung it up, brushed his teeth and then sat down to read about the news in England and the world.

He had just about finished the newspaper when there was a knock on his door. He wondered who it might be as he opened the door.

There was a tall white haired, but young looking man with tanned skin and an erect posture in a black suit standing in front of him with a smile on his face and an extended hand as he said in perfect English, "Inspector Grant? I'm Johann von Schoenfeld."

Steve was stunned. He didn't expect Dr. von Schoenfeld to come to meet him. It was about 30 minutes before nine. Steve recovered and shook Dr. von Schoenfeld's hand vigorously.

"Yes, I'm Steve Grant. Won't you please come in" Steve backed up into the room as the older man came forward with a slight limp.

Dr. von Schoenfeld noticed Steve looking at his right leg and quickly explained, "Oh, I sprained my knee two days ago playing a far too vigorous a game of tennis for my age. It will be okay though, I brought a cane to help me along today. I just wanted to meet you early and express my gratitude to you for saving my son's life and being so courteous to him and my daughter-in-law."

"I'm afraid that I wasn't the person," Steve said. "It was Mrs. Annie Elliott and her collie, Sean with the expertise of Dr. Jamie Macadam, an emergency doctor who arrived on the scene in a helicopter from his hospital in Edinburgh. They were the real heroes!"

Dr. von Schoenfeld looked at Steve with piercing pale blue eyes and said, "And you, too, all of you! Natalie has told me all about this band of brothers that you have put together to help my son and daughter-in-law. I am most indebted to you all and especially you for putting this team of experts together."

Dr. von Schoenfeld looked around the room and asked, "Is everything comfortable for you?"

"Yes, I walked down to the Markt Platz yesterday afternoon. I was very impressed. The food and drink were excellent and I've been thinking about visiting the Elisabeth Gasthausbrauerie tonight."

"Ach, ja, we enjoy visiting the old town once in a while," Dr. von Schoenfeld said. "I studied medicine here years ago and have just retired from active practice. I do a little consultation just to keep my hand in medicine. Occasionally, I spend time in the University Library where the Adler Buchs are kept. I've learned quite a bit about our family. We have an ancestor, Elsa who was a student of Martin Luther and friend of his wife, Katharina von Bora.

"If you would like, we have plenty of room at our farm

just outside of Marburg," he continued. "My wife, Ilsa and I would be delighted if you could visit with us and our family for a while. Dietrich's sister, Ingrid is home from the University for the summer and is at the church with my wife, Ilsa, Natalie and her parents. Carolyn and Christopher spent yesterday and last night with us. They will be leaving for Scotland right after the memorial services. They are all waiting at the church for you and me. We all would be delighted if you would drive with us out to the farm after the memorial services. I talked with Dietrich this morning when he called Natalie and he sounded just fine."

Steve raised one eyebrow and said, "I don't want to be any trouble for you, but if you have room, I would be delighted to visit with you for at least tonight before I return to Edinburgh tomorrow. I'll check out of the hotel after the services and follow you in my car if it's all right with you?"

"Okay!"

The two of them turned and Steve followed the doctor out of the room. The door lock clicked as it closed and Steve tried the handle to make sure it was secure.

They took the elevator to the ground floor and walked out of the hotel's front door onto Elisabeth Strasse. It took only a few minutes for them to walk the short distance to the cathedral. They entered the church through the south door and passed by President von Hindenburg's burial place and continued down the nave to the South Choir and St. John's Altar on the right side of the nave. As they approached, he saw Natalie lean toward an older lady that resembled her and whisper into her ear. It turned out to be her mother Maria Novak who was standing next to her husband, Jan, who was considerably taller than his wife, at least six feet four inches Steve thought. She smiled and waved at him and he did the same.

Ilsa, Dr. von Schoenfeld's wife and Ingrid, their daughter, appeared to be spitting images with blond hair, freckled faces and clear blue eyes. Carolyn and Christopher Rood were standing behind them smiling as they spied their new friend.

They were all wearing black clothes as befitted the occasion. There was a Lutheran pastor standing behind the altar in his vestments. The altar had a purple and gold altar cloth with a beautifully engraved brass urn resting upon it.

Steve discovered that the pastor was Peter Wallenfels who was a cousin of the von Schoenfelds and the Roods. He too was tall, about six feet, Steve guessed and with a military bearing that suggested military service— perhaps in the Luftwaffe, same as Dietrich. He had dark brown hair and also had blue eyes, slightly grey Steve noticed as he drew nearer to the group. They all had blue eyes except Natalie and her mother who had hazel eyes and a milky white complexion with dark hair. Natalie's father could have passed for a Wallenfels—probably a Sud Deutschlander in the Czech Republic—he surmised.

Steve and Johann stopped in front of the gathering of the family and Johann introduced Steve to everyone. They all shook hands and took their places kneeling before the altar. Peter Wallenfels began the mock memorial service. Everyone took their roles in the charade seriously and the women even had tears in their eyes as they listened to the eloquence of the pastor. Steve couldn't help but make hurried glances around the church while he bowed his head in reverence to the service. He tried to be as discreet as possible befitting his police training and he thought at one point that he saw someone suspicious in a grey suit with a swarthy complexion, but he finally concluded that it probably was just a slightly curious passer-by.

When the service was over, Peter Wallenfels picked up the brass urn that was supposed to contain Dietrich's ashes and gave it to Dr. von Schoenfeld. He carefully held it cradled in his right arm and hand. Carolyn and Christopher embraced and shook hands with their cousin Peter. Christopher's mother had been a Wallenfels before she married Christopher's father. They all filed out of the church in a solemn procession. It was then that he noticed the man in the grey suit watching them from just inside the church door.

After they had all gathered outside the Elisabeth Kirche, Steve explained that there had probably been an agent watching them inside the church, but he didn't know from which organization he was.

"Interpol, the Mossad, CIA, Bundes Nachtricten Dienst, Scotland Yard etc. were all on this case and working with each other trying to capture Mohammad and his son, Ahmed ali, but he had disappeared," he explained. "The thinking is that Mohammad is in Saudi Arabia and Ahmed in Prague. We think that Mohammad believes that he has killed Dietrich, but the man in the grey suit could be from the Muslim Brotherhood.

"They are after Natalie now and we have to spirit her away someplace out of Europe. We believe the cover story that she has gone into seclusion after her husband's death has gotten to Mohammad and her enemies will deduce that she will probably be with her own family—her parents probably. So the Novaks and von Schoenfeld family will have our people watching over them while we spirit Dietrich and Natalie out of Europe to the United States where they will be staying with the Roods. Dietrich can recover from his wounds and he and Natalie can catch their breath while we try to track down his assailants and arrest them.

"Natalie will be attending Kate's and my wedding and right afterwards, we'll arrange for her and Dietrich to vanish into thin air while we plant the story that she is in seclusion, mourning the loss of her husband. Carolyn and Christopher and we all feel that if they travel by automobile around Texas, they can hide in plain sight as just another tourist couple on their honeymoon. That is, until we feel that we know where Mohammad and Ahmed are, then we can lure them into the United States where they won't have the support system they have in Europe."

Carolyn and Christopher nodded their heads in agreement.

"We'll have them on friendly turf where we have the advantage and can arrest them," Steve continued. "In the process, we may be able to uncover more of their network inside Europe."

Thinking of what Dr. Fox had said, he added, "You know the old Irish story—when they're all chasing after the poor bloody fox, it's better to be dressed as a hound! Natalie and Dietrich will be supplied with new identities and passports. When they get to the United States, they will be provided with American clothes so they can blend into the crowds."

They all shook their heads, understanding what Steve had just said.

Steve then said in a firm voice, "It's vitally important that none of us speak foolishly of anything I have told you, even to your best friends! We must maintain the image that Dietrich is dead and that the family is in mourning and that no one knows where Natalie has gone into seclusion. We have to support the illusion that Natalie wants to be alone!"

Steve and the two Drs. Rood shook hands with every one of the family members and thanked Pastor Peter Wallenfels for his services. They all waited outside the Kirche while Steve, Dr. von Schoenfeld and Drs. Rood retrieved their cars from a nearby parking area.

Steve and Dr. von Schoenfeld walked with Carolyn and Christopher to their rented E46 BMW M3 CSL coupe that had a 3.2-liter, 391 h.p. engine that gave the vehicle super-fast acceleration and cornering with lightning fast gear shifting. Christopher had thought the autobahn would be an ideal road to test his dream car. Little did he know that he would soon have his chance.

As they were leaving, Carolyn and Christopher turned and embraced Johann and Steve and shook their hands. In turn, Steve and Johann wished them well on their trip back to Scotland before they returned to the United States. They waved to them as they left the parking lot.

12 THE CHASE

Christopher maneuvered his BMW out of the parking lot and into traffic. Then he noticed out of the corner of his eye, two identical black Audi A-6 four door sedans pull into traffic behind them. He casually mentioned to Carolyn about the two cars, and Carolyn turned to look at them.

"Isn't that a coincidence that two identical cars would pull into traffic just as we have done?"

"Maybe not so much of a coincidence as we think, babe. Let's keep an eye on them and see what they do." Carolyn nodded her head and they headed toward the Pilgrimstein and the Kurt Schumacher Brucke over the Lahn River toward the B-3 autobahn leading south to Frankfurt.

As Christopher melted into the south bound traffic on B-3 toward Frankfurt, Carolyn softly said, "Darling, those two cars are right behind us. Their windows are darkened, but the driver in the car right behind us looks Arabic."

Christopher looked into his rear view mirror and murmured, "Yeah!" Then, he looked at her and said, "Let's move into the high speed lane and see what this baby will do."

He spotted an opening in the traffic and shoved the BMW

into high gear and sped into the high speed traffic lane that was going about 90 miles per hour.

The car hummed swiftly with ease into the fast lane and Carolyn remarked, "Honey, they're right behind us and coming up rapidly."

As she spoke, the lead Audi quickly accelerated and passed them on the right and just as quickly moved in front of them and started to slow down. Christopher noticed that the second car had pulled up just behind them. Carolyn then noticed a black Mercedes S class sedan move suddenly into the high speed lane some distance behind the following Audi. Christopher decided that he would move to the right and pass the Audi in front of him. Just as he pulled to the right, the lead Audi accelerated and the Audi behind him moved up to his left to keep pace.

Suddenly a black Mercedes C class sedan pulled from the lane to his right quickly to get in front of him so that he had to slow down. He frowned and said to Carolyn, "Damn, we're being boxed in!"

As soon as he said that, he noticed that the Audi on his left had rolled down the passenger side window and a dark haired man was pointing a pistol at him and motioning him to move to the right and exit behind the Mercedes. Carolyn had already pulled her map out and told Christopher that the next exit was L-3125 just north of Gisselberg.

Christopher wrinkled his eyebrows and said, "Carolyn, I'm familiar with this area. I'm going to pretend to follow their directions and then I'm going to show them that this BMW is not quite what they think it is!"

With that, Christopher followed the Mercedes C class sedan into the right lane as if he were going to exit with it and the Audi kept pace beside him while the trailing Audi moved in close behind him, nearly on his bumper as they approached the exit. Christopher turned his blinkers on indicating that he was turning to exit and the Audi beside him on the left quickly slowed down to follow behind the Audi that was behind him. Christopher began his turn into the exit lane following slowly behind the Mercedes.

Christopher suddenly turned the steering wheel of the BMW to the left and jammed the accelerator to the floor. The BMW responded like a leopard leaving his spots behind and darted into the open highway. The two Audi automobiles jammed on their brakes, but it was too late. The lead Audi was already into the exit behind the Mercedes and the trailing Audi was reacting quickly to give chase.

Christopher and the pursuing Audi accelerated rapidly into the middle lane heading for the fast lane as Carolyn turned to look at the Mercedes and Audi on the off ramp.

She exclaimed, "There is a German police car just behind the Audi on the exit ramp and he is pulling both of the cars over."

Christopher muttered, "Good!"

Christopher was pulling away from the Audi as he noticed that the black Mercedes S class sedan was right behind the Audi and keeping pace with it. He glanced at Carolyn and said, "I wonder who those guys in that black Mercedes S are? Maybe they're just in the chase for the fun of it. They're not blinking their headlights for the Audi to get out of the way!"

Just as he said that, Christopher double clicked his headlights to the car in front of him and it dutifully moved into the middle lane to the right. Christopher sped up to 120 mph easily and put more distance between him and the two cars following behind.

Carolyn asked, "What are you going to do with those people following us?"

Christopher looked at her and winked. He said, "Wait and see. I know this area like the back of my hand. I've got a surprise for them!"

Gisselberg and Neiderweimar slid by as they sped down the autobahn leaving other automobiles in their dust as they passed the B-255 exit and across the Waldschlossen Brucke, past Wolfhausen and Weimar. The two cars following them were keeping pace although the Mercedes was deliberately lagging behind the Audi, but keeping them in sight. Cars in front of them were getting out of their way as Christopher double clicked his lights.

They passed Roth and Fronhausen and Christopher remarked, "It's strange that we haven't had any police cars challenge us!"

Carolyn wrinkled her nose and replied, "You're going too fast for everyone."

"Well, not for long," Christopher quipped, slowing the BMW down as they passed Sicherhausen and were coming up on the L-3356 exit just north of Stauffenberg. When they exited onto the L-3356 exit, Carolyn could see that the Audi and the Mercedes had slowed down and moved into the right lane to follow them down the exit onto the L-3356 roadway.

Christopher swung the BMW sharply to the right onto L-3356 and pushed the accelerator down. The car leaped onto the road and Christopher maneuvered the agile beast down the curvy road at a fast pace that kept him comfortably ahead of the pursuing Audi and Mercedes. He sped down L-3356 as it became Alten-Busecker Strasse leading into the village of Daubringen and then turned right onto Giessener Strasse.

Villagers watched in horror and got out of the way as the BMW sped past houses, pedestrians and bicyclers toward the Shafer Multikulti-Treff. By this time the Audi had caught up with them and the Mercedes had slowed down and was 100 yards behind the Audi. The driver of the Audi was dangerously close to the BMW and not particularly concerned about any pedestrians or dogs that might get in his way. Christopher could see the dark scowl on the driver's face.

Just as Christopher passed the Multikulti-Treff, Christopher gunned the engine and took a quick left turn down the Bomgasse with the Audi right behind. The driver of the Audi gunned his car and was close enough to ram the BMW when Christopher accelerated and took a sharp left turn as the road dead ended onto a small side road beside a deep ravine with a creek at its bottom. Carolyn screamed as he slammed his brakes and the BMW came to an abrupt halt.

The driver of the Audi was totally surprised and tried to

slam on his brakes, but it was too late. He suddenly saw that the upwardly inclined road in front of him had dead ended on the perpendicular road beside the deep creek and wide ravine. His eyes widened and he gasped, "Oh shat!" The Audi slid across the road and became airborne as it flew over the creek and slammed into the stone embankment on the other side of the creek and burst into a fireball as it exploded and fell into the creek.

The black Mercedes pulled up next to Carolyn and Christopher's BMW and the back door of the Mercedes opened. The man in the grey suit that they had seen at the Elisabeth Kirke got out and waved his arm. He had a smile on his face. The driver of the Mercedes opened and a man with blond hair in a dark blue suit got out and extended his hand to shake Christopher's hand. He introduced himself as Hans Bilder of the Bundes Nachtricten Dienst and the man in the grey suit as Ari Shapiro of the Israeli Mossad.

Ari spoke in perfect Cambridge English as he shook Christopher's hand and bowed toward Carolyn, "We've been watching over your family and you. We have had these members of the Muslim Brotherhood under joint surveillance for some time. These are bad characters, and you led them and us on a merry chase. We won't have to worry about these that crashed and we have the ones in the other Audi and Mercedes under arrest. They are being interrogated at this moment. We are also watching the Schoenfeld Estate and have been for some time."

"I'm glad," said Christopher.

Ari looked intently at Carolyn and then Christopher and said, "You know that they were going to kill you and probably sell your wife into slavery!"

Carolyn became ashen and started to shake. She barely was able to speak, "You're kidding, aren't you?"

"No," was his terse reply.

Hans then explained that they were going to provide escort for them to the Frankfurt Airport and make sure that they made their flight to Scotland on time.

Carolyn and Christopher sighed with relief and Christopher said in order to break the tenseness of the moment, "I hope I won't get a speeding ticket."

Everyone laughed and Hans said, "No, you won't get a speeding ticket, but we might think about a medal for helping us get these criminals."

During the ride to the airport, Carolyn admonished Christopher about not warning her prior to the abrupt stop.

He replied, "Sorry, I was somewhat preoccupied making certain that *we* stayed on the pavement and *they* ended up in the creek."

"I guess I'll forgive you this time," she said affectionately with a grin. "Just for the record," she added, "I would prefer that there is not a next time!"

13 THE SCHOENFELD ESTATE

Steve walked with Dr. von Schoenfeld over to his Mercedes GL 550 4-matic SUV. They got into it and returned to everyone waiting for them in front of the Elisabeth Kirche. They pulled up to the group and parked the silver grey wagon next to the curb. The size of the SUV would accommodate seven persons comfortably for short distances, but not for a long trip.

Everyone got into the SUV except Ingrid. She insisted that Steve sit next to her for the short excursion to his hotel so that he could retrieve his belongings, check out of the hotel and get his car from the garage so that he could follow them to the von Schoenfelds' farm. They all waved their goodbyes to Pastor Wallenfels as they left for Steve's hotel. Their SUV quickly made the short trip to the hotel and Steve disappeared inside after Dr. von Schoenfeld had parked his car in the parking garage.

It took Steve about ten minutes to get his bags, check out of his hotel and retrieve his rented car. When he drove up to the SUV, Ingrid was waiting for him. As she got into Steve's car, she explained that she had volunteered to be his navigator on the way to their farm and besides it left more room inside the SUV for everyone else!

Steve pulled his car out behind the silver grey SUV as they exited the hotel's garage and entered Elisabeth Strasse for the journey to the farm. They drove through the streets of Marburg and onto the autobahn that led north toward the von Schoenfeld farm. Steve tailed them with the expertise of a pursuing policeman and they soon broke into empty countryside with far stretching meadows that had even rows of plowed land that had been planted for various crops. An occasional woods dotted the countryside hills that rose between the nicely cultivated farmland.

Ten minutes later, the small caravan exited the autobahn and Steve noted the road so he could find his way back to the autobahn when he returned to Frankfurt the next day for his return trip to Edinburgh. Fifteen minutes later after a few twists and turns in the road, which Ingrid pointed out, they turned left onto a small road that aptly enough was named after his host's family. A few miles more and they entered a long curving driveway that led up a gentle hill to a chalet farmhouse that looked like it could accommodate a large family. There was a tennis court on the left side of the house, surrounded by a chain fence next to a swimming pool with a small waterfall off to the side. There was also a hot tub spa next to the swimming pool that looked like it could accommodate at least half a dozen tired tennis players!

Dr. von Schoenfeld pulled into a five car garage that had an old red Jaguar XKE convertible sports car that looked brand new despite its age. Steve particularly liked that antique automobile and guessed that it was a 1970 Jaguar. There was a Mercedes C class sedan next to the spot that Dr. von Schoenfeld pulled into and he motioned Steve into the spot next to his SUV.

After they got out of their cars, Ingrid offered to show him the guest room that he would occupy. As they entered the grey stone building with a dark blue slate roof and a turret just to the side of the entrance door, Ingrid leaned over to Steve and whispered into his ear as she pointed to the turret, "That's your guest room. It has three levels and the best view in the house and it has a stone spiral staircase!" She laughed as she said, "It has a small observatory on the third level with a telescope! Would you like me to show you how to use it tonight? It can track the Moon, Mars and Venus!"

Steve did not respond to her question and she looked puzzled. Then she said, "You're probably tired?"

They entered the house and off to the left of the foyer was an oak door to the turret guest room, and immediately to the right was a large double door that opened to reveal a spacious library with sliding library stairladder that could reach the top shelves.

"Obviously this was a well-read family!" thought Steve.

Ingrid motioned to the oak door and ran over and opened it for Steve to enter. Dr. von Schoenfeld continued into a Great Room with his guests. The Great Room looked like a medieval oak paneled room with large wooden beams and hanging tapestries. There was a statue of a knight with real shining armor guarding the entrance! The place looked positively steeped in chivalric history!

Natalie had broken off from the rest and was about to follow Ingrid and Steve into the guest room when Steve noticed that Dr. von Schoenfeld had turned, raised his hand to the side of his mouth and shouted to him, "Don't be concerned, Ingrid is a little flirt, but she's not dangerous!" Then he turned back to his guests and he and Ilsa followed them into the Great Room with its stuffed leather chairs, couch and comfortable atmosphere.

Natalie laughed with that remark and looked at Steve and winked. "See why I just love Dietrich and his family. They are all great fun and extremely loyal to each other."

Ingrid had pouted her lips out in a childish fashion and murmured, "He can't get used to the fact that I'm all grown up—well, almost!" She laughed then said, "But I love him so. He is just a little protective of me and is terribly concerned about Dietrich. He tries his best to cover up his anxiety!"

Natalie agreed and said, "He is such a dear, just like Dietrich. Now Ingrid, remember, I told you that Steve is engaged to be married to a wonderful woman."

"Yes, but he's not married yet," she said as she looked up coyly at Steve and slowly said, "And he's sooo handsome!" She drawled out the words and then giggled.

The three of them entered the large round room with a large round bed in the middle with curved wooden furniture around the circumference of the room. The floor was oak with a large round throw rug that embraced the bed. There was a large kleiderschrank and dresser with a curved mirror above it and a curved desk below a curved stained glass window. On the inside wall, a narrow stone staircase with a wrought iron hand rail curved up the wall to the next room where the dressing room, bathroom with its fully glassed in shower, and a curved linen closet were located. Another stained glass window showered multicolored rays of light across the wooden floor. An iron vertical staircase from that room led to a small library-study with a large curved window that circled the room 300 degrees just under the turret's conical roof with its interior wooden beams. There was a reflective astronomical telescope with an attached computer and digital camera that was pointed toward the curved glass window that peered out toward the blue sky. Obviously Dr. von Schoenfeld's family had wide interests!

Ingrid took great delight in showing Steve the guest room from top to bottom. Natalie said that she would stay in the bedroom while Ingrid showed off the rest of the unique turret. She had already seen it. After Ingrid returned with her guest to the bottom floor, Ingrid asked Steve if he wanted her to put away his clothes and he politely declined her offer saying that he would do it later.

Natalie got up from the round bed that she had been sitting on and said, "Let's go into the Great Room. I want you to speak with my parents and Frau Schoenfeld."

They left the room with Natalie leading the way and Ingrid trailing along behind Steve.

They all entered the room, walking past the knight in armor guarding the door and toward the families that were gathered around the bar at the other end of the large room with its stone fireplace and paneled walls. They were sipping wine and chatting in German when they entered the room, but when they spied Steve, they immediately switched to English without missing a sentence.

Dr. von Schoenfeld asked which wine they would like, and they all gave their preferences, and he dutifully poured them each a glass. Steve had selected a red burgundy and Natalie and Ingrid picked a Chardonnay. They all asked him about how Dietrich looked when he left Scotland for the memorial services and Steve told them all that he knew and described how well he had responded to Dr. Macadam's care. He repeated that they had to remain cautious when Natalie left in a few days to rejoin Dietrich.

Frau Schoenfeld mentioned that she had fixed roast beef for the evening meal with white asparagus and potato cakes. They were going to have strawberry shortcake in his honor to go along with the coffee and brandy. Steve suddenly became very hungry at the thought of the dinner. Ingrid looked at Steve and noticed the look in his eyes as her mother was describing the evening meal.

She giggled and said to her mother, "You are right. You always told me that the way to a man's heart was through his stomach!"

Mother and daughter looked at each other and smiled as if some great secret known only to females had suddenly been revealed! They all laughed and then turned toward the sofa and chairs in the room and sat down with the men pairing off into their corner next to the fireplace and the females to the more intimate leather sofas and chairs.

Jan, Natalie's father, asked Steve, "Have you planned how to track down Dietrich's assailant and corner him?"

"We're working on that and don't have all the details yet," Steve explained. "We first have to get the rat out of his hiding place before we can trap him. It was just a matter of time. Unfortunately, he is now after Natalie because he thinks that Dietrich is dead. We have covered Dietrich's tracks pretty well—even the Interpol thinks that he is dead. I'm not sure, but we may have been watched at the Elisabeth Kirche this morning.

"I don't know who all are watching us," Steve said with uncertainness in his voice. "All I know is that we must be careful because Natalie is still in danger!"

Just at that moment, his cell phone rang and Steve recognized the number and he excused himself and said, "Important call!" He then turned slightly and in muffled tones answered the phone. It was Kate and her voice was anxious.

"Steve, we just got a lead on Mohammad! The Mossad is reporting that they have gotten word out of Syria that Mohammad was killed this afternoon in a sudden attack by government forces. They believe it to be true. They know that he was working with some radical rebel forces, up to his old tricks of teaching them about IEDs! But they are not for sure. They haven't gotten a positive ID.

"Scotland Yard thinks that they have spotted Ahmed ali talking to a London Muslim cleric at the Black Friar pub off Queen Victoria Street near Temple on the East side of London. They are keeping a close watch on him. They have visual and electronic surveillance on Ahmed and the cleric. You know they have been having difficulty with the radical clerics using the mosques as cover while they recruit home grown suicide squads. They are concerned because Ahmed ali has been trained in explosives by his father and they sure don't want IEDs popping up all over London! I'll keep you informed. How did everything go with the memorial service?"

"Everything went well, darling, but I think that somebody's agent may have been observing us."

He continued, "I've left the hotel and am now the overnight guest of Dr. von Schoenfeld and his family. They live on a farm a few miles outside Marburg and they invited me to stay the night. Natalie let the cat out of the bag about our engagement and we have been the hot topic of conversation. I wish you were here to answer all of the questions that the ladies have!"

Kate's voice suddenly picked up, "What ladies?"

"You know, Natalie and her mother and Dietrich's mother and his sister. I don't know what to tell them other than we are deeply in love!"

"Oh, that was sweet of you to say," purred Kate, "I miss you so much."

"Well, I know that you will do just fine. You must tell me all about it when you get home. Our mothers are all wrapped up in this and I must tell you darling, that I am too! I am anxiously waiting to see you tomorrow. I've got a surprise for you! I hope you will like it! Is the farm comfortable? I know what a city person you are!"

Steve smiled to himself and replied, "Oh, I'll get along okay. I'm pretty tough!"

"Oh, you poor baby!" Kate replied, "It will just be for a night. I'm sure you can make it for one night. Talk to you later, I love you!"

"I love you too," Steve whispered.

Then they both hung up. Steve felt a little pang of guilt for not describing the farm house and the wonderful meal that he was anticipating.

He turned to Dr. von Schoenfeld and Jan Novak. "I'm sorry that I had to talk so long, but Kate just informed me that Mohammad, the man that attacked Dietrich, might be dead. The authorities received word from a very reliable source that he may have been killed in an explosion in Syria, but that his son has been spotted in London. They are not quite sure what that is all about, but London is too close to Edinburgh and they have increased the security for Dietrich. So, you shouldn't worry. Everything is well in hand and we may only have to worry about Ahmed. They don't think that he knows right now about his father. I believe that we can breathe a little easier now with this good news out of Syria about the possible death of Mohammad."

Steve looked at Jan and Johann and the strain that he had

noticed in their faces earlier appeared to be dissipated and they looked much relieved.

Dr. von Schoenfeld turned to his wife and shouted across the room, "Ladies, Inspector Grant has just gotten word from his office in Scotland that Dietrich's assailant has in all probability just been killed today in Syria. We can't let our guard down now; however, his son Ahmed ali has been seen in London apparently on other business rather than Dietrich and Natalie. I believe that we can sleep easier tonight with this news."

Ingrid smiled and let out a wild whoop and said, "All right!"

Ilsa and Maria looked at each other and then smiled at Natalie.

Maria hugged her daughter and whispered into her ear as only a mother could do, "It's going to just fine, dearest, just fine!"

Ingrid jumped up and down and hugged Natalie. Both of them had tears in their eyes, but they were joyful tears as sisters would share. Ilsa held both Maria's hand and Natalie's hand and muttered, "Gott sei dank!"

Ilsa put her arms around her daughter-in-law and her husband. Johann who had walked over to Natalie and Ilsa, put his arms around them both. Jan was hugging his wife. Steve stood there looking at this tender scene wishing that they had positive and irrefutable evidence that Mohammad was indeed dead! Ilsa broke the silence and said that she will be serving Champagne with dinner tonight and say a prayer to God for this good news. She broke away from her husband and walked over to Steve, hugged him and whispered, "Thank you, thank you, Steve for this wonderful news!"

At that moment, Steve's cell phone rang again. He excused himself and answered it and listened intently. His face darkened and then it quickly lit up as he said into his phone, "That is great news! They were caught completely unaware? You say that we are being watched over by the Bundes

Nachtricten Dienst? Well, that's good news. Where are you now? You're getting ready to board your flight? Well, both of you take care and we'll look forward to seeing you in Scotland and the United States."

With that, Grant hung up and turned to his hosts. "The Muslim Brotherhood tried to kidnap Carolyn and Christopher, but Christopher outwitted them. They're safe and the bad guys are either in jail or dead. That man in the grey suit at the church was with the Mossad! The Bundes Nachtrichten Dienst has everything well in hand and are watching over us all as we speak. Carolyn and Christopher are safely on their way to Scotland and then back home to Texas."

Ingrid smiled and let out another wild whoop and yelled, "Wow!"

She jumped up and down again and then hugged Steve. She looked up at him and declared, "They're my cousins!"

The dinner that Ilsa served in the dining room that night lived up to its billing!

Dr. von Schoenfeld said a heartfelt prayer of thanks before the dinner was served and gave a toast with the champagne for the joyous news. Everyone enjoyed each other's company during the meal. Maria, Ilsa and Natalie wanted to know all about Steve and Kate's wedding and their honeymoon plans. Steve said that he didn't know where Kate wanted to go, but he knew that they would like to go to the United States and pay their respects to King Peter in Libertyville and then go to Texas sometime after their wedding in Edinburgh.

"You'll all be receiving a wedding invitation," Steve said.

Natalie smiled, "I know that Dietrich would like to be there, but I'll be there for the both of us."

"I definitely want to be there, too, so I can get a good look at Kate," vowed Ingrid.

Everyone laughed. They were all in great spirits by the time an exceptionally good strawberry shortcake, coffee, and brandy were served.

The men retired to the Great Room while the ladies joined together to clean up the dining room, the dishes, and the kitchen before joining the men in the Great Room. Ilsa was still running her household as her mother had taught her!

After they joined the men, the conversation turned to breakfast tomorrow morning and Steve's departure. Steve had said when he was asked by Ilsa, that a light breakfast was all that he wanted for the trip and he didn't want to inconvenience anyone with his early departure. Johann said that he and his wife always got up early in the morning and that everyone else should say their goodnights now before going to bed, and they looked forward to everyone getting together again! They all said their good nights and wished Steve and Kate well in their marriage and their lives together.

They all, with the exception of Steve, climbed the winding stairs in the hall that led upstairs to the other bedrooms. Steve stood at the bottom of the stairs and waved at them as they disappeared toward their rooms.

Ingrid stopped on the stairs until everyone else had vanished and then she ran down the stairs, and up to him and threw her arms around him, kissed him on the mouth and whispered into his ear, "Thank you! Thank you for saving my brother. I love you!"

With that she ran back up the stairs and at the top of the stairs, turned, blew him a kiss and then disappeared down the upstairs hall to her bedroom. Steve turned, a little embarrassed at the display of puppy love and subconsciously half wished that he was Ingrid's age again, then walked toward the door to his bedroom and went to bed.

The next morning, the sun was already spreading a multicolored pattern over Steve's bedroom floor and bed when he woke up from a deep, but pleasant sleep. The bed covers were scattered around his twisted frame as he removed the pillow that he held over his eyes. He looked around the room and couldn't figure out where the top or the bottom of his bed was. He rubbed his eyes and looked at his stainless steel Rolex Submariner watch and was startled to see that it was already half past six! His flight to Edinburgh was at 12:30 that afternoon and Frankfurt was only about 97 kilometers from Marburg, but he knew that he should be there early and that he had to turn in his rental car and check his luggage.

He bolted from the bed, slid into his slippers, grabbed his shaving and toiletry kit, and sprinted up the spiral stone stairs to the second story bathroom. He shaved, slipped out of his pajamas, jumped into the round all glass shower, and turned the controls for the multishower heads that spewed out the welcome water that engulfed him. He shampooed his hair and picked up the new cake of English Lavender soap that Ingrid had made certain was in his shower the day before. How thoughtful and very German, he mused as the water that reflected the dancing colors from the rising sunlight coming through the stained glass window that poured through the clear, all-glass, large, round shower. It reminded him of the dancing multicolored lights in a discotheque!

After he had dressed and straightened his tie, he thought that he would sneak into the kitchen before anyone was up and not disturb them. He walked past the breakfast room on his way to the kitchen and noticed out of the corner of his eye that everyone was already in the breakfast room and Ilsa had his orange juice and coffee waiting for him. She said to him that she hoped that his breakfast would be adequate.

Across the table he spied Ingrid looking at him mischievously as she shouted, "Sleepyhead!"

Everyone, including Steve laughed as he seated himself down at the table where Ilsa had set the table for him next to Ingrid. Ilsa had sensed from Steve's remarks the night before that a poached egg with a croissant, orange juice and coffee with cream would be all that he would probably want.

Steve looked at Ilsa and said, "It's perfect!"

She smiled a self-satisfied smile and nodded to him.

He looked around the table and noticed that she had more food laid out in a buffet fashion that everyone else could choose. He thought to himself, "She read my mind!"

After breakfast they all shook hands and Natalie and Ingrid gave him a hug.

They said their good byes and Dr. von Schoenfeld walked with him to his room where he had already packed his bags. He excused himself to Johann and said that he had to retrieve his toiletry case that was still in the bathroom. He ran up the stairs and quickly brushed his teeth, washed his hands, grabbed his case and hurriedly descended the stairs and tucked the toiletry case into his bag. Dr. von Schoenfeld grabbed the bag as Steve picked up his briefcase and they left the room.

They turned toward the hall where everyone had gathered and Steve waved to his new found friends. Then he followed Johann through the opened front door and walked toward the garage to his rented C-class Mercedes. Johann clicked a remote control, and the garage doors opened and revealed the stable of cars that were lined up in a neat row.

When Steve pressed the car's electronic key, the trunk door opened and Dr. von Schoenfeld placed Steve's bag next to the briefcase that Steve had already placed in the trunk. He closed the trunk door and turned to Johann who shook his hand and thanked him again for all that he had done for his son and daughter-in-law. Ingrid threw her arms around him and kissed him on his cheek and then ran back to her father. Steve opened the door to the Mercedes and settled into the leather driver's seat, started the ignition and the car responded instantly to its driver with a soft purring roar to indicate that it was ready for the trip to Frankfurt International Airport.

Steve rolled down the driver's window and shook Johann's hand again. As he looked past Johann he could see that Ingrid had stepped into the driveway and was waving goodbye vigorously. He waved back to her, pressed the accelerator and the car slowly moved forward. Steve waved to Ingrid and her father again as the car picked up speed and he moved down the tree lined driveway toward Schoenfeld Lane and Frankfurt. He sighed and pondered the idea that he wanted

Kate and him to have a family like that!

14 LONDON—A GATHERING STORM

The morning dawn broke over Chelsea, a Kensington suburb southwest of Victoria Station. The small apartment, not too far from Hyde Park, was drab and dark, other than the small slit of sunlight that shined perilously through a narrow space between two halves of a blue curtain. The window looked down upon Milner Street.

Ahmed ali had just gotten up and poured a cup of dark Arabic coffee. He opened the curtain to let more sunlight into the apartment. He had been out late last night and had overslept. He usually got up early for his morning prayers. He always regretted it if he missed his morning or evening prayers. When he was in infidel countries, he tried to participate in as many daily prayers as he could so long that it did not attract attention to the fact that he was a devout Muslim working undercover for Allah! He wanted the English to believe that he was just a foreign visitor in London to absorb British culture.

He had been meeting with several imams of the mosques that had started to spring up over the English countryside like mushrooms. He had carried the good news that their Hamas comrades in Syria could expect a large shipment of Gadhafi weapons from Benghazi that would arrive by ship to Turkey sometime in September or October. The weapons would then be smuggled to Sunni rebel groups in Syria aligned with the Muslim Brotherhood. This would bolster their recruitment efforts.

It was the objective of the Muslim jihad to get as many immigrants into the western countries as soon as they could. If they could get cells led by jihadist imams into the various mosques, it would be easier to proselytize new young native born recruits into the jihadist movement worldwide.

Instead of bringing in trained Jihadist agents that could be easily spotted, they would create homegrown European and British citizens that could be converted into the Jihadist movement when they are impressionable teenagers or twenty year olds. Then they could be turned into trained jihadist assassins right under their European and British noses. They would become idealistic converts into immortals ready to kill infidels, become martyrs and obtain seventh heaven by sacrificing their own life for Allah!

The recruiting trip for the cause had been a great success and he had been informed that they were just about ready to set a group of "Manchurian candidates" loose in the United Kingdom. They would be more ruthless than the IRA when they terrorized the English on their home ground.

He thought, "The Imperial War Museum was not far away, maybe, just maybe the Muslim Jihads could teach these Brits and maybe the Yanks as well, something about warfare. Something that they could put in their war museum after Jihad had beaten them and converted the United Kingdom to their new Muslim faith!"

He was looking forward to visiting the United States where the Muslim immigration from various Muslim countries had been highly successful. They were even using the generous American subsidization of foreign immigration to make it easier to inculcate their culture and religion into the heartland of the United States where it would blossom like poisonous mushrooms, especially in the angry African-American population. There was already a militant attitude that had been prepared among the black youth and the Black Muslim movement. They could take advantage of their hatred of whites that had been building over the last few decades and then slide into a welfare state that made it easier to induce a favorable attitude among the population toward Sharia Law. He knew that moderate Muslims in the United States would not take an aggressive stance against militant jihad.

Ahmed had not told his sister that he was going to London and later in the year to the United States to coordinate more terrorist attacks on the unsuspecting Americans. After all, they had not experienced what the British had gone through with the I.R.A. The British were more prepared than the Americans. He knew that he would have to make a really big effort in the United States to terrorize them on their own turf. He knew that the Americans would be paralyzed since they had not really fought a war on their home ground in over a hundred years.

When home grown terror really begins in the United States, the average American will be totally confused! He laughed at the thought!

He and his father had arranged for a false report of his father's death on a remote field of fighting in Syria to be announced. They had already arranged for a mangled body of a warrior for Allah to be identified as his father by the Muslim Brotherhood. He knew that a little money and a quick funeral would cover their tracks and the NATO forces would not be able to confirm it. This way Mohammad would be able to disappear and everyone would let their guard down. When he got back to Prague and his father had let him know where he had gone underground, he would not let his sister, Rania know their father was still alive and warn Natalie in case she had heard of his death in Syria.

Ahmed finished dressing, ate a small biscuit and finished his cup of coffee. He had to hurry to make his train at Victoria Station. He would eat on the way. His trip would take him to Yorkshire, Birmingham and then to Manchester where he would meet with other imams that had been secreted into those towns. He was just locking the door to his rented apartment that the Muslim Jihad had provided for him, when he received a coded text message that would mean nothing to anyone other than him. He and his father had arranged a prearranged code that would let Ahmed know that his father was safely back in Jeddah, Saudi Arabia. He looked at it and smiled—everything had worked just as they planned. The message was short, but Ahmed recognized the prearranged code.

He took a taxi to Victoria Station and left a small tip for the driver. He smiled at the driver who appeared not to be impressed with the small tip. He picked up the small suitcase and ran through Victoria Station to the track where his train north was waiting. He noticed that he had a few minutes and took the time to purchase a few sandwiches and snacks for his trip at a small shop in the station. He then boarded the train and found his small compartment for the trip. He put his bag aside and settled down for the trip. He was still tired from the last few days work in the London area, but he was satisfied that everything was in place for the reign of terror there to begin within the next few years.

15 THE HOMECOMING

The airplane from Germany had just touched down as Steve reached for his cell phone. He was anxious to find out if anything new was on the horizon and he thought that he would let Kate know that he was back from Germany.

He dialed her private number at her apartment. It rang once and there was an immediate response.

"Hello, darling, I was hoping that you were home," Kate said. "Everything at the hospital is just fine, but Carolyn and Christopher have to get back to Austin after the wedding and Dr. Fox has to get back to his diggings at Fountains Abbey afterwards. They wish us all well and said they are looking forward to seeing us again in the United States. They are going with Natalie and Dietrich and Dr. Fox to Libertyville in October and hoped that we might be able to come at that time, but I did not want to commit us until I have discussed things with you," and then her voice trailed off and she said, "and your mother and aunt!"

"Well, I see that you have everything well in hand!" marveled Steve. "Marburg went well and there weren't any hitches at the church. I was certainly happy to hear that Carolyn and Christopher were able to make it safely back to

Scotland for our wedding after their hair raising chase on the autobahn. I was also glad to find out that the Mossad and the Bundes Nachtricten Dienst were silently chaperoning us in Germany. Listen, they are starting to empty out the airplane and I have to hang up. I'll clear customs and be at your apartment within an hour, I hope! Anything to drink?"

"Yes, a single malt Lismore—neat of course! I've got the glasses ready and some snacks before dinner." she replied. "Hurry, darling. Goodbye, 'til then."

"As quickly as possible." And then he hung up.

It took Steve about an hour to clear customs at the Edinburgh airport, get his car and drive to Kate's apartment in Edinburgh. He parked his car, retrieved his suitcase with the bottle of Mosel Riesling wine that he had picked up in Marburg for Kate and was getting ready to knock on Kate's door when it opened.

Kate was standing there in a stunning blue negligee that made her look ethereal. It appeared that a light from within her was creating a glow that wrapped around her golden hair and fell across the right side of her face and down upon her shoulders and breasts. Her blue eyes sparkled with excitement as she saw her fiancée who was half hidden by the darkness of the porch.

"I saw you drive up," she said.

Steve stood there completely dazed at the vision of loveliness that stood before him. He choked out the words, "Kate, you just take my breath away. I've been thinking of you every minute, I've missed you so much!"

She pulled him through the door and into the room. The door had no sooner closed than they both threw their arms around each other and he picked her up as her arms encircled his neck and he kissed her, first on her lips and then on her neck just below her left ear. She let out a soft gasp as her slippers fell to the floor.

He picked her up and carried her to the large mauve sofa next to the fireplace.

He cradled her in his arms as they lay down upon the sofa

and nestled into the warmth of each other's embrace. They kissed each other again and again, this time with a passion of two lovers separated far too long and she whispered, "My darling inspector, I adore you!"

With that, she untied Steve's tie and led him into her bedroom as she unbuttoned his jacket and let it slide onto the floor. When they reached the bed, they had both scrambled out their clothes, leaving them on the floor and they slid into the bed still embraced and with a desperate desire that consumed their every breath.

The soft pink light from the lamp next to their bed enveloped the two lovers as they lay breathlessly in each other's arms. An hour had passed since Steve had knocked on Kate's door and it seemed to them both that it had only been a few minutes and far too soon. He caressed her gently and brushed her hair from her eyes as he gazed into the soft blue gaze of his Kate. She trembled a bit as he pulled her closer and kissed her softly on her lips.

She murmured, "I'm afraid that the dinner I fixed for you is cold. I was hoping that you would like a filet mignon to go with your Scotch. I had it covered and could warm it if you wish."

Steve looked intently at her and said, "Yes, dear that would be fine, if you could be the dessert!"

She got up from the bed, took his hands and pulled him up towards her. He wrapped her in his arms and they kissed again. She nestled her face against his neck and whispered into his left ear as she touched his ear lobe with the tip of her tongue, "I think that can be arranged!"

The sun was already up and blazing through the windows in Kate's living room when the two lovers opened their eyes and looked at each other.

Kate laid her head against Steve's chest and took a big breath and sighed, "Morning has come far too soon. I would rather just spend the day here with you." She twisted her head up and looked into his eyes and with a conviction in her voice said, "I really missed you, darling, when you were in

Germany, more than at any time since I first met you three years ago."

He looked at her and with a surprised look on his face said, "Has it really been three years since we first met? It doesn't seem that long. Being with you has felt so comfortable—just like breathing!"

"Oh, darling, you always say the nicest things! I believe that I fell in love with you from that first day!"

He looked at her and said, "Walking through life with you will be the most wonderful thing to me. I just don't know what was wrong with me all these wasted years. I've been falling in love with you every day since I first saw you, but didn't realize it until this affair with Dietrich and Natalie. I guess their love for each other and their nearly losing each other during their honeymoon and through their ordeal, it brought home to me how much I love and need you . I just couldn't stand losing you!"

They both got up, showered together and made love to each other in the shower. They dressed, had breakfast and made plans to meet with the minister at the Holyrood Abbey Church in Edinburgh to arrange for their marriage ceremony. The wedding was just one week away and there was much to do.

His mother, aunt and Kate's mother had already talked to the Reverend Elliott and the three of them had an appointment to meet with him and the happy couple at Holyrood Abbey Church of Scotland that afternoon.

Steve's mother, aunt and Kate's mother had already met with Kate, and they had picked out the wedding dress for the marriage ceremony. The four of them had already picked out the flowers and made the wedding invitations for the friends and relatives of the bride and bridegroom!

The reception after the wedding was to be at Holyrood and they were concerned about the parking. The streets around the Abbey Church were narrow, but there was a convenient parking lot not too far away.

Carolyn and Christopher Rood were going to be there

with Natalie. Ed MacGregor and his family would be there as well. Jamie Macadam had insisted on being best man and he was going to bring a girlfriend, who was a nurse at the hospital, so she could be a bridesmaid. Natalie had arrived from Germany and was currently ensconced with Dietrich at the hospital. Even Dr. Fox was going to show up for their wedding. Christopher's family had historic connection with the storied church in the ancient past as did his wife Carolyn's family—the MacIntosh clan.

The surprise that Kate had been saving for Steve was revealed at the luncheon that afternoon when she and Steve met with both of their mothers and his aunt.

They had pooled their resources for Kate and Steve's honeymoon at the Romantik Hotel Beucour in the heart of the old town of Strasbourg, France in Alsace-Lorraine.

The week passed quickly and the wedding was a grand affair with Katie's and Steve's families there. Carolyn and Natalie looked radiant in their bridesmaid pastel dresses and Christopher stood next to them with Randall Fox close by. Dr. Macadam looked grand, but slightly uncomfortable in his tuxedo standing next to Steve, but he performed admirably as best man when Kate's father walked her down the aisle as they played the Wedding March by Mendelssohn. After the ceremony, Steve lifted Kate's veil and kissed so long that Jamie had to tap him on the shoulder so he could have his turn.

When Katie and Steve left the church after the wedding ceremony, they saw their friends outside and they threaded their way through the guests that lined both sides of the sidewalk. Steve could see out of the corner of his eye as he and Katie were just about to enter their car to depart for the reception that his college buddies, Inspector Ed MacGregor and Dr. Jamie Macadam had joined forces and were madly waving at them as they jointly picked up a bucket full of rice and showered them with an avalanche of the white stuff. He also saw the special Scotland Security Force agents interspersed through the guests and hanging around the church and its parking lot. He could hear Ed and Jamie shouting their congratulations above the other voices that joined in a chorus as the rice covered them from head to toe as they entered their decorated wedding limousine for the ride to their wedding reception.

The reception went until the early morning hours, and Steve and Kate were not disappointed. Family and friends kissed the bride and shook his hand until he felt like a politician. They were blissfully happy and wanted everyone to eat, dance and have a good time. But Natalie was not there. She had been safely whisked away by the Security Forces and was back at the hospital with Dietrich, safely protected.

In the early morning hours Steve and Kate went to Steve's apartment to get ready for the flight to Strasbourg for their honeymoon. By this time all of the rice had been shaken from their clothes and their bags were already packed for their flight.

At seven o'clock that morning, Carolyn, Natalie and Christopher had picked them up to take them to the airport where they met their immediate families and friends who had already gathered for their departure. They waved at everyone as they went through security on their way to the departure gate. No one had noticed the short older man with greying hair and dark complexion that was standing nonchalantly off to the side watching the disappearance of the newlyweds toward their flight. The old man was watching Natalie and the Roods with a great deal of interest.

He reached into his pocket and imperceptibly put his cell phone to his ear after he dialed a coded number and quietly said to the person on the other end of the line, "Ahmed, Natalie appears to be sad, but unsuspecting that she is in danger. Inspector Grant apparently has fallen for your father's ruse that he is dead and has dropped the case. He was just married to his secretary and they are leaving the country for their honeymoon! Natalie has apparently found some sympathy and protection with Maj. von Schoenfeld's American cousins. I will call and have our people in the

United States watch for them. I believe that she might be going to America to assuage her grief over her husband's death."

"Yes," he continued, "I will keep you informed. Tell your father that we will find an appropriate time and place to kidnap or kill her and her meddlesome American cousins!"

He then hung up the telephone and slipped it into his pocket and watched Natalie and the Roods walk toward Natalie's departure gate to Germany. He followed them and waited to see if she was really going to Germany.

Later that morning, Natalie departed for Marburg. Carolyn and Christopher hugged her just before she got on her flight to Germany. Carolyn had whispered into her ear that they were looking forward to seeing her and Dietrich in a few weeks. Christopher kissed her on the cheek and waved as she went through the gate to her plane escorted by two security agents.

Carolyn turned to Christopher and remarked that she was looking forward to seeing Natalie and Dietrich and that there were a lot of arrangements that she had to make since Christopher had his speaking engagement in New Orleans and Natalie and Dietrich would be joining them there. An hour later their plane was ready to depart for the United States and they settled into their first class seats for the long trip across the Atlantic.

Meanwhile the older man that had followed them to see if they were indeed going back to America slipped his cell phone out of his pocket and punched the telephone number for Ahmed. When Ahmed answered the phone the man apologized to Ahmed and said he was wrong about his hunch and that Natalie had boarded her flight to Germany and the Roods had boarded their flight to America. He said he watched both of their airplanes depart before making his call to him. He apologized again and then hung up.

16 STRASBOURG

Mohammad had just finished his morning prayers and was relaxing on the sofa in the living room of his spacious villa in the seaside resort of Jeddah, when his telephone rang. It was Ahmed.

"I hope that I haven't caught you at an inconvenient time, but I wanted to report that Natalie is in Germany with her family and the Bundes Nachtricten Dienst is watching over her and the Schoenfeld family. The Roods escaped our trap and are back in the United States and Inspector Grant and his wife have left for Strasbourg on their honeymoon, but my meetings in London went very well. We are all set to begin attacking British soldiers and police and indiscriminate bombings."

"Damn!"

"Father, don't you think that you are taking this Natalie business too seriously? Shouldn't we be focusing on our terror attacks against the infidels?"

"You weren't in Afghanistan when my mission was destroyed, and I was nearly killed and left with this painful limp by that bastard, Dietrich! I MUST have my revenge! I MUST destroy Natalie and stop the Schoenfeld bloodline!"

Ahmed started to argue, "But the security people of the

West are protecting them. Can't we wait while we concentrate on our larger enemy—the western infidels?"

"No, damn it!" There was a pause. "We can accomplish both goals. Where did you say Inspector Grant and his wife are?"

"Strasbourg."

"Let's do a bombing there and kill two birds with one stone! Besides Strasbourg is the capital of the European Union. What better place to begin our terror campaign against the West?"

"Alright," Ahmed sighed, "I'll get the ball rolling."

The flight to Strasbourg International Airport was uneventful and arrived shortly after noon. Katie and Steve claimed their baggage and were quickly passed through customs and security. Steve's credentials made it possible for him to clear those areas quickly. The downtown Romantik Hotel Beaucour was approximately 6.1 miles from the airport at 5 Rue Des Bauchers in old Strasbourg.

They caught a taxi for the short trip to the hotel. The drive was uneventful except that Katie was cuddling close to him and holding his hands in her lap. The driver parked his taxi in front of the hotel and after retrieving their baggage and opening the back door for them to get out, he handed their baggage to an older porter. He loaded the bags onto a cart that bore the name of the hotel and smiled at his new guests whom he surmised were newlyweds by the way they looked at each other.

Steve paid the fare and tip, and the couple followed the porter with their bags into the lobby where they were checked into the suite of rooms reserved for special guests and honeymooners. They decided, after checking into their rooms, to get a light lunch before settling down for an afternoon nap before dinner and looking around the old part of town, which was not far from the Rohan Palace and the center of the European Economic Union buildings. They were looking forward to walking later around the ancient city that was known for their fine restaurants and fare and as the

Venice of the North.

The porter opened the door to their suite and the warm comfortable interior invited them to enter the spacious rooms. Katie looked up at Steve and he winked at her as he scooped her up into his arms and carried her into the living room.

The elderly porter smiled but said nothing so as not to interfere in this magical moment for most honeymooners.

Steve slowly released his grip on her as she slid into an embrace and they unabashedly kissed again. The porter ignored them and took their bags into the bedroom where he placed them in the closet and reentered the living room where the couple had just rediscovered his appearance and blushed. The porter pretended not to notice and warmly congratulated them on their wedding and welcomed them to the hotel that he declared had been expressly designed for them.

It had been an old cane factory that had been redesigned into a hotel surrounding a courtyard with a fully modern interior and an ancient timber and stucco exterior that matched the ancient eighteenth century exteriors of the old town of Strasbourg.

Steve reached into his pocket and gave him a little bit bigger tip than he had intended, but he felt that the old man was sincerely appreciative of their visit to his town. The old man tipped his hat to the couple and bade them good luck and disappeared through the door which he locked on his way out. He had poked his head around the door just before he closed it and smiled as he placed a "Do Not Disturb" sign on the door handle.

Katie smiled a broad smile at her husband and her big blue eyes twinkled as she put her arms around him and stood on the tips of her toes and she kissed him softly on his lips and said, "This is just perfect!"

Katie and Steve pulled the covers down slowly as they got out of bed and Steve noted that the clock had aged by two hours since they had slid under the covers of their king sized bed. Katie put her slippers on and moved slowly toward the bathroom and shower. She stood for a second in front of the door wearing only a smile on her face as she motioned to Steve with a curling of her forefinger for him to join her in the shower. Steve gazed at his beautiful wife and sensed that she seemed to always read his thoughts. He obediently followed her into the large tiled shower that spewed water from five faucets like a waterfall.

By the time they had dressed, it was time for dinner. Katie had heard about the Au Pont Saint-Martin restaurant that was situated on one of the numerous small canals that gave Strasbourg the title of the "Venice of the North." It was within walking distance of their hotel and not too far from the Cathedrale Notre Dame de Strasbourg. As they leisurely strolled through the narrow ancient streets and medieval buildings, they noted that there were restaurants everywhere—they had heard that there were 126 restaurants—and every one of them they saw looked appealing!

There seemed to be quaint little shops as well as large shops that catered to every taste. It was certainly a honeymooners dream! They followed the small map that had been on the desk in their room for their convenience along with a list of the restaurants and shops with their telephone numbers. The desk had a small computer that was connected to the internet and they had researched everything about the city and its environs.

Katie had called and made dinner reservations for 7 p.m. and they punctually arrived after a leisurely stroll and an occasional investigation of some of the shops they passed on their way to the Au Pont Saint-Martin restaurant. They were pleasantly surprised at the quaint multistoried half-timbered and stucco ancient building that bordered the St. Martin bridge and snuggled between two canals so that every floor of the restaurant had a view of the canals and the swans that swam by calmly in their cool blue waters. They surmised that the building might have been an ancient mill just as their hotel had been a cane factory.

They were met at the entrance to the restaurant by a hostess in traditional dress with a bright white apron. She greeted them in perfect English, complimenting their promptness and their accents. She spoke several languages as did most of her fellow Alsatians. Also Strasbourg was the capital of the European Economic Union and there were people from all of Europe enjoying the comforts of their city!

The hostess surmised that they might be newlyweds by their behavior toward each other, so she escorted them to a particularly cozy table with an extraordinary view of the canal and the bridge. As they were being seated and given the unique menu with the city map on the opposite side, the steward appeared and they both ordered a single malt Scotch neat which appeared almost instantly from nowhere! They looked into each other's eyes and raised their glasses to toast their night.

Lights were beginning to appear around the city and their reflections were dancing on the canals. The candles in the restaurant were lit by unseen hands and a soft orange glow appeared in the room. Soft music drifted almost unnoticed through the small room where they were ensconced.

They placed their orders with the waitress when she appeared at just the right unhurried moment. They both ordered an entree of Soupe a l'oignon with a main dish of Escalope de Veau a la creme with a bottle of Gewurtztraminer wine and a dessert of Creme Brulee with Irish coffee.

The meal was served in an appropriate time that was comfortable to the couple as only a first class restaurant will do in order to make the meal appear to be unhurried. The maître d' used hand signals to let the servers know the appropriate time to pick up the dishes as the patrons were finished with a course and when to bring the next serving. Everything was done efficiently and with an expertise that is unique to Strasbourg.

Katie and Steve were so absorbed in each other that they

were held in a magic moment that would live in their hearts forever.

They drifted out of the restaurant and strolled over to the Cathedral of Notre Dame and went inside. There were only a few other young couples there, and Katie and Steve guessed were also newlyweds. The majesty of the interior was overwhelming and Katie and Steve embraced each other in silence and reverently renewed their oath of marriage and love to each other. They kissed in their embrace and exited the cathedral with their arms around each other.

It took them another hour to stroll nonchalantly back to their hotel. They entered the hotel and took the elevator to their floor and their room. As they opened the door to their suite, they were met by the soft glow of the interior lights and fresh bouquets of flowers that had been brought to their suite with a basket of fresh fruit that had been placed next to an attractive bouquet of freshly cut flowers on the dining room table.

Steve picked Katie up in his arms and kissed her softly on her lips and whispered, "I love you Kate!"

They entered the room, he kicked the door closed and carried her to the bedroom where the bed had been made and the sheets and covers had been turned back to reveal the traditional chocolates that were placed on their pillows.

He laid her softly on the bed and lay down with her in an embrace that enveloped her. They lay there in what seemed to be an instant, but was actually a half an hour. As he held her, he could see tears starting to cloud her eyes and a gentle trembling of her body lying close to his.

She looked up and into his eyes as she sobbed, "Steve, I love you so much. You have entered my soul and taken possession of my being. Please be careful, the world is dangerous with these Jihadists on the loose and you are my heart and soul!"

He wiped the tears softly with his hands and held her head in his hands and looked into her big blue eyes that were filled with tears and he said, "I'll be careful, dearest for the both of us. You are my life and my heart!"

The morning sun crept slowly across the lovers' eyes and Katie's eyes flickered open. She turned to Steve who was still blissfully asleep and whispered to herself as she looked at her husband's body still curled up next to her, that she must be in a dream that she had dreamt since she was a little girl and was looking for a knight on a white horse. She couldn't help but smile since her husband certainly was a knight of Saint John!

She shook him gently and with a soft caress of the hair across his eyes, she kissed him on his eyes and whispered into his ear, "Wake up dearest, the morning is half gone!"

He opened one eye and smiled. Then he held her closer in a warm embrace and kissed her on her lips and breasts and then whispered, "But not over!"

She laughed and then rolled him over and sat astride him and declared, "Action speaks louder than words!"

With that challenge they resumed their lovemaking where it had ended the night before.

The sun had risen to mid-morning when they had finished their love making and decided that a brunch was probably more appropriate than breakfast or lunch and they decided to get out of bed and take a shower and dress. Steve put his robe and his slippers on and went to the door to put a "Do Not Disturb" sign on the outside door handle only to discover that the sign that the elderly porter had placed there when they had first arrived had not been disturbed!

After they showered together, Steve shaved while Katie was fixing her makeup and combing her hair. They dressed and decided to go to one of the restaurants nearby, Restaurant de la Bourse, a short distance from their hotel.

They spent the rest of the day sightseeing, taking one of the sightseeing boats through the canals and ending up at the buildings of the European Parliament and dinner nearby at Le Jarden de le Europe. That night they decided they would start the next day by having a continental breakfast served in their room. The magic of the day had carried into their second night in romantic Strasbourg.

They rose early the next morning for their continental breakfast. They had barely gotten into their robes when there was a knock on the door and their breakfast had arrived at precisely 7:30 in the morning as they had requested. They thanked the maid who had arrived with their breakfast and a warm smile on her face.

Steve tried to tip her, but she smiled and said, "One day I'll be married and someone will serve me my breakfast on my honeymoon!" She blushed and then backed out of the door with a slight curtsy.

Katie and Steve looked at each other and smiled.

Katie ran up to him and threw her arms about him and kissed him. "I'm so glad we came here. This is truly a romantic town!"

They sat down at the table where the maid had placed their breakfast of orange juice, boiled egg, croissants, strawberry jam and coffee.

After they had dressed, Steve looked at a list of some of the sites and they agreed they would make a day of it and visit the Alsatian Museum, the Musee Historique, the Place de Austerlitz, the Museum of Fine Arts, Place Gutenburg, de Rohan Palace, and the Strasbourg Cathedral!

The weather was absolutely beautiful with not a cloud in the sky. The weather was a little cool for this late date in the month of June. It was Saturday June 30th and they both had to be back in the office in Edinburgh on Monday, July 2nd.

Their flight to Edinburgh was at 2 p.m. the next day and this was going to be their last day for any relaxation before going back to work!

They started out to meet their agenda, but there were so many shops in between the museums and their final destination at the cathedral. After buying some gifts for friends and relatives that they arranged to have shipped to their houses back home and taking the museum tours, they found themselves finally at the Strasbourg Cathedral de Notre Dame. It was more beautiful in the daytime than they had noticed during that first night of their stay in Strasbourg. It was originally begun in 1015 in the early Romanesque style and was finished in a late Gothic style. At 466 feet in height, it was the world's tallest building until surpassed by St. Nikolai's church in Hamburg, Germany in1874. It is still the sixth tallest church in the world and the highest still standing church built in the middle-ages. During World War II, the stained glass was stored in nearby salt mines to prevent any damage to the ancient masterpieces.

When they walked inside the massive cathedral, it took their breath away again. It was so much more majestic than it had appeared on that first night in town. The colors of the stain glass windows were inspiring and flooded the interior of the cathedral. The church was filled with worshippers and tourists. They held each other's hand tightly as they walked down the center aisle as if to cement their faith in each other and God.

Katie and Steve were silent and looked at each other as they had done in the Church of the Holyrood when they had pledged themselves to each other. Steve couldn't help it. Tears formed in his eyes as he looked at his beautiful Katie. She reached up and wiped the tears from his cheeks and kissed him, then she whispered, "me too!" and her words seemed to echo in the chamber of the Cathedral.

Suddenly, a beautiful little girl with dark hair and rosy cheeks and a pretty flowered dress and a bright red coat, walked up to them with a bouquet of roses and handed it to them.

"These are from Mohammad!"

Katie and Steve's faces grew pale and Katie gasped.

Two men in casual clothes moved in quickly to the child's side and grabbed her. They ripped the girl's coat off to reveal a suicide vest with explosives. It was wired with a remote detonator. The men clipped a couple of wires and removed the vest from the young girl who appeared frightened and bewildered.

She sobbed, "My mommy told me to give the pretty lady the flowers!"

One of the men introduced themselves as French security agents and explained that they had gotten wind of the terrorist plot to kill them and the people in the church just yesterday from the Mossad. They had infiltrated a jihadist cell in Strasbourg.

"We nabbed this girl's mother just as she was getting ready to detonate the suicide vest with her cell phone."

"You two are very lucky. This could have been a real disaster! We need to have you leave France immediately. There may be backup plans to kill you that we don't know about."

Katie was trembling and sobbing and Steve had his arms around her. He looked into her eyes and said, "Darling, it's going to be okay. We have to buck up and just realize that we're fortunate to have friends that care."

"We have a plane ready, sir and a bodyguard will escort you and you wife to the airport. We have already checked you out of your hotel and collected your belongings. They are on their way to the private plane that will fly you back to Edinburgh."

Then the policeman added, "Sorry to interrupt your honeymoon, inspector. We've been watching over you since you arrived."

They walked out of the church and into the cathedral square where a French police car was waiting. They got into the back seat of the car and Steve rolled down the window. They waved at the two security policemen who waved back. The car moved swiftly to the airport with sirens sounding.

Kate, still trembling, looked at Steve and said, "I hate to leave. Everything has been so perfect up until now and I do love you so!"

Steve said in a soft voice, "Me too! We're so lucky!"

When they arrived at the airport, the car moved to the hanger area where the private jet was waiting. They boarded the aircraft and sat down in their seats to await the takeoff for Scotland. They sat in silence for a few minutes and then Kate pressed her head against her husband's chest and quietly started to sob.

"What kind of mother would kill her own child just for revenge?"

Steve said nothing, but just held her closely and patted her shoulder gently.

The flight to Scotland was smooth and uneventful. In no time at all, the airplane was making its final approach into Edinburgh airport and touching down. The airplane rolled to a stop at its private hangar and Kate and Steve deplaned.

Their baggage was off loaded and a porter put the bags onto a cart and asked them to follow him. They made their way to the airport exit where they were surprised to find Ed MacGregor and Jamie Macadam waiting for them.

The usually reticent Dr. Macadam yelled at them both, "Glad you're back. We have all missed you both!"

Ed then threw his arms around his old college buddy and Kate and tried to make small talk. It was clear that they both had been badly shaken by the news of the attempt on their friends' lives.

"We just came down to kiss the bride and console her about getting such a dull husband!"

Katie and Steve burst out laughing and winked at each other! Jamie and Ed kissed Katie and shook Steve's hand vigorously.

Jamie said that Dietrich was doing well and is anxiously waiting for his bride to rejoin him tomorrow.

Steve looked at Jamie seriously and said, "When do you think we can let Natalie and Steve fly to New Orleans and rest for a while? We've been told by the Mossad that they are trying to get a lead on Mohammad and his son."

Ed and Jamie looked at each other. "Mohammad? We thought he was dead."

"So did everybody else," Steve Explained. "But we were told that the Mossad has evidence he was the mastermind behind the attempted attack in Strasbourg. They have already warned us that something evil is afoot in London and elsewhere and Scotland Yard is trying to get a handle on it.

They are watching the mosques carefully. Their opening salvo was to be the attack in France."

With that exchange, reality set in and Katie got very serious and said, "You know these jihadists will go after anyone to satisfy their ends. Everyone, and not just all of us who have had a part in thwarting these revenge attacks, is in danger. Just because Dietrich was a squadron leader of the flight that attacked and wiped out Mohammad's Taliban force that was laying IEDs on the road frequented by NATO forces and because we are protecting his family, Mohammad and his son Ahmed ali have taken it upon themselves to wipe us all out as a personal blood feud. I know that all of us in the West can't understand this logic, but Rudyard Kipling said it best when he said, "East is East and West is West and never the twain shall meet!"

She had a determined look in her eyes when she said, "This is one Scot that will move heaven and earth to protect my family and friends."

17 GOING UNDERCOVER

Natalie had just arrived at Edinburg International Airport from Germany in a private chartered jet on the afternoon of July 2nd. She was happy that she had the time to visit with her parents and Dietrich's family. They had all gotten along very well and she was sure that her parents were delighted with the Schoenfelds. She was absolutely positive that the Schoenfelds were happy with her. They knew their son very well and relied on his judgement.

The airplane was just arriving at its gate when she remembered the telephone call that she had received the previous afternoon in Marburg from her close friend in nursing school in Prague, Rania al Hussaini. Her voice had been anxious when she said that she was sorry that she could not attend the memorial services for Dietrich at the Elisabeth Kirche in Marburg, but she thought it best since she had discovered just recently that her father and brother were behind Dietrich's death and she was calling to warn her that they were also intent on murdering her just in case she was pregnant with Dietrich's child!

Rania explained that she had a horrific argument with her brother and father over her moderate stance on Islam and her determination to become a Czech citizen and blend into the

Czech culture. She had told them that she was not going to follow Sharia where it was in conflict with Czech Republic laws or customs, but she did not tell them that she intended to marry the Czech boy that she had been dating. He was very tolerant of her religion and agreed that they could marry and live together as a Christian and a peaceful Muslim doing God's will. They would raise their children with a tolerance of all the branches of the Jewish, Christian and Islamic traditions and all religions that were in peaceful harmony with each other in their love of the one Creator of us all.

Her father had argued that an ancient interpretation of Koranic text had admonished all true believers to kill all infidels wherever they are found, and she had retorted that an even more ancient interpretation of the same passage said that careful thought and reason should peaceably be used to persuade all infidels wherever they are found. And besides, her mother had been a Christian.

We had a back and forth argument that became more and more heated, with them laying out their extremist version of how the Jihadis would impose uncompromising and militant Islam upon the West; even to the point of turning Americans in America into unwitting mercenaries for the radical Islamic cause.

She said that her father had smiled and then laughed as he said that the infidels would buy their oil from their brother Muslims and then they would use the tribute the West would pay their brothers against the West. They would force them into conflicts that would bankrupt their economies rather than develop their own energy resources.

"My father had the cruelest smile on his face when he bragged that jihadist Islam even had Wahhabi sympathizers secreted in very high places within the American government!"

"I reminded both my father and brother that they should follow and obey the even more ancient adage that 'when in Rome, one should do as the Romans!'"

She explained that her brother and father were so angry

that she thought they might kill her!

"I decided not to have any further contact with them for everyone's sake and I'll be back in contact with you as soon as it is safe for the both of us."

She had quit her job at the hospital and was moving that day without leaving a forwarding address or telephone number! She and her fiancé were moving to the outskirts of Prague. Her father and brother did not know her fiancé's name and she was going to start using her fiancé's name and marry him as soon as possible!

She cautiously whispered to Natalie over the telephone to be on her guard. "My father and brother are just like my fanatical Nazi grandfather."

As she deplaned, Natalie now regretted that she had not asked Rania when and where her conversation with her father and brother had occurred, as the timing would be critical given the recent revelation that her father had possibly been killed in Syria. Rania had not even mentioned her fiancé's name.

She was happy to see that Katie and Steve were at the airport to meet her flight and she hugged and kissed them both. While they were on their way to the hospital to meet Dietrich, she relayed the telephone conversation that she had the day before with Rania.

Katie then told Natalie about the attack on them in Strasbourg and Natalie's face turned pale and she started to tremble.

"So Mohammad is still alive!"

"Yes," replied Katie, "And he has gone underground in Saudi Arabia behind the Crescent Curtain where these militant Jihadists know they can hide in safety. Members of the Muslim Brotherhood are wily and tenacious and arc not to be underestimated."

Steve knew that Katie was usually correct in her hunches and agreed with her.

He thought that they should all be doubly careful since they knew that Mohammad still had contacts in Edinburg and

Glasgow that were probably still watching for her.

The Jaguar arrived at the hospital and slid into its accustomed parking place.

The security people and Jamie were there to greet them. Jamie with his usual reticence waved at them and said, "Hi!" and then embraced Natalie and Katie, kissed them on their cheeks and warmly shook everyone's hands to welcome them back into the fold.

The security guards took Natalie's luggage and disappeared into the hospital with it. The three of them followed the fast moving security people to Natalie and Dietrich's apartment where they found Dietrich in good spirits and delighted to be reunited with his beautiful bride.

He gave his wife a hearty embrace and kissed her unabashedly on her lips in front of everyone. Natalie blushed but did not pull away. She was thrilled to be back safely with her husband. They all shook hands. Dietrich pointed out the Scotch that he had poured for Steve, Jamie and himself and the wine that he had chilled for the ladies.

Natalie and Katie looked quizzically at each other and then said simultaneously, "Where's our Scotch?"

Dietrich felt embarrassed at his obvious chauvinism and dutifully poured two more glasses of Scotch neat, but placed some seltzer water nearby just in case!

After this brief repartee, Steve related the conversation that Natalie had with Katie and him on their way from the airport to the hospital. They all expressed hope that Rania had been telling the truth and had safely gone underground with her fiancé. They thought that they should not take any chances and would rather wait for Rania to resurface, so they might be able to question her further about her father and brother and their possible whereabouts. If Rania and her fiancé were really in danger, they would also extend a security net around them.

Steve asked Jamie when he thought that Natalie and Dietrich could safely leave the hospital and leave for the United States to recuperate with their cousins Carolyn and

Christopher. Jamie replied that he thought in another week they could leave for Austin. But he suggested that they motor to Glasgow, then to Ayr to catch the Irish ferry to Belfast. From there they would catch a flight to Dublin and then on to Frankfort. There, they would board a jumbo jet to the United States.

Katie said that she could make all of the arrangements to have them safely leave Scotland and arrive in the United States.

After the friends had a light lunch of sandwiches and a fruit salad with greens and some good ale, Katie decided to call the United States and talk to Carolyn and Christopher Rood and make plans for Natalie and Dietrich to join them. She knew that it would be early in the morning in Austin, Texas, and she took the chance that she might catch them before they had a chance to begin their day.

The scrambled phone rang and Carolyn answered. "Hello," said Carolyn.

"Carolyn, I'm so glad that I reached you. Is Christopher there?"

"No, you just missed him. He had early rounds at the hospital and wanted to be there early to meet with his residents at the university. Congratulations again on your beautiful wedding. How was Strasbourg?"

"It was just too wonderful for words. Steve was just perfect! Except someone tried to kill us!"

"What!" said Carolyn incredulously, "You're kidding!"

"No, Mohammad is still alive!"

She then told Carolyn the whole story about Strasbourg and how lucky they had been.

Carolyn listened quietly and then she whispered with a shaking voice, "Then they're after all of us?"

"Looks that way!"

"Oh, my God!"

"Well..." and Kate trailed the word off and then added, "There has been some developments here that we wanted to discuss with you and Christopher. It seems that Natalie has heard from her friend Rania and that she and her father and brother got into a terrible argument, so she and her fiancé have left their apartment and gone underground in fear of their lives."

"Really?"

"Yes, we think so."

"We were wondering if it would be possible for Dietrich and Natalie to visit with you in Austin next week," Kate continued. "All of us here feel that it would be safer for them to be in the United States than here in Scotland or the UK."

"I can definitely answer for my husband and me, that it would be okay," Caroline replied. "In fact we have already discussed the issue."

"We'll be in New Orleans next week for a radiology seminar that Christopher has to attend since he is one of the lecturers," she continued. "Christopher has to meet with his business lawyer and friend in Atlanta on July 15th, just before the meeting. If Natalie and Dietrich flew to Atlanta, Christopher could meet them there and then they could fly to New Orleans together. We would be delighted if they could come to New Orleans and then drive back to Austin with us. We'll make their hotel reservations in Atlanta and New Orleans and get them nice accommodations in the same hotels where we'll be staying. I'll go ahead and include them in the advance dinner reservations that we already have. Actually, we'd love for the two of them to be our guests for a couple of months in Texas. That way they can meet some Texas Rangers, among other interesting folks and see the state. There's a lot of it to see!"

Carolyn was fairly bubbling with enthusiasm at the thought of seeing their cousins. "Besides," she said, "Christopher is being honored by the University of Texas Silver Spurs service organization for his community service in Austin. He will be honored during the halftime ceremonies of a home football game between the University of Texas Longhorns and the Baylor University Bears on Saturday, October 20th. They're old state rivals, you know? Kate, please call and let us know which flight they'll be on so Christopher can pick them up in Atlanta, and I can pick everyone up the next day at the New Orleans International Airport."

Kate replied that she would call them back on their secure line with all of the details of Natalie and Dietrich's flights.

The two friends said their goodbyes with Carolyn again graciously wishing Kate and Steve all of their best wishes for the coming years! She added that they were still hoping to see her and Steve in the United States.

Kate hung the telephone up and turned to Natalie and Dietrich and said enthusiastically, "Well, it's all set—except that you're going to Atlanta and then New Orleans first instead of Austin. It appears that Christopher has a business meeting in Atlanta on July 15th, and he will meet you there where you will spend the night.

"The three of you will fly the next day to New Orleans where Christopher will be lecturing at a radiology seminar. Carolyn will meet you at the airport in New Orleans and you will be their guests in New Orleans for a week before driving back to Austin with them. It also appears that you will not only meet some Texas Rangers, but will be seeing the University of Texas Longhorns battle the Baylor University Bears in October. Dr. Christopher Rood is being honored at the halftime ceremony for his community service on behalf of the University of Texas Silver Spurs, an honorary society! They are looking forward to being your hosts for a few months until Mohammad and his son Ahmed ali are apprehended."

Natalie clapped her hands together and said, "How wonderful, you know Dietrich trained in fighter tactics in Texas when he was a lieutenant! Now, I'll get to see the Wild West!"

Dietrich interrupted her and explained that the Indians were not on the warpath anymore and there were no more shoot-outs at the O.K. Corral and that the West is not as wild as it used to be.

She smiled, winked at Kate, then looked up at Dietrich and said, "But Kate said we were going to watch some bears fight some longhorns, didn't she?"

"Honey, it's a football game and that's the names of the two university's mascots."

Ignoring him, she postulated, "Maybe then, we should just go to Libertyville and see King Peter's tomb before he is moved to Belgrade."

The two of them didn't realize just how fateful those two events would be!

18 ATLANTA

Kate had just finished talking to Carolyn Rood and giving her all the details of Natalie and Dietrich's flights from Belfast to Atlanta and their flight on to New Orleans the next day. They would be leaving the hospital with Steve and Katie accompanying them to Glasgow and then onto the ferry to Belfast. Steve had thought it best for the four of them to appear to be on holiday together as friends. The weather was brisk so Dietrich and Steve could wear coats with pulled up collars and hats that would make it difficult for anyone to identify them.

The trip by automobile from Edinburg to Glasgow and then to Belfast by ferry went without a hitch and they arrived there on the morning of July 14, 2012.

They just had time to make their Lufthansa flight to Dublin and then on to Frankfurt and Atlanta.

Steve and Katie watched as Natalie and Dietrich went through security safely and on to the gate where they would presently board their flight to Dublin. Later after boarding the airplane, Dietrich and Natalie settled into their seats in Business Class so as to blend in with the usual commuters. Natalie took her scrambled cell phone from her purse and dialed Katie's scrambled cell phone.

"Is everything okay?" Natalie responded, "Yes, wish us luck!" Katie answered, "You both have all of our love and all of the luck that we have!"

"Call us when you arrive in Atlanta—no matter what the time!"

Natalie sobbed a bit and tears appeared in her eyes and she said softly, "We will and God bless you both. We'll miss you!"

With that, the two friends hung up. Katie turned to Steve and said wistfully, "I hope that all goes well with them, I really like them both."

Steve looked at her and held her close and kissed her on the cheek where a tear was just starting to run down. "They'll be just fine as long as they follow the precautions that we have discussed."

They walked to the airport exit and to the parking lot where they found their Jaguar waiting patiently for their return. It was time to get back to Scotland.

The flight to Dublin was uneventful. Natalie and Dietrich made their dawn Lufthansa connection to Frankfurt, which arrived promptly at 9 a.m. They also had no difficulty connecting with the Lufthansa flight to Atlanta where they were supposed to land just after 3:05 p.m. local time.

Once Natalie and Dietrich settled down in their comfortable seats in business class, Natalie smiled and reached over to hold Dietrich's hand. "How are you feeling? You're not too tired are you?"

Dietrich gripped her hand tightly to reassure her. "You're a dear. I'm just fine."

She smiled and looked back at him and nestled her head against his shoulder and closed her eyes with a growing sense of security. She could finally relax and feel that they were really back on their interrupted honeymoon, but that it was going to be a few months in the United States where they, hopefully, were not going to be subjected to the terror they had left behind.

A flight attendant came up to them and said to them, "Wie

sind Sie?"

Natalie was startled, and Dietrich replied, "Gut, danke. Und Sie?"

She laughed and replied in English, "I thought you might be German. I heard you whisper in a German accent to your wife. My name is Diane Braun. I'm really an American and I'm from New Orleans, but my family is from Germany. I grew up speaking German with a southern accent!" And then she laughed, "All of us Southerners love to talk and I thought that I spotted some new wedding rings."

Natalie smiled and thought that she just might like this America. Everyone is so friendly and appear to be from everywhere in the world!

The flight attendant patted Dietrich on the shoulder and leaned over to Natalie and said, "Honey, I have to get back to work, but I'll be back with some complimentary drinks for you and your new husband. Would champagne be okay?"

Natalie nodded and managed a weak "Yes."

The flight attendant disappeared almost as suddenly as she appeared. Natalie turned and looked inquiringly at Dietrich. He was smiling and said to her, "Relax darling, in the United States, everyone is friendly and proud of their heritage and even prouder to be a part of this melting pot they call America. You'll find that Southerners pride themselves in their hospitality to strangers, and they are really not as forward as they appear. They are honest and say what they think!"

She sighed in relief, nestled her head against his shoulder, and with a warmth of security drifted into a deep cozy sleep as she held her husband's hand.

The flight attendant returned after the airplane had reached cruising altitude with the two glasses of champagne that she had promised. She noticed that Natalie had drifted into a comfortable slumber and said softly that she would return later, but Dietrich looked up at her and said that it would be okay to leave her glass and that she would wake up in a few minutes.

She bent over and placed the glasses on the serving tray that Dietrich had lowered and whispered into his ear, "Congratulations, you've got a winner!"

He looked up at her and smiled, "I know!"

The flight attendant turned and walked down the aisle to the galley, then turned and waved at him and disappeared into her seat next to the galley. She would have a little time to get some rest for herself before she prepared the afternoon refreshments for her passengers.

The flight across the Atlantic was uneventful. Later the pilot announced that they would be flying over Greenland and Newfoundland, past New York and down the Appalachian chain of mountains to Atlanta.

We'll be flying at 45,000 feet where the flight will be smoother, and if we see any icebergs, we'll point them out to you."

It was about three hours later that the pilot announced there were three good- sized icebergs on the port side of the airplane and that they would soon be over Iceland and then Greenland. It was a marvelously clear day, so everyone could easily see them.

The flight attendant came by as they were looking at the icebergs and remarked that it was always thrilling to see the icebergs, but she couldn't help but think of the liner Titanic every time she saw them. Natalie whispered that the icebergs looked gigantic and she was glad that they were flying above them.

Diane smiled at them and said that lunch would be served shortly and handed them a menu. She turned and went down the aisle and join her fellow flight attendants.

An hour after lunch service, the captain announced that they were over Greenland, and not too long afterwards they were passing over St. John's Newfoundland. But by that time, the newlyweds were fast asleep and leaning on each other.

The airplane flew past the Saint Lawrence River Gulf and Estuary to the west and then down to Boston and Cape Cod when Natalie and Dietrich started to stir and wake up. Natalie looked out of her window at the white sand dunes of the Cape and the blue waters of the Bay and exclaimed, "Where are we?"

Dietrich replied, "We're just south of Boston and over Plymouth, where the Pilgrims landed and all that sand down there is Cape Cod where the Kennedys live." Dietrich looked at his wife and marveled at the excited look in her eyes. He explained, "Darling, we're in America!" She was just like a child that had blown out all of the candles on her birthday cake.

The captain came on the intercom again and told the passengers that they would fly over New York in a few minutes, and they would be able to see the Empire State Building, the Statue of Liberty, the new World Trade Center and Memorial to the September 11th victims.

The flight was going well when the pilot made another announcement, "We are going to skirt some dangerous high altitude thunderstorms over the Blue Ridge Mountains of the Appalachians. He explained that they had been cleared for a higher altitude which would swing their course further east closer to Atlanta than had been originally planned.

After taking a more southeasterly course, they flew east of the no fly zone over Washington, D.C., where they could see many of the buildings and monuments.

Natalie drew closer to the window and whispered to Dietrich, "Look, there is the Capitol building, the White House and the Washington Monument and Lincoln Memorial, Jefferson Memorial and Arlington Cemetery!" She was flushed with excitement at being able to see the entire breadth of the capital of the United States.

Dietrich had seen it all before and described the city and its environs. Just past Mount Vernon and Richmond, Virginia the mountains of the Appalachian Mountain chain slid into sight.

She was still looking out the window after having seen the Blue Ridge and Smokey Mountains of the Appalachian chain, when the pilot announced that they were going to pass to the north of Atlanta where the passengers on the left side of the aircraft could see the largest stone formation in the world outside of the sandstone mountain in Australia. The formation was Stone Mountain where Gutzon Borglum had carved the Confederate memorial on its side. He later carved the Mount Rushmore Presidential National Monument in South Dakota.

The announcement had stirred Natalie to consciousness and she looked up into Dietrich's blue eyes.

"Where are we?"

"We're coming into Atlanta," Dietrich replied.

She perked up and looked out of the window at the green forest that blanketed the ground beneath them and then she spotted Stone Mountain and Atlanta. She exclaimed that she didn't know that Atlanta was so big. Dietrich explained that it was a major transportation hub and boasted Hartsfield-Jackson International Airport, the busiest airport in the world!

For a while, the plane was in a holding pattern because of the heavy incoming traffic, but soon the captain announced that they were clear to land. The plane made a long looping approach slowly arching toward the ground and making a perfect, smooth landing.

After pulling up to the gate and stopping, the passengers filed out of the aircraft with their overhead baggage and exited the plane onto the gate ramp. Natalie immediately felt the warm blast of the Atlanta air as they ascended the ramp toward the air conditioned interior of the spacious airport. They cleared baggage and customs with no trouble and when they entered the airport lobby with their luggage, they saw Christopher smiling and waving at them. He was standing next to his business attorney and friend, Diamond Dave Berry and his wife, Debbie. Natalie and Dietrich walked over to their welcoming committee and Natalie ran up to Christopher, put her arms around him and kissed him on the cheek, saying that she was glad to see him.

Diamond Dave grinned and chided his old friend, "How

long has this been going on?"

Christopher, whom Diamond Dave called Fighter Doc, winced and punched him on the shoulder.

Christopher smiled and said, Welcome to America!" He then made all the introductions and they all shook hands like old friends.

Debbie was a knockout blonde with deep blue eyes. Diamond Dave was about six feet tall with black curly hair and a Clark Gable mustache. He had a tanned complexion and Natalie whispered to her husband that she thought he looked like Rhett Butler from the movie *Gone with the Wind*, and that his wife Debbie looked like Melanie! Dietrich agreed.

Diamond Dave announced that he had made dinner reservations at, appropriately enough, Pittypat's Porch, a *Gone with the Wind* themed restaurant right across the street from the Westin Peachtree Plaza Hotel where Natalie, Dietrich and Christopher would be staying for the night in adjoining rooms on the 45th floor.

No one noticed a handsome dark complected young man with black hair and green eyes watching them intently.

Everyone grabbed a bag and headed for Diamond Dave's black BMW X5M automobile. They arrived at the hotel and after parking, registering Natalie and Dietrich at the hotel, they all headed to each of their suites and dropped off their luggage. Christopher along with Diamond Dave and Debbie waited in the living room of Christopher's suite conversing while Natalie and Dietrich freshened up in their suite before going to Pittypat's Porch.

About 30 minutes before their reservations for dinner, Natalie and Dietrich feeling refreshed after showering and taking a short nap appeared at Christopher's door dressed in new light weight clothes appropriate for the occasion.

They knocked on the door and Diamond Dave answered it and when he saw Natalie and Dietrich, he softly whistled and said, "You two look fabulous! You don't look like you've just crossed the Atlantic Ocean!"

They walked across the street to the restaurant and were

greeted warmly by the maître d'. They were seated and immediately immersed in antebellum ambiance.

Then following an Old South style dinner, complete with fried chicken, barbecued ribs, fried green tomatoes, grits and mint juleps, the group retired to the Sun Dial Bar and Restaurant at the top of their hotel. It was a onetime architectural wonder that slowly rotates a full circle, giving everyone a superb view of Atlanta and the countryside. Natalie, falling in love with the idea of America, plied Debbie with a myriad of questions about the U.S., Georgia, and Atlanta in particular.

Toward the end of the evening after dinner drinks were polished off, they all left the rotating bar and took the elevator down to the 45th floor and the rooms where Christopher, Natalie and Dietrich were staying.

The next morning, Diamond Dave drove them to the airport to catch their noon flight to New Orleans.

19 NEW ORLEANS

Natalie, Dietrich and Christopher were all booked into business class on a non- stop Delta flight that would arrive at Louis Armstrong International Airport in New Orleans shortly before 1:00 p.m. Central Standard Time. Christopher had already called ahead to Carolyn, who would meet them at the airport.

Security at Hartsfield-Jackson International Airport was efficient with no nonsense. It was a reminder to the three of them about their current state of affairs with Mohammad and Ahmed and how the world had changed since the airline and cruise ship hijackings and terrorist bombings from decades ago. Diamond Dave waved at Christopher, Natalie and Dietrich as they entered the security line to get to their flight gate.

The dark haired young man with the green eyes from the day before, was standing close to the security entrance to the flight gates watching as Christopher, Natalie and Dietrich passed through security toward their gate. He held his cellphone close to his ear and called his confederate on the other side of the security that they were coming through and to follow them through the airport to their gate and see where they were going. Twenty minutes later, he received a call from his confederate, "They're going to New Orleans!" The man with the green eyes went over to the Delta counter and bought a ticket to New Orleans.

In contrast, their flight to New Orleans was made especially pleasant by the presence of Maura Fitzgerald, a senior flight attendant whom Christopher knew from previous flights and who had been good friends with Carolyn in Texas. A keen observer, Maura deduced from the even color skin under Natalie's wedding ring and how cozy Natalie and Dietrich were with one another that the two of them were newlyweds.

"As soon as we're airborne and the seat belt sign is turned off, I'll be back with a bottle of champagne on the house as a wedding gift," she told them.

"On the house, what does that mean?" she asked Dietrich. Dietrich and Christopher smiled then laughed.

"It means that it is free," Dietrich explained.

"Oh," she said sheepishly, "I guess I'll get used to American slang eventually."

Minutes later, with the plane starting to cruise at 30,000 feet, Maura was back with a bottle of champagne, three glasses and some cookies and handed them to Christopher and the wedding couple. "I'm sorry that we don't have some wedding cake, but I hope the cookies will do."

They all smiled and Dietrich said that they would. Maura turned and waved as she resumed her flight attendant duties.

The flight flew over the Mississippi River where it turned south on its approach into the New Orleans area. Natalie was astonished at the sight of the broad seemingly endless waterway.

"I had no idea that it was so big. It's bigger than the Rhine River!" She was no less amazed at the paddle wheel steamboat that eddied along in the water just south of Natchez, Mississippi. Natalie was delighted when Christopher mentioned that he thought that a riverboat ride was included in Carolyn's plans for them.

The New Orleans Louis Armstrong International Airport

FRANK R. FAUNCE AND JOE C. RUDÉ

came into view and the airplane began its final approach to the landing strip as the flight attendants collected all cups, napkins and glasses and stowed them in plastic bags. The airplane floated down to the runway and a perfect landing that barely shook the airplane as it rolled toward its parking gate. The airplane stopped just short of the gate as it was slowly guided to its berth. The plane stopped and the passengers began to deplane.

Christopher, Natalie and Dietrich got up and stretched and then gathered their carry-on bags and started for the exit. When they reached the exit, the pilot was standing next to Maura. He grinned and said to Dietrich and Natalie that he was sure glad that they had decided on New Orleans for their honeymoon and wished them the best.

Maura and the pilot both said, "Auf Wiedersehen!" as Maura embraced Natalie and wished them the best of luck as they exited the aircraft and stepped onto the ramp way toward the airport. She had no idea that they would need all the luck they could get!

Natalie immediately felt the humid warm blast of the New Orleans air as they started up the ramp. Dietrich held her hand as they entered into the air conditioned interior of the airport and headed for the baggage claim area. They had no trouble with their bags and when they entered the airport lobby they saw Carolyn waving a big sign at them. She rushed to Christopher, Natalie and Dietrich and the two women embraced each other.

Natalie declared that it was a lot warmer here than she had imagined and she was afraid that her clothes were not appropriate for the subtropical climate that she had suddenly encountered.

Christopher and Dietrich looked at each other and smiled; then, Christopher looked at Natalie and Carolyn and with a mocked New Orleans accent said to Natalie, "Honey chile, don't you worry none. All will be taken care of!"

Natalie looked at him, not quite understanding the accent or the joke that she had just heard. Carolyn frowned at her husband and said to Natalie, "He's just trying to be funny and imitate the New Orleans drawl for you and not doing a very good job at it!"

Carolyn grabbed Natalie by the arm and led her away toward the parking lot where their Mercedes SUV was parked. As they walked away, Carolyn muttered to Natalie, "I think that we are stuck with a couple of comedians!"

Christopher and Dietrich looked quizzically at each other and followed along behind them as they carried the luggage behind their wives looking like a couple of porters.

When they reached the automobile all three of them piled into the Mercedes SUV. Their wives were laughing and Carolyn said to Natalie that the first thing that they needed to do tomorrow morning was to get her and Dietrich a new wardrobe while Christopher gave his lecture to the Radiology convention. Christopher started the car and guided it onto Airline Drive and headed due east toward downtown New Orleans and their hotel, The Ritz Carlton, New Orleans. It is on Canal Street across from the old French Quarter and its fine restaurants.

The Ritz Carleton had been the large old historic Maison Blanc department store in a previous incarnation. After undergoing a renovation into a hotel and outfitted with a lushly landscaped central courtyard, it was closed for about a year in the wake of the considerable damage that had been caused by Hurricane Katrina.

A $106 million refurbishment had made it grander than ever with magnificent suites accoutered with floor to ceiling windows, bathrooms with soaking tubs and showers, Louis XVI style desks and furniture, CD/DVD libraries with surround sound and Venetian style beverage armoires.

Carolyn explained that they both had an executive suite on the same floor and access to the Ritz Carlton Club lounge. Carolyn further elaborated to Natalie and Dietrich that they had a late reservation at the Court of the Two Sisters Restaurant at 613 Rue Royale, just a short distance from their hotel. She had already ordered a fruit basket with an assortment of finger sandwiches and a chardonnay wine to be placed in their room so they wouldn't have any trouble relaxing and taking a soaking bath or a shower before they met for dinner later. She and Christopher had already registered them, and she handed Dietrich the two electronic keys to their suite.

Christopher guided the silver grey Mercedes SUV into the guest registration parking place and a porter immediately appeared to take their baggage to their rooms. Dietrich showed him the key to their rooms, and he disappeared with their luggage on his way to their suites. Christopher gave the parking attendant a key to the Mercedes and he drove it off to the parking garage, leaving the two couples standing in front of the entrance to the impressive hotel. They entered the stunning lobby and Christopher led them to the elevator that would take them to their suites.

The elevator rose quickly to the fifth floor where their suites were located. As they exited the elevator, Christopher turned to Dietrich and said, "You know that I talked to Dr. Macadam and he said that you were healing faster than he had expected. But you have been through a great deal of trauma and I'd like to take a look at you to see for myself how you're doing."

He murmured to Carolyn that they were going to Natalie and Dietrich's room so that he could examine Dietrich's wounds. He could plainly see that the gash he had on his neck below his left ear had closed with only a minimal amount of scarring, but still some slight swelling. It didn't look at all angry at first glance.

They walked down the hall to the right of the elevator to suite 557 and Dietrich opened the door with his electronic key and was pleased to see their luggage neatly placed on a luggage rack in the spacious closet. Natalie retrieved her vanity case and took it to the bathroom and unpacked its contents and placed them on the vanity table and returned the case to the closet and stowed it to one side.

Meanwhile, Christopher had taken Dietrich to the

bathroom and had him take off his shirt so that he could see the entry wound of the dagger that had wedged between the two ribs that prevented a mortal wound. When he removed the small bandage, he was astounded how well Dietrich was healing. He placed his ear against his back below his scapula and asked him to take a deep breath which Dietrich did. Christopher asked him if he felt any pain when he took the breath. Dietrich said no, but that he could feel that it wasn't normal yet.

"You're indeed lucky to have had an extremely skilled doctor like Dr. Macadam attending you so soon after the assault. He not only saved your life, but had minimized the healing period by acting so swiftly and carefully to stabilize you. You'll probably be well enough for normal but not excessive exercise in the next six weeks and should be completely healed within three months."

Dietrich put his shirt on and they rejoined Natalie and Carolyn. Carolyn had opened one of the bottles of Chardonnay and already poured the wine. When Dietrich and Christopher entered the living room of the suite, she gave them a glass of wine and proposed a toast to Natalie and Dietrich for his quick recovery and their stay in the United States on a continued recovery and honeymoon! She was inwardly pleased that the Luftwaffe had placed Dietrich on an extended six months secret leave of absence for his full recovery before reporting back to duty.

They drank the toast and Carolyn and Christopher excused themselves and went to their suite to rest before getting ready for the anticipated dinner that night. Natalie meanwhile turned to Dietrich back in their room and suggested that they both take a relaxing soaking bubble bath in the huge bath tub in their bathroom and then take a shower before going out to dinner.

Dietrich put his glass down and found a CD of Mozart music that they could relax with. He then silently walked over and grabbed Natalie's hand, picked up his glass and led her into the bathroom. He took her glass from her hand, put their glasses beside the tub, turned on the water to the tub and tested it with his hand for the right temperature. As the tub began to fill, he walked over to Natalie and silently looking into her hazel eyes began to undress her. She smiled at him and trembled a little as her clothes dropped to the floor, and she slipped into the water. She watched as he undressed and slid into the tub beside her.

He reached over the side of the tub and picked up the glasses and handed her glass to her. He tipped his glass to hers and when the glasses touched with a ring, he said, "Natalie, I love you more than life itself."

They must have soaked in their loving embrace for half an hour when they suddenly realized that they needed to get ready for dinner.

Natalie stepped out of the tub and into the shower where she shampooed her hair and washed her body. Dietrich, meanwhile finished shaving and entered the shower with Natalie and she washed him with her soft hands caressing him as she washed him from head to toe. After they finished their shower, Natalie dried her hair while Dietrich combed his hair and patted after shave lotion over his face and cologne over his body. She laughed at him for being so methodical in his grooming and after she finished drying her hair she walked over and held him in a tight embrace while she kissed him fervently on his lips and then nuzzled against his chest.

They stood there for a few minutes and then parted while she finished grooming and combing her hair and placing her makeup. She dressed in a smart lightweight delicately strapped blue dress and wore a single gold necklace around her neck with a single blue diamond surrounded in a small halo of blue topaz. Her shoes were small blue matching slippers with a slight lift to the heels. Her dark hair was parted on the left and her long hair waved loosely over her right eye and fell to her shoulders in a straight curl that caressed the top of her breasts and framed the diamond and topaz necklace.

He wore light weight dark blue slacks and black shoes with

a matching blue tie and a light cream colored sport coat that resembled a white dinner jacket but was more loosely cut. His white shirt had French cuffs that sported simple black oval cuff links with a small white Maltese cross in the middle. His blond hair was combed smartly back with a crease on the right side and a wave that curved over the left side of his head.

At eight-thirty that night, Carolyn and Christopher arrived at their door and they entered. When Carolyn saw Natalie, she exclaimed, "Natalie, you are simply gorgeous!"

Natalie could have said the same about Carolyn for she had combed her dark hair with a part to the right so that it fell to her shoulders in a soft halo around her face. It accentuated her green eyes that matched the emerald necklace around her neck. She also wore a lightly strapped emerald dress that complimented her figure. It flowed down from her small waist to below her knees and swished when she walked. Her shoes were light weight green slippers that were slightly elevated that boosted her height by two inches to about five feet five inches.

Christopher was dressed in a dark blue sport coat with light grey slacks and black shoes. He also had a white shirt with French cuffs and similar black oval cuff links with a small white Maltese cross in the middle. He wore a plain blue silk tie that matched his coat.

To the uninitiated, the similar cuff links would mean nothing, but to someone familiar with medieval history, it would identify the wearers as knights of the Order of Saint John.

Natalie hugged Carolyn and said that she thought that she was beautiful and that she adored her dress. She said she was looking forward to seeing the Court of the Two Sisters. Christopher turned toward her and read from the menu he had brought for them to peruse.

He explained that the two Creole sisters who owned a notions shop on the site of the restaurant gave it its name. The site at 613 Rue Royale had played a significant role in the history of old New Orleans.

The two sisters, Emma and Bertha Camors, who were born in 1858 and 1860 respectively, belonged to a proud and aristocratic Creole family and their notions shop, outfitted many of the city's finest women with formal gowns, lace and perfumes imported from Paris.

The foursome then walked the short distance to the restaurant where they were seated. The waiter handed a menu to them and they glanced down the list of food with French names that were described in English and French. Natalie and Dietrich looked down the list of foods available and gasped that it all looked good, but they couldn't decide.

Christopher explained that the restaurant frequently had that problem and they made their menu available as souvenirs so that customers could think about the menu before their arrival at the restaurant. The waiters were also very good at steering people toward the foods that they would enjoy.

It had taken them about ten minutes to get to the restaurant. Natalie and Dietrich were surprised at the size of the old residence that had been turned into a first class restaurant. They had walked through the large wrought iron gate into the massive courtyard that was surrounded by the ancient five storied residence with wrought iron balconies that overlooked the centrally located courtyard tables that had multicolored umbrellas protecting them. The courtyard had trees with Spanish moss dripping from their branches and potted plants and flowers of all kinds that lent an air of a French formal garden.

The maître d' signaled a waiter for glasses of spring water to be placed on their table. Their waiter suggested hors d'oeuvres to start the meal. He turned toward Carolyn and Natalie. Carolyn mentioned to the waiter that she was allergic to shell fish and he suggested either the Plaquemine fruit cocktail or the baked onion soup gratinee. Carolyn said she would take the onion soup and then he turned to Natalie, and she replied that she had never had Oysters Rockefeller so she would try them. Christopher and Dietrich agreed that they would have them as well.

Christopher ordered a bottle of Piesporter Goldtropfchen Kabinett and a bottle of California Merlot from the Russian River Valley.

They had hardly started their conversation about how beautiful the courtyard was, when soft music and the waiter with the hors d'oeuvre arrived at their table. A violinist was starting to wander around the courtyard playing soothing ballads. Carolyn and Christopher ordered the charbroiled tenderloin of beef and Natalie and Dietrich decided to order the Veal Royal Court as their entrees. The waiter poured them two more glasses of the Goltdropfchen and Carolyn and Christopher two more glasses of the Merlot.

When it came to dessert, everyone ordered the traditional New Orleans Bananas Foster which the waiter served table side flamed in brandy sauce over French vanilla ice cream.

Natalie was startled when the waiter lit the flame and the brandy ignited skyward. "I've seen this in the movies, but this is the first time for real!"

The waiter brought four small Hennessy XO cognacs and four demitasses of New Orleans coffee.

Dietrich leaned back in his chair and said to them all with a wink, "I think that I might be in heaven!"

Natalie wrinkled her nose and pouted her lips and said, "Don't you even think that!"

They all laughed and Natalie looked bewildered. Dietrich explained to her that it was just an American joke. She immediately regained her composure and playfully slapped her husband gently on the shoulder and joined in the laughter.

They returned to their hotel and took the elevator to the fifth floor and Carolyn said to Natalie and Dietrich when they reached their door that they should sleep in late and that she would be at their room around nine o'clock in the morning since Christopher had to get up early to go to his lecture in one of the meeting rooms at the Ritz. He would join them for lunch between his two lectures. Natalie and Dietrich replied that they would look forward to seeing her at that time. Dietrich opened their door and waved goodnight to Carolyn and Christopher and disappeared inside. Carolyn and Christopher went to their room grateful for the opportunity to get in bed earlier than usual.

The next morning rose with a burst of sunshine and a beautiful dark blue sky that reminded Natalie of the cool blue eyes of the Wallenfels and von Schoenfeld families that also was evident in Christopher's and Dietrich's eyes. Carolyn was punctual and knocked on their door just as she and Dietrich were finishing dressing for the day.

She was looking forward to visiting some of the chic clothing stores in old New Orleans just off Jackson Square and the Riverwalk with Carolyn and Dietrich.

Her husband like most husbands was not particularly thrilled with the notion of shopping with the two ladies that morning! He was greatly relieved when Carolyn announced to them that they wouldn't have time to go shopping that morning, but would have to delay their shopping until the afternoon since they would be meeting Christopher at Galatoires for lunch. Meanwhile Carolyn thought they would want to go to the world famous Cafe du Mond down by the Riverwalk and the Farmer's Market which in earlier days had been the site of the old slave market.

She knew most of the slave markets still in existence were in the Middle East and Africa!

Natalie and Carolyn were dressed in light weight sun dresses that revealed their slim figures and Dietrich was dressed in a polo shirt, light blue sport jacket and light colored slacks and comfortable loafers. He wanted to find a straw Panama hat that was prominent for the men of New Orleans. As they walked out of the front of the Ritz Carlton, they saw one of the streetcars made famous by Tennessee Williams' play and movie *A Streetcar Named Desire*!

It didn't take long for the trio to walk the short distance to the Cafe du Mond on Decatur Street next to the Jean Lafitte National Historic Park and order the famous cafe au lait and white powdered sugar beignets that was their trademark.

Natalie was delighted with the fluffy New Orleans fritters that were like no others in the world. Dietrich had found just the hat that he wanted on their way to the cafe. It was a plantation straw hat just like the one that Clark Gable had worn in the movie, *Gone with the Wind*.

As they sat in the shade of the cafe that was close to the Mississippi River, Natalie spied the old paddle wheel steamboat "Natchez" that was tied up at the riverboat wharf next to Woldenberg Park nearby. She pointed to it and exclaimed, "Do you think that we could go aboard and look at it? I have read that it was a gambling boat!"

Carolyn laughed and said, "Yes I think that it might be possible, but I don't know if there is still gambling onboard since Harrah's Casino and Hotel has been built down by the Hilton Hotel and Riverwalk Shopping Mall."

They were unaware of the handsome dark complected young man with green eyes and coal black hair sitting alone at a nearby table. He was staring intently at Natalie and silently drinking some creole coffee and nibbling on his beignet.

The boat had been recently restored and painted and made a two hour river tour daily. Carolyn suggested, "We could take a ride on it after we have lunch with Christopher and later go shopping. It's very popular and perhaps we should get tickets after we finish our breakfast and before we tour Jackson Square and look at some of the art galleries that surround it. It will be on our way through the Old French Quarter and back to our hotel."

Natalie happily anticipated going aboard a famous old boat for a ride on the Mississippi. She said, "It will be just like a trip into the past!"

They leisurely finished their beignets and coffee and sauntered over to the small ticket office in front of the "Natchez" and found that they were in luck.

There was a trip scheduled for that afternoon at 2:00 p.m. Dietrich insisted on buying the tickets for their excursion and put them into his pocket. They then turned their attention to

Jackson Square and wandered around it looking at the shops and artists' paintings that were displayed on the streets bordering the square much like the artists' galleries that surround the Left Bank and Montmartre in Paris.

They walked around the square and then strolled into the French Quarter down St. Peter Street to Bourbon Street. There they found some musicians playing New Orleans jazz in Preservation Hall on the corner of the two streets. They lingered a while listening to the rhythmic melodies that poured out of the open doors of the hall onto Bourbon Street. Carolyn reminded them that they had to hurry to meet Christopher at Galatoire's Restaurant on Bourbon Street. It was almost noon and it took them only about ten minutes to get to the restaurant even though they passed by many inviting shops.

They walked into the restaurant a few minutes past noon and found Christopher standing next to a table that he had saved for them. He waved at them. He gave Carolyn a kiss and a hug and then hugged Natalie. Dietrich pulled out chairs for Carolyn and Natalie to sit down.

"Whew!" Christopher gasped, "I'm glad that lecture's over. I only need to speak for three hours this afternoon!" Looking at Dietrich, he said, "I see that you've found the hat that you wanted."

"I made reservations for us at Brennan's this evening at eight o'clock. I'll be through at four this afternoon, will it be okay if we meet at Harrah's at four-thirty for drinks and a look at the Casino and discotheque?"

Everyone nodded their approval and they eagerly awaited the lunch that the waiters were beginning to serve. Nobody noticed the dark haired young man with the green eyes sitting at the next table.

The fare for the day was either char broiled breast of chicken or a filet mignon and they all decided on a lighter lunch of chicken which was served with a creole mustard and honey sauce and pasta bordelaise with broccoli au gratin. They chose a Robert Mondavi Fume Blanc wine and strawberries and cream for desert with a cup of New Orleans coffee.

While they were eating, they discussed the shopping spree which was the activity of the afternoon after the river boat cruise. Natalie and Carolyn were enthusiastically discussing the purchases they wanted to make while Dietrich and Christopher reminisced about their respective missions and escapades of their wars. Christopher's experiences in "Desert Storm" and Dietrich's in "Enduring Freedom."

The men both agreed that the current explosive world terrorism was similar to the barbarity of the Crusades that was fought a thousand years before by the Knights and their adversaries, the Assassins of old. Again, it appeared that the Muslim world had exploded in a fever of conquest and annihilation of their enemies. It was as if the clock had been turned back a thousand years!

Carolyn and Natalie were engaged in the more important tasks before them and did not want to dwell upon the politics and dangers of the world—it was far too depressing and besides, they were all supposed to be upbeat and positive and for the time being at least, forget all of the nonsense of the world and remember that they were on vacation! The ladies finally won over their husbands and they talked about listening to Bourbon Street jazz and enjoying the pleasures of immortal New Orleans that would never be conquered by either barbarity or nature's violence!

The luncheon was over and Christopher had to return to the podium and the trio waved goodbye to him.

They walked leisurely the short distance to the Riverboat Docks. They saw that many of the ladies were wearing wide curved brimmed straw bonnets with a satin ribbon and bow wrapped around its crown. Dietrich spied a stand where the bonnets were being sold that was next to the ticket office. He bought three tickets and treated each of them with a bonnet sporting a blue ribbon and bow.

A small crowd was standing in front of the Natchez and was just starting to board her when they arrived. They waited their turn and gingerly stepped onto the wooden gangplank that rose from the dock to the deck of the boat. As they stepped onto the deck of the old boat, they marveled at the newness of its appearance. It was as if time had evaporated and they had been transported to another century. The deck hands, hostesses and Captain with his officers were all dressed in period costumes just as it had been in antebellum times. They were conducted through a tour of the old riverboat and casino lounge with the gambling tables complete with an ancient roulette wheel and period cards and dice at the appropriate tables.

They toured the dining room and kitchen as well as some of the old state rooms with their antebellum furniture. They were barely aware that the paddle wheels were turning and the old boat was churning its way to the middle of the Mississippi River and even though the vessel had modern navigation instrumentation and safety devices, the age old boating practices of measuring speed and depth were reenacted for the crowd and a deckhand yelled out for the crowd, "Mark Twain," denoting the depth of the river at that point of its passage and assuring everyone that the depth was sufficient for safe navigation. The crowd clapped and cheered its approval and the crew smiled with the crowd's endorsement of their reenactment of an old nautical tradition.

Natalie looked up at her husband and then to Carolyn and said to them both, "Thank you, thank you! It was just as I dreamt it would be!" She said she felt just as if she had been transported into the middle of the Old South.

The trio went up onto the upper deck and watched the small towns bordering the Mississippi slip by as they looked at the map of their transit during the excursion. Soon, Mint Julips were being offered to the passengers to remind them of their experience aboard ship. They were a welcome relief to the passengers as the day had warmed considerably since the cool morning hours and the sun beat down upon them with no mercy. They were glad for the cool minty drink and the sunglasses that they were wearing.

Dietrich was delighted that he had his straw Panama hat and the ladies were certainly happy that they were wearing the straw broad brimmed bonnets that Dietrich had purchased for them just before boarding the boat. They had noticed that most of the passengers were buying them from a young black man that was selling the straw hats and bonnets just outside the ticket office.

The steamboat blew its steam whistle to alert the passengers that they were ending their trip and getting ready to dock at the wharf where they had begun their journey. As the boat slowed down and slid into its anchorage, the deck hands jumped ashore and tied the anchorage lines to the dock and swiftly moved the gangplank to its place on the dock for the passengers to disembark. The captain and his officers and hostesses dressed in antebellum costumes thanked their passengers for being their guests for two hours and wished them well on their way home and on their stay in their fair city. The passengers in turn replied how pleased they were with their experience and many took pictures of the captain and his crew and of the boat on which they had been passengers.

The trio looked back at the "Natchez" as they walked over to Woldenberg Park and sat down on one of the park benches.

"That was a real treat for me!" said Natalie as she looked at Carolyn and then her husband. "I never dreamed that New Orleans would be this beautiful! I just can't imagine that this city that had been so devastated just a few years ago could be restored so quickly. The citizens of New Orleans and Louisiana have certainly demonstrated their courage and resourcefulness."

Dietrich added, "It just shows what America can do when they are challenged!"

Carolyn smiled, "Just the American 'can do and never say die spirit.'" And then she added with a flip of her head, "America gets that from Texas!"

They walked down to the River Walk shops and Dietrich

persevered as his wife and Carolyn went from shop to shop and looked at and tried on many clothes and shoes before deciding on the ones that would be suitable for New Orleans and Austin. Natalie had even convinced him to try on some clothes that she thought might be suitable for him. He was surprised at how well she knew his likes, dislikes and his sizes. He acknowledged his wife's good taste and expert shopping skills that he wished he possessed. He was so glad she was his wife! They had asked the shops to send their purchases to their rooms at the Ritz-Carlton Hotel and paid extra for the privilege.

Before they knew it, it was almost four o'clock and they hurried to Harrah's Hotel and Casino. They were just going through the entrance to Harrah's when Carolyn shouted to them that she had spotted Christopher over by the concierge and they all waved at him. He came up to them and said he thought that it might be nice if they looked at the casino and played a couple of slot machines or perhaps blackjack. Christopher maintained that blackjack or twenty-one as some people called it, was the only game that the participants had a decent chance to win.

Carolyn snickered that was why they called it blackjack after the American slang word for being bludgeoned! Christopher blushed slightly and then remarked that his wife Carolyn always had a knack of cutting to the chase in a minimal amount of words. In other words—she was Scottish!

Carolyn replied, "Of course!"

They all laughed—even Natalie who was beginning to understand the playful banter between their American cousins.

They entered the Casino and walked among the tables with all of the chatter and noise that accompanies gambling. Everyone seemed to be enjoying themselves, particularly the little old ladies who were guarding their slot machines and cheering when the bells rang for a payoff. Dietrich suggested that they all sit down and play twenty-one after Christopher explained the game. Carolyn declined, saying she would observe silently since she didn't like to see grown adults cry. She smiled and winked at Natalie as she made the remarks. Natalie winked back and mentioned that she was looking forward to beating the men!

It didn't take too long for the age old specter of beginners luck to rear its head as Natalie beat the house seven straight times to the consternation of Christopher and Dietrich, who were only barely able to break even. Dietrich pronounced that he had had enough and declared that Natalie was the true champion of the family and Christopher shrugged his shoulders and gave up with barely a whimper.

Carolyn and Natalie laughed as Natalie swept up her winnings and went to the cashier to cash in her chips! The men cashed their remaining chips and both of them hugged Natalie and shook her hand in acknowledgement of her victory. They had left a tip to the dealer and they all thanked the young lady who had been dealing. Christopher looked at each other and winked, saying that it was a feminine conspiracy!

They had not noticed that they were being carefully watched by two tall swarthy men that were lingering near the edge of the room. The men whispered to each other and one of them left.

They walked around the casino and after watching the spirited and noisy repartee at the craps tables arrived at the roulette wheels where there was a fair number of people drowning their wagering sorrows in some tall glasses of Wild Turkey bourbon. There were even a fair number sharing their losses with Jack Daniels!

Finally Christopher said, "Before we go to dinner at Brennan's, let's go to the Masquerade Club here in the heart of Harrah's for a final drink before dinner and watch the youngsters dance to the disco music."

They asked one of the dealers for directions to the popular discotheque and following her guidance, they found themselves at the entrance to the upbeat club that was among the highest ranked discos in the country. They sat down at a table and almost instantly a pretty young waitress who looked most appealing in the barest of a costume asked them, "What is your pleasure?" They looked at each other and the two men declared that a single malt whiskey neat would do just fine and the ladies said that a whiskey sour would suit them. The waitress asked if they wanted to keep a tab and Christopher said that they only wanted one drink and would pay for the drinks immediately.

The drinks appeared as if out of nowhere and the waitress smiled pleasantly as Christopher gave her a sizable tip. Carolyn frowned in her best Scottish fashion as if it were too much, but the waitress only smiled at them all and thanked them very much.

They took their drinks and toasted each other and glanced at the gyrating young bodies keeping time to the rhythms that were bouncing off the walls of the club.

Natalie shouted over the noise, "This is the most exciting club that I could ever imagine!" She couldn't believe that there were so many attractive young people that could crowd into such a small amount of space between each other!

The handsome young man with black hair, green eyes and dark complexion from Atlanta walked over to their table and held out his hand and asked Natalie to dance with him. She looked up at him with a bewildered look on her face and held her left hand up to show him her wedding ring.

He laughed and grabbed her hand and pulled her up toward him and wrapped his arms around her and started to push her into the crowded dancers. She tried to pull away from his grip as Dietrich and Christopher in unison leaped to her rescue.

Natalie exhaled to reduce the young man's hold around her waist and slipped down exposing his head and neck just as Christopher hit him with a karate chop that staggered him. The dancers around the fracas started to clear away screaming. The young man's hand loosened and Natalie broke free just as the two swarthy men from the casino came over to aid the young man. One was carrying a large towel that had been soaked in chloroform.

Dietrich grabbed the man with the towel and pushed it into his face as he tripped him to the floor and jumped on him pressing the towel hard over his nose and mouth and holding him down with the other hand. The crowd moved away rapidly.

Christopher had already given the young man a kick to his stomach that rendered him unconscious on the floor. Christopher, just in time, grabbed the other man's hand that was holding a knife. He kicked the man in the groin and as the man bent over, he gave his forearm above the hand holding the knife a karate chop that broke it with a sickening crunch. The man winced, dropped the knife, just as Christopher landed a deadly chop to the man's larynx. He dropped to the floor unconscious gasping for air.

Suddenly, while the attack was going on, Maura Fitzgerald appeared from nowhere to help Carolyn whisk Natalie away from the scene and out of the discotheque that had suddenly become a pandemonium.

Police appeared from nowhere to empty the casino and control the fleeing customers. The three men were cuffed and put in ambulances on gurneys when they arrived. The ambulances sped off to the hospital with a police escort.

As soon as the casino was empty, Maura came back into the casino with Carolyn and an almost hysterical Natalie. She took charge of the scene and went over, flashed a wallet with a shield and started conversing with the police and two other men in dark blue suits. She turned and walked calmly over to the two couples.

She was smiling as she put her arms around a shaking Natalie.

"Everything's going to be fine. Don't you know that there are angels watching over all of you?"

She then turned and walked over to Christopher and Dietrich who were still flushed from their spirited defense of Natalie.

"You guys were too fast for us."

"What do you mean, us?" Christopher gasped as he looked at his old friend and then turned to look at Carolyn who had a quizzical look on her face.

"Who are you? I thought that you were a flight attendant!"

"Among other things," she laughed. "We see a lot of people on flights between Atlanta and New Orleans."

"We?"

"Yeah, me and those two guys in blue suits. We're the guardian angels!"

Maura, Dietrich and Christopher walked over to Carolyn and Natalie and Maura said, "I apologize for us not intervening sooner, but we just ID'd those other guys a few minutes before the fracas began. We've been watching them since you entered Harrah's. We figured out who the guy with the green eyes was while he was on his later flight from Atlanta. The three of them followed you into the casino. It might be a wise idea for you to leave town after you finish your visit tomorrow and get on to Texas."

She turned to Natalie and Dietrich. "We picked up the surveillance ball since you've arrived in the United States. Our overseas friends have been with you in the background ever since you boarded your flight in Ireland. We'll be over your shoulder all the time, even tonight and tomorrow and your trip to Texas. Keep your dinner date at Brennan's Restaurant tonight and act as if nothing has happened tomorrow." She smiled at them.

The two couples nodded their heads and said in unison, "Yes, ma'am."

Maura embraced them all and then went over to talk to the two men in blue suits. She turned and waved to them and they waved back.

The two couples found their way to the plaza outside the hotel and walked quietly toward Canal Street and to the Ritz Carlton Hotel where they went back to their rooms to refresh and get into appropriate clothes for dinner at Brennan's.

They later exited the hotel and walked across Canal Street to Royal Street and just a few blocks to Brennan's Restaurant.

They entered the restaurant and were immediately seated at their table. The maître d' gave them their menus and they ordered four glasses of Kendall-Jackson Chardonnay and a waiter brought a small plate of dinner rolls and fresh butter along with the wine to their table. They looked over the menu and decided a small cup of Creole onion soup would do nicely for an appetizer followed with a Brennan salad of Romaine lettuce with Brennan's famous Creole dressing with grated Parmesan cheese and croutons.

Carolyn and Natalie decided on the Trout Pecan while Christopher settled on Brennan's Blackened Redfish and Dietrich wanted the Grilled Filet of Salmon Audubon named after the famous painter and naturalist of the nineteenth century who had roamed the Bayou country around New Orleans. They were starting to feel better after everything that had happened just a little while ago.

Natalie quipped, "I don't know if I'll get my appetite back or not! I just can't get over what happened tonight." She screwed her mouth around and rasped, "Ugh, those guys were terrible. I just had to take a shower to wash their presence off of me!"

Dietrich and Christopher said in unison, "Yeah, me too!" as they looked at their bruised hands. That broke the seriousness of the situation and they all laughed letting out some of their tension and anxiety.

"Did you see that big guy with a towel? It had chloroform on it. They were trying to kidnap you, Natalie," Dietrich said.

She started to shudder and Dietrich put his arm around her and he said, "Yeah, I really laid him out!"

Natalie then laughed and winked at Christopher, "You both really laid them out! I thought that one guy whose arm you broke was laid out permanently!"

With that the tension was broken, and the four comrades decided that they would be able to eat their meals.

The dinner was served with the finesse of a Parisian restaurant. The restaurant was famous for its seafood and it met everyone's expectations. For dessert, the ladies decided on Crepes Fitzgerald for Carolyn and Crepes Bridget for Natalie.

The two men decided on a split of the Creole Chocolate Suicide Cake as a pact between cousins! Coffee au lait with Grand Marnier brandy was served with the desserts.

Feeling full, but satisfied, they returned to the Ritz-Carlton in good humor and ready for a good night's sleep.

After the sun woke them up the next morning, the two couples showered and dressed for their tour of New Orleans. They all met in Carolyn and Christopher's suite and discussed their agenda for the day.

Christopher mentioned that there were cemetery tours and Voodoo tours. He said the old St. Louis Cemetery #1 at 425 Basin Street which was established in 1789 was near at hand in the French Quarter. He suggested that they could easily walk there from the hotel after breakfast at Brennan's by walking a short distance down Canal Street to Basin Street and turning north and walking another four blocks to Conti Street where the cemetery is located. They could wander through the old graves and perhaps take a tour.

He said, "You never can tell when you might run across one of the famous funeral processions or an occasional ghost!"

Natalie gasped, "You don't mean real ghosts, do you?"

Everyone laughed, but then Christopher's face became serious and he said in a low tone of voice, "I really don't know! There have been reports of strange happenings on a dark night among the trees with their Spanish moss masking a full moon or a night with a dense bayou fog muffling the sounds of the city except for the occasional hooting of an owl. But I do suggest that we visit the cemetery in the morning when the sun is up and the birds are chirping among the oak trees."

Natalie's eyes had been opening wider and wider as Christopher was describing the possibilities of ghosts and the hair was standing up on the nape her neck with every detail. Christopher also noticed a strange hypnotic glaze in

Dietrich's eyes as if he were trying to remember that early morning feeling that he experienced in the Saint Mary Chapel among the thirteen sycamores that had embraced the moon that night.

Dietrich's shoulders trembled a bit and Christopher decided that he had gone too far and he quickly interrupted the trance that he had created by laughing and saying, "I guess I scared you both!"

Carolyn looked at her husband in sympathy with Natalie and Dietrich, and said, "There you go again, always fooling!"

The trance was broken, but Natalie and Dietrich had already put their arms around each other's waists in a mutually supporting embrace and laughed, but it wasn't convincing.

Carolyn took her husband's hand and pushed him toward the door, quipping, "Well, we might as well all go back to bed since my husband has scared the Hell out of all of us."

She looked up at Christopher and said," Well, are you through? Can we go now and get some breakfast?"

Carolyn kissed Natalie on her cheek as she embraced them both and said, "Let's go over to Brennan's for breakfast. I've already called them and they are expecting us. You'll love their pick-me-up breakfasts before we walk over to the St. Louis Cemetery."

Natalie and Dietrich responded that they were ready for the day!

They entered the restaurant and the maître d' was waiting for them or at least it seemed so. All the restaurants in New Orleans gave their customers that Southern hospitality feeling that they were in business just to please each and every one of their customers or friends as they described them! They were quickly seated and the waiter brought them the menu. They all chose "Eggs Hussarde," one of the dishes that had put "Breakfast at Brennan's" on the restauranteur map! It was poached eggs atop Holland rusks, Canadian bacon and Marchand de Vin sauce topped with Hollandaise Sauce and served with the required Gewurtztraminer Spatlese wine and

New Orleans coffee!

After they had finished their hearty breakfast and looked at the city map they had gotten from the Ritz-Carlton Hotel concierge, they decided they would walk down Bourbon Street and look into the shops until they got to Saint Louis Street. St. Louis Street would take them directly to the cemetery. The walk would do them good after their delicious and filling breakfast!

The cemetery was surrounded by an ancient iron spiked fence and contained mausoleums of all types from the fancy to those that were plain and strictly utilitarian. Many of the mausoleums had decorative flower arrangements left by friends or relatives and all of the tombs were well maintained and in good repair. Obviously, the citizens and families had great respect for the past!

As they walked among the graves and the trees with their Spanish moss, neatly trimmed bushes along with flowering plants and trees that demonstrated the meticulous gardening and attention to detail that was evident throughout the city, they believed New Orleans to truly be a garden city!

Natalie remarked to her companions that she could now understand how the people of New Orleans could celebrate a funeral procession with music and dancing! The whole city celebrated the joy of life as well as the solemnity of death as part of the same process of existence. They exited the cemetery with a better grasp of the totality of this truly remarkable town.

They walked to the Mercedes Benz Superdome stadium at the corner of Girod and LaSalle streets. Stadiums were named today after sponsoring corporations rather than people or places as it was done in the past. There was no doubt that the United States had transformed itself into a corporate entity rather than a nation of people proud of their history!

They were able to enter the gigantic arena of sports that had housed thousands of people during hurricane Katrina and it took their breath away. It looked as though an entire village would fit under its massive dome! After taking in the scope of this magnificent edifice that would rival any of the ancient marvels of the world, they departed the domed stadium and walked to the acclaimed National World War II Museum which focuses on the contributions of the United States to the victory of the Allies in World War II and more particularly the landings at Normandy on June sixth 1944. It was designated by Congress as the nation's World War II Museum in 2003 and dedicated by the Presidents Bush.

The museum has several World War II aircraft, both Allied as well as Axis suspended from the ceiling as if they were flying their missions, including fighters and bombers. There was also a TBF Avenger similar to the one flown by President George H.W. Bush during the Pacific campaign off Okinawa in that war. Both of the Presidents Bush were fighter pilots. President Kennedy had been a commander of a PT boat during that war in the Pacific.

Americans have always embraced their military heroes from the time of George Washington to George Bush. And most American presidents have served honorably in their nation's military before they became president and commander-in-chief of all the nation's armed forces. The museum is constantly expanding.

They entered the museum not knowing what to expect, but after three hours of touring that seemed to have evaporated much too quickly, they could see that it would take a week or longer to appreciate all of the wonders that the museum housed. It certainly compared to England's Imperial War Museum! The interactive and multimedia displays and dozens of video oral histories and personal stories were haunting—especially for the two warriors that held Natalie's and Carolyn's hands.

Now that they were ready to leave, it was afternoon and the sun was starting its slow descent into the west. They decided that rather than go back to their hotel, they would find a nice restaurant on the waterfront close to the convention center. They decided on the Hilton New Orleans Riverside Hotel where they had a beautiful restaurant,

Drago's Seafood Restaurant, with a breathtaking view of the Mississippi River and the boats moving on the river. It was located just north of the Riverside Market Place on Poydras Street.

It didn't take long for them to arrive at Convention Center Boulevard. Christopher remarked to his fellow walkers that some years ago he had received the key to the city of New Orleans when Mr. Morial had been mayor. Carolyn remarked that Christopher had spoken that time at a radiology convention about some of his research at the University of Texas.

Natalie thought to herself, "Hmm, a doctor, military flyer, researcher, university professor and lecturer, connoisseur of the arts, historian, author, martial arts champion and my new cousin!"

They reached Poydras Street in no time and entered the hotel. They found the restaurant with its view of the river and ordered four Glenlivet single malt Scotch whiskeys neat and sat down in some comfortable leather chairs to sip the Scotch and watch the ships as they moved up and down the Mississippi River. The cruise ships docked nearby and they had hoped to see one, but those docks were empty that night. Christopher walked over to the maître d' and made their reservations and was told that if they wanted to eat early, he would accommodate them early for dinner in about a half an hour. Christopher nodded his head and replied that that would be fine and then he turned and returned to his party to watch the sun sink into the river.

One half hour later, a waiter from the restaurant, came to their table and said that they had a table for them and were ready to take their orders. Christopher was glad they were able to get in early since they had a long trip tomorrow to Austin. They were all seated at a comfortable table by a large plate glass window that overlooked the river. They had an excellent view and they were all delighted at their good fortune. Dietrich looked at Natalie with a dreamy look that always accompanied two newly wed lovers. She returned his glance with a wistful smile that spoke a thousand words of understanding.

Carolyn saw the exchange and silently tugged on Christopher's arm to get his attention. He leaned down and she kissed him softly on his cheek and whispered into his ear as they looked toward the two newlyweds, "Remember, darling?" and Christopher softly whispered, "Yes!"

The waiter returned with four glasses of water and a menu. They ordered their meals and Christopher said that he was going whole hog with his order. Natalie turned to Carolyn and lightly whispered, "What does it mean to go whole hog?" Carolyn held back any laughter and calmly whispered back, "In Texas it means to go all the way for something or order everything!"

Natalie looked confused and then her eyes lit up and she whispered to Carolyn, "You mean that it would be okay for me to say that I go whole hog for Dietrich!"

Carolyn couldn't restrain herself anymore and laughed, "Yes!"

Dietrich and Christopher turned their heads at the same time towards the two wives and Christopher said, "What's up?"

Carolyn held her fingers softly to her lips and said, "Nothing, just girl talk!" And with that, everyone laughed.

The meal was served and when it came time for the dessert, they all decided on the apple cobbler with cream and cafe au lait with Hennessey brandy.

By this time a crescent moon had risen and was casting its reflection on the meandering waters of the Mississippi River. Christopher complained that he had eaten too much and Natalie and Dietrich asked if they could walk over to Woldenberg Park next to the Spanish Plaza and sit for a few minutes in the light breeze that was rippling the water of the river and bringing the soft melodies of New Orleans jazz to the park. They all agreed that that would be a perfect setting for the end of a beautiful day. It didn't occur to them that a crescent moon was the symbol of Islam!

They sat quietly in the park with its oak trees heavy with shadowy Spanish moss. The moon glowed brightly in the night sky and the two couples held hands and the ladies rested their heads on their husband's shoulder and dreamt sweet thoughts of the romantic moon that was gazing down just for them.

They sat in silent bliss and then Dietrich softly said, "It's beginning to get chilly, do you think we should go back to our hotel."

They all nodded their heads in agreement and walked slowly and quietly back to the hotel and to their rooms. When they had exited the elevator on their floor, Carolyn suggested, "Shall we all meet in our room for breakfast. We'll order a light Continental Breakfast for four and meet, say, around seven o'clock tomorrow morning. That will give us plenty of time to get packed and check out of our rooms after breakfast and maybe reach Houston or maybe even Austin in good time tomorrow."

They all agreed and Carolyn and Christopher watched Natalie and Dietrich walk to their room holding each other's hand. When they reached their room the couple turned and waved at Carolyn and Christopher and disappeared into their suite.

Carolyn and Christopher lingered at their door still gazing down the hallway when she put her arm around Christopher's waist and looked up at his blue eyes and said as she gently squeezed him, "It has been a good day, hasn't it?"

He looked into her emerald eyes and thought he saw a slight tear just at the corner of her eyes. Saying nothing, he opened their door, then reached down and picked her up and kissed her. Then he walked into the room with her in his arms, closed the door and carried her to their bedroom. As they entered the room, he pulled her up to his face and kissed her passionately on her lips, then he nuzzled her ear and whispered, "I love you more each day." And then he carried her to their bed and gently laid her down and lay down beside her.

20 BERLIN

B erlin is a city of 3.3 million people with 4.9 million inhabitants in its metropolitan area. It is the capital of Germany and is surrounded by the Federal State of Brandenburg. It is large enough to hide the remnants of the Black September Organization that terrorized the Munich Olympics. Ahmed ali and his father, Mohammad, were staying at the Hotel Adlon Kempinski on Unter den Linden Strasse in the heart of Berlin where it is possible to hide in plain sight. Mohammad had shaved his beard that he had grown while he was in Syria and Ahmed had only a small mustache that made him resemble Adolph Hitler.

They had met some of their fellow Muslim Brotherhood comrades the day before in the Tiergarten where they had discussed future terrorist bombings in Germany, France and the United States to coordinate with the bombings planned for London. The group had met earlier with some Chechen terrorists that called themselves Freedom Fighters that were planning similar bombings in Russia. It was the intent of the jihadists to strike terror and fear around the world and keep the West off guard so that the Brotherhood with their terrorist allies could methodically subvert the "Arab Spring" into the desired Caliphate from Gibraltar to China.

They were meeting in Germany to discuss ways and means of undermining the government of the Chancellor of Germany, Angela Merkel. The Brotherhood feared her for her strong stance against militant Muslims and her insistence on obeying German law, language and customs for everyone living in Germany regardless of their background. She was looked upon admiringly by people in the Western World as the Iron Chancellor and in the United Kingdom as the Margaret Thatcher of Germany.

The meeting had concluded with the formation of organizational planning committees for coordinated terror plots on western countries by the various Jihadist groups that were represented by members that had met together in the Tiergarten the day before. Mohammad and Ahmed were satisfied with the unity of purpose these groups had shown and they knew that their Wahhabi supporters would approve of their planned and coordinated attacks on the West.

Mohammad and Ahmed spent an uneventful night in their hotel room and decided the next morning to have breakfast at Cafe' Einstein on Unter den Linden Strasse where they could discuss their plans and their efforts to kill Natalie if she were pregnant or sell her into slavery in one of the many slave markets in Africa or the Middle East.

And the slave trade is still profitable. Mauretania just south of Morocco in West Africa has open slave markets and estimated to have as high as a 20 percent population of slaves. As recently as 1950, Saudi Arabia's slave population was estimated to be 450,000 people!

The Arabian Peninsula and the Muslim world has been very active in recent years in slavery, sex trafficking and abduction for servitude and human organs for transplant. There has been Christian abduction and slave trading in the Muslim world for centuries, right up to modern times.

Recently, Jamat-ud Daawa in Pakistan with ties to al Qaida has been suspected of Christian abduction and slave trading. The Clinton Global Initiative had highlighted an estimated 20 million people worldwide including the Americas and the

Caribbean that have been victims in some form of modern day slavery or prostitution. President Obama had spoken out about ending the injustice and outrage of human trafficking.

Mohammad and Ahmed ali had seated themselves at a table outside of the restaurant and when a waiter presented them with a menu, they glanced at it and ordered only assorted fruit with strudel and dark black coffee.

Mohammad was visibly disturbed when his son told him that they had bungled the job of kidnapping Natalie in New Orleans. "I would remind you that it's likely that she is being protected by her cousins in the United States, Homeland Security agents or the police."

"I don't know," Ahmed ali replied. "There was a man with her in Atlanta when she arrived and stayed with her when she and her cousin arrived in New Orleans. He acted like a body guard, but he seemed too intimate."

"She probably has a new boyfriend!" Mohammad fumed. "And with her husband barely buried and with her carrying on in public with the consent of her cousins. It's that way in the West and why they must be destroyed!"

Too flippantly, Ahmed ali replied, "Well, life goes on."

His voice rising, Mohammad demanded, "No, it doesn't! I want her abducted or killed! Use propofol next time instead of chloroform, It's quicker! And make sure she is isolated and alone, separated from her boyfriend and cousins, not like the way you tried in New Orleans. He pointed his finger at Ahmed and shook it in his face, "Next time isolate her! Have you alerted all of our agents in the United States?"

"No, not yet," Ahmed ali whispered sheepishly. "Just Atlanta."

Mohammad slammed his fist on the table so hard that the dishes rattled and heads turned towards them. Mohammad looked up and noticed an officer of the Bundespolizei watching them intently. He had seated himself at a table a few meters away and was talking on a cell phone. That prompted Mohammad to quickly switch from Arabic to German and begin talking about touring various places in Berlin that were usually frequented by foreign tourists.

Ahmed picked up the ruse immediately and began chatting in German about various possible tourist spots that might be interesting to visit.

They finished their meal quickly and Mohammad motioned to the waiter for their bill and promptly paid for their breakfast, in cash and with a small tip. They casually strolled down the avenue toward their hotel and noticed that the policeman did not get up from his table, but continued talking on his phone.

Ahmed breathed a sigh of relief and said, "I guess he wasn't paying any attention to us."

Mohammad replied, "I wouldn't be too sure of that. It's time for us to leave this country and for you to get back to Prague and convince your sister of the error of her ways in any way that you can and for me to get back to Jeddah."

Then he looked intently into his son's eyes and was adamant. "I want to know where Natalie is at all times! Do not disappoint me! See if you can get your sister to give us any information on her whereabouts now. Use whatever means possible without killing her. She may be valuable in the future! As for her Czech friend, it would be nice to find out who he is and eliminate him."

Ahmed nodded, "I'll have my agents watching for Natalie at the major American airports such as Boston, New York, Los Angeles, San Francisco, Atlanta, and Chicago, among other places."

"Don't forget Austin, San Antonio, Corpus Christi, Dallas-Fort Worth and Houston."

The policeman that was still sitting at his table at the Cafe' Einstein and was watching Mohammad and Ahmed ali as they walked away from their table and down the boulevard.

"They are leaving for their hotel now," the policeman said into his cell phone. "I believe I got the entire conversation recorded. The first part was in Arabic and they were discussing abducting someone named Natalie and when they noticed me, they switched to German."

"Sehr gut!" replied his supervisor.

Mohammad and Ahmed walked to their hotel, went to their room and quickly packed their bags. After they paid their bill in cash, they took a taxi to Schoenfeld Airport. Mohammad couldn't help but think of the irony that he was using an airport named for his enemy's family to escape from this infidel country. And after embracing each other, they went to their respective departure gates for Prague and Jeddah.

The last thing that Mohammad said to his son before they parted was, "Let me know the whereabouts of Natalie. I want to personally see that she and her meddling American cousins die!"

21 TEXAS

The next morning the Roods and the von Schoenfelds left New Orleans in Christopher's silver grey 2012 GL Class Mercedes-Benz SUV for Carolyn and Christopher's home in Austin. Christopher had insisted on paying the hotel bill as a token of their congratulations on Dietrich's recovery and the resumption of their interrupted honeymoon. They were getting away later than they had anticipated. It was eight-thirty in the morning and Christopher was anxious to leave.

The route would take them through the Cajun bayou country of southern Louisiana, through Metairie and Kenner on Interstate 10 to Baton Rouge and then west onto Interstate 10W to Texas.

From Baton Rouge, they traveled through Lafayette, Lake Charles and onto the High Bridge over the Calcasieu River and Lake Charles. The span was so high that Natalie remarked that it looked like a roller coaster! They crossed the Sabine River just west of Lake Charles, entered Texas and crossed the Texas bayou lands, the rich oil fields that surrounded Beaumont and Port Arthur.

They then passed over the San Jacinto River where Texas won its independence from Mexico. Scots Irish General Sam

Houston and his Texican Army defeated General Santa Anna, the dictator of Mexico, and his much larger force in an early morning surprise attack. Texas became an independent country for some time before joining the United States as the Lone Star state after the US-Mexican War. Texas still uses its former national flag as its state flag!

They continued their journey westward on Interstate 10 into the city of Houston with its harbor and the old city of Galveston located south of Houston on an island connected to the mainland and Houston by a causeway. Galveston is home to a branch of the University of Texas Medical School. Christopher spent part of his education there before going to Corpus Christi where he met Carolyn. The National Aeronautics and Space Administration (NASA) Center is between Galveston and Houston.

They pressed on and drove the last 200 miles on Interstate 10 west to their destination of Austin where the Roods lived in a Swiss styled chateau on a peninsula called Point Venture that sticks out into Lake Travis west of the city.

It had taken ten hours to reach the Rood House on Lake Travis and everyone was exhausted and famished from the trip. They were ready to relax out on one of the cantilevered porches that jutted out from the backside of the chateau and wrapped around the western side of the house. It afforded them an exhilarating view of the lake as the sun was beginning to set in the west.

Christopher parked the SUV in the large six-car garage built into the side of a limestone cliff just to the side of the chateau. The chateau was free standing on huge concrete pillars sunk into the earth below the cliff and it was reached from the side of the cliff where the garage was located by a wide concrete bridge with two gargoyles peering into the gorge on either side of the bridge that led to the front entrance of the chateau. Christopher had designed it to resemble the bridge over the gorge to Roslyn Castle in Scotland.

He had parked the vehicle next to the classic 1970 beige

Mercedes Benz 280 SL convertible that he owned when he met Carolyn in Corpus Christi. He kept the automobile for sentimental reasons and also because it was a much sought after antique classic car! Parked next to the SL was a brand new early release BMW Z4 35i roadster that he had just purchased at a good price from a friend that owned a dealership in Austin. Carolyn's Mercedes C 350 four door sedan was parked next to Christopher's latest acquisition.

They crossed over the concrete bridge past the stone gargoyles keeping guard at the front door. Carolyn punched in the access code and placed her thumb onto the security sensor that read her thumbprint and allowed the door to be opened. Security cameras peered down on them from concealed locations and recorded everyone. Carolyn opened the door and they stepped into the entrance foyer that was actually on the third floor of the five storied chateau. Balthazar, the large grey family cat was there to greet them all!

Christopher and Dietrich carried the luggage up the stairs on the left past an elevator to the balcony and sitting area that was just off a hallway leading to the guest rooms. They dropped the Rood's luggage on the floor just in front of the first guest room and placed the Schoenfelds' luggage in the first guest room. Natalie and Dietrich noticed that there was a placard on their door that declared the guest room was the German Room.

Christopher explained that all of the guest rooms had names and he and Carolyn thought this room would be appropriate for them. Natalie thanked them and Carolyn said they would see them downstairs shortly after they had a chance to recover from the trip. Carolyn and Christopher then picked up their luggage and went upstairs to their bedroom and Balthazar followed Natalie into their room.

After a half hour, Carolyn came to the Schoenfelds' room and Natalie with Balthazar joined her as they went downstairs to the kitchen. After about fifteen minutes, Christopher joined Dietrich and they went downstairs to the kitchen on the third floor where their wives were already preparing dinner. Carolyn asked Christopher to take Dietrich down to the wine cellar and pick out a special champagne for their homecoming.

Carolyn and Natalie had already prepared some finger sandwiches and a garden salad with a vinaigrette sauce by the time Christopher and Dietrich had returned with some iced champagne from the refrigerated wine cellar. The meal was just perfect to watch the sun set into the lake and the thin crescent moon rise high into the night sky from across the eastern side of the lake. Christopher had taken a bottle of 2004 Roederer Cristal Champagne from the walk in refrigerator in his wine cellar that kept his wines at just the right temperature.

The house was designed so that Carolyn could look from the kitchen through the dining room past the third floor deck where they were dining, and see the massive stone fireplace at the far side of the Great Room. There was a medieval armored chest plate and shield with crossed broadswords above the mantle of the fireplace. On the mantle of the massive fireplace was a large model ship of Columbus' flagship Santa Maria with its unfurled sails emblazoned with the red Templar Cross of the Knights Templar.

Just past the stair steps to the Great Room and the grandfather clock and close to the French doors leading to the outside deck was a large twelve foot long brown leather couch facing toward the fireplace. It had a red fox fur satin lined blanket draped over its back and throw pillows laid randomly down its twelve foot length. There was a large oval cherry wood coffee table with a glass top and a two foot high round blown glass hurricane lamp with a large white candle.

The two couples sat in four of the wrought iron chairs with soft pillows that were placed around the glass topped wrought iron table on the deck, eating their dinner and discussing their stay in New Orleans. The light meal was excellent and Carolyn remarked to her guests that the evening sky with the pink clouds silhouetted against the setting sun, "topped off the meal and ended the day perfectly!" She was telling their guests that they would have to do some shopping in Austin and get some more lighter clothing for the next few months they would be in the hot Texas Summer sun.

Since they were in ranch country, Christopher said that they would have to get some regular Texas attire consisting of blue jeans long enough to roll up and show off their boots and to show off the large silver buckled belt that they absolutely had to wear with the jeans and the long sleeved light weight Scottish plaid shirt that was required. And to top it off, they needed a dove grey Stetson hat with a genuine Texas crease!

Carolyn listened to Christopher's description of what they should wear and studied the startled look and open mouth that Natalie wore on her face. Finally she had to break her silence and tell Christopher, "Don't frighten our guests with all that cowboy talk. They can wear what they want to!"

Natalie quickly turned toward Carolyn and exclaimed, "Oh no, it sounds just super. Just like in the movies. I've always been fascinated by American movies and the Wild West and now we're here at last!"

Carolyn looked at her husband, rolled her eyes at him and then looked at Natalie and exclaimed, "Honey, it's not all that wild today. Most of the time people wear regular clothes."

The great deck with its various bird feeders was perched high enough among the top branches of the trees in the back yard for the guests to feel as if they were sitting in a tree house looking out over the lake. The trees rose skyward from the back yard with its various flower gardens that sloped down to the edge of the lake where the gazebo and boat house were located.

Carolyn and Christopher were water skiing enthusiasts and frequently had friends from the university over for an evening meal after a day of skiing on the lake. They had a small picnic area in the garden next to the gazebo, a private secluded sandy beach, and boathouse. Sheltered walkways meandered through the several different gardens located around the house.

By this time, the bright crescent moon had risen high in the night sky and the Milky Way was shining brightly above their heads. Carolyn turned to Natalie and Dietrich and asked if they were ready for bed. Natalie and Dietrich nodded their heads.

They all rose from the table and picked up their plates and glasses and took them into the kitchen through the French doors.

Christopher explained that the floor above them had four guest rooms that were similar except for the decorations and furniture and the next floor up was Carolyn's and his bedroom. The four walked up to the guest rooms on the fourth floor. The German Room was the first guest room on the corner of a sitting area with a small library and balcony that overlooked the Great Room with its high beamed ceiling.

It was adjacent to the Scotland room where Carolyn said they kept all of the ghosts! The other two rooms were the Swiss Room to commemorate Christopher's climbing of the Matterhorn and the Mexico Room to celebrate their many trips to Mexico when they were residents in Corpus Christi. The floor where Carolyn and Christopher's bedroom was located was just above this floor.

All of the guest rooms were large with a large bedroom and bed, sitting room with sofa, chairs, desk, television and walk in closets and a private bath and shower. There was also a smaller private deck that was located outside their bedroom and sitting room. The backside of the house facing toward the lake had large floor to ceiling glass windows for all of the various rooms on the five floors of the house.

The windows were all covered with vertical louvered blinds and pull curtains to keep the sunlight out when desired. But that wasn't all! Christopher explained to Natalie and Dietrich that each room had its own small kitchenette just off the sitting room with a fully stocked refrigerator and pantry, a dishwasher and a small bar with various wines, beer, whiskeys and liqueurs!

Natalie and Dietrich looked at their host and smiled.

Natalie said, "You and Carolyn are spoiling us, it's like a dream! Thank you for giving us this opportunity for a real honeymoon!"

Christopher blushed at her remarks and said, "Shucks ma'am, that's just the way we do things here in Texas!"

They all laughed and Carolyn and Christopher turned toward the stairs and waved goodnight to their guests as they walked up the stairs to their bedroom.

The next morning after breakfast, Carolyn and Christopher took the newlyweds on a Cook's tour of their house. Even though it was quite large, it was laid out in a convenient manner. They were led up the stairs that led from one floor of the house to another, even though there was an elevator with an iron grated door that went from the sub-basement to the fifth floor where the master bedroom was located.

The master bedroom had its own adjoining office with a walnut paneled library, and a bath with a dressing room with two cedar paneled walk-in clothes closets adjacent to it. The master bathroom had a large walk-in shower for two and a large Jacuzzi that looked out toward the lake through a sliding glass door that led to another small private outside deck. The dressing room was next to the two walk-in clothes closets. One for Carolyn and the other for Christopher.

The library next to the bedroom was off a small hall with walls harboring some of Christopher's photographs. The hall led to a narrow spiral staircase that went up to a small astronomical library that contained a reflecting telescope. The sloping roof over that small library was glass with a curtain that could be opened to observe the stars or closed to keep the sun out. It also had a large plate glass window that looked out over Lake Travis.

The sub-basement held a temperature and humidity controlled wine cellar, storage rooms, and a large photography studio. It had a ceiling that was twenty feet high. The studio glass windows looked out over the gardens and lawn that surrounded the house. It was large enough to accommodate the large collection of artwork and cameras that Christopher had collected over the years in pursuit of his hobby.

In a corner of that large open studio was a full-size pool table and display cases that held keepsakes of their lives. Balthazar liked to sleep on the pool table and, because of his age, spent a lot of his time there.

One area of the studio was devoted to the Hospitaller Order of Saint John and its Stroh Library in honor of Colonel Oscar Stroh who had been a staff officer of General Douglas MacArthur and a professor at the United States Army War College in Carlisle, Pennsylvania. He had been a very close friend of theirs.

Christopher also had a collection of American and German military guns, swords, knives and a replica of an original Order of Saint John Crusader Sword that had been crafted by Ed Halligan, a famous knife maker from Coweta County, Georgia.

An Achievement and Coat of Arms granted to him by the Royal College of Arms in London, England was hanging on the wall next to photographs that were taken when he had served as a flight surgeon and weapons systems officer in a Phantom II jet warplane. He had a fully flyable fan jet model of the plane that he had flown in Desert Storm prominently displayed—it was painted with the camouflage and markings, including the kills of the original plane.

The basement was basically a large art gallery that contained his collections of sculptures and paintings by various famous artists. He favored Remington paintings and sculptures of the old west, but he had quite a few from Europe and Asia.

He also had a large collection of photographs of old and recent photographers. They were all hanging on the walls and partitions in the gallery according to the artists and their periods of time. He favored Ansel Adam's photography, but had quite a few of his own photographs including his published works displayed.

Tucked in the corner of the gallery were a few of the older cameras from the 1800s, tastefully displayed. Various new, old and ancient sculptures were displayed scattered among the paintings and photographs. All of the works of art had pinpoint lighting from the ceiling that could illuminate each of them individually or collectively.

The entire house was decorated with furniture, paintings and tapestries from all over the world where the Roods had traveled. They were particularly fond of antiques and some were museum pieces.

After the Cook's tour of the house, they decided that it would be nice to have lunch and relax down by the gazebo and boat dock where the picnic area of the garden was located.

Carolyn had ordered two large pizzas from a nearby restaurant in Lakeway on the other side of the peninsula from Point Venture where they were located.

After the pizzas arrived, they took the elevator to the sub-basement which was the bottom floor of the chateau and walked down one of the paths through the gardens to the picnic area.

It was a beautiful clear blue day that was typical of the Hill Country of Texas.

The birds and a few occasional hawks were patrolling the skies and lake. Hummingbirds had staked out their claim to the gardens adjacent to the picnic table that Carolyn and Natalie had prepared with linens and eating utensils.

It was bright enough outside for everyone to wear sunglasses and Christopher had brought some Leica zoom binoculars to watch the speedboats with their cargoes of youngsters and the ever present water skiers.

The Roods had their own speedboat safely cocooned and elevated above the water in their boathouse and had not yet brought it out for the summer. It was a sea blue and white Chris Craft Launch 22 that was over eight feet wide and twenty-three and a half feet long with a Volvo 5.7 GIC inboard engine with Heritage trim.

It was very fast and seated five people comfortably. Christopher confided to Dietrich that he would contact his dealer to come out and get the boat ready for the summer. With all that had happened in the last few months, he had neglected the boat!

Natalie declared that she was famished and could eat one of the giant pizzas all by herself. Of course, she had no such intention and Dietrich smiled because her bubbling enthusiasm was one of the things about her that he adored.

Carolyn brought out a bottle of Australian Merlot and a pitcher of spring water that was famous in the area from the refrigerator next to the built in barbecue near the picnic gazebo and the stone retaining wall encompassing the area.

Natalie and Carolyn both wore light sun dresses and the wide brimmed straw sun hats they had bought in New Orleans and open sandals. Dietrich and Christopher were dressed in white boating slacks with brightly colored polo shirts and white canvas boating shoes. They wore no hats and Carolyn mentioned that it might be prudent for them to stay in the shade of the umbrella covered table. The breeze was brisk enough that it kept pestering insects away.

The ice cold water and lightly chilled Merlot went just right with the two pizzas. There were no leftovers to the lunch and the foursome were satisfied to lie on the chaise lounge chairs that they had placed facing toward the lake and watch the passing boat traffic. The college kids were out on summer vacation and loudly expressing their joy at playing in the water.

Dietrich was watching the boats and suddenly yelled to Christopher to pick up his binoculars. He was looking at a speedboat that had a young man with binoculars looking their way. He had noticed that he had been in the same place for about 30 minutes and was almost continuously looking their way.

Christopher picked up his glasses and zoomed in on his face. "He looks like a college kid"

Dietrich exclaimed, "Look, he must have spotted us. We

must have spooked him. He's starting to leave."

Christopher turned to Dietrich and said softly, "Don't tell the girls."

"I won't, but we better notify Steve what has happened."

"Okay." Christopher took his scrambled phone and called Steve.

"Hi, Christopher, what's happening?"

Christopher filled in Steve and he replied, "Yes, we knew about everything since you arrived in the United States, but not about the guy you just spotted watching your house. We'll get on it right away and I'll call you back when we find out anything. You know we've been watching everything and it might be just a college kid watching for girls. One of our angels is probably checking it out right now."

"Okay," and they hung up.

Dietrich asked Christopher, "What did he say?"

"He said they would check it out and call back."

Twenty minutes later, Christopher's cell phone rang and it was Steve.

"It was a college kid and we scared the hell out of him. He had seen one of the Texas Ranger's boats assigned to the case approaching him and he fled like a bat, but we got him. He's plenty scared now, so you won't see him again."

"Okay, thank you, give our best to Kate," and then they hung up.

Christopher turned to Dietrich and told him what Steve said.

"I'm glad," Dietrich said, "but don't tell Carolyn and Natalie, they'll laugh at us."

Later that afternoon Christopher answered a telephone call from his attorney and old friend Diamond Dave in Atlanta. David was anxious to inform Christopher on the state of his investments in and about Atlanta. He expanded on their business discussions they had in Atlanta and that the retirement home and village project was now to the point where ground could be broken, but he needed his okay and that the Emergency Care Centers in which he and his business partner were involved, needed to expand. David had a few questions that he needed to ask Christopher to make sure that everything would run smoothly and besides he was anxious to see how his old friend was after his trip to New Orleans!

Christopher gave his opinions on the business projects and explained to David that he couldn't come to Atlanta again just yet since his guests were going to be visiting with him for several weeks and trusted him to proceed as they planned. He said that everything was well with his cousins from Germany and he thought that his presentations on the research that he was involved with at the University of Texas had been well received in New Orleans.

David informed him that he had a promising lead on a piece of Scottish property he and Carolyn had been looking at in Scotland—a 50 acre tract overlooking Loch Moy and the island where Moy Castle, the original seat of the chiefs of the MacIntosh clan in Inverness, was located.

"I know how much Carolyn wants to build there," David said, "but I'll have to go over to Scotland to check on all of the details of the purchase and what it will take to build the kind of house that she is thinking about. I just got a call that the owner is ready to deal, and that it's available at a fair price."

"Thank you, so much," Christopher replied. "Carolyn will be delighted about that land being available. Make all of the usual arrangements and keep me informed."

Christopher had not told David about the intricacies of the mysterious visit that he and Carolyn had suddenly made to Edinburgh and Germany. David knew that they frequently visited Europe and especially Scotland and Germany in particular, so he was not surprised. He didn't ask any questions since he knew that his friend would tell him what was happening when he thought the time was right.

The two old friends said their goodbyes and hung up. Christopher thought to himself that he was lucky to have a friend like David who never asked questions that he thought might be inappropriate, but would wait patiently for the right time when they could discuss whatever issues were necessary. He knew that David would always come to his aid if necessary and vice versa.

"Who was that?" Carolyn asked.

Christopher replied, "It was Diamond Dave and he just wanted us to know that everything in Atlanta was going as planned and that he would pursue buying the land in Scotland."

"That's nice," Carolyn replied. "Did you tell him hello for me?"

Christopher had to admit that it had slipped his mind. Carolyn looked at him and a slight frown crossed her eyebrows for an instant, but then she smiled, realizing that husbands were frequently guilty of such inadvertent lapses!

The evening crept upon the Roods and their two guests more quickly than they had all expected and after dinner, Dietrich said that the time differences between Europe and the United States and all the activities in New Orleans in addition to the long trip to Texas was beginning to catch up with them and he thought that he would go to bed early.

Natalie followed up her husband and said, "Me too. I'm a little tired as well!"

Dietrich took Natalie's hand and led her to the stairway to their floor and waved goodnight to Carolyn and Christopher who looked at each other and smiled knowingly.

Carolyn looked up at Christopher and flashed her green eyes at him as she grabbed his hand and led him off toward the elevator to their bedroom. She flicked her eyelids rapidly, looked up demurely and murmured, imitating Natalie, "Me too!"

The next morning, in the large heavy old wooden king-sized bed, Carolyn rolled over to Christopher who was staring out the window at the birds and squirrels that were playing among the tree branches of the trees overlooking the deck outside their bedroom window. The sun was just coming up on the opposite side of the house and casting its shadow across the trees.

"You know, Natalie and Dietrich seemed to be interested in the Texas Rangers. Do you think they would be interested in going to Waco and visit the Ranger Hall of Fame and Museum?" Christopher asked.

Carolyn replied that she thought they would, but that perhaps they could do that in a couple of weeks after she made arrangements for them to meet with a real life Texas Ranger when they visited the museum.

Meanwhile, she thought it would be fun to take them to Corpus Christi to see Padre Island and the hospital and medical center where they had first met. And maybe, she thought, they could stop off at Bandera just northwest of San Antonio on their way to Corpus Christi since it is the recognized cowboy capital of the world and has played such a significant role in the history of Texas.

Carolyn and Christopher dressed and went downstairs to the kitchen to find that Natalie had just finished fixing breakfast for everyone and was just coming up to see what had been keeping them!

Carolyn smiled and asked if she had any difficulty finding everything and Natalie smiled back and said, "No, the kitchen was well organized and I've fixed a fresh fruit salad and Eggs Benedict with some lovely Piesporter Goldtrophchen wine that I found. I understand from previous conversations that they are a favorite with you and Christopher." She had even found some avocados to go with the Eggs Benedict. Natalie said that she had remembered Carolyn mentioning that she and Christopher had enjoyed this breakfast from their visits to their apartment in San Francisco.

Dietrich was seated at the small breakfast table in the breakfast nook and was already at work tasting some large strawberries that Carolyn had found at the Fresh Market and stored in the refrigerator before they had left for New Orleans. As the trio entered the nook, Dietrich stood up to help seat his wife and Carolyn.

The coffee was brewing and the aroma of the freshly

ground coffee beans were swirling around the table. They all sat down at the table and Christopher poured the coffee for Carolyn and Natalie and then for himself.

Dietrich had already poured his coffee and was busy adding some cream to it when he asked, "Do you think that it would be okay to do a little water skiing?"

Christopher replied that he would call the Yacht Club and have the mechanic come by this afternoon if possible and get the boat ready. He said that they were very efficient helping members get ready for the summer. If everyone wanted, maybe they could just relax today and swim from the pier and sandy beach next to it. The sun would probably be warm today and they could just hang around in swim suits and lounging attire.

They slowly ate their breakfasts and Carolyn, who is an excellent cook—really a chef—remarked how well the food tasted and that Natalie had really out done herself. She was duly impressed! She turned to Dietrich and remarked that he was indeed fortunate. He had not only married a beautiful woman, but an excellent cook as well.

Natalie blushed and turned her head and said to Carolyn, "That is indeed a compliment, especially coming from you!"

Carolyn blushed a little.

With that little bit of repartee, they all smiled and Dietrich declared, "Christopher, you and I are the lucky ones!"

Natalie and Carolyn nodded their heads vigorously in agreement.

The two couples spent the day at their little beachside resort, swimming and lying in the sun with a little time walking through the meticulous gardens that surrounded the house. The two couples walked through the gardens with the affectionate holding of hands that were usually the custom of young lovers. It was apparent that the Roods, who were not quite a decade older than the von Schoenfelds, still had not lost the bloom of their youth that had characterized their marriage.

The mechanic from the yacht club had arrived shortly

after lunch with his crew of three to ready the Chris Craft skiing boat, test the engines that hummed agreeably when started and check all of the safety gear that were required by law. They even filled the tank and tested the boat during a short run around the peninsula.

They then went over all of the safety rules for cruising the lake and took the two couples for a short cruise to check each of them to see if they could handle the boat and the rules of navigation and courtesy while skiing. They were thorough before issuing them the permit required for the season.

They all decided that the next few days after that would be devoted to improving their skills at water skiing.

Carolyn had called that afternoon to a friend in the Texas State Historical Association to arrange for a genuine Texas Ranger to meet them in two weeks at the Texas Ranger Hall of Fame and Museum in Waco. She had asked her friend if the Ranger could wear his uniform and holster a revolver. Her friend Susan Howard laughed and told her that it was no problem and many of them relished the idea of carrying a Colt seven and one-half inch barreled Peacemaker revolver along with a Stetson hat and familiar boots.

Christopher, one evening as they sat on the deck sipping some wine and looking at the lake, reveled Natalie and Dietrich with stories about Texas. Carolyn had heard them all a thousand times it seemed, but indulged him in his whimsy.

He talked about Manuel T. Gonzaullas who was a famous Texas Ranger that spawned the legendary phrase that it only took one Ranger to quell one riot.

Texas has delighted in their Lone Star flag and their reputation not to mess with Texas and without missing a beat, he told a story about the independent nature of Texans.

It was during the late 1960s that a dredging of the Mansfield Cut channel between the Gulf of Mexico and the Laguna Madre through the barrier Padre Island, that the automatic dredging machine dug so deeply, that gold and tarnished silver coins and artifacts spewed forth into the air, onto the sandy beach in such numbers that the dredge had to be shut down. What was left of the Spanish Galleon Santa Maria de Yciar was destroyed. A recent hurricane uncovered one of the three ancient treasure ships near the Mansfield Cut.

In 1967, a salvage firm, without the proper licensing, recovered items from the galleon, including silver and gold coins, gold jewelry, cannonballs, astrolabes and other artifacts. The company, supposedly from Gary, Indiana, recovered so much treasure that the word spread quickly to Austin, and the state of Texas sued the salvage firm. Only part of the treasure was returned.

The treasure fleet had set sail from Veracruz on April 9, 1554, for Spain loaded with plunder of the conquistadors. It has been said that it was the richest treasure fleet that ever sailed for Spain! A violent storm scattered the fleet and several galleons went down off the southern coast of Texas near Port Mansfield and Padre Island. Three ships reached Spain and one limped back to Veracruz. Three ships were wrecked off Padre Island—the Santa Maria de Yciar, the San Esteban and the Espiritu Santo. Three hundred survivors including soldiers, sailors, priests, women and children were attacked by Karankawa Indians as they fled down the island. Only two men survived, one of them a priest for which the island is named.

When news of the disaster reached Mexico, a salvage expedition was started.

The Spanish had native divers from Yucatan bring up gold and silver from the San Esteban, which had been easily found since its masts were above water. They found the other two galleons by dragging a chain between the two ships. The recovered treasure was catalogued and sent on to Seville, Spain.

In 1904, Alex Meuly of Corpus Christi claimed that he found the remains of the galleons 420 feet from shore and 35 miles down the island from Corpus Christi near Port Mansfield. Stories of gold and silver coins that have washed ashore in the sand dunes of the island after a severe storm have been legendary.

Spanish doubloons dated 1525 were found so often in one sand dune after any violent storm that it was called Money Hill!

The story about the salvage company in 1967 goes that the Texas Governor sent the Texas Rangers to Padre Island to secure the artifacts and treasure. By this time much of the treasure and artifacts had been transported to a warehouse in Gary, Indiana, and the state of Texas sued the company for the return of the artifacts. Texas A&M University marine scientists and archeologists were sent down to the area to initiate a scientific investigation and recovery of the area and the artifacts that remained.

Negotiations between the company and the state of Texas were not going rapidly enough so the Texas governor decided to appeal to the governor of Indiana directly for help to recover the artifacts. Apparently, that did not produce any speedy results, so the Texas governor sent the Texas Rangers along with some 16-wheeler trucks to Indiana, and over a weekend, in the dark of night, the artifacts were loaded onto the trucks and returned to Texas. The Texas governor then called the Indiana governor the next week after the midnight raid trucks had crossed back over the Texas state line and told him that he no longer needed his help! So rumor has it, but it speaks volumes about the tenacity and spirit of Texas independence and its citizens!

22 AUSTIN

Later that afternoon, Carolyn tried to call their friend Dr. Fox, but he had not yet returned from England. His housekeeper, Mary Stuart, said that she did not know exactly when he might return and she reminded Carolyn, as they all knew, that he could at times be unpredictable if he was engrossed in a particular dig or research. She and Christopher decided that they would call again the day before their trip to San Antonio, Bandera, and Corpus Christi. Perhaps they could pick him up later in the month or in August when they were going to Waco. Salado, where Dr. Fox lived, was on the way!

They spent the next two weeks enjoying Lake Travis and its environs around the peninsula. Christopher had called a friend who had a Jet Ski and Dietrich delighted in showing Natalie the finer points of jet skiing as they went on excursions around the Lake. Natalie and Carolyn had bought some new bikini swim suits and other boating apparel on one of their shopping trips into Austin. When the two got back to Rood House, they changed into their new clothes and showed them off to their husbands. When they got to the bikinis, Christopher declared that they both looked so beautiful that they would probably be arrested for causing a riot!

Dietrich merely whistled his approval and suggested that except when they were on the beach or in the boat, it might be wise to wear a light long shirt over the bikinis! One afternoon, after swimming, Natalie and Carolyn put the suggested shirts over their bikinis with an appropriate scarf around their necks, and the two couples took the Chris-Craft to the marina of the yacht club where they all enjoyed a refreshing lunch!

Carolyn and Christopher had taken Natalie and Dietrich into Austin several times over the next few weeks to Town Lake with its park and to the various restaurants, stores and shops so they could purchase any odds and ends. The morning of the day before their planned week long trip to Corpus Christi, Christopher again called his old friend, Dr. Fox, and the housekeeper informed him that Dr. Fox had not yet returned, but had left a message for her that he would probably be back from England in a couple of weeks and that he had not forgotten about Libertyville or the Baylor-Texas game.

Christopher laughed and remarked to Mrs. Stuart that if Dr. Fox called to tell him they were all going to Corpus Christi and were sorry he missed the trip, and to ask him to give them a call when he got back so they could pick him up and they could all visit the Texas Ranger Museum. She replied that she would give him the message and wished them well on their trip.

Christopher thanked her and then hung up the telephone. He turned to Carolyn who was standing next to him and said, "Well, I guess that Randall has found something interesting at the dig, he won't be back for a few more weeks and Mrs. Stuart said that she would have him call us as soon as he has returned."

Carolyn shrugged her shoulders and said, "That's too bad, I think he would have enjoyed the trip. We better get a move on, though, since we have a lot to see today in Austin."

That day, they had all planned to see the vast main campus

of the University of Texas, their old alma mater. They had wandered through the campus which took the better part of a day.

Christopher drove to the parking lot of the Darrell K. Royal-Texas Memorial Stadium which has a seating capacity of 100,119 persons, the largest football only stadium in the state of Texas. The parking lot was convenient to the sport complex where it was located and also the main campus. Christopher and Carolyn wanted their guests to see the stadium where Christopher was going to be honored at halftime ceremonies of the October 20th Baylor-Texas game by the Texas Silver Spurs.

Dr. Fox was going to join the two couples for the ceremonies. Besides, Natalie had never seen an American college football game and the Texas Longhorns and the Baylor Bears were listed in the top ten collegiate football teams in the country going into the 2012 season. Christopher assured them the game would be one of the highlights of the year.

When Natalie and Dietrich saw the stadium, they were awestruck and Dietrich declared that it was big enough for a small airplane to land on the field. He did not realize at the time how prophetic his statement was!

Behind the art museum at the corner of 21st Street and Speedway is the Perry-Castaneda Library, the main central library for the University of Texas which houses nearly eight million volumes and is the fifth largest library among academic institutions in the United States and is the eleventh largest overall in the country. It was purely unintentional, but the footprint of the library resembles the shape of the state!

The two couples toured the library after seeing the art museum since it was on their way to the main building on campus where the imposing Texas Tower is located overlooking the campus. The main building's tower is 307 feet high and has 28 floors or 30 if you count the carillon room above its huge clock which can be seen from all corners of the campus. The 56 Burleson Bells from the old Victorian-

Gothic Main building which was built in 1882, is the largest in Texas.

There are two elevators to the 27th floor and another elevator to the 28th floor observation deck. The observation deck affords a grand view of the forty acre campus and stadium.

The two couples finished their tour of the campus after taking the elevator to the observation deck. Carolyn and Christopher had seen the tower while they were students at the university, but Christopher was the only one that had actually been to the observation deck before. The two couples marveled at the view which allowed them to see miles into the distance beyond the campus. Carolyn remarked to everyone that they had a good view of the football stadium from the deck.

By the time they had left the tower, the sun was starting to set in the west toward the Administration Building with its extremely large parking lots that took the overflow traffic from the well-attended football games and the student body during daytime class room hours.

When they finally got back to Lake Travis and Rood House at Point Venture, they were exhausted so Carolyn made a light dinner of orange roughy and rice with a mixed fruit salad and a light Chardonnay and settled for Hennessey Brandy and coffee in the Great Room before retiring for the night. They talked about the trip they were going on the next day through San Marcos and New Braunfels to San Antonio, Bandera, and then Corpus Christi and Padre Island. Natalie also wanted to see the Wildlife Bird Reservation outside Port Aransas and Port Lavaca. It was one of the largest bird sanctuaries in the world! Carolyn had already mapped out the week long adventure and its itinerary.

With the vision of their new adventure the next day, they finished their drinks and waved goodnight to each other and retired to their respective bedrooms to get a good night's sleep for tomorrow.

23 SAN ANTONIO

They were all up at the crack of dawn and Carolyn had prepared breakfast and two lunch baskets for their trip. They ate the breakfast, cleaned the dishes and took the lunch baskets to the Rood's Mercedes SUV. They had already packed their clothes the day before and loaded them into the SUV. They were planning on a picnic lunch in one of New Braunfels' parks before heading into San Antonio. Christopher went back to the house to check that nothing had been left behind when the telephone rang.

It was Steve Grant and he apologized for calling so early, but that he had just received a message from the Bundes Nachtricten Dienst that Ahmed and Mohammad had been spotted at a restaurant in Berlin by a policeman that thought they were behaving suspiciously and speaking Arabic.

He took a photo of them and forwarded it through channels, but they had disappeared before they could be arrested. It was a definite ID Steve said firmly, "Please, be on the alert!"

Christopher said they would be cautious. Then they said their goodbyes and Christopher returned to the SUV and whispered to Dietrich, "They've definitely identified Ahmed and Mohammad in Berlin. Don't say anything to Carolyn and

Natalie just yet."

Dietrich nodded his head that he understood.

Interstate Highway 35 from Austin to San Antonio went through San Marcos and New Braunfels before it joined with Loop 410 around San Antonio. They would take the remainder of the day getting there and show Natalie and Dietrich those two cites before going on to the Hilton Hotel on the River Walk of the San Antonio River next to the famous Alamo.

The Hill Country is unique for its fusion of Spanish and Central European (German, Swiss, Austrian, Polish and Czech) influences in food, beer, wine, architecture and music that form a distinctive Texan culture that is separate from the state's Southern and Southwestern influences. The accordion of the German settlers was popularized in the Tejano music of the 19th century. These Central European settlers not only brought their culture, but their language is still heard in the smaller towns. German is still spoken and taught in Fredericksburg and New Braunfels which were settled by the Germans in the 1840s at the time of the Texas Republic! Braunfels means brown rock in German and New Braunfels is named for Braunfels, Germany. New Braunfels has a large German Texan community. New Braunfels' newspaper is the Herald- Zeitung!

They reached San Marcos in less than an hour. It is part of the Austin metropolitan area and was founded on the banks of the San Marcos River whose headwaters are fed by the San Marcos Springs from the Edwards aquifer. The clear cool water flows through the city and its parks. The site of the city reaches back in history over 10,000 years to the Clovis culture. Texas State University-San Marcos is located there. In the 1960s, because of the clear waters, Aquarena Springs and Wonder World were established there. Many famous people including the 36th president of the United States, Lyndon Baines Johnson, attended college there. They stopped at Sewell Park for a few minutes to have a picnic lunch so Carolyn, who was the navigator for the trip, could get her maps in order and to take a look at the beautiful San Marcos River.

They were back on Interstate 35 and in less than 45 minutes were past Live Oak and Windcrest and through Alamo Heights to the downtown area of San Antonio where the Alamo, River Walk, Old San Antonio historic district and outdoor theatre, Hemisfair Park, the Tower of the Americas and San Antonio Convention Center are all located within walking distance of each other!

Christopher drove to the Hilton Palacio del Rio Hotel where they had reservations for the night. They pulled up to the hotel's entrance where they were met by a valet and doorman who took their bags which were promptly whisked off to the registration desk inside the lobby of the spacious hotel. Christopher and Dietrich took their personal belongings to the registration desk where their wives were already standing. A pretty young lady who spoke with a slight Spanish accent looked up at Christopher and smiled. She said that Carolyn had already given her the reservation confirmations for the night and all that she needed was his identification and credit card.

Christopher handed his military identification card since this was a major military town in the United States and where the Joint Military Academy of Health Sciences was located at Fort Sam Houston.

She looked at his credit card and noted the Fort Sam Houston Officers Club logo on his Visa card and that his military identification card identified him as a Colonel in the United States Air Force. Dietrich had handed his military identification card and credit card to her as well before Christopher could explain to him that he was covering both hotel bills.

She noted that he was Maj. Hans Zimmermann in the German Luftwaffe.

Christopher stared at the cards that Dietrich had laid down and pushed them back toward Dietrich, saying he would be paying for both rooms. Then he laughed, "My treat, major!"

Carolyn turned quickly, but didn't say a word. Natalie paid no attention to what had just occurred.

The receptionist's back suddenly stiffened and a serious look flashed across her face. She looked at both men and said, "Sirs, your rooms are adjacent to each other and are ready now! I'm sorry for the slight delay." She swiped Christopher's credit card and handed it back to him along with two electronic keys to Dietrich and two electronic keys to Christopher. She then looked swiftly to the young man who was holding the cart with their bags and said, "Please take these two officers and their wives to their rooms!"

Dietrich looked at Christopher and whispered, "I thought our rooms would be ready at three o'clock and it's only a little past one?"

Christopher smiled and winked at him as he whispered back, "She's been in the military, probably Air Force!"

Meanwhile Carolyn and Natalie had noticed that something had happened, but they didn't understand what and Carolyn asked Christopher, "What was going on?"

Dietrich and Christopher both smiled at their wives quizzical looks and Dietrich blurted out, "Privilege of rank!"

They all laughed as they followed the young man with their bags into the elevator. The elevator rose rapidly to their floor and he took them down to their rooms overlooking the beautiful River Walk and its gardens.

As he unlocked their rooms, he looked at the two couples trying to figure out who they were, and said, "These are rooms that we normally hold for celebrities or VIPs!" "Should I know you?"

Christopher replied, "Nope, we're just two Air Force officers!"

The young man shook his head and turned around to take their bags into their rooms. Christopher took the moment to tell the two ladies that he would explain all about what happened when they had settled into their rooms.

Christopher generously tipped the young man who looked

at him closely and said, "Give me time, it'll come to me who you are!" He then nodded to both Carolyn and Christopher and closed the door behind him when he left the room.

Carolyn then insisted on knowing what went on at the registration desk when the receptionist saw that Dietrich and he were ranking Air Force officers and gave them special attention.

"It's because we both have such beautiful wives!" Christopher said.

Carolyn blushed and then hit him softly on the shoulder and walked into the bathroom to straighten up her hair.

Christopher unlocked his side of the door that connected their two rooms and knocked on it. In a few moments, Dietrich unlocked their side of the double doors and opened it. Natalie and Dietrich smiled at each other and Christopher said to Dietrich, "Okay, give."

Once inside Carolyn and Christopher's room, Dietrich took out his wallet and picked up Natalie's bag to show them the new fake identification cards that had been issued in alias names and addresses for them. "I just wanted to show you our new identities if you need to introduce us to anyone who doesn't know what's going on. Steve Grant gave them to us in Edinburgh."

Christopher glanced over to Carolyn who was smiling.

Carolyn put a finger to her head and said, "Yes, I know. Kate told me and I guess…" she paused looking at her husband, "I forgot to tell you about their new identity and credit cards."

She then turned to Natalie and Dietrich and said, "Kate informed me what Steve was doing and that's why we haven't let you use your new cards and to pay everything in cash. We didn't want anyone to guess who you really are."

Christopher interjected, "I knew that Steve didn't want you to pay for anything except in cash, but I didn't think about new identity cards and credit cards. You surprised me with that fake military ID and credit card from the Luftwaffe. The Luftwaffe certainly thinks of everything."

Dietrich laughed, "It wasn't the Luftwaffe or Steve. It was Kate!"

Laughing they all walked into von Schoenfeld's room and noticed that Dietrich had already poured four drinks, neat, and they were lined up on the serving table next to the bar.

"I couldn't find any unblended Scotch, but they had Makers Mark bourbon," Dietrich said. "Is that okay?"

"Sure!" replied Christopher just as Carolyn entered the room and said, "Got one for me, Dietrich? With a little branch?"

And then she smiled and said, "That's Texan for water."

By this time Natalie had entered the room and added, "Make it the same for me!" She was beginning to act like a Texan!

But even in the midst of their vacation gaiety, they all knew that the bogus identification and credit cards could give Natalie and Dietrich real life-saving anonymity.

The two couples sat down around the table and talked about what they wanted to do the rest of the day. Dietrich said that he wanted to see the famous Alamo where brave Texans had died to give General Sam Houston time to gather an army to defeat General Santa Anna at San Jacinto. William Travis, Davy Crockett, James Bowie and 112 Texan, Tejanos and Scots-Irish volunteers perished. It was located just a few blocks from the River Walk.

Natalie responded that she had seen the Tower of the Americas on the Hemisfair grounds on the way to the hotel and wondered if they could visit it since she had heard so much in Prague about it. It is a 750-foot observation tower/restaurant built for the World's Hemisfair '68. The tower was the tallest observation tower in the United States until 1996.

Carolyn wanted to show them the restored old village of San Antonio with its shops, historic buildings and the River Walk outdoor theatre.

Christopher said that they would enjoy a ride on a riverboat and dinner at a River Walk restaurant. He thought that they might enjoy stopping off first at the Esquire Tavern, the oldest bar on the River Walk with the longest wooden bar in Texas, over 100 feet long! This should be followed by some margaritas and Texas chili, at Barribas Cantina.

Natalie clapped her hands and said, "Okay, let's do everything!"

So they did it all and returned exhausted to their rooms for a nightcap of Hennessey and a good night's sleep.

The next morning they had breakfast in their rooms and strolled down the River Walk in the early morning sunshine with the birds chirping their morning songs. It reminded Carolyn of the decks that hung out and under the tree branches outside of their house.

When they returned to their rooms, they called the porter and he collected their baggage and took it down to their waiting Mercedes SUV. Christopher had already paid the hotel bill electronically before they had left their rooms. He tipped the porter, doorman and valet respectively and they all got into their vehicle for the drive over to Bandera and then on to Corpus Christi.

Christopher explained that he had to drop by his office at the South Texas Medical Center to check on some on-going research in which his residents were involved. Christopher drove to the medical center and turned into the Medical School Parking Garage A and parked in his assigned faculty parking space. He asked Natalie and Dietrich if they wanted to accompany him to his office and get a look at the University of Texas Medical Center where he worked. They answered that they would and they followed Christopher and Carolyn to the University of Texas Medical School.

Christopher took the outside walk rather than the tunnel to the medical school. They walked past the Academic and Administration Building and Christopher pointed out the Methodist Hospital to their left and the University Hospital behind the Texas Medical School Building. Much of his research was at the University Hospital and Methodist Hospital he said. He mentioned that the Dolph Briscoe Jr.

Library on the other side of the Medical School and the University of Texas Dental School was a frequent gathering place for the students and residents to study.

They walked into the Medical School and to Christopher's office. As they entered, Christopher's secretary, Samantha Gruenwald, looked up and smiled. "Long time, no see!"

Christopher smiled back and introduced Natalie and Dietrich. Samantha, or Sam as Christopher called her, seemed glad to see her boss. She told him that the new three dimensional computerized equipment had just been delivered and was already installed, so that the research for which he had received a large grant could be commenced as soon as he got back from his three-week vacation. She also mentioned that Dr. Harries from Atlanta had called and said that he would call you back as soon as you got back from your vacation. He said that he had made all the arrangements for Libertyville.

She further added, "Oh, there was a telephone call for you from a Dr. Smythe of the Venerable Order of Saint John. He asked about you and your cousin, Natalie. I told him that I didn't know anything about your relatives and that you were on vacation. He said that he would get in touch with you later. When I asked him if he wanted to leave a message, he said no and that he would call you back at another time. He sounded strange and with an accent that didn't sound English. I also noticed that the call was from Prague, Czech Republic."

Christopher raised his eyebrows and muttered under his breath, "Mohammad up to his old tricks!" He looked at Dietrich and then back to Sam, and said, "Good girl, probably some solicitor!" And then he winked at her. "If he should call back, don't tell him anything about Dietrich or Natalie. After all, Dietrich isn't supposed to be alive!"

She nodded and said that she understood.

Samantha Gruenwald had been Christopher's devoted secretary and confidant for years and was discreet about Dr. Rood's business and his investigations. She said, "If you want,

Perhaps it will help him in his investigations!"

Christopher told her that it would be good of her to do that and for her to give his and Carolyn's best to Steve and his new wife Katie Sue. He knew that by this time, she and Steve's secretary and wife had become very good long distance friends!

Christopher quickly looked over a stack of mail and concluded that it could wait until he returned to work next week. Carolyn and Natalie were exchanging recipes with Samantha and Dietrich was looking out of a window that overlooked the South Texas Medical Center. He appeared to be very bored about the recipe talk.

Christopher walked over to Dietrich and patted him on the shoulder and said, "It looks as though our good friend, Smythe knows that Natalie is in Texas and was on a fishing expedition when he called my office and talked to Sam."

Dietrich appeared uneasy.

"You shouldn't have any concerns, Sam is very good at keeping these persistent types at bay! Let's not worry about him and just go on down to Corpus Christi and enjoy ourselves."

The ladies finished exchanging recipes when Christopher announced to them that he had caught up on the news for the time being and that they should be on their way to Bandera for a light lunch and a look around the city. They said their farewells to Sam and she congratulated them on their wedding and wished them well with their visit to the United States.

The two couples said their goodbyes to Samantha, went to the garage and their car and then headed west to Highway 16-Bandera Road where they exited north towards Bandera. The area around Bandera Pass had been the demarcation point between the settlers and the Indians.

In 1843, forty Texas Rangers lead by Colonel Jack Hays were ambushed in the pass by a superior force of Comanche warriors and would have been massacred if it had not been for the fact that the Rangers were armed by the new Colt Walker revolver which surprised the Indians with its superior firepower. Five Rangers lost their lives and scores of Indians including their chief lost their lives. The day of the repeating revolver had arrived!

Bandera later became the staging area for driving vast herds of Texas cattle north along the Western Trail to Dodge City, Kansas. In 1874, the first of many herds, estimated at 6 million cattle over the next 20 years travelled the trail to Dodge City. The city prospered and in 1890 an ornate courthouse was built.

The San Antonio highway was built in 1936 and by 1948 there were 17 "dude" ranches catering to the booming tourist trade. The dude ranch owners proclaimed Bandera as the Cowboy Capital of the World and that year organized its first "Stompede."

Mansfield Park had held its first rodeo in 1924 and became the training ground for future rodeo champions. Western movies were filmed there and famous riders, ropers and gunslingers performed for the tourist crowds. Some of the old stores, post office, mill, cotton gin, and a bed and breakfast—the "Mansion"—is in Bandera, as well as the several "honky-tonks" that are attractions for artists, musicians, cowboys and ranchers that mingle with the tourists.

In a little less than an hour the two couples found themselves in Bandera. They parked their SUV and wandered around the small town and had a quick lunch in one of the honky-tonks just to say that they had been in an old time saloon. Natalie and Dietrich even bought a couple of real Texas Stetsons and convinced Carolyn and Christopher that they needed the legendary Stetsons before they could enter the saloon, so they could have a real cowboy lunch and take pictures of each other. Carolyn and Christopher declined to tell them that they already had theirs at home!

After lunch they got back into the SUV for the long trek down Interstate 37 to Corpus Christi.

24 MEXICO CITY

Mohammad and Ahmed ali were looking out of their hotel room at the Four Seasons Hotel on the Paseo de la Reforma just 500 steps from the Chapultepec Park and the exclusive Polanco neighborhood and the Zona Rosa. The view of the fountain and courtyard were magnificent, but their minds were on the report from one of their agents in Austin, Texas.

He had been taking photographs of Natalie and her cousin, Carolyn, as they were shopping for a trip to Corpus Christi. The agent had followed them and entered the shop where they were shopping after noticing them walking down the street while he was driving by. All of the Brotherhood agents in Texas had been on the alert since photographs of Natalie had been distributed to them. They had been put on the alert since Mohammad had ordered his son to have all members of the Brotherhood in Texas look for her.

He had been close enough to Carolyn and Natalie to hear Carolyn talking to Natalie about diving on the oil rigs off the coast of Corpus Christi. They were looking at various bathing suits and clothes for that purpose. He had heard Carolyn say that her husband Christopher was keen to see the famous aircraft carrier, Lexington which was on permanent station there and that she was looking forward to the trip.

At about that time, Carolyn had noticed the young man watching them and they hurriedly left the shop with their purchases. He had not followed them in order to divert attention from himself and not arouse suspicion.

He sent the pictures to the Brotherhood headquarters in a mosque in Houston.

They had verified Carolyn's and Natalie's identification and forwarded the information to Ahmed and Mohammad in Mexico City.

Ahmed had remarked to his father that maybe they should also kidnap Carolyn and sell her as well as Natalie to the slave markets since she was also beautiful.

Mohammad went ballistic over that remark and quickly reprimanded him for the suggestion since they did not want to create an uproar like the Holloway case in Aruba. It was one thing to kidnap Natalie and quite another one to kidnap a prominent American citizen. It was okay to kill Americans, but kidnapping them in America was far too risky.

Ahmed nodded that he agreed with his father.

Mohammad then said that the best thing would be try to kidnap her while they were diving on the oil rigs since they were in international waters. The trick would be if there were no other boats around, then they could board Natalie's boat like pirates and take her by gunpoint, kill the others, and sink their boat. That way there would be no witnesses and she and her cousins would simply disappear. At least until they might find some of the bodies later and everyone would just assume that she was lost at sea and not look for her. If there were other boats around, it might cause a major problem, since they would have to kill more people and take more hostages. No, if they could not isolate them at the rigs, they could wait until she was isolated at the Lexington and take her there.

"Tell your agents in Corpus Christi to be discreet and if plan one at the rigs doesn't happen, then we can go to plan two at the Lexington," Mohammad told Ahmad. "Use two or possibly three agents and when she is isolated, use a fast acting sedative like propofol injected into her arm to make it appear that she's fainted and then they can safely take her off the carrier with no one the wiser."

He added, "Tell them to be patient and follow her until the right moment when she is most vulnerable and isolated, by herself, before they acted. If need be, after she's injected, they can prevent anyone nearby who tries to interfere by showing them fake IDs and pretending to be related. We don't want a scuffle!"

He continued, "After they abduct her, bring her to me here in Mexico City for the necessary physical examination before we dispose of her. I want to personally tell her of her fate in the slave or transplant markets of the Middle East." Then he added, "We may even want to have our way with her!"

And then he winked at his son.

25 CORPUS CHRISTI

It took them about three hours to reach Lake Corpus Christi and then to Calallen past Nueces Bay to Corpus Christi. Christopher decided to drive past Spohn Hospital and Driscoll Hospital after viewing downtown Corpus Christi and the marina on Shoreline Drive. They turned off Shoreline Boulevard into the driveway of the Omni Corpus Christi Hotel on North Shoreline Boulevard. After parking the SUV in front of the hotel, Christopher asked the valet if they could keep their vehicle parked there for a half hour until they checked into their suites since they wanted to drive around the city for a while until coming back for dinner.

The valet nodded his agreement and Christopher tipped him ten dollars for his courtesy. Their bags were taken to the Registration Desk and they checked into two adjacent Bayview Suites.

The pretty registration clerk smiled at the two couples as they checked in. She noticed the military identification cards that Christopher and Dietrich showed her and asked them if they were going out to the Naval Air Station. They answered that they were merely on vacation and not on duty assignments.

She remarked that the two suites had 875 square feet of area and a large living and dining room, kitchenette, wet bar, bedroom with king size bed, bathroom and a private balcony overlooking Corpus Christi Bay, the Marina and the USS Lexington of World War II fame.

Christopher nodded his approval and she then swiped his credit card and gave them their respective electronic keys and motioned to a bellhop to take their bags to their rooms. The couples followed him to the elevator and up to their rooms on the fourteenth floor. Christopher tipped the bellhop after he placed their bags in their respective rooms.

After going to their rooms, Christopher called the Republic of Texas Bar and Grill in the hotel and made reservations for four at nine o'clock that night.

Twenty minutes later, Natalie and Dietrich knocked on Carolyn and Christopher's door.

Carolyn answered the door and said, "Come on in and have a Scotch. I've already poured some Lismore, neat, with soda on the side. Christopher is still in the bathroom trying to look wonderful for the evening. You know how husbands are!"

She winked at Natalie and she replied, "I certainly do!"

Dietrich remained nonplussed and did not respond, but instead walked over to his drink and took a sip and then walked over to Natalie with her drink in his hand, kissed her and then handed her drink to her and quietly said, "I forgive you both!"

About this time Christopher entered the room and said, "What did I miss," when he saw the looks on Carolyn's and Natalie's faces.

Carolyn looked up at her husband as she handed him his drink and replied, "Not a thing!" and then she smiled and put her arm around her husband's waist and gave him a gentle hug.

After they finished their drinks, they walked down to the elevator and took it to the lobby where they went out to their waiting car. They got into the SUV and drove down Shoreline

Boulevard past Sherrill and McCaughan Parks to Morgan Avenue where the new Spohn Shoreline Hospital is and turned right onto Morgan Avenue down to the old Spohn Hospital where Christopher had been a resident.

After seeing that hospital, Christopher retraced his way back to Shoreline Drive to Ocean Drive and turned south so Natalie and Dietrich could see Cole Park with its amphitheater and down to Rossiter Street where he turned right and went to South Alameda Street where Driscoll Children's Hospital and the old Ada Wilson Hospital are located. Those were the hospitals where Carolyn had done her residency.

He then went down South Alameda Street to where Doddridge Street intersected and turned left until he got back onto Ocean Drive so that they could see the Bay again. They continued across a bridge to where the old Corpus Christi Junior College had been that is now Texas A&M University-Corpus Christi.

As they continued down Ocean Drive to South Padre Island Drive, they saw the Naval Air Station where the movie actor, Tyrone Power had taken flight training before heading to the South Pacific. He had been a Marine Corps aviator during World War II.

They headed down South Padre Island Drive to Padre Ballie Park where they noticed that the sea breeze had picked up. They turned into the entrance and drove down to the beach. The sun was just starting to dip toward the horizon with a red glow casting its color onto the whitecaps that were beginning to break with the incoming tide and increased winds. It was absolutely beautiful and a fitting end to a day long drive from San Antonio.

When they got out of the SUV and walked down to the sea, they took off their shoes and held them in their hands as they walked into the breaking surf. Dietrich and Christopher wrapped their arms around their wives' waists and held them close as they peered into the orange ball of the setting sun.

They all took a deep breath of the refreshing sea breeze

and turned and walked back to the SUV. There were some towels in the back of the SUV and they dried their feet. Carolyn had anticipated this possibility. They put their shoes on and got back into the vehicle and drove back to Corpus Christi and their suites at the Omni Corpus Christi Hotel.

Christopher had some Lismore Scotch waiting for Natalie and Dietrich when they knocked on his door. The ladies had changed into light weight strapped summer evening dresses. They looked exceptionally beautiful, Christopher thought as he handed the wives their drinks.

Carolyn was wearing a beautiful emerald green dress that enhanced the green of her eyes that seemed blue during daylight hours but now sparkled like emeralds. Natalie wore a crisp light blue evening dress that embraced her tanned shoulders and dark brown hair that fell over one shoulder.

Dietrich and Christopher were dressed in ivory white dinner jackets and midnight blue trousers. Their summer weight white shirts with French cuffs and cufflinks were left open at the collar in deference to the semitropical weather in Corpus Christi and the casual atmosphere of the restaurant they were going to.

They both wore Order of Saint John cufflinks. Christopher's bore the familiar plain white Maltese cross on a red ground while Dietrich's was a white Maltese cross with the Prussian Eagle interposed between the arms of the white cross on a black ground. Each branch of the Order of Saint John had their own specific type of Maltese cross.

Dietrich raised his glass in a salute to Texas and their hosts and they all sipped the Scotch that tasted somehow better now that they had arrived at their hotel.

When they arrived at the Republic of Texas Bar and Grill, they were promptly seated at a table for four next to the glass windows that afforded a panoramic view of Corpus Christi Bay and the Marina. They could clearly see the yachts that were lined up evenly in their berths and the USS Lexington standing majestically in the distance at its dock.

Natalie remarked at the beauty of the view of the bay and

the sparkling lights that seemed to dance on the rippling waves of water. They could see the running lights of a few sailboats that were out for an evening sail in the almost full moon that was rising above the water in the bay.

It was Tuesday the 28th day of August and the weather was magnificently clear with a brilliant canopy of bright stars. Christopher asked if they wanted to go sailing in the bay and the Laguna Madre the next day and take a picnic lunch on Padre Island, perhaps down by Port Aransas and the bird sanctuary where the largest birds in Texas, the whooping crane could be seen or did they want to tour the USS Lexington with its interactive exhibits that would probably consume the better part of the day.

Natalie declared that she would rather sail and see the whooping cranes while Dietrich calmly said that he would like to see the World War II aircraft carrier, but that he would yield to Natalie's wishes if it was okay with Carolyn. Carolyn smiled and shook her head agreeing with Natalie, and Natalie clapped her hands in delight. Christopher smiled and said that he would make all the arrangements for the next morning if Carolyn and Natalie would make the arrangements for the picnic luncheon.

The waiter arrived shortly after the decision was made for the next day's excursion and gave them a menu for dinner and asked if they wanted any appetizers or aperitif. They looked at their menus and decided on the Carnitas, for openers.

Christopher suggested a glass of Merlot wine and they all agreed. The waiter departed and soon returned with the wine while they discussed what they wanted for their meals.

It all looked appetizing. Carolyn and Natalie agreed that they would like to have the Texas Bob White Quail with Wild Rice Pilaf. Dietrich and Christopher split their decision. Dietrich chose the Veal Osso Bucco with a side of Wilted Spinach Salad. Christopher chose the Broken Arrow Ranch Venison Grilled 10 ounce Loin Cut with a Caesar Salad.

Carolyn and Natalie said that they would like a Piesporter

Michelsberg wine for their dinner while Dietrich and Christopher said they would stay with the Merlot. They all agreed on Hennessey Brandy and coffee with Key Lime Pie for dessert. Christopher said that he had been told by some of the doctors at the South Texas Medical Center about Corpus Christi restaurants and they all swore by this restaurant.

They soon found that the doctors had not been wrong. Their meals were excellent and they felt good after the long day's trip and Christopher left a more than generous tip and praised the waiters for their excellent service.

When they arrived back at their rooms, Dietrich stretched his arms and announced that the day had been wonderful, but tiring and he was ready for a good night's sleep. They all agreed that they were ready for bed and Carolyn invited them to their room for breakfast, but not until nine o'clock in the morning. Christopher added that everyone should be ready in boating attire and deck shoes!

They then waved goodnight as they went into their respective rooms for a welcome sleep.

As Carolyn and Christopher entered their rooms, Carolyn announced that she was ready for bed. They undressed and just left their clothes on the sofa. They walked over to the bed. Carolyn then turned and walked over to the light next to the living room couch and turned it off. The room was immediately engulfed in darkness as she sauntered over to the large glass doors that led to their balcony and opened the drapes to the view of the bay and its sparkling lights. The moon was a quarter of the way in its transit of the night sky and its illumination spread into the room leaving a soft light across Carolyn and falling onto the carpeted floor. Carolyn looked over to Christopher and smiled. She then turned, walked back to him and they slipped under the covers and she wrapped her arms around her husband.

Meanwhile Natalie and Dietrich had entered their rooms and turned on the lights. Dietrich sat down on the couch, took off his shoes and laid his coat on the back of the couch.

He leaned back and put feet on the coffee table in front of the couch and sighed, "Boy, am I exhausted!"

Natalie, who had pulled the drapes open and slid the glass door to their private balcony back to reveal the magnificent harbor view, turned and said, "What did you say dear?"

Dietrich turned and saw that his wife had stepped out onto the balcony and yelled to her, "I said that I was exhausted!"

Natalie saw that their balcony was isolated from the other balconies and afforded them a completely private view of the marina and the night sky. The moon was absolutely beautiful with not a cloud in the sky. The stars hung in the sky like Christmas lights and the sky was unusually dark for a night with a near full moon.

Natalie turned toward Dietrich with a sly grin on her face and twitched her nose and motioned for Dietrich to join her. Dietrich walked out onto the balcony and his feet felt cold on the matted concrete floor. Natalie put her arm around Dietrich waist and for a few minutes they stood there looking at the moon and harbor lights.

She then turned and disappeared into the suite. He was looking out toward the harbor when the interior lights went out. He turned and saw Natalie standing in a shaft of moonlight that flooded through the glass door and windows into the suite. It was then that he noticed that she had only slippers on. She was naked and looking absolutely gorgeous in the soft moonlight. She had loosened her hair and it had tumbled over her shoulders onto her breasts. She motioned for him to come inside.

Dietrich stood there for a moment. She took his breath away and he suddenly didn't feel tired at all.

She moved slowly toward him and put her arms around his neck and pulled his face down to hers. She had to stand on the tips of her bare toes to reach him.

They embraced and kept their kiss for a few minutes before she started to unbutton his shirt and slowly undressed him.

They kissed passionately for several minutes with the soft breeze from the bay enveloping them in the moonlight. He turned her around gently caressed her. She took his hand and led him to their bed where they slid under the covers and made passionate love until they fell asleep in each other's arms. Morning came too soon and the sunrise was bright enough to cast its shadows onto the deck.

At nine o'clock, Natalie and Dietrich knocked on Carolyn and Christopher's door and Christopher opened it and cheerfully said, "I hope that the two of you had a good night's sleep?"

Natalie cast her eyes downward as she smiled and said that they had a wonderful night's sleep and they both declared that they were famished and ready for a day of sailing and bird watching.

Carolyn yelled from the kitchenette and said that the waiter had just brought up their breakfasts and that she was just finishing putting a morning bouquet of yellow roses on the table. She had ordered them from the florists and Christopher had already made the arrangements for a small sloop rigged boat with a mainsail and a jib.

He said that it was a typical Bermuda sloop with a Marconi mainsail rig and a small jib sail. It was a 34-foot Catalina sloop named *Winds of Corpus Christi*.

Dietrich remarked that he had sailed a similar boat when he was young and vacationing in Geneva. He said that he really enjoyed Lake Geneva and those summers so long ago. He remembered that you could always find your way back to Geneva by seeing the Jet d'Eau Fountain which was at the juncture of where Lake Geneva empties into the Rhone River. It jets water 459 feet into the air and can be seen from all over the city and from an altitude of 33,000 feet. It is lit at night.

Christopher said that Carolyn and he had always enjoyed sailing in the bay and Laguna Madre since the winds in Corpus Christi were constant and sailing was always good. He had brought with him a Leica digital camera that he said could also take pictures underwater and two Leica binoculars for viewing the birds and the scenery around the Bay.

Carolyn looked at Natalie and smiled.

Natalie blurted out, "You mean the girls in their bathing suits don't you?"

Christopher looked sheepish and said, "Well yes, that too!"

Natalie replied, "Well, Carolyn and I have our bikinis on under these sailing shorts and blouses and that will have to do for the both of you!"

Carolyn said that she hoped that a breakfast of poached eggs and toast with a fruit salad and orange juice and coffee would be okay. She had also ordered a noon picnic lunch with egg salad and tuna salad sandwiches with potato chips and pretzels along with some Sam Adams beer and ale to drink. It had been delivered earlier from the hotel's kitchen and she had it packed over the beer cans on ice in the large ice cooler that had been delivered from the Corpus Christi Bay Yacht Club.

Christopher announced that if they got back early enough, they would be able to watch the Midget Ocean Racing Fleet races that are held every Wednesday night. The yacht club promotes sailing in the Coastal Bend area of Texas.

He then mentioned that the Corpus Christi Buccaneer Days Carnival celebrated its 75th year on April 9th, 2012, to commemorate the invasion of Corpus Christi Bay by the pirate Jean Lafitte and his crew of cutthroats in 1821—and possibly stashing $500,000 in gold along the coast. He said that next year the celebration would be held on May 3rd, 2013, and maybe they could all get together for it.

Dietrich replied, "Why not?"

They ate their breakfast leisurely in the suite and then put their gear together and left for the yacht club that was just behind their hotel. They walked down the pier to the slip where the *Winds of Corpus Christi* was docked and placed all their gear in the cabin. Carolyn put the lunches in the refrigerator and placed the sheets that Natalie and Carolyn had brought on which to sunbathe onto the gimbaled table.

Dietrich untied the mooring lines as Christopher raised the foresail. Dietrich took the helm and the wind gently caught the sail. He deftly maneuvered the boat from the dock towards the open water of Corpus Christi Bay. Christopher then raised the mainsail and the *Winds of Corpus Christi* began a long swift reach toward the middle of the bay.

The day went pretty much as they had planned and the blue and white sloop sailed perfectly and swiftly before the constant breeze. They arrived outside the Wildlife Bird sanctuary where they had a little snack of cheese sticks and ale. As they were finishing their repast, they were able to spot some whooping cranes in flight and takes some pictures. The sun became warm and the breeze was welcome. The two wives disappeared below decks to the main cabin and peeled off their outer clothes to their bikini swimming suits and laid them neatly on the galley table next to the sheets.

Christopher popped his head through the cabin door and asked them if they wanted him to place the inflatable mattress on the foredeck.

"No, not just yet. Maybe later after lunch. We want to look at the birds and the other boats."

Christopher nodded his head and went back out on deck and resumed his sailor duties. The two ladies poured sun screen and lotion over each other. Natalie remarked to Carolyn how beautiful she looked in her new bikini.

Carolyn blushed and said, "I didn't have the courage to wear a bikini until you insisted during our Austin shopping spree. I hope that Christopher likes it. I think you look better in yours. Mine looks like a Mother Hubbard next to yours."

"Mother Hubbard, what does that mean?"

"You know, more matronly."

Natalie looked at her and remarked, "I have an extra one just like the one I have on except it's green not blue like the one I have on. I haven't worn it. Try it on and see what you think, it will probably fit you. I have it in my bag and you're welcome to it."

Natalie walked over to her bag and pulled out her other bikini and gave it to Carolyn.

Carolyn took it and disappeared into the foc'sle cabin bedroom and closed the door behind her. When she came out a few minutes later, she said, "What do you think?"

"You're going to wow both Christopher and Dietrich!" Natalie said. Then she added, "Is wow the correct word?"

"I hope so," she replied as she looked down at the bikini. Natalie kissed her on the cheek and said, "Everything will be just fine."

They put their blouses on over their bathing suits and buttoned them at the waist. They decided not to wear their straw hats since the wind was quite strong.

They climbed up the stairs to the main deck and Christopher and Dietrich both did a double take and Dietrich whistled and said, "You both look positively ravishing!"

The two ladies smiled and looked at each other as the wind caught their blouses and exposed their bikinis and their hair was swept around their shoulders.

Christopher said, "You both would make a great picture!" And then, he took a picture of them.

After an hour of sailing and watching the birds, they decided that it was time for lunch. Meanwhile Christopher and Dietrich had furled the sails and dropped a sand anchor fore and aft. The boat stabilized and gently rolled with the very slight waves in the bay. It was noontime and the surface of the water was almost flat as the wind had slowed to a slight breeze—almost calm. They joined their wives in the cabin and Dietrich remarked how good the lunch looked.

They looked at their wives and Christopher chimed in that they both looked beautiful, but should be careful to use enough lotion or keep their blouses on since the sun was overhead.

The beer was ice cold and tasted good with their lunch. Just as they finished their meal, the wind started to pick up and they hurriedly cleaned up the table and galley and put the empty paper plates and beer cans into a plastic waste bag to dispose of back at the marina.

The two men went on deck and hauled the anchors on board and unfurled the sails and trimmed them. Soon they were back sailing smoothly toward Mustang Island. The ladies reappeared on deck with their blouses on but loosely buttoned.

They tacked north towards Aransas Pass where they could do some more bird watching. Natalie said that she thought that she had seen some whooping cranes and some pelicans. The seagulls were swooping down to the water and picking up unlucky fish that were too close to the surface.

Christopher got out his camera and started taking pictures of the birds. Dietrich was at the helm and kept the boat on a steady course. The ladies were watching all of the action through the binoculars and remarking how close the birds came to their boat.

Christopher turned to Dietrich and then to Carolyn and Natalie and said, "What do you think, would all of you like to do some snorkeling at the oil rigs?"

In unison, everyone said, "Yes!"

"Okay let's head for Aransas Pass."

Dietrich turned the wheel at the helm and tacked toward the East and Aransas Pass. They soon arrived, furled the sails, and secured them. They started their auxiliary engines, cleared the pass and headed for the open sea.

"Sure glad we have auxiliary engines, it made it a lot easier to get through the pass," Christopher said.

Dietrich agreed and after raising their sails again, they headed for the rig about 15 miles off the coast. They had not noticed the fishing boat that had followed them through the pass. The three men with black hair and beards with swarthy complexions were keeping their boat well astern of the *Winds of Corpus Christi.*

As Aransas Pass disappeared over the horizon and the oil rigs appeared on the horizon, a yacht coming from the rigs sailed past them with several college kids on board. They were drinking Lone Star beer from cans and a couple of the boys were throwing the empty cans over board. One of the girls that were on board went over to them and was waving her hand and yelling at them. They could barely hear her remarks, but it was obvious that she was castigating them for throwing the beer cans overboard.

Natalie ran over to Dietrich and whispered into his ear, "They're not wearing any clothes!"

"I noticed," Dietrich replied, raising an eyebrow. "We're in international waters and they can legally do whatever they want as long as they don't break international law which does not address clothing."

"Oh! I didn't know," replied Natalie.

Carolyn and Christopher smiled. And then Christopher pointed to the oil rigs and said, "It looks like we're going to have company at the rigs."

They all looked in the direction of the rigs and saw that there were three other boats clustered around the rigs that acted as artificial reefs that attracted the multicolored fish that inhabited the shores of the Gulf of Mexico.

As they approached a rig, Dietrich adroitly maneuvered their boat close to it as Christopher dropped the sails and furled them. He then dropped their sand anchors and the boat slowly stopped and snuggled in close to the rig. They dropped their diving buoy and anchor indicating that divers were below.

The fishing boat trailing them had also stopped and dropped its anchor. The men aboard had their binoculars trained on the *Winds of Corpus Christi*.

Christopher had been watching them for the last fifteen minutes. He turned to Dietrich and remarked, "What do you think of that fishing boat behind us?"

Dietrich turned and looked through his binoculars at the boat. "I don't like the looks of the crew. They don't look like fishermen to me. What do you think?"

Christopher paused and then said, "Let's watch them and make sure they are really fishing. You know that boat stopped about two hundred yards astern, but I don't see any fishing gear. They seem to be watching us. We will continue to keep a watch on deck."

Christopher went below decks and came up with four sets of snorkeling gear. He had arranged with the yacht club for the gear when he chartered the boat earlier.

Dietrich had picked a spot sufficiently away from the others just in case they might be spear fishing, but in a few minutes they quickly became aware that everyone was sightseeing with cameras and not spear guns.

Christopher said that he would trade off with Dietrich staying as watch on deck while the others were diving. Dietrich then told Carolyn and Natalie that he would go initially with them and then later trade off with Christopher.

Christopher whispered to Dietrich, "Let's keep our suspicions to ourselves and not tell Carolyn and Natalie just yet."

The three of them then got into the water with their gear. They adjusted their masks, took a deep breath and descended into the water to look at the many fish that were swimming around the barnacled substructure of the rig.

A few minutes later one of the more colorful small fish came up to Natalie's mask and peered inside. It startled her and she rose to the surface and took a deep breath. She started to laugh and turned toward Christopher who was watching anxiously from the deck and yelled, "I've just been kissed by a fish!"

They both laughed and Christopher yelled back, "Don't tell Dietrich. He'll be jealous."

She laughed again, waved, took a deep breath and disappeared beneath the water and found Dietrich pointing out some of the fish to Carolyn. She swam up to him and hugged one of his arms. She then swam to Carolyn and motioned for her to surface. The three of them surfaced and she told them what had happened.

Dietrich raised an eyebrow and said, "As long as it's only a fish." And then, he laughed and disappeared under the water to take some photographs with the Leica in its underwater camera case that Christopher had lent him.

Later, Dietrich exchanged places with Christopher and Dietrich handed him the camera just before he descended beneath the slightly rolling water to take more pictures.

After about a half an hour more of snorkeling, they decided that it was time to head back to Corpus Christi. Two of the other boats were weighing anchor and they decided to do the same. They weighed anchor and Dietrich decided to use the auxiliary engines to go with them.

The three boats including the *Winds of Corpus Christi* all passed the anchored fishing boat.

The bearded man at the helm of the fishing boat snarled at his comrades in Arabic, "Those infidels are damn lucky. If they had been alone, we could have boarded their boat, killed the men, kidnapped the women and then sunk their boat in deeper water where it would never be found. We missed our chance today. Damn those other boats."

He slammed his fist into the palm of his other hand and then muttered, "Tomorrow, they won't be so lucky, we'll get her then!"

The three boats headed for Aransas Pass, but the fishing boat stayed in place. The bearded man at the helm then spun the wheel around towards Aransas Pass, picked up his cell phone and called Ahmed. When Ahmed answered the phone, he said, "I couldn't isolate them so we could grab her. There were three other boats with them at the rigs the entire time, and they left a guard on deck to act as a look out."

There was a pause as if he were listening and then he said, arguing, into the phone, "Why don't we just kill them, it would be easier than kidnapping her. We wouldn't have to get so close to them or isolate her."

There was another long pause. After the man hung up, he said to the crew that they were going to try again tomorrow and they were instructed to go to Aransas Pass, return the fishing boat to the boat rental firm and then return to the rooms they had there. They would receive their instructions later from Ahmed after he talked to his father, Mohammad.

After the *Winds of Corpus Christi* cleared Aransas Pass, Christopher and Dietrich turned off the auxiliary engines and raised their sails. Suddenly the wind shifted and picked up. Dietrich and Christopher decided they had better move back into calmer waters since the waves were beginning to break over the bow of the boat and they were far out into the bay. They turned about and headed toward calmer water. Natalie and Carolyn decided they could probably sunbathe.

They took off their shirts and put them on the benches in the cabin and then went to the foredeck where Christopher had tied down an inflatable mattress covered with a fitted sheet. They then stretched out on it. The breezes were calmer and the water had flattened out to smooth swells.

The waves were now almost dead calm. They undid the top and back straps of their bikini tops so that there would be no white line where they tanned. The two husbands were already in their swim suits and were busy handling the steering and the lines as they tacked across the bay. Then they sailed over to a secluded part of Oso Bay near the Pharaoh Valley subdivision known as the Hans and Pat Suter Wildlife Refuge, famous for sea bird watching. They released the anchor chains fore and aft after furling the sails. It was a sheltered cove and the boat slid to a halt and stabilized itself, swinging gently in the light breeze.

The sun was warm and Carolyn and Natalie asked their husbands to rub some more lotion on their backs and legs so they wouldn't burn and then join them in sunbathing. Christopher and Dietrich peeled off their shirts and rubbed the tanning lotion profusely over their bodies and then went to the foredeck where Natalie and Carolyn were lying on the blankets they had spread out. They heard their husbands approaching and as they turned to look at them they clutched the bikini tops to keep their breasts covered.

Natalie said they looked handsome in their bathing suits and they both smiled. Dietrich ignored the remark and said that they would rub the lotion on their backs if they turned over onto their stomachs. The two wives agreed and turned over.

Dietrich and Christopher stood over their wives and dripped the lotion on their wives' backs, legs and arms. Both ladies squealed as the cold liquid fell on their warm bodies, but it felt good as their husbands rubbed the lotion over their bodies. Christopher and Dietrich knelt over their wives and the lotion was cool to their warm backs, arms and legs as their husbands massaged the liquid into their skin.

Natalie then turned over and let her bikini top fall to the side and onto the sheet. She looked up at Dietrich and curled her finger toward him and said, "And now the front!"

Carolyn and Christopher were surprised and it showed on their faces as they gasped. Natalie quickly explained that nudity while sunbathing in Europe was commonplace. Dietrich began applying lotion on Natalie and massaging her as he softly explained that in the United States it wasn't legal to sunbathe in the nude in public and that she would have to put her top back on.

Natalie started to complain and Dietrich turned to Carolyn and said, "Is that true?"

Carolyn then looked up at Christopher and then back to Natalie and said, "It's true that you can only sunbathe nude in private or certain selected areas in Texas."

Natalie said that it didn't make any sense to her, but she would comply with the law to please Dietrich and Carolyn and started to put her top on, then she pouted her lips and turned to Carolyn and pleaded, "What about those two ladies we saw in the boat that were naked? Besides, I'll look like a zebra and won't have an even tan!"

Carolyn looked up sheepishly at Christopher and then Dietrich, shrugged her shoulders. She paused and then looked back up to her husband and as Christopher leaned down, she whispered into his ear, "Darling ... she does make a lot of sense!"

Christopher looked at Dietrich and then at Carolyn, shrugged his shoulders and silently began rubbing the lotion onto Carolyn's back.

Natalie smiled and laid her bikini top back on the sheet.

The sun was beginning to go down as they pulled the *Winds of Corpus Christi* into its slip at the Marina. They had already put their clothes on by the time they sailed into the marina and were glad they had put some sun screen on, but the tips of all of their noses were slightly red.

They walked wearily back to the hotel and their rooms exhausted and slightly sunburned. They thought that they would order dinner in their rooms and Natalie insisted that they have the dinner served in their suite that night and for Carolyn and Christopher to come back early so they could watch the boat races from their balcony and have some Scotch and hors d'oeuvres.

Carolyn and Christopher went to their room, showered and took a short nap after which they dressed casually and went to the von Schoenfelds' room where they were greeted by Natalie. They too had showered and were also dressed casually. The hors d'oeuvres were laid out on a table on the balcony along with the Scotch. Dietrich poured a Scotch for both of them and proceeded to talk about the kind of small boat sailing races that he had participated in as a youth during his summers in Switzerland.

They had a front row seat from the balcony for the monthly small boat match races that were commencing. They all enjoyed sailing and they gathered on the balcony where they could sit and watch the swift piloting and maneuvering that these races afforded the young skippers of these sailing boats.

Dietrich delighted in explaining the finer points of sailing to their guests. Natalie hung on every word that her husband was saying and didn't have the heart to tell him that she was a sailing champion in her youth in the Czech Republic. She pondered how she was going to let him teach her how to sail and how fast a pupil she would be!

When the dinner arrived at eight o'clock, they decided to eat in the small dining room next to the living room in their suite. The dinner was perfect since they had a light lunch and a strenuous day sailing. Everyone was satisfied and, when they got to the Grand Marnier, Christopher proposed a toast to the honeymooners. He and Carolyn touched their glasses to the glasses of their cousins and, after drinking their toast, took their leave. They waved goodnight to Natalie and Dietrich as they trudged down to their rooms tired, but happy.

Tomorrow was to be their last day in Corpus Christi before they left the following morning to go back to Austin. The two couples met each other the next morning for breakfast at eight o'clock at the Glass Pavilion Restaurant in the hotel.

Dietrich and Christopher were talking about the USS Lexington and its record during World War II during the course of their breakfast. The Lexington had started with the name of Cabot when news of the sinking of the original Lexington was announced at the shipyard. Immediately, the Cabot's name was changed to the Lexington to commemorate that carrier and to confuse the enemy. The original Lexington had been reported by the Japanese as being sunk and then reappearing so many times that it had acquired the nickname of the ghost. The ship's crew later called it the Blue Ghost because of its dark blue camouflage.

The USS Lexington Museum was just a short distance from their hotel, so they decided to walk to it.

The Lexington has a MEGA theatre in the forward aircraft elevator space. It is similar to an IMAX theatre. Recently the catapult room was added as one of the attractions. Both Christopher and Dietrich expressed a desire to see this feature.

The ship also had a major role in the film, *Pearl Harbor.*

The morning breezes had picked up from yesterday's mild breezes and the ladies had to wear a silk scarf around their heads to keep their hair from being tossed about by the wind. The two couples walked together down Shoreline Drive to the Lexington Museum and bought their tickets for entry. They then walked up the gangplank and were given a catalogue of the various exhibits and aircraft that were displayed. At different places there were interactive displays that told the entire history of the famed aircraft carrier and its many missions. They even had the chance to experience the flight of a fighter aircraft being launched and recovered from a flight simulator.

Carolyn and Natalie, contrary to the expectations of their husbands, were delighted at experiencing the flight simulator. They were surprised at their wives' aptitude and interest. During the tour of the carrier, they took advantage of the restaurant on board to have lunch and drink Coca Cola directly from an old bottle similar to one used during World War II!

Christopher lifted up one of the new Coke bottles to see if the inscription of the bottling company and date was on the bottom of the bottle. He was disappointed and said that it wasn't like it used to be and then he told the story about his diving on the wrecks of sunken World War II ships in Truk Lagoon in the South Pacific.

He said that he found an old case of Coca Cola bottles still filled with Coke lying in the sand just off the beach at Tarawa Island where one of the bloodiest battles in the Pacific took place in the early years of island hopping during the war.

With that being said, he took out his catalogue and said, "You know they have some old World War II carrier aircraft in the main hangar deck. I'd like to see if they have an Avenger TBF on display there. Would anyone like to go with me to the hangar?"

Natalie raised her arm enthusiastically and said, "Me, I'd like to go."

Dietrich asked if they had any jets and Christopher said that they did.

"Do they have any Phantoms?"

Christopher nodded, "Yes."

"Carolyn, would you like to go with me to see the aircraft that Christopher flew in Desert Storm that is similar to the Tornado that I flew in Afghanistan?"

Carolyn looked up at Dietrich and smiled, "Yes."

They agreed to meet back in the restaurant in half an hour after they had finished looking at the airplanes. Christopher circled where the jets were on one of the two maps of the carrier that he had and gave it to Dietrich. Dietrich grabbed Carolyn's arm and they started walking toward the deck where the jets were located. Natalie and Christopher walked toward the main hangar deck where the World War II aircraft and Avenger TBF were.

Neither couple had noticed the two well dressed, clean shaved Arabic young men watching the two couples as they got up and went to their respective hangars. The young men smiled at each other and followed casually behind Natalie and Christopher.

Christopher led Natalie down the stairway to the main hangar deck where the World War II aircraft were lined up neatly in rows. There were placards next to the aircraft with details of their history and performance during the war. The Avenger TBF was located at the far end of the hangar next to a Douglas Dauntless dive bomber and a F6F Grumman Hellcat aircraft. They walked over to the Avenger TBF and Natalie strolled past it and was looking at the smaller Hellcats about thirty feet away. The hangar was almost empty with just a few old timers on the other side of the hangar reminiscing over the stories their fathers had told them about flying their missions from these carriers.

They were both engrossed in reading the placards and examining the aircraft. Christopher was looking at the Avenger placard and had not noticed that Natalie wasn't with him.

Natalie had just leaned down to look at the hook under the Hellcat that was used to capture the aircraft when it landed, when the two young men grabbed her, one from behind who tried to cover her mouth with a handkerchief with one hand while he held her hands behind her back with the other hand. The other man approached her from the front with a needle and syringe filled with propofol to inject into her arm.

Neither of them had anticipated Natalie's stiff resistance. She used her athletic skills and quickly raised to her full height which caught the man behind unaware and she bit his hand as he was trying to cover her mouth. He yelled and she screamed and kicked the other man in the groin.

Christopher swiftly reacted to her scream, looked up, and leaped almost instantaneously like a cat, analyzing the situation as he grabbed the stabilizer of the Avenger and spun himself across the floor toward Natalie and the two men. They had not counted on the athletic ability and size of their adversaries.

Natalie had just kicked the man with the syringe in his groin and Christopher slid on his back beneath him as he started to bend over in pain. Christopher kicked his right foot upward toward the bent over assailant and delivered a strong blow to the man's throat with his foot. The man with the needle collapsed in an unconscious mass onto the hangar deck.

The man trying to handle Natalie was surprised at her strength as she twisted him around and grabbed his hair and snapped his head downward toward her bent knee. His head hit her knee with a terrible thud and he fell to the hangar deck in a heap. The man was dazed, but realized his desperate situation. He staggered to his knees and let out another yell as he turned to see Christopher's angry face coming toward him and immediately took to his heels. He ran through the people that were beginning to gather and darted up the stairway to flee the scene and ran into the arms of two security guards who handcuffed his hands behind his back and put him down on the deck.

Christopher immediately turned to Natalie and put his arms around a sobbing, but not hysterical Natalie and asked her how she was doing as he glanced down at the unconscious man and syringe lying on the deck. He guessed it contained propofol, a very effective and quick sedative. She looked into Christopher's blue eyes and said loudly, "We sure took care of them, didn't we?"

The small crowd that had gathered around applauded the two valiant combatants while a security guard who had just arrived kneeled down, placed the unconscious man's hands behind his back and handcuffed him for the Corpus Christi police that were on their way.

Meanwhile, Christopher put his finger to his mouth and told Natalie not to say anything. As the security guard was handcuffing the assailant, Christopher grabbed Natalie's hand and they silently walked quickly away past the people who had gathered. When the security man got to his feet, they were gone!

They left the area and walked quickly to the hangar deck where Carolyn and Dietrich were. Christopher had already called on his scrambled cell phone the emergency number that Inspector Grant had given him for Texas and was surprised when the young lady who answered said, "Texas Rangers, Lieutenant Stewart's office, what's up, Dr. Rood?"

He filled her in on what had just happened and she told him to leave the area immediately before the Corpus Christi police arrived and that she'll take care of everything. She told him they should go to their hotel and behave as though nothing had happened and then leave for Austin the next morning.

When they found Carolyn and Dietrich, they explained to them what had just happened and how well Natalie had performed. Dietrich embraced his wife and Carolyn, who was wide eyed, gasped, "Honey you might have been killed!" Christopher held her tight and reassured her that he and Natalie were shaken, but okay.

"These men were on a mission to abduct Natalie and not to kill her," Christopher explained. "And the Texas Rangers are our guardian angels now; they will take care of everything. We were told to leave immediately and not to talk to anyone. We are to return to our hotel rooms as if nothing had happened and leave for home without any fanfare tomorrow morning."

They walked back to their rooms and decided that they would have their dinner from room service in Carolyn and Christopher's room after Natalie and Christopher had a chance to shower and change into clean clothes after their ordeal. When they finished their dinner and had a chance to review the day, they decided to leave early for the trip back to Austin.

The next morning came swiftly and the two couples had a quick breakfast at Morsels, a small breakfast and lunch restaurant in the Omni Hotel, and left for Austin.

They took their time going back to Austin so they could distill yesterday's events, taking the scenic coastal route to Victoria and Lavaca Bay. They passed the bird sanctuaries with their palm trees and live oaks, the mesquite groves dotting the grasslands, and then stopped for lunch in Victoria. After lunch, they visited Lavaca Bay and spent some time watching the peaceful surf lapping against the sand and taking pictures as an occasional pelican or whooping crane passed by.

The long trip back to Austin was uneventful and soothing. They were tired and hungry when they finally pulled into the garage at Rood House on Point Venture. The orange sun was just beginning its plunge into the waters of Lake Travis.

As they trudged across the bridge to the house, Dietrich noticed that the gargoyles had their perpetual grin and stared outward for any enemies that might approach the stronghold of the chalet. Carolyn had already punched in the security password and thumbprint analyzer and opened the front door. The unseen security cameras had already identified the entering faces and stored their images.

They entered into the foyer off the Great Room and Christopher echoed everyone's thoughts and sighed, "It's great to be home and what's for dinner?"

Everyone grinned as they dropped their bags and belongings onto the wooden floor.

Carolyn and Natalie walked over to the large leather sofa in the Great room and fell into its comfortable softness. They both looked up to their husbands and Carolyn sighed, "Let's just have one of those icebox pizzas and some Merlot and go to bed. "I'm pooped!"

They all agreed and Christopher walked into the kitchen and got a large frozen pizza with everything on it and popped it into the oven for the required time. He took an Australian Merlot from the wine rack and opened it just as Carolyn came into the kitchen and said, "Let's have some wine now while we wait for the pizza and we can eat it in the Great Room so Natalie and Dietrich don't have to stir from that comfortable sofa and fox fur."

He agreed and they took some glasses and the wine bottle and placed them on the large oval glass topped coffee table with the large hurricane lamp which he promptly lit. He poured the wine into the glasses and handed them to everyone and they sat down next to the von Schoenfelds on the big comfortable brown leather sofa and waited for the bell to ring when the pizza was done.

They had consumed one bottle of wine by the time the oven bell rang, so Christopher went to the kitchen, took the pizza out of the oven, cut it into eight big wedges, which he placed on a large pizza plate. He brought it all to the coffee table with another bottle of Merlot and four large linen napkins and then announced to everyone that they were going to have to use their fingers, Texas style. Then he winked and sat down next to Carolyn. They all finished dinner silently while watching the hypnotizing flickering flame of the candle in the lamp.

When they were through, Carolyn and Christopher got up from the sofa and she grabbed Christopher's hand and announced that they were going to bed and said, "Goodnight all!" And then they took the elevator to their bedroom.

Meanwhile, back at the Four Seasons Hotel in Mexico City, Ahmed was answering a telephone call from Corpus Christi. Mohammad was sitting on a sofa smoking a strong Latakia cigar from Syria waiting for the news of their success in Texas.

As Ahmed listened, his eyes widened, and his face drained of blood and turned pale. The depth of their failure to apprehend Natalie or kill her new boyfriend or her cousins was beginning to put fear into his heart over what his father's reaction to the bad news might be. He silently hung up the telephone and turned to his father who had a questioning look on his face. Ahmed uttered only three words before the full wrath of his father's rage and emotion enveloped him like a tornado. "Corpus Christi failed."

After Mohammad's ranting had subsided and Ahmed had expected the worst, he was surprised to hear his father say, "They have failed, but we will not!"

Ahmed related the full story about the oil rig crowded with boats and how Natalie and Christopher had thwarted her abduction, and all of their agents involved in Port Aransas and Corpus Christi had been captured by the Texas Rangers.

Mohammad had quieted down and with piercing wild eyes, he calmly said to his frightened son, "If the mountain will not come to Mohammad, then Mohammad will go to the mountain!"

He then looked his son squarely in his eyes and said to him, "We will kill them all—Natalie and her new boyfriend, her meddling cousins in Texas and a lot more. We will make the Twin Towers in New York look like child's play and the two of us will be the ultimate martyrs for our cause!"

Ahmed was shocked by the crazy look in his father's eyes and his dark countenance, but all he could reply was, "As Allah wills!"

26 SALADO AND THE TEXAS RANGERS

The next morning was a Friday and Christopher thought that he might be able to reach Randall Fox if he called his house before he had a chance to get away. It was seven o'clock and everyone else was still asleep after the trip home from Corpus Christi yesterday. He had quietly tiptoed past the Great Room into the kitchen in his bathrobe and fixed a pot of coffee.

He and Carolyn kept extra bathrobes in a closet in the bathroom off the hall next to the Great Room in case they had early breakfasts. As he strolled past the bathroom, he had noticed that Natalie and Dietrich were in bathrobes from that closet. They were still sound asleep nestled under the fox fur blanket on the leather couch and Balthazar only lifted his head up and then laid it back down on the fox fur blanket and closed his eyes. The candle was still burning with a faint vanilla odor.

He heard the telephone ring when he dialed his old friend's number on the 1970s styled dial phone in the kitchen. When Randall answered, "Is that you Christopher?" he didn't have time to answer before Randall continued, "You'll never guess what has just been developed?" Before Christopher could answer again, his friend answered his own question. "It's a rifle that can't miss! It just can't miss!"

Christopher asserted himself, "Hold it, Randy. Slow down and tell me what this is all about."

He could hear his old friend take in a deep breath and then slowly say, "A scientist named John McHale, who is also an avid hunter, has invented a high technology rifle that cannot miss—even out to 1,000 yards and in the hands of any amateur!"

"I got my hands on one of these rifles the other day from a friend of mine who is on the Board of Directors of the Tracking Point Corporation that is beginning to manufacture these rifles for hunting. They sell for $25,000 and I've got one! Of course not everyone can buy one. You have to have a special background check and be cleared by every agency imaginable.

"Hell, the military is camping out here in Austin to get this gun." Without pausing to let Christopher speak, he continued, "You won't believe your eyes. It delivers an effective range to 1,000 yards and works with Android and iOS smart phones and tablets. Wind speed is the only data you'll manually input to the scope using a toggle button. Chris, I've even got a silencer so nobody can even hear it coming! And the best part is that they are making them here in Texas."

Randall stopped talking and there was a long silence on the other end of the phone. "Did you hear what I said, Chris. This means that we can finally get us a twelve point deer the next time we go hunting!"

Another long silence and then Christopher slowly said, "I just wanted to make sure that you were finished, Randall. You know that sometimes it's hard to get a word in edgewise when I'm speaking to you. Our conversations sometimes resemble monologues rather than dialogues!"

Christopher could hear a gulp on the other end of the line and then Randall said, "I know, I apologize. It's just that sometimes I get so excited about ideas and things that my words tumble all over themselves."

Christopher replied to his old friend, "That may be why you're not married, you know." There was another long silence and he knew that his old friend was remembering back many years when his wife and children had left him.

Christopher knew as soon as he had said it that he should not have. Randall never mentions his marriage and most people don't know that he was once married and had children.

Soon, Randall was back on the phone in his usual professorial manner and said, "I'm happy that you and Carolyn are bringing your cousins to pick me up next weekend so that we all can go visit the Ranger Museum. You know, I always get a kick learning about the exploits of a true patriotic police force. You did know that they are really working for the Republic of Texas!"

Christopher replied that he was looking forward to seeing him and that he is sure that his cousin Dietrich would love to get a chance at firing his new rifle. He is a hunter, too.

He heard his friend brighten up a bit as he enthusiastically said, "Really, is he really interested in guns and hunting?"

Christopher affirmed that he was and that he would give him a call before they drove up to Salado this next weekend. His friend said goodbye and clicked the receiver of his telephone down.

Carolyn had already entered the kitchen when he hung up the phone. She was clutching her robe as she whispered that Natalie and Dietrich were still asleep on the couch. Christopher replied that he hoped that he didn't wake everyone when he made the coffee and was talking to Randall.

"No, just me, when you got up" Carolyn whispered.

Christopher had already had three cups of coffee when his telephone rang and he quickly picked up the phone before it could ring again. He answered softly, "Hello, this is Dr. Rood, what can I do for you?"

The voice on the other end of the telephone was his good

friend and fellow professor, Dr. William E. Harries, a professor at Emory University in Atlanta, Georgia. Carolyn at that point decided that she would get dressed and fix breakfast and whispered into Christopher's ear not to talk too long or loud. She then kissed his ear, wrapped her robe around her and hurried off toward the elevator down the hall and to their bedroom.

Christopher turned toward Carolyn as she left and blew her a kiss. He turned back to his conversation and told Bill that he had been wondering about the plans for Libertyville. His friend Bill was the spitting image of the early 20th century English actor Ronald Coleman.

They were discussing King Peter II and how he had miraculously escaped from his palace in Belgrade to England during World War II and that in the 1960s he and his cabinet officers were living in exile in the United States. He had never abdicated his throne and refused the solicitations of Tito, dictator of communist Yugoslavia.

King Peter II died in a Denver hospital at age 47 after a failed liver transplant and at his request was interred in Saint Sava Monastery Chapel in Libertyville, Illinois. He was the only king to be buried in the United States. His loyal members in Canada and the United States had placed a memorial plaque in his honor at Saint Sava and were going to pay their last respects with a pilgrimage to his tomb in September 2012 before his body was to be disinterred and sent back to Belgrade, Serbia to be reinterred with his family in the royal tombs there.

Colonel Harries was calling Christopher to confirm the ceremonies and pilgrimage to Libertyville set for Saturday, September 22, 2012. Christopher told him that he and Carolyn as well as two cousins from Europe would be there for the ceremonies. They had planned to place a wreath next to the tomb in the chapel. Members of the Order from the United States and Canada were going to be present as a last memorial and farewell to the king's presence in America.

Christopher and Bill had finished their conversation and

hung up when he heard Carolyn's voice from the kitchen telling him that Natalie and Dietrich were getting dressed and he should too. She asked him who it was. She had returned fully dressed and without interrupting him had started fixing breakfast. He informed her that it was Bill Harries and she replied, "How are Lucille and Bill?"

He told her that they were doing well and that he was just checking to make sure that we were all set for the pilgrimage. Carolyn said that she thought so and that Dietrich and Natalie had expressed an interest in going to Libertyville since it was just north of Chicago. Neither of them had been to the Chicago area and they wanted to see what it was like as well as pay their respects to King Peter before he finally returned to his native land from his long exile.

He told her that he had earlier talked with Randall Fox before Bill had called and that he was anxious for us to pick him up at his small ranch outside Salado so he can show us a new gun that he has acquired. "I told him that Dietrich and I would probably be interested in shooting it."

Carolyn asked, "What's so interesting about the gun?"

Christopher whispered into her ear, "It's worth $25,000."

She whistled and said, "Yeah, I would like to see that gun!"

Later, Christopher told Natalie and Dietrich over breakfast that they were going to make a day trip out of their visit to Waco and the Texas Ranger Museum and that Dr. Randall Fox, whom they met in Edinburg had invited them to his ranch outside Salado where he wanted to show them a new gun.

Carolyn interjected, "It's worth $25.000."

Natalie and Dietrich looked at each other and simultaneously said, "Why?"

They all laughed at that and Christopher replied that Randall was always interested in the latest technologies and he claims that this rifle can't miss a target even at a thousand yards.

Dietrich took a deep breath and said, "This, I've got to

see!"

They spent the weekend recuperating from Corpus Christi and exploring the Hill Country around Lake Travis. Natalie exclaimed that she had fallen in love with Texas and couldn't figure out why anyone would want to live elsewhere.

Carolyn looked her in the eyes and said, "Wait until the temperatures reach 105 degrees Fahrenheit!"

The next week Christopher went back to work while Carolyn, Dietrich and Natalie spent their time water skiing, sailing, swimming, sunbathing, picnics on their private beach and exploring the gardens and grounds of Rood House, looking at Christopher and Carolyn's extensive collections, antiques, paintings, artwork and reading from the Rood's extensive library, watching old movies on Turner Classic Movies and watching Robert Osborne and Ben Mankiewicz introduce old films and interview movie stars. They were particularly interested in listening to the famous movie star and director Drew Barrymore's discussions with Robert Osborne about the essential films and her remembrances of her famous family.

The time flew by and suddenly, it was Saturday, September 8th, and they were on their way to Salado. The sky was clear without a cloud in the deep blue sky that stretched endlessly from horizon to horizon with the flat tops of the clumps of Mesquite trees that would appear from time to time. Natalie thought, "No wonder they call it the "Big Sky Country!"

They headed north from Austin on Interstate 35 to Salado where they exited right onto South Stagecoach Road. The historic Old Stagecoach Inn on South Stagecoach Road is where Sam Houston and other dignitaries have stayed and is on the road that the original stagecoaches traveled. The famous Chisholm Trail heading north passed alongside this road. You can even stay in the same room that General, Governor and President Sam Houston stayed in. They stopped at the Historic Old Stagecoach Inn and had a late brunch at 11:00 a.m. when the dining room opened. After their meal, they headed north across the Salado Creek toward

Killeen about ten miles to Dr. Fox's forty-acre ranch which he lovingly called the "Back Forty Ranch."

Dr. Fox heard them drive up and was out on the front porch of the sprawling ranch house that turned out to be mainly a large paneled and beamed library with three bedrooms of moderate size, a large kitchen and dining room with a large dining table that rarely had guests. It was more likely to have papers and scientific journals spread on it. The front of the house looked out toward a Mesquite Grove in the distance which was on the edge of the forty-acre spread. A large porch dominated the front of the house and had several rocking chairs and a large bench sitting on it. It faced north so the prevailing westerly wind would not blow directly onto the porch. There was a small visitor's cottage with two moderate rooms, a bath and kitchenette with an adjoining small dining room. He had said that he built it so that his children could visit with him, but they seldom did, perhaps because he was frequently gone, either lecturing or at one of his digs somewhere in the world.

He greeted them wearing his typical dove grey Texas Stetson hat, but he was dressed in an old sport coat and slacks with an Ivy League long sleeve oxford cloth button down collar shirt and tie with the familiar rancher's boots. He was a dichotomy of dress which spoke volumes about him.

His house keeper, Mrs. Stuart, a neighbor, had dropped by to take a look at the visiting foreigners. She had met Carolyn and Christopher on many occasions when they had passed through the area and visited with him. It was then that she would come over and cook meals for Randall's guests so that they wouldn't suffer indigestion from meals that he might prepare. She looked at Natalie and Dietrich and shook their hands and said to Dietrich, "You sure have a pretty wife."

Dietrich nodded his head in agreement.

"Well, I have to be going, chores don't wait, you know."

She waved at everybody and climbed into an old Ford pickup truck and rumbled down the driveway toward her house.

"She just wanted to meet you folks," Randall explained to Natalie and Dietrich.

"She's wanted to meet you and make sure that I wouldn't forget to take you to dinner at the Old Stagecoach Inn."

He pushed them into the library where he had placed the revolutionary rifle on the top of a large table that he used for his research. Christopher looked at the electronic bolt action rifle that could be programmed to fire for its master and no other and also to take out a target at a thousand yards with just a squeeze of the trigger. The rifle used a laser and a GPS scope that could align the target with the bore of the weapon and calculate a trajectory to hit the target with mathematical precision. It used specially made ammunition just for this specific rifle and all that needed to be done was to enter the velocity and direction of the prevailing winds between the shooter and his target. There was an electronic device that measured the local conditions down to a breath!

Randall took the weapon out onto the front porch and asked Dietrich and Christopher to peer through a spotting scope that he had set up to align with a target 1,000 yards away over by the Mesquite grove. He explained that the weapon had a hair trigger setting and a stabilizing electronic mechanism just like the stable-cam digital cameras have so pictures would not be blurred.

He wanted them to try three shots each at the two targets he had set up. One for each of them. He cautioned not to be surprised if the weapon did not fire precisely when they squeezed the trigger; there may be a very slight delay while the rifle is calculating just the right moment in the sway of the rifle barrel so as to afford the best hit. He wanted them to fire three carefully aimed shots at their respective targets, then he would drive them in his Jeep Wrangler over to the targets to see how they had done. He entered a specific code into the weapon for each of them so that the rifle would fire and then wrote down the code.

Dietrich went first, and when he squeezed off the first round after Randall had shown him how to enter the wind velocity into the rifle, he was surprised how quiet the weapon was with hardly any recoil! Dietrich fired two more rounds and handed the weapon off to Christopher who entered his code into the rifle and squeezed off three rounds in quick succession. He said to both Dietrich and Randall that he thought he had been too quick on the trigger.

Randall laughed and said, "Let's go see!"

They jumped into the Jeep Wrangler and headed across the field toward the grove of Mesquite trees. When they reached their targets they were surprised that Randall had already written their names on the targets that he had assigned to them.

Dietrich ran over to his target and exclaimed, "I have only one hit, but it's dead center in the bullseye."

Randall took out a magnifying glass and said, "Look at it again."

To Dietrich's surprise, he could see all three hits with only a hair breadth between the shots. Christopher looked at his target and it exhibited very similar results!

The two shooters shook their heads and Dietrich exclaimed that if he had not seen it, he would not have believed it. He said, "This weapon has changed the whole scope of warfare!"

Randall looked at him and squinted his eyes and said, "I thought we were talking about deer hunting!"

This provoked a minute of silence and then they all three agreed that the world had suddenly changed— hopefully for the better.

They got back into the Jeep with their targets and sped back to the ranch house. When they got there they showed the targets to their wives and they all stood in somberness realizing what the future could hold. Randall immediately took the rifle to a secret hiding place and came back with a pitcher of local German beer.

Dr. Fox said, "Here, this should get us in a frame of mind so we can enjoy the Ranger museum."

They drank the wonderful local brew that was made by the

descendants of the German settlers and he was right. The beer did make them feel better!

Dr. Fox had brought out a box that held a commemorative 1876 Colt Peacemaker revolver with a 7-1/2 inch barrel. The case contained a rawhide covered book with the history of the Texas Rangers and a genuine Ranger lone star badge made from a Mexican five pesos silver coin. He said that this weapon had been a favorite of the Rangers since 1876 and some still wear it in a high set holster rig as they did when riding on a horse—especially during official ceremonies.

Christopher and Dietrich handled the revolver and noted its superb balance and pointing characteristics.

Natalie was watching them and came over and asked, "May I handle it? I've always wanted to see a real cowboy gun and hold it!" She tried to twirl it as they did in the movies and remarked how heavy it seemed.

Randall came over and said, "Ma'am, let me show you how it's done."

With that she handed the gun to him and he proceeded to twirl it in several different directions forwards and backwards and then flipped it into the air and snatched it expertly out of the air and continued its spin before rolling it over and handing it back to her.

She took it and handed it to her husband and clapped her hands together as she exclaimed, "That's how I've seen it done in the western movies!" She put her arms around Randall's neck and kissed him on the cheek!

He pulled shyly away and turned red. He looked down at the floor and kicked his boot at the floor and muttered, "Shucks, that ain't nothin', Ma'am!" They all laughed.

Randall then mentioned he understood that Maj. Al Jones, the Commander of Company "F" of the Rangers that was co-headquartered in San Antonio and Waco and worked with the Texas Ranger Hall of Fame and Museum in Waco had arranged for Natalie and Dietrich to meet with Ranger Lieutenant, Bob Stewart at the Museum at two o'clock this afternoon. He suggested they get there early since it was not considered wise to keep a Ranger waiting!

Christopher blurted out, "That's the guy that's been assigned to watch over Natalie and Dietrich while they're in Texas! It's his office number that Inspector Grant gave me in Edinburgh and it was his secretary that I talked to in Corpus Christi that squared everything for us!"

Carolyn looked up and said, "He must have a secretary like Kate."

Randall seemed to already know this and replied, "She is," and then disappeared with the revolver and reappeared in three minutes ready to go. They all got into the Mercedes SUV for the excursion to Waco.

They got back onto Interstate 35 and were soon passing through Temple toward Waco just a few minutes more down the road. It took them about an hour to get to the museum that was located adjacent to Interstate 35 in Waco. They parked the car in the parking lot and got out. It was just one-thirty. They had made it with time to spare!

They paid their seven dollar admission fee and entered the one story enormous ranch house style building with its broad porch and gabled roof and several wings. They were surprised at the number of displays with guns, artwork, sculptures and artifacts that told the Ranger story. It has the Armstrong Research Center located adjacent to the museum that was added in 1976. It has a library and gift shop as well. In 1997, the Texas Legislature met and designated the renamed Texas Ranger Research Center as the official repository for archives and memorabilia related to the Texas Rangers Service. Outside the building is a statue of a lone Ranger on a horse holding the Lone Star state flag. The museum even sponsors a Junior Ranger program!

As they looked around the museum, they spotted a tall lanky man with a blue suit, cowboy boots and a dust grey Stetson hat. He was handsome and had the look of a John Wayne with a set jaw. He looked kind, but definitely appeared to be someone not to fool around with! He appeared to be looking for someone.

They walked over to him and, as they approached, his tight lips broke into a smile and he said, "You all must be the professors with the foreign dignitaries I'm supposed to look after while they're in Texas. Maj. Jones wants me to show you around the Hall of Fame and the museum. I'm Lieutenant Stewart of the Texas Rangers. They told me that you would have a beautiful woman in tow!"

He looked straight into Natalie's hazel eyes and then into Carolyn's blue green eyes and said, "But they didn't tell me that there would be two beautiful women!"

He then turned toward Dietrich and said, "You must be her husband," as he motioned toward Natalie. "Then you're Maj. Dietrich von Schoenfeld of the German Air Force!"

"How did you know?" Dietrich asked.

He smiled and pointed toward Randall and said, "He told me you'd be tall, good looking and wearing boots and a Texas Stetson." Then he motioned toward Christopher and said, "And Dr. Rood, everybody around Austin and these parts knows him. He and his pretty wife have had their pictures in the papers a lot of times and besides, I met him and his wife once at a Texas Silver Spurs shindig!"

He shook each of their hands, taking care to be gentle with his handshake with Carolyn and Natalie. He then asked Randall if he had tried out his new Tracking Point XS2 rifle with the silencer! He said that the two of them should go hunting sometime because he would sure like to try out that new gun. Randall grinned and said that if he wanted, he was sure welcome to come out to the Back Forty Ranch and try it out anytime. The Ranger tipped his hat and said that he would give him a call.

Natalie and Dietrich were amazed at the Ranger's instant identification of all of them, but then it was probably deductive reasoning along with careful observation and a good memory along with a little prior research before the meeting!

Lt. Stewart took his time and showed them around the

entire Hall of Fame and the museum. At one of the displays, he remarked that the Rangers had served under five national flags and was a unique Division in the Department of Public Safety for Texas. It had always been a paramilitary organization since its inception by Stephen F. Austin in 1823. He remarked that the Colt "Walker" revolver of Mexican War fame had been named for a famous Texas Ranger. Finally, they finished their tour and the von Schoenfelds knew they had met a true Texas Ranger officer and he had totally charmed everyone.

Natalie had even confided to Carolyn that she had previously thought that the Texas Rangers were rough, uneducated, poorly dressed cowboys with no manners at all and now she knew that nothing could be farther from the truth!

It was five o'clock and the museum was closing. They all shook Lt. Stewart's hand and thanked him for taking the time to show them around. Natalie whispered into his ear as she shook his hand that she was going to tell all of her girlfriends back home that she had met a real Texas Ranger and was thrilled at the opportunity!

He smiled and quietly said, "Thank you ma'am."

They waved goodbye to Lt. Stewart as they got into their SUV and headed toward Interstate 35 and the drive back to Salado and dinner at the Old Stagecoach Inn.

After dinner, they drove to Randall's ranch and he welcomed them into the living room with a large stone fireplace and brown leather couches and chairs. The coffee table and furniture were made from light Mesquite Wood that had a honey brown color. The wooden dark oak planked floor had a large multicolored Navajo Indian Rug that had been purchased in Santa Fe, New Mexico. A large Spanish metal chandelier with flame like lights illuminated the room in a soft amber glow that matched the full moon outside.

They sat down and Randall disappeared into the kitchen and returned with five small snifters on a dark wooden tray and a bottle of Maracame Gran Platino Tequila Blanco. He placed it on the large Mesquite coffee table with a glass top and asked them if they would try a sip of this special Tequila. He looked at each of them as he poured the liquor into the glasses and then he proposed a toast to the newlyweds and to their future family and happiness. As he looked at Natalie and Dietrich, Natalie thought she could see a faraway look in his eyes as he said future family and happiness.

They slowly drank the Tequila and it flowed smoothly down their throats with a soft warmness that did not burn. He asked them if they would like some more and they said that what they had was enough since they had a long drive home.

With that he drained his glass and threw it into the fireplace and invited his guests to do the same when they finished draining their glasses so as not to tempt the fates about his toast! As each one finished their glass, they followed suit and hurled their glasses into the fireplace.

Randall turned the topic of conversation to the upcoming Memorial Pilgrimage to Saint Sava Chapel on the 22nd of September and the Baylor-Texas football game on the 20th of October when Christopher was going to be honored for his services to the community.

They all told Randall that they had a wonderful time at the Museum and Christopher and Dietrich expressed their amazement over the XS2 rifle and that they would have to schedule a hunt sometime during next year's hunting season. Dietrich chimed in and said to let him know and he would try to get another leave of absence.

Natalie upon hearing that said, "Don't leave me out, I love Texas too!"

Randall asked them to wait. He had a surprise for them. He disappeared into the hallway and returned in a couple of minutes with the presentation case that contained the Commemorative Texas Ranger Colt 76 Peacemaker with the 7-1/2 inch barrel that he had earlier showed them. The case now had a blue satin ribbon and bow wrapped around it with a handwritten card to the newlyweds celebrating their marriage and an official certificate from the governor of Texas granting them honorary citizenship in the great state of Texas and honorary membership in the Texas Rangers!

Randall remarked that only twenty-five of these presentation Colt revolvers commemorating the founding of the Texas Rangers were ever made by Colt and it was his honor to present the gun and for the governor, their certificates of honorary Texas citizenship and honorary membership into the Texas Rangers. He remarked that the blue ribbon represented the Blue Bonnet flowers of Texas and the blue flecks in Natalie's hazel eyes!

Natalie and Dietrich were stunned and overwhelmed by the governor's and Randall's generosity and his efforts in welcoming them to Texas! Natalie burst into tears and ran to Randall, threw her arms around him and kissed him on his cheek. Dietrich stammered his appreciation and shook Randall's hand exclaiming that they would never forget him. They never dreamed just how true that thought would be!

They walked toward the SUV and Christopher and Dietrich shook Randall's hand again and said goodbye. Natalie and Carolyn hugged him and said their goodbyes and they got into the SUV. As they pulled away, they could see Randall in the driveway waving goodbye and they all waved back as they disappeared into the night. They all knew that they had all just left a loyal friend.

27 LIBERTYVILLE

The airplane was beginning its slow descent into the Chicago metro area and O'Hare International Airport—at times the busiest in the world! The flight attendants had already cleared the cabins and all of the tray tables had been elevated and locked. The buckles were locked and all of the seats were in their upright positions. Everyone was holding their breath as the plane flew through the darkened clouds of a thunderstorm that was buffeting the aircraft as it descended on instruments and computers. The pilots had assured everyone that it was just routine as lightning flashed outside and its rumble sounded too close for comfort.

Dietrich and the others in their entourage except Natalie were calm. She was holding her hands together and squeezing them so that her knuckles were white. Her face was calm without a hint of fear, but her hands gave her away! They had traveled all over the world and had flown under severe conditions before and they knew that O'Hare was a safe airport to land at and with all the safety equipment imaginable.

Dietrich and Christopher had flown on dangerous missions in their respective Air Forces where the odds on their lives had been assessed as "not worth a plugged nickel." The Captain announced that they were approaching the runway and would soon land. Everyone heard the wheels go down and lock into position and then the plane started into a long glide that finally terminated with all of the wheels touching down simultaneously and the aircraft rolling smoothly down the runway and gradually slowing down without the brakes squealing until the aircraft came almost to a halt and then moved smoothly off the main runway and headed toward its gate.

Christopher and Dietrich quietly smiled and looked at each other, knowingly.

The pilot was surely trained in the Air Force and not the Navy since naval aviators always land fast and hard waiting for the restraining hook on an aircraft carrier to grab them and slow them down to a halt. Their pilots, they surmised, were probably multiengine aviators since fighter pilots tended to get down fast and exit the main runway at a higher speed and as fast as possible!

They chuckled and Dietrich said in German that he knew what Christopher was thinking and they both laughed together at their private joke. They looked over at Natalie and her breathing was slower now and color had returned to her knuckles. Carolyn was fixing her hair and Randall was asleep! They shook Randall gently and he snorted as he woke up. He rubbed his eyes and looked about and then he said, "Are we here?" and then the two couples started laughing and Carolyn assured Randall that they had arrived and that the airplane was getting ready to dock at their gate.

As soon as the aircraft had stopped, a few ambitious individuals anxious to exit the aircraft, stood up and tried to squeeze forward with their carry-on bag to a better starting position to begin the race out of the airplane and into the crowded corridors of the airport. They would race toward the baggage claim areas where they could get the best positions to retrieve their baggage and then sprint to their parked cars and get into a slow moving line to exit the airport and file into the clogged traffic heading toward their home.

The two couples and Randall waited patiently for the sprinters to pass by and then they got up and walked leisurely down the airplane's aisle toward the exit which was almost empty of passengers. They all thanked the pilot and flight attendant at the exit for their safe flight and Randall said to the pilot as he exited, "Nice flight and landing, captain, Air Force, I presume?"

The pilot looked at him quizzically and replied, "Yes, multiengine—how did you know?"

Randall smiled and said, "We have to stick together!" shook his hand and thanked the flight attendant and walked down the gangway toward the gate, leaving the pilot with a puzzled look on his face.

Christopher and Dietrich who had been watching Randall, smiled and Dietrich said to Christopher, "He wasn't asleep was he?"

Christopher replied, "Yes. But his ears are always awake!"

They found the baggage claim area and saw their bags coming down the chute just as they walked up to the carousel. They retrieved their bags and walked to the exit door. It was four o'clock in the afternoon on the 21st of September and they had reservations at the O'Hare Airport Hilton Hotel which was just across from the airport.

They easily crossed the street and walked to the lobby. Once inside the hotel they all walked up to the reception counter where they confirmed their reservations and the receptionist gave them their electronic keys. Their rooms had already been paid by the Order. Christopher left a message for Colonel Harries and his wife Lucille to call him as soon as they checked in and were settled in their room so they could all go down to the bar and have a drink together. He said that he wanted to introduce him to his cousins who were part of the Johanniter Order of Saint John.

They walked down to their respective rooms. The rooms were down at the end of a corridor not far from the elevators. There were three rooms, two across from one another and the third at the end was a suite with a bedroom and bath and a separate living room and bar. The one at the end was Carolyn and Christopher's rooms and Natalie and Dietrich's room were opposite to Randall's room. Those rooms did not have a living room, but did have a sitting area and a bar along with a bedroom and bath. Carolyn asked everyone to get settled in their rooms and in a half an hour for them to come to their room for some finger sandwiches and beer that she would order from room service. They all agreed.

A half hour later, they had assembled in Carolyn and Christopher's room and were just beginning to pour the beer when the telephone rang. It was Bill Harries. He told Christopher that they had just arrived and were putting their clothes into the closet and dresser. Christopher informed them that everyone was with him in his room. He gave Bill the room number and told him to bring Lucille and come to the room as soon as they could. Bill said that they would and they hung up.

There was a knock on the door fifteen minutes later and Lucille and Bill entered the hotel room. Lucille was tall and slender as was Bill. They were in their early sixties and their hair was starting to grey. Lucille was a pretty North Carolina lady with brunette hair that was carefully combed and set in a loose swirl that hung gracefully below her ears. She was dressed in a summer weight blue patterned dress and matching shoes that revealed the dignity of the Old South.

Bill was tall and slender with an athletic build that reflected his youth in sports. He had joined the Navy after graduation from college at North Carolina and served with distinction as an officer for two years. He entered Emory Dental School in Atlanta where he excelled. His practice in Atlanta was highly successful and his investments were rewarding. He had remained in the Reserves, but had switched to the Army Air Force and then to the Army when the Air Force separated from the Army. It was the Army where he had been given several commands as a reserve officer and risen quickly to the rank of full colonel. He was also in the Hospitaller Order of

Saint John with the rank of Bailiff. His hair was beginning to grey and he wore a mustache that was well groomed and with his military erect stature, he looked every inch a Southern colonel.

He was a member of the Atlanta City Gate Old Guard that protected the city of Atlanta during the War Between the States and was now an honorary society composed of southern military officers that hold formations and attend Atlanta military functions in their white military uniforms. He was also a member of the Sons of the American Revolution and the Society of the Cincinnati which was formed by George Washington and Lafayette for officers that served in the Revolutionary War. Only their descendants can belong and it's a very special group that has its national headquarters in Washington, DC.

His family had served in all of the branches of military service and served in all of the military conflicts and wars that the United States had been in. He reflected the Southern tradition of service to their state and nation. He, like Christopher, had an Achievement and his own Coat of Arms, but Bill's was from the Lord Lyon College of Heraldry in Edinburgh. Bill had also been a professor at Emory Dental School until it was closed in 1989.

Christopher introduced Natalie and Dietrich to Lucille and Bill and, of course, they knew Dr. Fox from the Hospitaller Order of Saint John. They talked about the things that were going on in the Middle East and how King Peter II had shinnied down a drain pipe of the Royal Palace in Belgrade to avoid capture by the Nazis and their Muslim SS allies. He then escaped with the help of English commandos.

King Peter II and his advisors had opposed the policies of the Regent Prince Paul, a cousin of his father. His father, King Alexander I, had been assassinated in Marseille on October 9, 1934, by a Macedonian terrorist working with Croatian separatists. His eldest son Peter was crowned King, but because he was 11 years old at the time, King Alexander's cousin Prince Paul was made regent until King Peter II came of age. Regent Paul had declared that the Kingdom of Yugoslavia would join Hitler's Tripartite Pact on March 25, 1941.

Two days later King Peter II, at age 17, was declared of age and participated in a British supported coup d'état opposing the pact with Hitler. Hitler immediately invaded Yugoslavia and the Royal Yugoslavian military resisted until April 17, 1941. This delayed Hitler's Operation Barbarossa into Russia. The English smuggled the young king and his ministers through the Greek Islands to Palestine, then to Cairo and Gibraltar, and finally to London in June 1941 where he and his government, along with other governments occupied by the Nazis, went into exile during the war.

He met his wife, Princess Alexandra of Greece and Denmark, in England where they were married. He became a Knight and Associate Bailiff Grand Cross of the Venerable Order of Saint John on June 21, 1943, during his exile in England in the early 1940s. He resisted the political efforts of many postwar politicians to force him to abdicate or to come to an agreement with the communist dictator of Yugoslavia, Josip Broz Tito.

King Peter II was betrayed by the allies, and Tito gained recognition at the Teheran Conference on December 1, 1943. King Peter II never did yield and instead migrated to the United States to live in exile and seek a way to regain his throne.

He never abdicated his throne and was a recognized king up to his death in 1970 at a Denver, Colorado, hospital after a failed liver transplant. When he realized that he was dying, he chose a Serbian Orthodox Saint Sava monastery chapel in Libertyville as his place of burial rather than a communist Yugoslavia. He is a hero to the American-Serbian community of the United States and to the loyal Serbs in Serbia.

Bill Harries reminded his friends that they had to be at the Saint Sava Monastery Chapel by 10:00 a.m. the next day for the ceremony at eleven o'clock and it took a little over an hour to drive to Libertyville which is north of the airport. He said that he had rented a van that would accommodate everyone and they should leave by no later than 8:30 a.m. the next day if we were going to make it on time. They decided to eat that night in their rooms with room service and to stop at a restaurant on the way tomorrow morning. They could eat downtown in Chicago tomorrow night. Bill said that he would make that reservation for everyone to make sure that they had a good table. By the time they agreed on the schedule it was six o'clock and they needed to get to bed early if they were going to get enough sleep. Lucille and Bill said their goodbyes to everyone and went to their room.

Christopher asked his friends if it would be all right to eat in their suite tonight and they agreed if they could share the expenses. Christopher waved his hand and said that would make the calculations too complicated and that he would simply write it off on his taxes. Carolyn looked at him and said, "Good luck!"

They all looked at the menu in the room and decided that they would rather go downstairs to the Gaslight Club Restaurant and have a good Chicago Porterhouse Steak with all of the trimmings. They called Bill and Lucille and met them in the lobby. When they all arrived at the restaurant, they saw that the soft lights and ambiance along with the piano player playing soft relaxing dinner music was just the ticket! The table had candelabras to enhance the effect. They chose a table not too far from the grand piano, but far enough to have a conversation. They were seated and the waiter brought their menus. The meal went splendidly and they went back to their rooms and tumbled into their beds like children.

They were all up early and dressed for the memorial service in their traditional Sunday clothes and met downstairs in the lobby at 8:30 a.m. as they had arranged the evening before. The weather was still cold and rainy but there were occasional patches of blue sky. Dr. Harries drove the rented van to the front of the hotel and they all piled in. The drive to Libertyville was faster than they had anticipated. It took them only forty minutes due to the light Saturday morning traffic.

When they entered the city limits, they found a "House of Pancakes" restaurant that served a variety of pancakes from the Belgium waffles to the traditional American stack of pancakes and butter with maple Syrup. They all had a hearty breakfast and then they noticed the time.

They just had time to get to the Saint Sava Chapel on the outskirts of town.

When they drove up to the small parking lot, they could already spot some of the members of the Order of Saint John gathering on the front lawn of the chapel. Since Christopher and Bill had a part in the ceremonies, they and their wives joined Randall and the others. Natalie and Dietrich walked along behind them.

Dietrich was wearing a fedora hat and a trench coat with collar raised to protect against the wind and possible rain. Randall was talking to Dietrich as they were walking and mentioned, "One of the interesting things about King Peter's burial at Saint Sava was that most of his ministers who had gone into exile with him are buried in the churchyard outside the chapel. Since we have some time before the ceremonies, now was probably the best time to look at their gravestones and get some pictures."

Natalie said that she wasn't interested in the gravestones, but Dietrich said he was and that he and Randall were going to take a look at the monuments and get some pictures. Besides, Dietrich was not supposed to be seen with Natalie. That was not part of the plan to trap Mohammad and Ahmed.

She hurried along and caught up with Carolyn and said, "Oh, Dietrich and Randall are going to get some pictures of some old gravestones in the churchyard. They said that they would be outside the chapel when the ceremonies began."

Carolyn looked at her and replied, "I hope that you are right. You know, that once Randall gets started, he is so absorbed in the topic, that he could give a dissertation for hours!"

Natalie replied, "I hate to tell you this, but Dietrich is no better. He is so into this Saint John and Knights Templar business with the Crusades and Middle Ages that sometimes I believe that he wishes that he had lived then instead of now!"

Carolyn looked at Natalie and shrugged her shoulders, "Christopher is the same way. I guess that we'll just have to grin and bear that burden!"

She had no sooner said that and they both heard Dr. Harries begin the opening speeches before the presentation of the Saint John White Maltese Cross wreath at the side of King Peter's sarcophagus. Carolyn and Natalie pressed forward so they could see.

The speeches went by rather rapidly and the flower displays and cards from well-wishers were placed next to the four foot high wreathe by the boys from the monastery and the little girls from the area dressed in their traditional Serbian garb.

Christopher turned around and motioned for Carolyn to come forward since some photographers wanted some pictures of Bill and Lucille with Carolyn and him. Carolyn told Natalie that they should move forward. As she left, a void was made, and some visitors behind her pushed her forward and forced her into the area just behind Carolyn and Christopher.

She felt embarrassed to be pushed into the limelight and tried to wriggle loose, but it was no use. Cameras were flashing and Christopher and Bill were waving at the on lookers. Finally it was over and the people behind her were starting to leave and she could wriggle loose and step outside the Chapel where Dietrich and Randall were standing with sheepish looks on their faces.

Both of them apologized profusely to Natalie and Dietrich grabbed her hand and held her close as the crowds moved past them and began to dissipate. Natalie told him that it was alright and that they didn't want him to be recognized or in any pictures anyway.

Soon Lucille and Bill with Carolyn and Christopher

reappeared and they all went into the now nearly empty chapel. They all took pictures of the wreath and flowers with cards expressing their love of King Peter II and wishing him well on his return to his native land and royal entombment. It was as if he could somehow hear their wishes. He was a hero to them and they would miss him!

If only the King's family could see how loved he was by the Serbian Community in America. He was widely respected for his stand against the Nazis and Communists and his compassion for American generosity. If only he could have seen how he was admired by his Order and his fellow Serbs!

The three couples and Randall returned to the van and started back towards Chicago. It had been a grand affair and a pilgrimage that would last in the memories of the members of the Order of Saint John.

It took them a little longer to get to their rooms to freshen up and change their clothes for the trip into Chicago to see the elevated railway, the downtown stores and the Water Tower, Lakeshore Drive, Soldiers Field and Park, the Field Museum with its dinosaur displays and the German World War II Submarine that was captured to get its Enigma Machine, the University of Chicago Field House where the first controlled atomic chain reaction was done, Northwestern University in Evanston, the Chicago River which is dyed Green on Saint Patrick's Day, the Sears Tower, and the baseball fields of the Chicago Cubs and the Chicago White Sox. Most of all, they enjoyed dinner in a downtown Italian Restaurant where they served Chicago's famous deep dish pizza that tasted like heaven on earth!

It was a tall order, but with due diligence, they made it and returned to their hotel exhausted but happy. It was a whirlwind sightseeing tour that Bill gave everyone along with its history. Bill was familiar with Chicago from his time in the Navy at the Great Lakes Naval Air Station where he first learned to fly.

Natalie was sure by now that fate had selected her to be surrounded by pilots who were members of the Order of

Saint John. It was her destiny! When she asked Randall if he was a pilot, he said emphatically, "No, but I'm a good passenger!" She felt somehow saved and greatly relieved!

They all thanked Bill and Lucille when they returned to their hotel and went up to Carolyn and Christopher's room and drank a toast to the Order of Saint John and to King Peter II.

Bill said that he and Lucille had an early morning flight to Atlanta the next morning and would say their farewells now and wished everybody a good flight back to Austin. He said that they were happy to finally meet Natalie and Dietrich whom Carolyn and Christopher had talked so much about and that they would love for them to visit them in Atlanta where everything is green!

The two couples and Randall left Chicago behind the next day and landed at the Austin airport at 3 p.m. right on time. Randall said goodbye to his old and new friends and waved to them as he left the baggage area and trudged toward the parking lot where his Jeep Wrangler was parked.

Dietrich remarked as Randall disappeared, "He certainly is a fascinating curmudgeon of a professor. I like him!"

Natalie chimed in, "Me too."

Christopher said of his friend, "There isn't a thing that he wouldn't do for his friends. It's too bad that he lives out there all by himself on that lonely patch of land!"

They found their Mercedes SUV and finally arrived at Rood House on Point Venture and parked the car in the garage and carried their luggage across the gargoyled bridge into the house and dropped them on the floor in the foyer. They collapsed on the big overstuffed couch in the Great Room and Carolyn brought a big tray with a pitcher and four glasses of lemonade which they all drank down in relief and just sat there in silence staring at the big fireplace. Balthazar had come into the Great Room and jumped onto Natalie's lap and waited patiently for her to rub his head.

Finally Christopher broke the silence and said, "Now that was a very busy trip!" They all nodded their heads in agreement and Christopher poured another round of lemonade for everyone.

28 THE BIG GAME

The next day, the two couples slept late and did not get up before nine o'clock in the morning. By this time, the birds in the trees behind Rood House had already had their breakfasts and were busy chattering at the squirrels that were trying to invade their feeding trays and generally annoy them. The bird houses and feeding trays where Carolyn had carefully laid out seed and food for the neighborhood birds were located at strategic spots around the decks.

The two couples wandered into the kitchen still dressed in their night attire and robes with a sleepy look on their faces. The two husbands still had early morning stubble on their faces where they had not shaved. Carolyn and Natalie proceeded to prepare breakfast as Christopher perused the morning newspaper and Dietrich was following the flying antics of the birds as they dived on the squirrels. He took an interest in their tactics as if they were fighter pilots! Balthazar just watched them intently.

Christopher had just turned to the sports page and noted that the Texas football teams were all doing well for this early in the season and the big homecoming game between the University of Texas and Baylor was less than four weeks away. Natalie was just pouring the coffee when her cell phone rang. She turned away and spoke in a low muffled voice. Then all of a sudden she said in a loud voice, "Are you absolutely sure!" Then there was a long pause as she was listening to the voice on the other end of the telephone. By this time Carolyn, Christopher and Dietrich had looked up and were watching Natalie.

She had a surprised and somewhat horrified look on her face and then she started to cry. It appeared from the conversation that the voice on the other end of the line was trying to console her. Another long pause and then Natalie said, "Thank you and God bless you! Auf Wiedersehen!"

She wiped the tears from her eyes as she looked up into six inquiring eyes. Dietrich ran over to her and put his arms around her shoulders and led her over to the kitchen table. They all sat around her as she explained, "That was Rania! She called me to say that there was a picture of me with Carolyn and Christopher at Saint Sava Serbian Orthodox Monastery Chapel in Libertyville in the Czech version of the German newsmagazine, Der Spiegel. She said that it was on the front page and identified Carolyn, Christopher and me and the Harries at the memorial services for King Peter II. The article told the story about King Peter II and his return next year to Serbia and burial in the Royal Family Mausoleum in Oplenac on May 26, 2013. She said that she and her fiancé were hiding out and she was pretending to be his wife so that her brother Ahmed couldn't find her. She quit her job and they moved outside Prague. She said that Ahmed was sure to see the story and tell his father. She never told Ahmed or her father her fiancée's name. She was terribly afraid for my life and she told me that she didn't want me to wind up like Dietrich! I'm sorry that I broke out crying like that, but when she mentioned Dietrich, I just couldn't help myself!"

Dietrich consoled her, "Well, at least, she and the world think I'm dead and our little ruse has worked. Darling, I think that your impromptu tears sold the story. Rania will certainly corroborate the fiction that I'm dead if need be."

Natalie looked up at him and softly said with a trembling lip, "I hope that it will never be true. I love you too much!"

Carolyn and Christopher went over to her and patted her on her shoulder.

Christopher said, "Look it's a lovely day just meant for motor boating and lying in the sun! Let's eat breakfast and not worry just yet. We'll call Steve in Edinburgh and he'll alert Interpol, the Mossad and everyone else. We'll just wait for our flies to enter the web!"

Natalie said, "I just know that Rania is our friend and that she has broken completely with her family. She is a good nurse and kind hearted and I'm sure, is my friend!"

With that, Christopher disappeared into his library to call Steve and let him know what had just happened. They talked for quite a while and Steve told Christopher that Katie was calling all of the agencies right now to put everyone on the alert. He told Christopher that all of the airports and major port cities would be given photos of Mohammad and Ahmed so they can be picked up on surveillance cameras with photo ID and agents will be briefed. They would also find Rania and quietly protect her and her fiancé if necessary without their knowing.

Steve explained, "The CBP also were using MQ-9 Guardian surveillance drones that had a service ceiling of 50,000 feet and an operational altitude of 25,000 feet. These unmanned aircraft were equipped with GA-ASI's Lynx synthetic aperture radar and Raytheon's MTS-B electro optical infrared sensors. They also were equipped with ultra-high resolution digital cameras that had steady cam and face recognition capability from an altitude of 50,000 feet! They had an operational endurance of 14 hours fully loaded. The CBP also told us they were going to use an MQ-9 Guardian high altitude surveillance drone that was stationed at the Naval Air Station in Corpus Christi, Texas, to help Homeland Security and the CBP track down Mohammad and Ahmed if they came across the United States southern border in Texas."

He told Christopher that Mossad agents in the United States are already probably getting an alert—especially those in Texas! And then he laughed, "Don't worry, we're on it and I'll personally keep you informed. And besides, Kate and I want to meet some Rangers also."

"When did you say that you were going to receive your recognition from the Silver Spurs?"

Christopher replied, "Well, the big game and the halftime ceremony is on Saturday, October 20th. You can stay with us at our house. Let me know and I'll pick you up at Austin International Airport."

Steve replied, "Will do, I'll talk to Kate and let you know."

With that, they ended their conversation and Christopher walked back into the kitchen and announced, "Everything has been taken care of and I've invited Kate and Steve to join us for the big game. He'll call us back and let us know when he's arriving." He laughed and then said, "I guess I'd better call Randall before he gets off somewhere and let him know that Kate and Steve are going to want to see his friend, Lt. Bob Stewart!"

They all sat down at the kitchen table and each pondered the events of the morning in their own minds as they silently ate their breakfasts. Finally, Christopher broke the silence and said, "You know, I think that Steve might be interested in that new rifle that Randall has—you know the electronic XS2 Tracking Point rifle. What do you think, Dietrich?"

Dietrich replied, "Yes, I think so. I'd like to try it again, when we have a little more time. Perhaps when he comes down for the game and before we see Lt. Stewart again in Waco."

Christopher replied that he would look around and perhaps find a range that would do. Perhaps at the old Bergstrom Air Force Base on State Highway 71, seven miles east of Austin.

Carolyn knew that her husband, Dietrich, and Randall were interested in guns as most men seemed to be and she could only sympathize with Katie when she arrived with

Steve. She knew that she would have to plan a day so that the boys could get together. Maybe she could arrange to have Lt. Stewart go with them and "kill several birds with one stone!"

She decided to push all thoughts of violence and danger away and suggested that they might go down to their beach and picnic area for a little sunbathing with sandwiches and beer. Perhaps they could take a boat ride over to the yacht club for evening dinner and then some quiet brandies on the deck outside the Great Room so they could watch the nearly full moon that would turn into a harvest moon on this next Sunday, the 30th of September. Everyone agreed that would make for a pleasant quiet and relaxing day that they could all use!

The day went as planned and the two couples fell into a pleasant routine for the next 3 ½ weeks before the game. Christopher had his usual routine with his teaching, his practice and research. The Silver Spurs had been in contact with him so they could all meet with various dignitaries and rehearse the halftime proceedings and awards. There was going to be a designated area for friends and relatives of Dr. Christopher Rood. There was going to be enough room for Carolyn, Natalie, Dietrich, Kate, Steve, and Dr. Fox. They would all have to be in their seats at least one half hour before halftime. The plan was to meet Dr. Fox in the stadium parking lot and then go on to the stadium and take their seats for the big game. Dr. Fox was to follow them back to Rood House that night so they could meet Lt. Stewart the next day for their marksmanship outing.

Dr. Fox was going to bring plenty of matched ammunition for the affair. He had called Lt. Bob Stewart to arrange for him to meet with him and his friends, Inspector Steve Grant and his wife at Dr. Rood's house. Lt. Stewart said that he would talk to his wife about the meeting planned for the next day after the Texas-Baylor game. Carolyn, Natalie and Katie were going to prepare a fantastic lunch for everyone at the outing.

Katie had called a few days after their initial conversation with Steve to tell him about Rania's telephone call. She arranged for Steve and her to fly into Austin-Bergstrom International Airport on Monday, the 15th of October, so they would have plenty of time to become acclimated to the difference in time and change in climate. Besides Katie wanted to try out her new bathing suit and test her water skiing expertise. It had been a few years since she had waterskied and she was ready for some warm weather. It had been a little chilly in Edinburgh the last few weeks.

Katie and Steve's flight from Scotland arrived in Austin at six o'clock on the afternoon of the 15th, right on schedule after a layover in Atlanta. Christopher was there to pick them up at the airport and they drove to Lake Travis and Rood House at Point Venture.

This was their first trip to Texas, and Katie and Steve had not quite expected the warm 80 and 90 degree Fahrenheit temperatures. Katie said that it was pleasant, but realized that they were going to have to do some shopping in Austin soon after their arrival. The only clothing that she was sure that she would not have to replace was her bikini!

It was like a homecoming when Katie and Steve arrived at Rood House. As soon as they came through the front door, they were met with cries of happiness at their arrival and Natalie and Katie embraced each other and compared their wedding rings. Dietrich whispered to Christopher and Steve that it was a "girl thing!" Carolyn embraced Katie and welcomed her to Rood House and Texas. Katie immediately noticed that a lot of the furniture and fixtures were from Scotland!

Carolyn had already prepared a round of Scotch whiskey for everyone out on the deck around the large wrought iron table with a glass top. Neat, of course!

Christopher and Dietrich along with Steve took their bags up the stairs to their rooms down the hall from Natalie's and Dietrich's. Christopher declared that it would only be appropriate that they should occupy the Scotland Room! Their rooms all had a deck balcony looking out over Lake

Travis.

The "boys" walked back down the stairs after dropping off the luggage and joined their wives who were already exchanging stories and ideas about how to spend the next two weeks that Katie and Steve had in Texas. Katie was saying that she would be happy to just spend her time at Lake Travis waterskiing and lying on the beach in her bikini and making love to Steve at night!

The husbands arrived just as Katie was making her last remark. She looked up and saw the husbands as they walked through the door. She felt the warm rush of blood to her face as she began blushing.

Steve said, "What did you say?" and before she could answer, Natalie replied, "The same thing that we are all thinking!" and then the wives giggled their approval.

Christopher looked at Katie and then Steve and with a playful twinkle in his eye, mentioned that Natalie and Dietrich believed that sunbathing should only be done in the nude!

Katie looked shocked and then said, "You mean that I can't wear my bikini!"

Steve then looked at Katie, laughed and then winked at her and said, "Yes, but only while waterskiing!"

Katie looked stunned for a second and then laughed. She looked into Steve's eyes and firmly said, "That's okay with me!"

Steve looked quizzically at her and said, "You know dear, that there has been a surveillance drone over this house since the day after the Corpus Christi affair"

Katie put her hand over her mouth as if she had not known and stammered, "I hope we catch those two wretches quickly so they won't spoil our vacation!" She laughed and then they all burst out in laughter!

They sat down with their wives and everyone had just finished drinking their first Scotch, while Natalie and Katie were talking about their honeymoons and were beginning their second Scotch when the telephone rang. Carolyn answered the phone and the caller on the other end asked for

Inspector Grant. It was Inspector Ed MacGregor.

Steve answered the phone and said in a cheerful way, "What's up?"

Ed replied that the surveillance cameras at Laredo, Texas, just identified Mohammad al Hussaini and Ahmed al Hussaini crossing the border in separate vehicles about two hours ago, but they got away in the crowd. Evidently, the ID didn't process rapidly enough and they switched to other vehicles. "You know that the Mexican border just is not as secure as the Americans would like it to be. They are just not prepared for the middle eastern terrorists!"

The expression on Steve's face did not change and he replied, "Thanks Ed, it is okay! I appreciate your calling. Keep me informed!"

Carolyn, sensing something, asked Steve if everything was okay and in a nonchalant manner he replied that everything was fine and just a few details at his office needed his approval. He turned toward the table he had just left and sat down and picked up the conversation where it had left off.

A veal parmesan dinner was served with mashed potatoes and green beans that Natalie and Carolyn prepared while Katie pitched in with the dessert of chocolate mousse with Irish coffee. After dinner they all stretched and yawned and agreed that it was time to go to bed. Katie and Steve expressed that it was such a lovely evening with good friends and they thanked Carolyn and Christopher for such wonderful accommodations. Carolyn told everyone that they should sleep in late since Christopher had the next two weeks off for all of the festivities and the homecoming game.

They all walked to their separate bedrooms and waved goodnight to each other. Steve opened the door and picked up Kate and held her tightly in his arms as he walked into the room. Katie tilted her head toward Steve and kissed him tenderly on his lips and then brushed his ear with her lips and whispered, "They're here aren't they?"

He turned his head until their eyes met and he replied, "Yep!"

The next few days were busy with reports coming in to Steve from all of the resources that he had through Scotland Yard, Interpol and the Mossad. Katie and Steve were keeping everything quiet from the inhabitants of Rood House.

Katie had kept her usual cheery countenance and went shopping early the next day with Carolyn and Natalie. She wanted to do the shopping and get back to Point Venture before noon. Steve went with them supposedly because Katie wanted to make sure his new clothes fit. Actually, he was guarding the ladies.

Katie knew his measurements precisely. They managed to buy a new wardrobe for her and Steve quickly. She made light talk about their two week vacation; she was determined to keep a stiff Scottish upper lip and spent her time with small talk while everyone enjoyed the few remaining days before the big ballgame, sunbathing, swimming, waterskiing, and enjoying the secluded beach and gardens of Rood House.

Steve made sure that they kept everyone around the relative safety of the Rood House and Point Venture to make sure that Natalie or Dietrich would not be an easy target. They were still sure that the two terrorists knew nothing of Dietrich's presence there.

Friday before game day finally arrived, and Steve received word from the Texas Rangers just before noon that they had been informed by the Mossad that five Muslim terrorist suspects had been seen yesterday by one of their agents, entering a warehouse in Dallas. The warehouse was a storage area where an advertising agency kept supplies they used for large holiday parades. The Mossad agent had watched the five men enter the warehouse, but only four men came out and left.

When the Rangers got there, the Mossad agent told the Rangers that he had been watching the activities of a Dallas mosque and had followed the five Muslims to the warehouse. The Rangers looked at each other and one of them said, "What are we waiting for? Let's go inside."

They entered the building together with the Mossad agent

and found no one there. It was filled with inflatable animals and clowns used in parades and were folded and stored for future use.

The CBP had a MQ-9 Guardian surveillance drone over the area at the request of the Texas Rangers and it had spotted the five Muslims enter the warehouse and the Mossad agent who was watching them. It had also taken photos of the four Muslims when they left the warehouse, the two Rangers when they had arrived, and a black homeless man that had left through a back door of the warehouse just before the Rangers had arrived.

When the CBP saw the computer analysis of the drone's digital camera's download of a face shot of the black man at the warehouse, the computer recognized the man as Ahmed even though he had attempted to disguise himself. But why did Ahmed take a chance on being spotted in Dallas that had unusually heavy security systems similar to the ones in London? They had checked with the company that owned the warehouse and they were clean!

Steve decided to inform his fellow members of the Order of Saint John what has been happening since they had arrived on Monday. He and Katie took the time after lunch to sit down with everyone in the Great Room of the chalet to make the revelations known.

Steve told them everything he knew and said that Lt. Stewart had been assigned by the Rangers, at his request, to be with them all day Saturday through the homecoming festivities, the game with its halftime ceremonies, and until the time that Mohammad and Ahmed were apprehended.

He said that Lt. Stewart had volunteered when he was filled in about what was going on and who was involved. Needless to say, his family will not be with him during this time and everyone in the state, the CBP, Texas Rangers and the Homeland Security forces that are now in play are on a high state of alert!

Christopher said, "Now I know why I hadn't heard back from Dr. Fox or Lt. Stewart!"

Steve answered, "Yes, and even though you probably didn't notice, there has been a surveillance drone over this house since the alert went out!"

Katie and the other ladies looked at each other and then Katie broke their silence and said, "Even while we've been sun bathing and waterskiing."

Natalie flushed and then said softly, "Even at night?"

Dietrich looked at Steve with a wry smile on his face and Steve replied, "Yes, you know the drones also have night vision!"

Dietrich looked up at everyone and said, "You don't know it, but MQ-9 Guardian drones have been assigned to my 51 Squadron back in Germany and when I return to active duty, I'll probably be trained to fly these aircraft." And then he looked at Natalie and winked and the added, "I'll probably do some of my training here in Texas. Maybe even in Corpus Christi. Would you like to come with me back to Texas?"

Natalie could not believe her ears and jumped up and clapped her hands together and said with an almost Texas accent, "Would I ever!"

Rood House woke up early the next morning so that they could all get down to the field for the big game and be in their places for all of the events. They parked the Mercedes SUV in the designated parking space that the university had assigned for the VIPs that were going to be in the halftime ceremonies. Lt. Stewart was already there in his uniform and wearing his 7-1/2 inch peacemaker with stag horn pistol grips. They all felt safe now that he was there with them.

A few minutes later, Dr. Fox pulled up in his white Jeep Wrangler Safari SUV with a tan hardtop and smoked side windows that shaded and hid its interior. He had a front license plate with a white Maltese cross in the middle signifying the Order of Saint John. His vehicle was covered with the dust from the "Back Forty" ranch. Somehow it looked incongruent!

Randall jumped out of his car and greeted his comrades and Lt. Stewart.

When he saw the Ranger in uniform, he asked, "What's going on?"

Steve quickly filled him in on all of the details that had happened over the last few days and that Lt. Stewart had been assigned at his own request to watch over us all!

Randall said, "Well I guess that things are coming into focus! Where to now?"

Dietrich had been listening to all of this and asked, "Before we are seated in the stadium, would it be okay for Dr. Fox and me to go over to the Perry-Castaneda Library where they have a book concerning the Holy Grail and Saint Mary Chapel that I have been wanting to show him."

Natalie protested, "But darling, that can wait until later. The traffic will increase and the crowds will be starting to enter the stadium soon."

Dietrich said, "What do you think, Steve? It won't take half an hour. I know exactly where it is. I looked it up on the library's web site!"

Steve turned to Lt. Stewart and asked him, "What do you think, lieutenant?"

Lt. Stewart answered, "I think it will be safe if we get everyone seated in their designated seats where more Rangers are situated. But I'm going with you and Dr. Fox!"

Natalie pouted about Dietrich leaving her for only a while, but recovered and hugged her husband and said, "Okay, if you must!"

They all walked down to the VIP area where Lt. Stewart introduced them to the other Rangers and explained to them that he, Dr. Fox and Dietrich were going to walk over to the Library for a half an hour and then return shortly.

They nodded their heads in approval at the lieutenant and everyone sat down in their designated seats. Dietrich said goodbye and turned toward Natalie as he started to walk away with his two companions and blew her a kiss.

The three walked back to the parking lot which was filled and crowds just beginning to fill the stadium.

Kick-off was in about a half an hour. They were just about

to step across San Jacinto toward 21st Street and the library when they spotted a grey Ford F-250 truck with a large covered bed and a red construction company sign on the door traveling south on San Jacinto.

As it flashed by, Dietrich turned to Dr. Fox and Lt. Stewart and exclaimed, "I think that was Mr. Smythe driving that truck." He paused, corrected himself, and continued, "I mean Mohammad is driving that grey Ford truck!"

The three of them turned their heads quickly and looked down the street and watched as it turned down San Jacinto and then it turned right onto Martin Luther King Street past the Brazos Garage and the Blanton Museum of Art.

Lt. Stewart said, "Are you sure?"

"I'm sure of it. That is the man who tried to kill me!"

With that, Dr. Fox said to the two of them, "Wait a minute!" and he ran over to his Jeep, opened the back door and pulled out a black leather covered case and a pair of binoculars, closed the rear door, and locked it. "Let's run down to the corner and see where it is going!"

The three of them sprinted down to the corner just in time to see the grey truck turn left into the entrance of the large Administration Building parking lot opposite University Street and disappear among the already parked vehicles.

Dr. Fox yelled, "Let's get over to Speedway Street and to the roof of the Perry-Castaneda Library as quickly as possible and see if we can spot them in the parking lot and see where they go."

Lt. Stewart broke out into a sprint and Dietrich was right with him. Dr. Fox was trailing them, but not far. The younger men were in excellent condition and Dr. Fox was holding his own. They arrived at the front door and Dietrich noticed the case that Dr. Fox was holding and said, "Here, let me carry that!"

Dr. Fox, who was breathing more heavily than the other two, gasped, "Thanks!"

They passed the security guard, headed for an elevator, and quickly went to the top floor where they found a stairway to the roof of the building. They ran to the south side of the roof where Dietrich's keen eyes spotted the truck which had parked just east and next to the University of Texas Administration Building in an area roped off with yellow construction signs and tape.

Dr. Fox handed Dietrich the Leica high magnification spotting binoculars that he used to spot deer and occasionally look at the moon.

Dietrich took the binoculars and quickly focused it on the two men that had gotten out of the truck and identified that the older man was indeed Mohammad al Hussaini, but he didn't know who the younger man was.

Lt. Stewart asked for the binoculars and then focused them on the two men. He said crisply, "The older man is Mohammad and the younger one is his son, Ahmed! He is the one who was at the warehouse that we ID'd from the drone photos and the photos that we got from Laredo."

He immediately called the Ranger watch center that had been established at the stadium. Maj. Jones, commander of Company F, answered the call and Lt. Stewart described the scene.

Maj. Jones asked him if he had control of the situation and whether he needed backup. Lt. Stewart in true Ranger fashion said, "No, let's not spook them. Who knows what they have down there. If that truck is filled with explosives, they could easily bring down the Administration Building. We know that Mohammad is an expert in explosives."

Maj. Jones asked if he should call in a SWAT unit.

Lt. Stewart said, "No, that would create a disturbance and possibly a riot. Let's keep this low key for now and see what they are up to."

They hung up and Lt. Stewart said to Dietrich and Randall, "We are going to observe for a while to see what is going on and then possibly later call in some snipers."

Dr. Fox looked at Dietrich and then Lt. Stewart and calmly said, "That won't be necessary, I brought my XS-2 and plenty of ammunition."

He pointed to the black case and said, "I've been practicing and I think I can hit any target up to three quarters of a mile!"

"You mean that you have that rifle in that case!" said Lt. Stewart.

Randall looked into the lieutenant's eyes and coldly replied, "Yes, and I know how to use it!"

"You're deputized!"

The three men returned their gaze to the two men who were uncovering something in the back of the truck. They could see something that looked like a large bear's face. The younger man went to the door of the truck's cab and pulled out what looked like a hunting vest and put it on.

Dietrich took the binoculars and gasped as he saw Ahmed pull a Baylor windbreaker over the vest. "He just put on a suicide vest with a hand button attached. I've seen them in Afghanistan and he could detonate that vest with just the push of a button."

"He has just raised the level of danger to a catastrophic level if that truck is loaded with plastic explosives."

Just as Dietrich made his remarks a loud noise went up in the stadium as the opening kickoff was made and the game started between the ranked Texas team and the ranked Baylor Bears that had defeated the Texas Longhorns for the last two years.

They looked back at the two men as they pulled out a large balloon that looked like a bear and laid it out on the pavement behind the truck. The bear was folded so that it could be easily inflated and it was painted in the colors of Baylor University and the bear had a large Yellow "B" on the front of a green vest on its chest.

Dietrich zoomed the binoculars to full power as he saw the men attach a hose to the bear and begin inflating the bear with helium.

Dietrich could see a large basket filled with plastic explosives and what appeared to be small metal strips that resembled daggers.

"Shrapnel," Dietrich whispered to his friends. "Those bastards have explosives in that basket with metal shrapnel! They intend to float that thing over the stadium and explode it at halftime when the Silver Spur ceremonies are occurring! They know that Carolyn and Natalie will be standing with Christopher when he receives his award! They plan on killing thousands of people in the stands as well! I think that Ahmed is going to martyr himself and detonate the explosives himself when that Baylor Bear balloon is guided by him over the middle of the stadium. They have thought of everything including the drift of the westerly wind that will float the balloon over the stadium with just a minimal help from that small engine with a propeller attached to the basket. He's going to ride that damned thing to his seventh heaven!"

Then Dietrich said, "Wait a minute! Mohammad is walking away toward the main campus. Lt. Stewart, here you take the binoculars and watch Mohammad and see where he goes. I'll keep my eyes on Ahmed."

He looked at Randall and asked, "Do you think you could make a shot and hit Ahmed from this distance?"

Randall replied, "No, it's too dangerous. The balloon should float close to us as it goes toward the stadium and I'm sure I could get a clean shot at him then since he won't have his finger on the detonation button and will be steering the balloon. We can have Mohammad picked up later by your men, Bob."

Randall was now calling Lt. Stewart by his first name as comrades in arms do when in combat action.

The balloon was almost halfway filled and beginning to take shape. Randall estimated that it would be about 30 or 40 feet tall when fully inflated. The game was fully underway and by now it was in the second quarter. They could see the score board and Texas was leading, but barely. It was going to be a close game and the fans had been on their feet most of the game so far.

Bob was watching Mohammad as he made his way across the campus and headed toward the main building and the

Texas Tower. Bob informed his comrades that Mohammad was now in the main building.

He remarked, "That son of a bitch is going to watch this whole thing from the top of the tower. He is going to watch his son explode that bomb over the stadium!"

Randall replied, "Not if I can help it!"

He had unpacked his rifle, loaded it and turned on the weapon. He punched in his personal code and held the handgrip so that his fingerprints could be read allowing the weapon to function. He then fed in the numbers for the prevailing wind velocities that he read off his mini iPad after he had blue-toothed it to the weapon. He now synchronized its GPS and fed into the computer the rifle's coordinates and the projected trajectory of the balloon's path toward the stadium.

The balloon was now filled to capacity with the hose detached and Ahmed was standing in the basket that was under the bear balloon. He was standing on the plastic explosives ready to release the balloon from the bed of the truck.

The final minutes of the first half were winding down with Texas barely leading by a touchdown and the crowd was roaring. Dietrich had called Natalie on his cell phone and made his apologies for not being with her, assuring her that he would be joining her before the second half started.

He told her that the research that he and Dr. Fox were doing was almost complete. She had started to scold him and then remembered what Carolyn had said to her about husbands that were intent.

She took a deep breath and calmly told him to take his time and she would be waiting for him to join her.

He said goodbye to her and marveled about how lucky he was. He turned to Randall and his eyes pleaded with anxiety as he asked, "Are you sure that you can pull this off?"

Randall looked at him with a warm confidence, as he said firmly, "Yes, of course!"

Bob announced to his companions that Mohammad had

just arrived at the observation deck at the top of the tower and that he had a pair of binoculars around his neck and was looking toward the stadium. He has an ear piece in his ear.

He had a cell phone in one hand as he watched the final seconds of the first half elapse. The bands came onto the field and played their respective fight songs and then a platform was brought onto the field and the VIPs of the Texas Silver Spurs came onto the field to the applause of the 101,355 fans that were in the stands.

Dietrich could see that Carolyn, Christopher and Natalie were on the platform with the dignitaries and the speeches were beginning. He also noticed that Ahmed had released the Baylor Bear balloon and it rose rapidly and the westerly breeze caught it and started it toward the stadium.

He could see Ahmed steering the balloon between the library and the Blanton Art Museum toward the stadium.

Randall was tracking him with his rifle that he had balanced on a swivel tripod. Randall had the telescopic sight on maximum magnification and its electronic cross hairs fully centered on Ahmed's forehead.

He was waiting for Ahmed to stand a little more erect.

The balloon was just passing over the Blanton Museum and approaching the dormitories when Ahmed stood up and Randall squeezed the trigger.

The shot was muffled by the silencer on the rifle and a small round dot of red blood appeared on Ahmed's forehead. A bewildered and silent look appeared on Ahmed's face as he began a slow slump and sat down on the explosives as his last breath left his lungs. Then his body lurched forward into the balloon's rigging making it appear as if he were waving.

Lt. Bob Stewart was watching Mohammad with his binoculars trained on his face.

Randall had already swiveled the rifle so that the electronic cross hairs of the rifle's telescopic sight were focused squarely on the little patch of hair filling the space between Mohammad's eyes.

Bob saw a triumphant smile disappear from Mohammad's

face as he watched in horror and confusion as his son slumped onto the explosives.

Mohammad quickly turned his binoculars over to the roof of the library and saw the three men on its roof. Bob saw Mohammad stop and mouth the single word, "Dietrich," as a small red round dot appeared on his forehead dead center between his eyes and the back of his head exploded in a pinkish red shower of blood, bone and brains as he fell backwards against the wall of the tower.

Dietrich and Bob raised their arms above their heads and screamed, "YES!"

They turned to a calm Dr. Fox and Lt. Stewart said, "Best damned shooting I've ever seen!"

Dr. Fox replied, "Not me, it was the rifle!"

Lt. Stewart then looked each of his companions sternly in their eyes and softly said, "None of us can tell anyone exactly what happened. The story must be that a madman and his son were killed when they attempted to bring rifles to the Texas Tower and that the Rangers thwarted their attempt. We can't allow the real story to get out; otherwise, the public will be afraid to enter any stadium for a ball game!"

They all nodded to each other and swiftly agreed.

Lt. Stewart then added, "The Air Force Special Operations Command will quietly recover the balloon and disarm the explosives or destroy it. The cover story will be that the balloon was just a college prank and the unknown student that pulled it off had escaped."

Lt. Stewart then called the governor and informed him what had happened and then turned to his companions and explained to them that everything had been handled and the public will never know. The Air Force Special Forces will take control of the balloon.

Bob walked over to Randall and he handled the miracle rifle to him; he cradled it in his hands and then drew it up to his shoulder to check its balance.

The rifle was flashing a red error light signifying that it would not function in a stranger's hands!

Bob laughed and gave it back to Randall. He said to Randall and Dietrich, "I just gotta have one of those!"

The balloon with its cargo of explosives and a dead terrorist was just beginning to float across the stadium at a height of one hundred feet when the Baylor fans started to cheer the impromptu surprise of their mascot above the field.

The fans rose to their feet at the assumed prank of some Baylor fraternity and its lone passenger who was kneeling forward in the basket caught in the rigging under the bear with his hand waving in the air.

It took ten minutes for all of the commotion to die down after the balloon had drifted past the stadium and toward the east just north of Bergstrom International Airport where the Air Force Special Forces Command and Control Center was going to carefully and safely direct the operation that would either land or destroy the balloon with its deadly cargo well out of town and in the secluded area of Camp Swift thirty-seven miles east of Austin.

After Randall packed his rifle back into its protective case, Lt. Stewart called Maj. Jones and told him that he could stand down the Rangers—the threat had been eliminated, the governor had been informed and they could pick up the remains of a terrorist over at the Texas Tower and another terrorist at Camp Swift a few miles east of town.

The three men walked silently down the stairs from the roof of the Perry-Castaneda Library toward the elevator which took them to the street level and out to Twenty-first Street where they walked toward the stadium.

They walked to the parking lot where Randall's Jeep was located. He walked over to it and unlocked the back door and placed the rifle into its hiding place beneath the carpet. Then he locked the door and rejoined his companions and said to Bob and Dietrich, "Let's take Sunday off, and we can all try the rifle out on Monday!"

"Tomorrow is God's Day and America's tomorrow for all of us!"

They rejoined their friends in the VIP seats and Natalie

ran toward Dietrich when she saw him and wrapped her arms around him.

She told him she was so glad he was back and the game was terribly exciting! "Did you see that huge Baylor Bear balloon that some prankster flew over the stadium at halftime?"

She said she was proud to be a member of his family and she was as thrilled as Carolyn at Christopher's recognition by the Texas Silver Spurs for his outstanding civic action.

He kissed her and said that he wanted to go over and congratulate Christopher and apologize for missing the ceremony.

As Dietrich and Natalie complimented the couple on Christopher's recognition, Christopher looked up at Dietrich and whispered, "They were here?"

Dietrich nodded and then leaned over to Carolyn and Christopher and whispered, "The danger has been eliminated permanently!"

"The balloon?" Christopher asked.

Dietrich responded, "Yes, and with the help of Randall's rifle."

Christopher had guessed that the balloon was more than people thought. He knew they would get the full story later.

Dietrich walked over to Kate and Steve where Natalie was talking to Kate.

He put his arm around Natalie's waist and said to them, "Natalie and I are forever grateful for everything that the both of you have done for us and for saving my life. I just want you to know that the danger is over and that Mohammad and Ahmed are dead, thanks to the both of you and your efforts."

Meanwhile, Maj. Jones had called the Air Force Special Operations Command and advised them that the balloon was now drifting east over the city of Austin at about two to three hundred feet altitude. He was told by Col. George Armstrong that their Special Forces Team was now in sight of the balloon that was drifting just past U.S. Highway 35 and was headed along MLK Boulevard toward Bastrop.

"It appears that it is maintaining its altitude or maybe rising just a little from the afternoon heat. We'll keep you informed on our progress as it heads into the countryside. We're going to try and engage it somewhere west of Texas State Highway 95 and Camp Swift. Camp Swift has been notified and an alert has been issued to clear the canyon and surrounding area where we are going to disarm or drop the balloon. If we have to destroy the balloon, it will be in a military reservation where explosions are not unusual. We can't let it descend into an inhabited area where there is some danger. We are putting all airline flights into Bergstrom International Airport into a holding pattern until this balloon is neutralized."

"Roger that. Watch out for a possible trigger on the bottom of the gondola," replied Maj. Jones. Then he hung up and turned to Sgt. Tommy Wise and murmured almost under his breath, "Good luck, they're going to need it!"

Camp Swift is a Texas National Guard military training reservation that consists of 56,000 acres that has a deep canyon and heavily wooded area in the middle of the training area. The canyon is bordered by steep limestone walls with 45-degree sloping forested sides that descend into a valley with a creek at its bottom. In 1944, during World War II, the 10th Mountain Division trained there.

The Air Force HH-60G Pave Hawk helicopter that was the US Air Force Special Forces prime recovery operations aircraft was keeping pace with the Baylor Bear balloon drifting eastward twenty miles west of Sayersville when the commander of the aircraft, Maj. Jimmy Perkins spoke into his headset to his crew of four, "Heads up, we're going to start the recovery."

Sgt. Kerry Kilgore, who had been a star athlete at Purdue University and who Maj. Perkins called "Reddy" had just put his harness on and attached it to the winch cable. He replied matter-of-factly into his headset, "Roger that! I've got the tow cable attached and I'm ready to go."

Maj. Perkins smiled at his copilot, Capt. Richard Shimer, who he called "Dick," then he tersely said to Sgt. Kilgore, "Reddy, just remember, don't go lower than the top edge of the gondola. If you do and any trigger is activated, we're all 'tits up'. We have to let the full length of the tow cable play out to keep us away from the balloon as much as possible."

"Roger that," he replied as he stepped out of the side hatch of the helicopter and the lowering began. They were about three hundred feet above the balloon, and the special baffled helicopter blades of this unique special rescue helicopter kept the downward air turbulence out to the sides of the balloon allowing St. Kilgore to descend safely to the gondola. When he got to the edge of the gondola, he was able to see Ahmed's body entangled in the rigging with the backside of his head blown away. He immediately thought, "whew, bad day!" as he hooked the towing cable into cable rigging connections at the leading edge of the gondola.

"Done, it's hooked up," he barked into his headset.

"Not so fast," replied Maj. Perkins. "We're going to lower you a few more feet so you can carefully look to see if there actually is a trigger mechanism on the bottom of the gondola or anywhere else."

"Roger that. I didn't see any trigger in the gondola other than the button on this poor sap's suicide vest."

Reddy slowly slid below the gondola so he could get a clear view of the bottom surface.

"Yep, there's one on the bottom of the gondola. Haul me up. Let's get me the hell out of here! Terri would not appreciate this thing blowing up!"

Maj. Perkins paused and then said into his headset, "Well that takes care of any idea of disarming and landing that damned balloon. Guys, we're going to have to blow it!"

Maj. Perkins turned to Capt. Shimer and winked as he said into his headset, "Col. Armstrong, it's armed and we're going to have to blow it in the canyon at Camp Swift. We're hooked up and ready to tow it to the canyon. Over."

"Roger that, you're cleared to blow it. Good luck! Out,"

replied Col. Armstrong.

Back in the chopper, Sgt. Kilgore said to his fellow crew members, "That poor son of a bitch down there didn't have a chance to blow that balloon. Somebody got him square between the eyes!"

He then turned to check his twin fifty caliber machine guns that he was going to use to chop up all of the helium compartments of the balloon and drop it into the middle of the Camp Swift canyon. That would activate the trigger on the bottom of the gondola and blow up the balloon.

They slowly began towing the balloon toward the large canyon where it could be safely dropped and detonated.

As they approached the canyon, Maj. Perkins said to Sgt. Kilgore, "What do you think, Reddy? Let me know when we are in a safe area in the middle of the canyon."

"Roger that, looking good, major!" He then added, "Captain, could you come back here and unhook the cable to the bear balloon just before Maj. Perkins peels away, giving me a good shot at the bear?"

He looked up from his computerized twin machine guns to see a smiling Capt. Shimer already in place to cut their target loose.

Lt. Charles Masters, who they called "Shorty," even though he was over six feet tall, was the blond-haired flight engineer. He had already computed when to release the balloon and suddenly barked into his headset, "Now!"

Capt. Shimer released the balloon just as Maj. Perkins lit the "afterburner" and the Pave Hawk obediently peeled away to give Reddy a clear shot. The automatic targeting system acquired the balloon and the machine guns chattered and chewed up the bear, and it dropped like a stone exactly into the middle of the deep canyon.

An enormous explosion and fireball lifted high up into the air as the shrapnel tore into the sides of the limestone canyon. The blast concussion wave reached the screaming helicopter and shook it.

Dick looked at Reddy and Shorty and breathed into his

headset, "Damn, I'm glad that didn't explode in Darrell Royal Stadium!"

All four crew members simultaneously said, "Amen!"

At Darrell K. Royal Stadium there was a flash of distant light toward the eastern horizon, followed by a rumbling sound like thunder. The sky was clear and the fans had almost cleared the stadium. Natalie turned toward her husband.

She held her hand to her lips and happy tears were beginning to well up in her eyes as she realized what had happened and the danger was finally over.

Kate held her husband's hand and Steve replied that he was happy for them and that Kate and he had found new friends they will cherish forever.

The game had been as thrilling as everyone had thought it would be, and Texas squeaked out a last minute victory. The final score was 56 to 50, the highest scoring game between the two teams since 1950!

The story of the balloon was hushed for national security reasons and was reported as a prank by an unknown Baylor student.

Steve and Katie stayed a couple more weeks with their new friends, Natalie, Dietrich, and their hospitable hosts— the Roods. They were able to safely visit Waco and the Texas Ranger Museum and enjoy a real Texas rodeo and outdoor barbecue, thanks to Lt. Bob Stewart and the Texas Rangers!

29 EPILOGUE

The early morning dew had not yet evaporated when Ed MacGregor's police car with Natalie and Dietrich as passengers rolled into the Elliotts' driveway with Sean running alongside it and barking a welcome to his old friend.

Annie and her children, Brian and Susan came outside when they heard the barking. They recognized Ed's car and walked over to the driver's side and Ed stuck his head out of the window and said, "Annie, I've got a couple of old friends of yours, both whom you'll recognize from that fateful day in June."

About this time, Annie's husband Sam had come outside and when he recognized Ed, he walked over and shook Ed's hand. He said, "I know you've always fancied Annie since we were all children in school together, but what brings you out here today?"

Ed laughed, but inwardly he knew that he had always had a secret crush on Annie and was jealous of Sam and his good fortune!

He and his passengers got out of the car and he reintroduced Natalie and Dietrich to the Elliott family.

Natalie shook their hands and said that she was forever

indebted to them all and then she shook Sean's paw and said to him, "You precious dog for saving my husband's life, Thank You!" She patted his head and Sean nearly wagged his tail off.

Dietrich shook their hands and thanked them all for saving his life and then he shook Sean's paw as well.

Annie invited them in for tea, which she served in the breakfast room. Susan whispered to her mother that Dietrich was handsome and then she blushed.

Brian smiled at Natalie.

Annie agreed with Susan and then dismissed the children outside to play with Sean, who was still wagging his tail as he and his playmates went outside.

Sam said that they were all glad to see him up and well. They asked Ed if they had ever found out who had assaulted Dietrich and Ed informed them that the would-be assassins were caught and are dead. Sam said, "Good riddance, we don't need their sort running around amuck, destroying the children and good people of the world!"

Natalie said that Dr. Macadam had told them how kind you were and that your quick action had saved her husband's life!"

Annie said, "That sounds like Jamie, he's always modest about his accomplishments."

They spoke for a while as they finished their tea and then Natalie turned to Annie and said quietly, "You know, if it weren't for you and your family, Dietrich and I wouldn't be expecting a child!"

Annie looked up with a surprised look on her face and in a hushed voice stammered, "You're expecting a baby? When is it due? Is it a boy or a girl?"

Dietrich turned toward his wife and Annie and then Sam and Ed and proudly explained, "We just found out last week."

Sam reached out for Dietrich's hand and shook it heartedly and looked at Annie and then at Natalie and Dietrich and said, "Congratulations, that's wonderful, we are so happy for you."

Ed shook their hands and embraced Natalie, "We are all pleased at the good news and then he added, what names have you picked out?"

Natalie blushed and said, "We think if it's a girl that we'll name her Annie and if it's a boy we'll name him Sam. Would you mind terribly being Godparents?"

Annie and Sam were speechless for a moment. They looked at each other and together they said, "We'll be happy to be Godparents!"

Ed, Natalie and Dietrich walked with the Elliott family to the police car where they embraced the children and patted Sean's head.

They again thanked Annie and Sam before getting into the police car.

As Ed drove the car down the road towards Temple, Ed, Natalie and Dietrich leaned out of their windows and waved their farewells to the Elliotts who had gathered at the driveway's entrance and were waving back to them as they disappeared down the road.

Dietrich turned and said to Ed that he and Natalie had promised themselves that they would go back to Scotland and thank the Elliotts and him for doing everything that they had done.

Ed smiled and said, "By the way, what was that all about at the Abbey Chapel?"

Dietrich looked at him and said that it was just a dream and that it would be another 200 years before someone else could test his theories.

Ed replied that was too bad, but that he had kept his stick with its lens and had collected a copy of the crime scene photos that Sgt. Smedley had taken.

Dietrich asked, "Did he take any pictures of the tiles on the floor where I had swept it clean?"

Ed answered, "Yes, I looked at all of them, but couldn't figure it out. Anyway, I saved them all for you and as soon as we get back to Temple, I'll give them back to you!"

Dietrich turned to Natalie and smiled. He kissed her hand and then he said to her, "The games afoot again, my dear Watson!"

Natalie looked into Dietrich's blue eyes, carefully placed her hands over his ears and tenderly kissed him square on his mouth.

ABOUT THE AUTHORS

FRANK R. FAUNCE

 Frank R. Faunce, DDS, is a retired colonel in the United States Army. He was an associate professor and department chair at Emory University School of Dentistry in Atlanta, Georgia. He was the command dental surgeon of the Third United States Army and served overseas in that capacity in most of the Middle Eastern countries and in East Africa. He was commissioned as a captain during the Vietnam War and was activated for duty during Operation Desert Storm. His last assignment overseas was in Mogadishu, Somalia.

Dr. Faunce completed his residency in pediatric dentistry at the University of Texas Dental Branch in Houston. He served as deputy director of the Dental Division of the Academy of Health Care Sciences at Fort Sam Houston in San Antonio, Texas, and on special assignment to the United States Army Institute for Dental Research at Walter Reed Army Hospital in Washington, DC. He also has been a consultant to Congress for Technology Assessment. He commanded the 333rd Medical Detachment in Savannah, Georgia, and has been awarded the Meritorious Service Medal with 3 Oak Leaf Clusters and the Presidential Order of Military Medical Merit.

He has written many scientific papers and articles and a textbook on aesthetic dentistry, and was a consultant to the American Dental Association on aesthetic dentistry. He was president of the Academy of Dentistry International and is a

Fellow of the International College of Dentists, the American College of Dentists, the European Academy of Prosthetics, and American Academy of Pediatric Dentistry. He has several patents and has lectured extensively at universities in the United States, Canada, Mexico, Europe and Asia. He is a Distinguished Alumnus of Indiana University School of Dentistry and Marion High School in Marion, Indiana, and Honorary Citizen of New Orleans.

Dr. Faunce's military experience and travels throughout Europe and North America provided the background for this timely novel that is replete with vivid imagery that gives the reader a sense of being there. He is now working on the sequels to *Mystery at the Thirteen Sycamores.*

JOE C. RUDÉ III

Joe C. Rudé III, MD, grew up in Austin, Texas, and attended the University of Texas. While there, he won the Texas State Judo Championship and became a second-degree black belt. After medical school and internship, he joined the United States Air Force and served in Vietnam as a flight surgeon, flying 48 combat missions as the weapons systems officer in the back seat of F-4 Phantoms. For this he was awarded the Air Medal with two Oak Leaf Clusters.

After a radiology residency and fellowship at Emory University, Dr. Rudé practiced diagnostic and interventional radiology for 37 years in Atlanta, Georgia. During that time, he was elected chief-of-staff and was appointed to the Board of Trustees of one of his hospitals and served as a clinical associate professor at both the Emory University School of

Medicine and the School of Dentistry. Dr. Rudé has been a member of many medical societies including being a Fellow of the Royal Society of Medicine and an Honorary Fellow of the Academy of Dentistry International.

Always an inveterate traveler with experience in scuba diving and mountaineering, Dr. Rudé was accepted as a Fellow of the Explorer's Club in New York and has participated in ten Flag Expeditions from the Andes Mountains in Peru to the highlands and coral reefs of New Guinea. He is also a Fellow of the Royal Geographical Society in London. Dr. Rudé has held multiple offices in many genealogical and heraldic organizations, and was awarded several knighthoods. Since retiring he has devoted much time to writing, publishing a fine art photography book, and producing art center exhibitions.

Made in the USA
Monee, IL
07 May 2022

96001162R00198